THE BODY IN THE BED

by

JONATHAN B ZEITLIN

Copyright © 2020 Jonathan Ben Zeitlin
All rights reserved

Cover art by Susan Darlene Faw

THE BODY IN THE BED

Author's Note

I thought about saying merely that all characters in this book are fictional, and any resemblance to persons living or dead is purely coincidental, but then I decided it wasn't good enough.

I staged this novel in Gilbert County, Georgia. If you're from Georgia, you probably know there is no Gilbert County in real life. Gilbert County is a fictional county somewhere between Houston and Bibb Counties, in middle Georgia.

Some of you may wonder why I didn't set my novel in a real county; after all, I spent most of my life in Georgia and certainly could have painted a realistic picture.

The way I see it, this is a novel. It's fiction and intended to be a light-hearted and funny read. The purpose of all fiction is to entertain and, sometimes, to educate.

Many of the characters are ridiculous, including some of the law enforcement officers. That's the beauty of fiction; I can write whatever I want. Ridiculous characters are fun to read about (and fun to invent). Cops are normal people just like the rest of us; some are good, some are great, and some have challenges. And, as any writer knows, the best characters are flawed.

I have watched as law enforcement officers are vilified in the press, demonized by certain factions of the public, used as punching bags by candidates for political office. That's real life, not fiction, and I refuse to let anyone read my book and impute some of the ridiculous behavior I describe by my fictional characters to any real departments or real officers. They get enough unfair criticism as it is. Thus, Gilbert County.

I've spent almost thirty years in law enforcement with a big chunk of it in Georgia. The large majority of Georgia's law enforcement officers demonstrate only the strongest moral and ethical character and are role models for the rest of the United States.

I assure you, my Readers, the personalities in this book were drawn completely from my imagination and do not represent, in any way, the real cops of Georgia.

JONATHAN B. ZEITLIN

I hope you enjoy my novel. If you do, and you haven't yet read the first book in the series, *The Body in the Hole*, I encourage you to do so.

You can always reach me at zeitlinfiction@gmail.com, and you can always reach Yvgeny at pushingdaisiesforcash@yahoo.com.

THE BODY IN THE BED

JONATHAN B. ZEITLIN

CHAPTER ONE

╬

Cars started swerving toward the curb as the sound of sirens grew. Yvgeny slowed Cerberus, his late model Cadillac hearse, and looked into his rear-view mirror, his eyes wide and a smile on his face. Brianna, his new girlfriend, eyed him with disgust.
"What are you so excited about?"
"Are you kidding me? Fresh meat!"
"Seriously? Someone could be dying!"
Yvgeny continued looking into his mirror, gleefully smacking his steering wheel with his palms and bouncing in his seat, then he gushed,
"I know! Oooh, goody, goody!"
Finally, the ambulance came into view, and Yvgeny rolled forward a few feet and cut his wheel, angling his hearse for a quick getaway. As the ambulance passed, Yvgeny accelerated and fell behind it.
"What are you doing?"
"The early bird gets the corpse!"
Brianna stuffed another piece of nicotine gum into her mouth and tried to hide her face as they passed the other motorists, still perched on the shoulder and watching them in disbelief. Cerberus garnered quite a bit of attention, especially when tail-gaiting an ambulance.
It wasn't long before the ambulance turned onto a side street very familiar to Yvgeny. He slowed, and when the ambulance pulled into the circular driveway, Yvgeny raised, then dropped a balled fist, yelling, "cha-ching!"
The ambulance had pulled into the driveway of the Sunset Manor Assisted Living Center.

THE BODY IN THE BED

Brianna glared at him, chomping and smacking her nicotine gum.

"Now what? Are you going to run inside and hand out business cards?"

Yvgeny leaned back in his seat, a satisfied smile on his face.

"Not necessary. This is our turf! Mama knows the manager. She sends the woman to her beautician once a month for the works, and I get to stack our brochures and cards on the front desk. Oh, and she puts in a plug for us whenever someone konks."

Brianna turned and looked out the window, muttering, "Heartwarming."

Yvgeny leaned back and sighed, then muttered, "Easy money!"

Yvgeny pressed a button on his steering wheel and after the beep, he slowly uttered, "Call Mama."

The Bluetooth system connected him with the landline at Schmidt and Sons Mortuary, where he and his mother lived. The mortuary was a beautiful and imposing structure in downtown Comstock, and was one of the oldest standing buildings in town. It was originally built to be the estate of Julius Weaver, a local farming magnate. It was completed just before the turn of the century, and he died soon after, having enjoyed the place for only a few years.

After a whole lot of bad luck, including the advent of the First World War and then the Great Depression, the property changed hands several times, eventually landing in the lap of Eldred Schmidt. Old man Weaver must have been rolling in his coffin when Eldred converted the place to a mortuary.

The original Eldred Schmidt retired in 1936, assuming his sons would take over the business just like he had been grooming them to do. However, when the time came, two of the three children refused and moved away; only Eldred Junior stayed behind. A few years later, and in keeping with the luck of the Schmidt family, the other sons were all drafted into the Second World War, and never came home. Only Eldred Junior and Eldred Senior survived.

Eldred Junior was already ancient by the time young Yvgeny met him so many years ago. Today, the entire Schmidt family was buried in a choice spot in the cemetery behind Schmidt and Sons.

Yvgeny's father had been Eldred Junior's understudy for many years, and when Eldred Junior finally died, at a very old age, his father took over the business. Yvgeny's father taught him everything he knew about running a mortuary and handling dead bodies, and when he died, Yvgeny took Schmidt and Sons over.

Yvgeny spent most of his formative years in and around the place, making him an unusual and unpopular child in his neighborhood and at school. While other young children played with stuffed teddy bears and dolls, Yvgeny spent his time with the dead bodies his father brought home for embalming, burial, and cremation.

They became his only friends, and because they couldn't go outside to play with him, Yvgeny spent most of his childhood years in and around the old Victorian structure.

Yvgeny was still a young boy when he came upon old man Schmidt's steamer trunks, hidden away two generations earlier, lost and forgotten in a musty corner of the attic. He held his breath as he dragged them out and over to a window, and with the sunlight streaming in, he opened the first trunk and was delighted to find it full of ancient formal wear, all in impeccable condition, having survived the ages. And of course they survived! What else would one expect from a master mortician? Not one moth hole, not the slightest musty scent.

Morning coats, top hats, cravats; the Victorian finery left young Yvgeny jubilant and dewey-eyed. He tried on all the outfits, spending hours in front of his mirror modeling the best of late 19th century fashion. Of course, none of it fit his small child's frame, but it didn't matter. Young Yvgeny knew one day it would all fit him perfectly, and he would be able to bring a new level of poise and aplomb to the world.

Now a full-grown man, he still reveled in his outfits. To him, modern suits simply had no class, no *panache*. Sure, he was able to supplement his wardrobe via the various online marketplaces for Victorian formal wear, but his daily workhorses were the items he pulled from those chests so many years ago.

Also hidden within those ancient clothes was a mint second printing of Sir Arthur Conan Doyle's *The Adventures*

THE BODY IN THE BED

of Sherlock Holmes. A strapping, young, and mustachioed Holmes was depicted on the cover wearing his trademark cap and overcoat. A young and impressionable Yvgeny fell into both the book and the wardrobe with gusto. Every client his father brought home to embalm became his Watson.

The phone rang several times before his mother answered.

"Mama, there's fresh meat at Sunset Manor."

Brianna's mouth fell open and she turned away, closing her eyes in disgust.

His mother chuckled and said, "Excellent! I will give Beatrice a call. Oh, and there's still a few bouquets from the Hiram funeral, I will pluck out whatever still looks pretty and put together a nice wreath for you to bring her."

"Perfect, Mama. Toodles!"

Yvgeny pressed the red button and ended the call. Brianna continued looking out the window, but muttered, "How can you be so sure someone's dead? Maybe they just fell, or they're having a heart attack."

Yvgeny shook his head vigorously, smiling.

"Nope. Look around. No fire truck. No cop car. Just an ambulance. When it's just one ambulance, he's worm food."

"What about the sirens?"

Yvgeny waved a dismissive hand and said, "All show."

Yvgeny let another self-satisfied smile escape, then he motioned with his chin toward the commotion.

"Just look at those guys. One's on his cell phone, and the other is screwing around with his clipboard. And do you see anyone running out the front door yelling and screaming? Nope. Trust me. He's DRT."

"Do I even want to know?"

"Dead Right There."

Brianna just sighed and shook her head.

As the paramedics finally brought out the collapsible gurney from the back of the ambulance, Yvgeny turned to Brianna and asked, "Ready for some pizza?"

"What do I see in you," Brianna said, dryly. "Aren't you going to go in and pay your respects?"

Yvgeny narrowed his eyes.

"Of course not! Mama will call over here, tell her 'sorry for your loss,' yadda, yadda, yadda, these guys will haul the body over to the morgue, and when Mama's done making the wreath, I'll pop by and drop it off on my way."

"On your way?"

"Right. On my way to the morgue. Are you paying attention?"

Brianna shook her head, speechless, then looked out the window.

When they returned to Schmidt and Sons, his mother was in the main receiving room, her head bowed over the table working on a large wreath. She had gathered the best of the week-old flowers from the Hiram funeral and was cobbling them together into something new. She was concentrating so hard that she didn't realize they had arrived. As Yvgeny watched, Mama leaned back, resting her hand on her walking cane which was standing beside her on its four rubber pads. She inspected her work, then smiled proudly.

Yvgeny inspected the wreath with a smile.

"Mama, that funeral was a week ago! How did you get the flowers to look so alive?"

Mama glanced over at Yvgeny, still smiling.

"A spritz of sugar water twice a day adds a week!"

Brianna remained outside, smoking a cigarette. When his mother glanced over Yvgeny's shoulder and saw her, her smile faltered.

"Still with the *wieloryb*. And always with the cigarettes."

"Focus, Mama. What did Beatrice say?"

His mother glanced back at Brianna one more time, pursed her lips, and looked away, making a strangled sound in her throat. Just as she turned, Brianna flicked her cigarette onto the lawn and let herself inside.

"Earnest Ledbetter. He was on hospice. Kicked the bucket this morning. Most of his extended family's in Atlanta. The cops will handle the notification today. The family only visited the guy a couple times over the last year, so she doesn't think they're close."

THE BODY IN THE BED

"Great." Yvgeny said, dejection in his voice.

"I think his daughter is local, though."

Yvgeny looked up hopefully.

"Money?"

"She rents."

Yvgeny frowned.

"Job?"

"She's in retail."

Yvgeny sighed.

"Insurance?"

"Not sure," Mama said with a shrug.

"Friends?"

"Apparently he had plenty at the Sunset."

"Well, at least we got something."

There was always more money to be made when a family lost a loved one they actually loved. If the survivors were estranged from the decedent, Yvgeny knew he would be looking at far fewer dollars in his pocket. A survivor with a house usually had more money than a renter, and if the dead guy had friends, that meant maybe a better turn out at the party, and a fatter check at the end of the day.

"Don't forget to take care of Beatrice."

"Of course, Mama."

Instead of smiling, his mother shook her head, then gazed out the window, a vision of dejection.

"What is it now, Mama?"

"Nothing."

Still the downcast face. Yvgeny steeled himself, then said, "Mama?"

"It's just, well, remember the good old days, when your father was still around and it was just us and that scoundrel Lenny Updike? Things were so much easier back then. Even Warner Robins was too far to haul a body."

Lenny Updike used to be their only competition for funerals. Like two gas stations sharing a busy intersection, Lenny's and Schmidt's were constantly battling for business.

"Yes, Mama, I remember."

"Now they're coming all the way from Atlanta."

"I know, Mama, times are tougher now."

She sighed and looked down to pick at her cuticles.

"Encroachment," his mother added, "that's what it is. All

anyone cares about is the bottom line. Remember the Raj Brothers?"

When the Raj Brothers Mortuary in Locust Grove tried to grossly underbid a job and get a piece of Yvgeny's action, Yvgeny did a little Google research, hoping to dig up some dirt. He discovered the Raj brothers were actually the Singh brothers. The word "raj" was a Hindi word meaning "king."

However, this, alone, did not make for a compelling argument for the Georgia State Board of Funeral Services to censure him. After all, a Singh pretending to be a Raj was no worse than Yvgeny operating as a Schmidt.

Fortunately, he also discovered their licenses issued by the Funeral Board had expired. One phone call was all it took. Yvgeny won the job, but the experience was the last straw for Yvgeny and his mother. It was their wake-up call- the good old days were over.

His mother sighed loudly, then leaned in her chair and reached for her cane.

"Every day, more rules, more laws. Back in the day, you could just dump a guy in a hole, fill it up with dirt. And Heaven forbid you cremate a guy. Now you have to dig out pacemakers, metal plates, fillings; hell, you'd have to run a magnet over them to figure it out!"

Yvgeny nodded sagely.

"And the paperwork! Don't even get me started."

If she only knew, Yvgeny thought to himself. Yvgeny collected the fillings like the law required, but he kept them in a special coffee can he hid in a place Mama would never think to look. Whenever the can was full, he paid one of his friends a visit who would quietly hand him a pile of cash in exchange for all his dental gold.

Waste not, want not!

"Not to mention," his mother continued, "the special requests. Egad, the requests! 'Bury him with his favorite pipe;' 'bury her in her favorite dress.' Oh, and, 'Bury him facing east. Or west.' And don't even get me started with the foreigners. Next thing you know, we'll be making mummies!"

Yvgeny let her rant, choosing to remain silent. He checked his watch. After another sigh, his mother looked over at him.

"Oh, my *tygrysek*, what is this world coming to? I feel like a stranger on my own planet."

THE BODY IN THE BED

Next comes anger. I've seen this before, Yvgeny thought.

"That Lenny Updike. Such a big shot!" she growled, smacking her cane against the floor. "Now it's pay-to-play for every carcass. Swimming upstream, now, you hear me?"

She was right, of course. Beautician visits were no longer enough to tip the scales for new business. Now it had to be visits combined with Amazon gift cards, home baked pies, thoughtful holiday cards, you name it. The mortuary science schools were spitting out graduates by the hundreds, and the burial business had become a dog-eat-dog field full of young and hungry morticians, and the encroachment never ended.

In a recent visit to Beatrice's Body Farm (Yvgeny's moniker for Sunset Manor), he walked in to find Beatrice watching television on a forty-two inch plasma screen on the wall in the lobby, installed personally by Lenny Updike. He even added a golden name plate to the bottom of the set that read *Courtesy of Lenny Updike Mortuary.* It was only a matter of time before Beatrice and the Sunset's residents (and his future clients) succumbed to the wooing of Yvgeny's competitors.

"When you bring the bouquet, you can ask about setting something up."

"As I always do, Mama."

He stood and she sat, both silent. Yvgeny could tell she wasn't finished, and he waited, somewhat impatiently, for her to come out with it. He knew from experience that when she carried that pensive expression, something distasteful was on its way. He checked his watch one more time, an old Laco, a gift from a former client, then glanced outside toward Brianna.

"Your father, may his memory be a blessing, he wouldn't have me working my fingers to the bone creating wreaths and hawking our wares like some door to door Amway salesman. So much for my golden years."

Yvgeny grimaced. With every year, his mother's medication got a little stronger, and she got a little less lucid, a little more unstable. And even more bitter.

"Of course, Mama. My goal is to make you suffer."

"That's right, Yvgeny, make jokes out of my suffering. You're all I have left, and all you have to offer is sarcasm. But it's ok, I forgive you. In fact, I blame myself. Where did I go wrong?"

Still clutching her cane, his mother struggled to her feet and stormed away, smacking her cane on the heart of pine floors and muttering. Yvgeny watched her slowly take the stairs to her room, then he shrugged his shoulders, scooped up the wreath and left. When Brianna joined him just outside the kitchen, he muttered, "Got it," then they headed back toward Cerberus.

The Sunset Manor Assisted Living Center occupied a lovely corner in downtown Comstock at the intersection of Main and Elm. Its façade was modeled after a southern plantation house with an ample wraparound and columned porch. Potted ferns were hung at regular intervals. The rocking chairs were all filled with old men and women watching traffic and speaking softly.

As Yvgeny parked Cerberus outside, he muttered, "Ah, fruit of the womb. You may only see toothless geriatrics, but I see nothing but future clients!"

Brianna served him with another look of disgust, then shook her head. She reached into her purse and this time withdrew her electronic cigarette, took a deep drag, then exhaled. She glanced at him one more time and said, "You're a mess."

Yvgeny just smiled, collected his wreath from the back seat, and emerged from Cerberus. He placed his stovepipe hat upon his head, canted it just enough to capture the debonair look of a true Southern gentleman, then straightened his morning coat. Looking in his reflection captured in the tinted windows of the hearse, he ensured his Victorian finery was impeccable.

He turned, checked his profile, adjusted his crimson cravat, then with a smile and nod, he made for the door. Brianna took another drag from her e-cigarette, then oozed out of the car. She had to grab the lip of the roof with one hand, and push off the dash board with the other. She usually had to rock back and forth several times to generate enough momentum to get out.

By the time she emerged, Yvgeny was already climbing the stairs to the porch. Two old men nearest to the door stopped rocking and watched him carefully. One of them finally gathered up enough courage to call out in a cracking voice,

THE BODY IN THE BED

"Pickup?"

Yvgeny brandished the wreath and called out, "Delivery!"

Beatrice must have been waiting for him, because he didn't have to knock before she came stumbling out, her hair a mess, wearing a dress that hadn't been in style since Jimmy Carter was president. At seventy, she was one of the youngest occupants at Sunset Manor, and as proprietor, she took her job seriously.

"Ah, Geny, you're here." Looking down at the wreath, she cocked her head and smiled, adding, "Aww, you're so sweet, so kind. Such a good boy!"

Beatrice squeezed his arm and ushered them both inside. The foyer was as cold as a meat locker. Brianna immediately shivered and clutched her sides.

"I just spoke with your dear mother. Such a lovely woman!"

Beatrice motioned for them to follow her up the stairs, and Yvgeny hesitated. He had watched the ambulance arrive hours earlier, so the dearly departed should have been on ice at the county morgue by now.

"Beatrice, where are we going?"

"Oh dear, I forgot to tell you, the ambulance left without picking him up. They got called away to some big accident on the highway. They said poor Mr. Ledbetter would have to wait."

Yvgeny frowned a moment, then muttered, "Ah, the living always seem to take priority over the dead," then smiled and said, "No problem! Saves me a trip down to County."

Beatrice gave him an odd look, then gestured for them to follow her up the stairs and down the hall.

"So, how's your lovely mother doing, Geny?" Beatrice asked with the tone of a concerned relative. Yvgeny shrugged and kept walking, as if the shrug was sufficient to convey a response. When he caught Brianna's raised eyebrow, he added, "Same as ever, she's a stubborn bulldog of a woman."

"Oh, that's nice."

Yvgeny glanced at Brianna and rolled his eyes, and Brianna elbowed him in the side. Beatrice turned a corner, proceeding down another corridor. They passed a woman standing still, bony hands grasping an aluminum walker. She wore fuzzy slippers and a bathrobe. She did not smile as they approached. In fact, she did not seem to notice them at all.

The second story had the feel of a hotel; as they walked, they had to step over dirty breakfast dishes piled on the floor between some of the doors. Several of the rooms were open and a housekeeper wandered in and out, fetching supplies from her cart.

Finally, they stopped outside one of the doors toward the end of the hallway. Beatrice opened the door, beckoned for them to enter, then said, "OK, come on out when you're finished, I'll be just down the hall!"

Beatrice clearly did not want to cross the threshold, nor did she even glance inside. Yvgeny understood completely, and, as he imagined would be much to Beatrice's relief, shut the door in her face.

Once the door was shut, Brianna reached into her purse and produced her e-cigarette. Yvgeny raised his eyebrows but said nothing, instead turning toward his client. While Yvgeny observed the body, Brianna pressed herself against the furthest wall, trying not to look, but unable to turn away.

He was in his pajamas, his lips bluish. His arms were folded over his chest, which Yvgeny assumed was a pose initiated by a good-intentioned resident. Although it was obvious the man was dead, Yvgeny's old training kicked in, and he reached down and checked the carotid artery for a pulse.

One can never be too careful!

On his nightstand was a clock radio, a collection of prescription bottles, and a mug of coffee, half full. Yvgeny stuck his finger into the coffee, then put his finger in his mouth.

Yuck. Way too sweet.

Yvgeny lifted the sheets and peeked beneath. He inspected a little more closely, lifting up the man's shirt to check for lividity. Brianna made a soft heaving sound, then turned away. The movement caused Yvgeny to look over, and for a moment he was distracted by the view presented by Brianna's back side. He smiled, then grudgingly returned his attention to the dead body.

Yvgeny took one more half-hearted glance under the man's shirt, then re-arranged the shirt and sheets and stood up

THE BODY IN THE BED

straight. Nothing seemed amiss, so he snatched the stack of papers at the foot of the bed, thumbed through them, then smiled; Beatrice helpfully had left a copy of the hospice agreement for him. He turned to Brianna, drank in her Rubenesque figure, then held up the papers and called out, "Confirmed hospice. No coroner required. It's my lucky day!"

Brianna turned slightly green and turned to look out the window while Yvgeny produced his iPhone and started photographing the body. She heard the frequent clicking and glanced over.

"Why are you taking pictures? Is that some kind of legal thing?"

Yvgeny turned to the nightstand, and, while snapping a few more shots of the prescription jars, he clucked his tongue and said, "A picture's worth a thousand words! And of course, my dear, I like to take before and after shots, you know, for my scrap book!"

Brianna's face froze, unable to produce a response.

Yvgeny maintained a scrap book containing some of his more impressive jobs. It was a collection only those "in the industry" could appreciate. Before and after shots, in Yvgeny's opinion, were the best way to showcase his particular talents. Unfortunately, there was only one place where his expertise could be truly appreciated: mortician school!

For two days each semester, Yvgeny drove up to Macon, Georgia, to give a two-day seminar to a special class of seniors at the illustrious Harrison Hills School of Mortuary Science. HHMS had one of the best reputations in the region, and it was well deserved. With his scrapbook tucked under his arm, he joined one of his favorite colleagues in the business, Louise Humperdink, and commandeered her class, *Advanced Principles of Restorative Art*. He would walk her students through his scrapbook, using Louise's ELMO projector to zoom in on every detail, and expand on some of his tricks and strategies for bringing the dead to life.

Yvgeny shook himself out of his musings and glanced over at Brianna, this time trying to remain professional and not stare directly at her body.

Perhaps one day, he thought, *she'll be ready to appreciate my masterpieces.*

JONATHAN B. ZEITLIN

Yvgeny took a second glance at some of the prescription bottles, looked around one more time, then clapped his hands together.

"Come on!"

Brianna waddled behind Yvgeny as he left the room, hospice agreement in hand. Beatrice had tactfully placed herself in a Queen Anne upholstered chair at the end of the hall, clearly in an attempt to prevent any of her residents from getting too close.

When she saw them emerge from Mr. Ledbetter's room, Beatrice lumbered to her feet and walked toward them. She called out, "Is everything OK?"

"Sure is, I have the hospice order here, I just need the contact information for his next of kin, and of course I need to collect the m- m- the, uh," Yvgeny looked down at the order, scanned the first few lines, then nodded, "Mr. Ledbetter."

"Of course."

Beatrice arrived at the entrance to the room, then checked her watch. Her face lit up.

"Actually, it's almost three p.m. If you don't mind waiting a few minutes, every Tuesday we have Madame Jezelda over for psychic readings. The whole place lines up for her! You could take Mr. Ledbetter away and nobody would even notice."

Beatrice glanced over Yvgeny's shoulder into Earnest's room, frowned, then shouldered past him.

"Jezelda? The psycho on Seventh Street?" Yvgeny asked, as Beatrice briskly walked into Mr. Ledbetter's room and around the bed.

"You mean psychic," she called out, teeth bared in a fake smile.

Yvgeny paused, then nodded and said, "sure, psychic."

Beatrice returned to the hallway, Earnest's coffee mug in hand.

"You're not a believer? But you've obviously heard of her?"

Yvgeny snickered.

"Who hasn't? Her picture is on every bus stop bench in town!"

He looked around, then muttered, "pure quackery."

Beatrice raised her eyebrows. "Quackery? I've seen her in action. She's the real thing. She can see the future!"

16

THE BODY IN THE BED

With significant effort, Yvgeny restrained from responding, turning slightly purple.

"What's she charge?"

"Twenty bucks," Brianna blurted out, and when Yvgeny twirled around to glare at her, she raised her voice.

"So what? It's *my* money."

"Might as well toss coins in a well," Yvgeny muttered.

Brianna glared at Yvgeny, and grumbled, "Funny, she said I should give *you* a chance. How's that for quackery?"

Yvgeny's glare softened and he muttered, "Well, maybe she's not a complete quack."

Having been subdued by Brianna, Yvgeny checked his watch, then nodded at Beatrice.

"OK, Ms. Beatrice, so, three p.m.? That's only ten minutes away. I will make all the preparations and return with a gurney at, say, 3:15?"

Beatrice raised a hand in triumph and said, "Perfect!"

They filed out behind Beatrice as she went down the circular stairs and back out onto the porch. Another short flight led down to the grass, and on either side of the railing were large pots full of blooming petunias. Beatrice poured out the coffee into one of the pots, then placed the mug on the railing. She pulled a card from her pocket and handed it over to Brianna, and said, "Jeanine Ledbetter, his daughter. I wrote his son's information on the back."

Yvgeny nodded and after a few more pleasantries, he and Brianna returned to Cerberus. He could feel the uneasy looks from the old people in their rocking chairs.

"What were you going to call him?" Brianna asked.

"What are you talking about?"

"You told Beatrice you were going to collect the m- m- Mr. Ledbetter. What were you going to say?"

Yvgeny opened his mouth, then closed it.

"You were going to call him meat, weren't you? Collect the *meat*? Are you serious?"

Yvgeny shrugged.

"Meat in motion, my dear, that's all we are. And after we die, we're just meat."

Brianna stared at him in amazement as he turned and fiddled with the rear gate of Cerberus. Then he sat against the gate and called the next of kin to close the deal. There was no answer, so he left a message, then tried the son, with the same result. He sighed, then shrugged.

Doesn't matter, the job's already 99% mine.

The vast majority of the time, it was first come, first serve. Grieving family members almost never conduct a feverish round of price shopping in deciding who would bury their loved one. Not to mention, in this case, Yvgeny already had the body. What kind of family would yank a body away from him to take it to another mortuary to save a few bucks? It almost never happened.

The body had to go somewhere, and usually the man with the meat was the man with the deal.

Yvgeny slid out the collapsible gurney he kept in back for just such an occasion.

As he dropped the wheels into place on the gurney, one of the elderly residents shuffled by Cerberus and planted himself close to the street, nervously switching his weight from one foot to another. The unusual behavior caught Yvgeny's attention, and he turned several times to look at the old man. Each time, he caught the old man looking back at him, making Yvgeny even more suspicious.

The man repeatedly checked his watch, then scanned the streets. Yvgeny put his hands on his hips, glaring at the man.

I know what's happening here.

As he expected, a few minutes later, an older, brown panel van pulled up and parked across the street. While he watched, a middle-aged Indian man emerged and came around the front of the van. He was wearing jeans and a navy laboratory style coat. He looked around, then approached the elderly man and handed him something. The surreptitious nature of the exchange caused Yvgeny to narrow his eyes.

"What's that all about?" Brianna asked.

Yvgeny didn't take his eyes away, snarling, "I know exactly what this is about. Wait here."

When the elderly man saw him coming, he shuffled away as fast as he could. Yvgeny didn't pay any attention to him, as his eyes were fixed on the Indian man.

"Well, well, paying off moles now, is that the depths to which you have stooped?"

The Indian male laughed and squared off with Yvgeny.

THE BODY IN THE BED

"Beats chasing ambulances, freak."

"Listen, Raj, Singh, whoever you are, this is my turf. Why don't you scurry up to Macon where there's enough bodies for everyone?"

"Don't you worry about my business, *vella*. And it's the Raj Brothers, not Singh! Maybe I should call you Eldred!"

"Look, whoever you are, you're too late. First come, first serve, so push off. I got dibs!"

The Indian man looked past Yvgeny toward the porch, over to Cerberus, then sighed.

"You got lucky this time, *vella*, but your luck will run out!"

"Yeah, yeah, and when yours runs out, you can always shutter that taxidermy salon of yours and buy a 7 Eleven!"

The Indian spouted off angrily to Yvgeny in his mother tongue, then stormed back to his van. Yvgeny returned to the back of Cerberus and posted beside Brianna.

"What was that about?"

"Nothing, just a sore loser."

Promptly at three p.m., Jezelda pulled up in her BMW five-series sedan. She claimed to be a Haitian voodoo priestess, but Yvgeny knew better. Her multicolored flowing skirts and head kerchief was nothing more than a costume. She marched up the driveway and when she saw Yvgeny and Brianna, she headed their way. Yvgeny turned and pretended to be busy with a corner of the gurney.

"Brianna, my *bèl ti fi*, how you doing?"

Brianna smiled, and then Jezelda looked over at Yvgeny. Yvgeny did not look up until Brianna's elbow connected with his ribs. He forced a smile and then, with his arms crossed, motioned with his head toward her car and asked, "Nice car, how many crystal balls did you have to rub to afford it?"

Jezelda stared at him, then motioned to his hearse, and asked, "and how many ditches you dig for that *korbiyar*?"

She looked at her watch, then announced, "I'm late," kissed Brianna on the cheek, then pushed past Yvgeny and headed toward the front door of Sunset Manor.

"Do you always have to be such a jerk?"

"Of course not. I *choose* to be such a jerk!"

A few minutes later, the front door flew open and Jezelda came stumbling out, wailing. She took several steps away from the door, fell onto her knees in the grass, then pressed her face against the ground as if in prayer.

Brianna ran toward her, and Yvgeny started at the sound of the door, bumping his head on the top of his hearse. When he saw Jezelda on the grass, he also headed in her direction, a smirk on his face. Jezelda had been trailed out of the door by Beatrice and several of Sunset Manor's elderly guests. One of them was holding out her iPhone, recording the event for posterity.

Brianna got to Jezelda first. She put her hand on Jezelda's back and asked, "What's wrong? What happened?"

"Death! Murder! It's here, I can feel it! *Ghede Nibo* tell me! He tell me through his *chevals*, they speak with the voice of the murdered, and they speaking to me, they says he be killed!"

Yvgeny's smirk broadened into a smile as he listened to her hysterical tirade. Beatrice came up and perched beside Brianna.

"Jezelda, whatever is the matter?"

Jezelda just wailed and buried her face further into the grass. Beatrice looked over at Brianna and Yvgeny; when she realized Yvgeny was smiling, her face clouded with confusion.

Brianna replied, "She was saying something about murder."

Beatrice's cheeks reddened and for a moment she seemed fearful. Then she shook it off and her eyes narrowed. She glanced back down with a sympathetic expression.

"Poor dear, she didn't even make it past the lobby, she just looked around as if she heard something, then she went crazy."

Jezelda looked up, turned back toward the house, nodded her head, and, with tears streaming down her face, turned to Beatrice and said, "Death! There's death inside!"

Beatrice put a soft hand on her shoulder and said, "Yes, Jezelda, a man died here this morning. He's still upstairs. Yvgeny is here to pick him up. He was very sick, Jezelda, he wasn't murdered."

"Murder! Cold blooded murder, *Ghede Nibo*, he used his *chevals*, his *chevals* spoke to me in *his* voice, the voice of the dead, the murdered man!"

Beatrice, now blushing slightly, tried to bring Jezelda to her feet, but she wouldn't budge. She blotted at her forehead

THE BODY IN THE BED

from the effort, then scanned the lawn, hoping Jezelda wasn't making too much of a spectacle.

Jezelda wailed again, but then finally started to climb to her feet. Beatrice seemed relieved. Jezelda turned to Yvgeny and pointed a dark finger at him. "Don't you take that body, you go fetch the police. This is a murder!"

"Jezelda, my dear, please, you're making such a fuss!"

Beatrice continued trying to hush Jezelda.

Yvgeny looked down at Jezelda's finger, then used one of his own to push it aside.

"Right. Murder. If you're talking to the dead guy, why don't you just tell him to call 911?"

Jezelda fell out of character for a moment, long enough to make an obscene gesture toward Yvgeny, then her eyes rolled back into her head and in a loud and theatric voice she cried,

"By knife, by gun, by stone, you kill,
It force your hand,
Destroy your will,
Jealousy, anger, desperation, madness,
They eats your soul,
Leaving only sadness."

Jezelda turned in a circle, looking at the three of them, then lurched across the grass toward her car. Beatrice watched her, relieved, then realized she was holding a wad of cash. She started walking after her.

"Jezelda, but you aren't finished yet!" Beatrice called out to her, waving a wad of money in her hand.

Jezelda stopped and glanced back at Beatrice and the money in her hand, quickly returned to snatch the money, then resumed her trek across the grass. Without turning around, Jezelda raised a hand and yelled, "Must get to my house, the *Loa* need a sacrifice!" A moment later she was gone, leaving only some greasy skids in the street from her rapid acceleration away from the crime scene. Yvgeny turned to Beatrice and said, "Well, that was fun!"

"Oh, I just don't know what got into her! Carrying on like that won't be good for her business."

"Are you kidding me? She's a flim-flam artist; that was pure marketing!" Yvgeny said.

Beatrice shook her head.

Yvgeny looked quizzically at Brianna, and, seeing the concern on her face, he shrugged, then returned to his hearse to get his gurney, leaving Brianna and Beatrice on the lawn, their faces full of pity and indecision.

When Yvgeny wheeled his gurney back up the sidewalk, humming a breathy tune, he stopped to look at them both. Brianna had tears welling in her eyes, and Beatrice was comforting her.

"Oh, come on, are you serious? She's a lunatic! Brianna- you going to help me with this?"

Both ladies just stared at him in disbelief.

"Fine, I'll do it myself."

He kicked the front wheels over the threshold and wheeled the gurney inside. Instead of being unobtrusive and unnoticed, as was the plan, he wheeled it toward the staircase through a throng of elderly people, some with canes, some on crutches, some in wheel chairs. As they milled about, Yvgeny began calling out, "Step aside, meat wagon coming through!"

As he pushed through the crowd, some crossed their heart. Others stared at the wall, oblivious to everything. One woman in a wheel chair was staring out into space with a broad smile on her face. As he passed by, she took in a deep breath and called out, "Meat wagon coming through!"

Yvgeny navigated to the first step, then kicked a pedal beside one of the wheels and the gurney collapsed. It was very light, and easy enough to break down to carry up the stairs. Of course, once he strapped the old man onto it, Brianna would have to help him lug it back down the stairs.

As he hefted up the gurney, one voice carried over the generally soft and brittle murmur of the ancient voices.

"Better call the coroner!"

Yvgeny turned toward the voice, but saw nothing but a sea of elderly white faces.

"Who said that?"

"Over here, sport!"

Yvgeny scanned the crowd, and after a moment, he saw a commotion toward the back of the atrium. He heard some muffled curses, then picked out an old man as he pushed his way through the geriatric horde. The man that stepped clear

THE BODY IN THE BED

of the group was clearly in his eighties, wearing a plaid flannel shirt and jeans kept up with a pair of red suspenders. He was a little stooped but didn't have a cane. He wore his gray hair in a flat top and had a well-trimmed mustache.

"Luther P. Telfair, at your service!"

Yvgeny smiled and said, "Well, Luther, a coroner notification is standard procedure for a nursing home like this -"

"This ain't no nursing home, sport, this here's an assisted living center. Look around, we ain't a bunch of damn gummers."

"OK, whatever it is, I'm sure Beatrice already notified the coroner."

"Yessir, and the coroner's going to have to call the GBI, you got a witness saying this here's a murder!"

Yvgeny sighed.

"A witness? Jezelda's nuts, that guy was on hospice, he already had one foot in the grave. There's no way the Georgia Bureau of Investigation is going to -"

"Don't matter, sport. Murder's murder. Guy jumps off a cliff, and you shoot him in the head on his way down, it's still murder, and you're going to jail."

Yvgeny took a deep breath, stuck an index finger in his ear and scratched.

"What are you, some kind of expert?"

The whispers and murmurs suddenly stopped as all eyes turned to Luther P. Telfair. One of the women standing nearby turned to Yvgeny and asked, incredulous, "You don't know Chief Telfair?"

"Don't ring a bell. Should it?" Yvgeny asked, inspecting his finger, then switching ears.

The old woman cleared her throat and recited, "Henry County Police Department's longest serving officer ever: fifty-seven years!"

Another old woman stepped forward, smiled at her friend, then announced, "Got him a commendation signed by President George H.W. Bush hisself, yes he did!"

A collective croon of respect washed over the group. The recipient blushed slightly, then straightened his back.

"Hash marks all the way past my elbow."

"Huh?"

"Hash marks. Where you been, sonny boy? Under a rock? You get a hash mark on your sleeve for every four years' service. I had 'em up past my elbow."

"I see. Congratulations. Now if you'll excuse me, I have a client to tend to."

Luther shuffled a little closer, and, after a conspiratorial glance over each shoulder, leaned in and whispered, still loud enough for the entire room to hear him, "You and me need to talk."

Yvgeny shrugged, then rubbed his index fingers on his pants. He noticed hearing aids in each ear as the old man turned left, then right.

"OK, follow me upstairs."

"I don't do stairs. I'll take the elevator."

Yvgeny cursed under his breath.

"You have an elevator?"

THE BODY IN THE BED

CHAPTER TWO

✟

"So, what is it we need to talk about?"

Luther walked ahead toward Earnest's room while Yvgeny dropped the wheels down and started pushing the gurney again.

Luther stopped outside Earnest's closed door and leaned across the gurney separating him from Yvgeny.

"Motive, sport, if you have a motive, you might have a murder."

"That's great, Luther, very helpful."

Luther cocked his head and asked, "Ain't *you* an uppity sumbitch! Got plenty of motive here. Sex, money, love, power. Fifty-seven years on the force, and every crime I ever saw started over one of those."

"You kidding me? This guy's like ninety years old. He might have money, but -"

"Eighty-four. Three years younger than me. And he had it all, sport, trust me."

Luther started to bob his head and beat box, then started rapping.

"He had it all, my friend, way back in the day,
Had money, had girls, that was just his way.
Back when I was little, he used to say,
Work hard when you're young, then you'll get to play!"

All Yvgeny could do was stare. The old man wiped his mouth, then cleared his throat.

"Words to live by, right there."

Yvgeny finally composed himself and asked, "You're a poet?"

Luther smiled, revealing a set of stained, brown teeth. His original set, not aftermarket, like most of the corpses that end up on his table.

"Nope. That was the one and only Junior G, straight outta' Macon."

"An eighty-seven year old man that listens to rap?"

"Junior's pe-paw, Grady, used to live at the Sunset. Good man. Junior used to come pay his respects, before he became a celebrity. He brought his pe-paw a bunch of his CDs once, and I got hooked."

Yvgeny stared at him a moment, then said, "Wait a minute. You're serious?"

"Everyone's got their vices, sport. I got your attention now?"

Yvgeny crossed his arms and said, "I'm listening."

"Earnest was in banking. Lost his wife back in the nineties. He got along OK for a while, but then he had a stroke. Made it tough for him, and his two kids, well, they was better at spending *his* money than making their own. They didn't want to take care of him, either, so they just stuck him in here. 'Bout three years ago, I reckon."

Luther licked his lips, pursed them a few times, then continued.

"Ernie, he was tough as nails. Taught his left side to work again, yessir, started walking again, started talking again, started doing everything again."

The old man emphasized his last comment with an elbow nudge into Yvgeny's ribs and a conspiratorial wink, causing Yvgeny to turn slightly pale.

"Anyway, he wasn't perfect, but he made the best of it. He talked a little funny after the stroke. He told the ladies he was British. Ha!"

He slapped one of his legs, then squinted at Yvgeny a moment, shaking his head.

"Boy, he was a real player around here. Sealed the deal like nobody's business. Bought Viagra in bulk, if you catch my drift."

Yvgeny winced, but tried to remain stoic.

"So, sex, there's your first motive," Luther said with a smile, a satisfied look on his face, then he continued.

"Money, too. That's always a motive. Ernie was like most of us, we only see the good in our kids until it's too late. They convinced him he needed to be in a place like this, dropped him off, then they told him they'd take care of the payments. What'd he do? He handed over his checkbook. Boy, was that a mistake!"

Luther shifted his weight and looked away, down the hall. His words grew softer.

"When you're locked up like that, it's hard to know what's happening with your money. Most of us ain't big on computers, don't really trust the interwebs."

Luther turned and looked at Yvgeny, shaking his head.

"I remember when his son dropped him off, he was driving an old beat up Ford Ranger. Didn't see them again for about a year, and only then because they needed his signature on something."

"They blew through his checking accounts, then they came back to get his savings. A few weeks ago, that putz showed up in a fancy new Mercedes. You think that ass wipe earned it?"

Luther's cheeks reddened and he punched a fist into his open hand several times. He started to pace back and forth in the hallway in front of Earnest's door.

"Back in my day, I'd have cuffed his ass right there in the yard. And ooh, Ernie was hot. And then, then he found out from Beatrice that she hadn't gotten a payment from him in a few months."

Yvgeny asked, "Then what happened?"

Luther shrugged.

"The next day, Ernie called his accountant. Cut them both off. And then he changed his will. He was a sucker, but he wasn't a dummy."

After a pregnant pause, the old chief said, "There's your money."

Yvgeny remained quiet. The old man fidgeted while he leaned on the wall, then said, more softly, "Love and power, those are more difficult around here. Money can get you some of each, but it ain't the real thing."

"What do you mean?"

"Well, none of us really work anymore, and we ain't royalty, so power's kind of a relative concept at this stage. And love? Well, we tend to take it day by day. We ain't much for planning futures, especially with each other."

"That's a fair point. So, in this case, sex or money."

JONATHAN B. ZEITLIN

"Now you're catching on."

Luther turned and finally opened Earnest's door and walked inside. Yvgeny followed him, pushing his gurney. Luther walked toward the nightstand while Yvgeny looked on. Luther took each medicine bottle and brought them up, one at a time, to inspect. His vision was terrible, and he had to hold each bottle just a few inches from his face to read the label. He grinned upon reading the first one, then shook the bottle, the pills inside rattling like a maraca.

"What I tell you? The little blue pills! That horn dog!"

Yvgeny moved closer.

Luther hunted around the nightstand, then started rubbing it.

"What are you doing?" Yvgeny asked.

"There was something here. A cup, or a mug. Where'd it go?"

Yvgeny leaned in and saw the coffee mug had left a ring on the wood.

"Coffee mug. It was here earlier. Beatrice took it away."

Luther stood a moment, deep in thought, then straightened up and turned to the bed. He bent over slightly to look at Earnest's face, then lifted the sheets to look underneath. He grunted occasionally as he worked. Then he lifted the eyelids and studied his eyes.

"Cancer. He didn't have much longer. Poor bastard."

As Luther continued inspecting the body, Yvgeny wandered toward the dresser and opened the first drawer. Inside were a collection of socks and a dinner plate, likely filched from the kitchen downstairs. On the plate there was a wedding ring, a wad of cash, and a few credit cards. Yvgeny glanced over his shoulder at Luther, still hunched over the body, then pocketed the cash and the ring. He left the cards- not worth the risk.

"Well, hard to say, you'd need an autopsy to make sure," the old man said to himself.

"Autopsy?" Yvgeny asked, "What are you talking about?"

Movement outside got Yvgeny's attention, and he turned to look out the window. A cherry red older model conversion van was backing into the driveway of Sunset Manor. Yvgeny sighed. The driver gunned the accelerator, the glass packs rumbling, before turning off the engine. Jimmy Flowers, in

THE BODY IN THE BED

the flesh.

"Oh goody, the coroner's here."

Luther looked at Yvgeny, then out the window.

"That ain't the sheriff!" Luther said.

"Sorry, the *deputy* coroner is here."

"That dandy?"

Luther pinched his lips together in the universal expression of distaste, then took one more look around the room.

"Well, so much for proving a murder."

Yvgeny put his hands on his hips, turned to Luther, and said, "Look, Luther, this ain't no murder, and even if it was, he was already on his way out the door. He needs to go in the ground before the end of the week or it's going to be closed casket, if you know what I'm saying."

"Listen here, sport, it's a murder until the coroner says otherwise. And until he says otherwise, Earnest goes to Macon, you feel me?"

"Have you met Jimmy? It's a wonder he was able to find this place at all."

"Yeah? Well, *you* didn't see the elevator!" Luther scoffed.

A few minutes later, the door to Earnest's room opened up, and Jimmy Flowers walked inside. Flowers wore a pair of jeans and a Hawaiian shirt, unbuttoned halfway, exposing a carpet of shiny black hair. He sported a thick mustache, and an affable smile. Flowers was a diehard Tom Selleck fan and a *Magnum, PI*, aficionado. He specifically chose the color of his van to match Magnum's Ferrari. Behind him huffed Beatrice, winded from having to take the stairs again. She leaned against the threshold of Earnest's room, and in between gasps, she was trying to speak with Flowers.

"Dr. Flowers, there's really nothing to see, I only called because the law requires it, seriously, you're wasting your time. Besides, Geny is here, he can just take the body and be on his way -"

Beatrice continued babbling at Flowers, but Flowers was laser focused on Yvgeny.

"Well, well, well, the undertaker himself."

"Good Lord, Flowers, who called *you*?"

Flowers straightened up, placed his hand over his heart, and with a self-righteous snort said, "I am the deputy coroner and it is my solemn responsibility to declare whether this death requires a referral to the medical examiner!"

Luther looked the doctor up and down, rolled his eyes, and walked toward the door. Ignoring Flowers, the old man turned back to Yvgeny and said, "Motive, sport. It's all about motive," then with a wink, he was gone.

"What was that about?" Flowers and Beatrice both asked.

"Don't worry about it."

Yvgeny smiled at Beatrice as he grabbed the door knob and slowly closed the door in Beatrice's face.

"I'm sorry, official business, my dear. Be out in a jiff!"

Yvgeny turned back to Flowers with his arms crossed over his chest.

"Look, Flowers, just do your hocus pocus and go, I gotta get this guy in the fridge before the flies start to hatch."

"Save your theatrics for someone else, Geny. I know your shuck and jive."

Yvgeny watched as the doctor glanced around the room, disinterestedly picked up one of the bottles on the nightstand, then looked at the body.

"Anyone touch him?"

"Yes, we cuddled for a while, then I made sure he was wearing something nice so he'd be presentable for you."

Flowers glared at Yvgeny, but didn't respond. Yvgeny looked outside to check on Brianna.

"Seriously, what was that old fart talking about, 'motive?' Something you ain't telling me?"

"No, he was just saying you never have a murder without motive."

"Right. So, this is the guy Jezelda was carrying on about?"

Yvgeny opened his mouth to begin unraveling a new story, then closed it. Flowers might already have spoken to Beatrice. Or Brianna.

"She was claiming some spirits visited her and told her he was murdered."

Yvgeny tried to sound as flippant as possible, but it fell flat. Flowers made a sound in his throat, then turned back to the body.

"You know what, I bet the sheriff would let me do this one _"

"No way, Flowers, this one's mine. I was here first!"

THE BODY IN THE BED

Flowers smiled and said, "It don't work that way, Geny, and you know it. This looks like a natural, and he's on hospice, but all things considered, I betcha the GBI would let me do a limited autopsy. That's $600 bucks for about three hours' work!"

"Well, a decent funeral will net me over $4,000, minimum, so step off, cowboy."

"You know how silly that sounds coming out of your mouth, with that Russian accent of yours?"

"It's Polish, you idiot."

Although Yvgeny was born and raised in the United States, his parents were first generation Americans, having left communist Poland before he was born. Unfortunately, they never taught him their mother tongue, so he only learned English from birth, but with his parents' accent. He absorbed their culture, but not the language itself, much to his frustration.

"Whatever," Flowers said as he opened his phone and started scrolling through his address book. Speaking to himself, he muttered, "suspicious natural, just tell 'em a psychic said it was murder, but ain't no evidence, that should do it."

He placed the phone to his ear, then glanced over at Yvgeny.

"If I get a green light, I'll be done tonight, you can probably get him by eight." Then he straightened up and said, "Hi, Sheriff?"

Yvgeny let out a frustrated breath and went back to the drawers, opened up the second one. Shirts. He opened the third as he heard Flowers say, "Yes, just a limited should be enough for us to close the book on it."

Yvgeny grumbled to himself wordlessly and opened another drawer. He wrinkled his nose in disgust as he found a bottle of lubricant laying on top of some folded pants. He'd seen enough.

"Nope, no need to notify the GBI yet." After a pause, he said, "Of course, I will let them know." Then he ended the call.

"Jackpot!" Flowers called out as he shut his flip phone and stuffed it back into his pocket. "I got the green light for a limited. Come on, let me borrow that cart of yours."

Yvgeny hesitated, and Flowers let out a chortle and said, "Are you kidding me? You already have it up here, just give me a hand with the body. Damn, Geny, you always have to be like this?"

Yvgeny moved in closer with a sigh and stepped on the wheel brakes of the cart, then grabbed Earnest's feet. Flowers called out, "One, two, three, heave!" then they both lifted him up and dropped him on the gurney. As Flowers strapped him down under a sheet, Yvgeny sniffed, squinted his eyes, then leaned in and sniffed again.

"Damn, Flowers, it's not even four p.m. and you're already in the sauce?"

"It's my after shave."

"Yeah, right, *eau de* gin and tonic."

"Whatever," Flowers responded, then he turned and grabbed the prescription bottles from the nightstand.

"You really think you'll be done with him tonight?"

Flowers looked at his watch, then back at the body.

"Just like I said. I'm just going to run blood work, maybe take a tissue sample, do a quick external examination. Probably finish around eight."

"Why can't you just do all that here?"

"You kidding me? In the middle of a nursing home?"

"Assisted living center."

"Whatever."

"What you're trying to say is you shouldn't perform autopsies when you're drunk."

"Stick it, undertaker."

Yvgeny trailed behind Flowers as he struggled to push the cart toward the door, the small wheels digging into the carpet. Once he finally got it into the hall, he stopped and turned back to Yvgeny.

"Um, maybe you can give the sheriff's office a call. Boss wants me to let the detectives know I'm taking Earnest here over to the shop."

"Any reason why *you* can't do that?"

"Because I kind of got my hands full!" Flowers cried out, filled with righteous indignation. Then Flowers patted Earnest on his chest and added, more calmly, "Besides, the more I can focus on looking under the hood, the quicker I can finish and the quicker you can do whatever it is you do."

THE BODY IN THE BED

Yvgeny tried to be rational. *If this idiot goes to the cops, they'd definitely open a case, and I'll never get the body back.*

Besides, closed casket was always bad for business. Sure, it's less work for me, but it's all about the benjamins.

Yvgeny sighed, then grudgingly nodded his head.

"I suppose I can notify them."

Flowers sneered, "That's great, Geny, you're a real pal."

When Flowers pushed the body through the front door and onto the porch, all heads turned. Beatrice had been chatting with Brianna, but when she saw Flowers at the helm of the gurney, she squinted and started following him down the handicapped ramp on one side of the stairs.

"What are you doing?" Beatrice snipped.

Flowers stopped, then glanced over at Yvgeny.

"What do you mean?"

"What are *you* doing with him? Shouldn't Geny be taking him?"

Yvgeny moved next to Flowers at the bottom of the porch and waved his arm theatrically toward Flowers.

"Master deputy coroner has determined there is sufficient evidence to justify an autopsy, based on the musings of a half-baked crackpot."

Flowers pursed his lips and started to protest, but his words were drowned out by Beatrice.

"That's ridiculous!" Beatrice cried, her cheeks coloring.

Yvgeny and Flowers shrugged their shoulders in unison, then Yvgeny replied, "Well, Madame, *you* were the one that called him."

"It's the law, but I didn't think -"

Yvgeny interrupted her to say, "but don't worry, Dr. Ginsu has assured me he will bring me whatever's left once he finishes with him."

Those within earshot winced, and one made the sign of the cross on his chest.

"Have some respect for the dead, young man," Beatrice chided. Then she turned to Flowers and added, "and please be quick and respectful with him. In fact, are you sure you have to touch him at all? Can't Geny just take a look?"

Flowers puffed up indignantly.

"Sorry, he's an undertaker, not a physician like me."

"Physician? Right. And Jezelda is a real voodoo priestess.

Imagine if you two joined forces. Every time you killed a patient, she could bring them back to life as a zombie with some of her hocus pocus. Hell, you could make your own army! Take over the world!"

"Keep it up, undertaker," Flowers said, "and you'll get this guy back in little chunks. It'll be a human jigsaw puzzle. You'll need a hundred bottles of Elmer's to glue him back together."

Flowers turned with a huff and pushed off with the gurney. Yvgeny followed from a distance, but then diverted from Flowers's path to join Brianna and Beatrice on the lawn. Beatrice's cheeks were red and tears welled in her eyes. Her hands shook.

While Yvgeny still watched from a distance, Flowers secured Earnest in the back of his converted van, then swerved onto the street, horns blaring behind him from the erratic move. Everyone watched him leave, then turned back to Yvgeny, who straightened his morning coat and turned to face Brianna.

"What happened?" Brianna asked.

Yvgeny looked at Beatrice and said, "Well, *someone* called the coroner's office."

Beatrice said, "Of course, I had to do it by law, but I didn't think he was going to *take* him!"

Yvgeny, bemused, spoke slowly.

"Well, I guess -"

"And he was on hospice, for heaven's sake!"

"Yes, but -"

"The only reason I called was that Earnest's doctor wasn't around."

"I know, but -"

"And Jezelda, well, people will start to talk, you know how it is in Comstock!"

Yvgeny closed his mouth and waited. Beatrice marched across the lawn in a huff, and Brianna and Yvgeny watched her until she clomped up the stairs and through the door. She almost knocked over Luther, who had just opened the door to come outside.

"So, Flowers is taking him to the shop?" Brianna asked.

"Yup. And we'll get the leftovers when he's done."

"Why was she so upset?" Brianna asked.

THE BODY IN THE BED

Yvgeny, who was watching Luther shuffle toward them, just shrugged and said, "Dunno."

Luther arrived, then stuck his thumbs behind his suspenders and grinned.

"Well, that was fun!"

Brianna, unsatisfied, turned back to Yvgeny.

"I'm confused, why did Flowers take him again?"

Luther turned to Brianna and snapped his suspenders with his thumbs.

"Earnest was on hospice. That means his doctor can just sign the certificate and he goes in the ground. No inquest, no autopsy. But Earnest left us while the doctor wasn't around to sign the death certificate."

Luther turned to Yvgeny, then Brianna, who was still furrowing her brow.

"So, 'cause the doctor wasn't here, they had to call the coroner," then, with an eye roll, Luther added, "or in this case, the deputy coroner. But even if the doctor was here, if he thought the death was suspicious in any way, he'd probably call the ME."

"A coroner *and* a medical examiner?"

"Georgia law says the sheriff can be the coroner. Coroner ain't gotta be a doctor."

"I'm confused." Brianna said.

"Gilbert County is unique, my dear," Yvgeny said, putting his arm around her. "It's one of the few counties in the state where the coroner- well, the deputy coroner, is also on the GBI contract. God help us, but Flowers actually has the authority to conduct an autopsy on behalf of the county. How insane is that?"

As Yvgeny shuddered, Luther asked, "Did he tell the sheriff yet?"

"Yes, but he roped me into notifying our good friends at the Gilbert County Sheriff's Department, Office of Investigations."

"You mean those two-"

"Yes, those two."

Yvgeny turned back to Luther.

"Well, it's been a pleasure. Really."

Yvgeny then turned toward Brianna and held out his arm.

"Now then, my dear, shall we pay our fine law enforcement

friends a visit?"

Once they shut the doors of Cerberus and got on the road, Brianna turned to Yvgeny, and asked, "Why are *we* going? Why can't Flowers report the autopsy himself? It's just a phone call, right?"

Yvgeny took a deep breath.

"Flowers asked me to call, and it's a good thing, trust me. You want that clown reporting an autopsy? Next thing you know, there will be a line of police cars outside his office, and we'll never get that body!"

"So what?"

"So what? Are you kidding me? That means no funeral. That means no money. And if the cops get involved, the GBI's going to carve him up like a turkey. They'll be tossing his organs on a scale, then shoving them back inside. Do you know how much work it will be to piece things back together? I mean, really!"

"So just do closed casket."

Yvgeny shook his head slowly.

"Oh, my dear, think about it. If all those geezers show up to the funeral and all they see is a wooden box, what will they think?"

Brianna stared at him blankly. Yvgeny sighed.

"But, if they see the old man looking like a million bucks, who do you think they will want embalming them when *they're* ready for *their* dirt nap?"

Brianna shuddered and remained quiet for the rest of the drive.

The Gilbert County Sheriff's Department's Headquarters was down the street in the heart of Comstock. Within that building sat the Office of Investigations, home to the county's two detectives, Harry Newsome and Bubba Johnson. For run of the mill investigations, they split the county, geographically, but shared the cases coming out of the county seat, Comstock. In bigger cases, like murders or one of the other "seven deadlies," they banded together.

Yvgeny and the two detectives shared a mutual dislike and mistrust for each other based on their prior interactions. The detectives believed Yvgeny interfered with a murder investigation from the previous year, even went so far as to arrest him and his gravedigger, Alfred, although both were

THE BODY IN THE BED

later released without charges.

Yvgeny, on the other hand, thought the detectives were incompetent boors, and the mistrust of the police he acquired from his parents only magnified his feelings. Having grown up in communist Poland, Yvgeny's parents had grown accustomed to crooked cops; paying bribes to avoid jail for imagined crimes was standard fare.

"Why couldn't we just do this with a phone call?"

Yvgeny snorted and shook his head with a smile. Yvgeny considered himself old fashioned, and of course, as a Sherlock Holmes aficionado, he knew the great detective would never do such a thing by telephone.

"Oh, my dear, there's a right way and a wrong way. Trust me."

On their way inside the precinct, Yvgeny turned to Brianna and muttered, "Here goes nothing," then painted a look of nonchalance on his face as he stepped inside.

A woman dressed neck to ankle in navy polyester looked up from her post at the front desk. Her eyebrows were penciled on and her eye shadow was a bright French blue. Yvgeny remembered her from his last visit to the station.

Maxine, I believe.

He approached the desk with a practiced air of disinterest.

"Maxine, I believe?"

Glancing down at her nameplate, all he saw was her last name, Baker.

"I wish to deliver a message to Detective Newsome."

Yvgeny began chanting to himself, *don't be here, don't be here!*

Maxine appeared to remember him, too, and she pursed her lips as if she had bitten into a lemon. She turned to her phone panel and put on her headset without a word to Yvgeny. She pressed several buttons, adjusted the microphone of her headset, then pressed a button and leaned forward.

"Yeah, Harry, that guy is here again, the one with all the dead people. I ain't even gonna *try* pronouncing his name."

She listened a moment, then glanced back at Yvgeny, inspected him up and down, and then nodded to herself.

"Yeah, that's about right."

A moment later she turned back to Yvgeny and said, "He'll

be right out."

"Fantastic."

A moment later, Harry Newsome appeared. He looked like a Wild West sheriff's deputy straight out of central casting, with a bushy mustache, deep set eyes, and longish graying hair. He wore cowboy boots, jeans, and a flannel shirt. His badge was clipped to his belt, next to his Glock. He was not smiling.

"Well, well, well, Count Dracula and his lovely assistant." He turned to Brianna, said "Ma'm."

"Lovely to see you again too, inspector," Yvgeny said.

Yvgeny preferred inspector to detective, just as he preferred undertaker to mortician, constable to officer, verbal anachronisms originating from his parents' archaic English. Most of their language study consisted of old books and movies they scrounged after fleeing communist Poland: another curse left to him by his parents.

Of course, it wasn't all their fault. Yvgeny also picked up some of his linguistic peculiarities from his avid reading of Sir Doyle's works, all in their original text. He always kept one of his dog-eared copies on his nightstand, and on his shelves, he displayed multiple copies and versions of his short stories and full-length novels.

"To what do I owe this high honor? You come to tell me you've solved another murder?"

"Ah, inspector, resentment is unbecoming on you."

For a moment, Newsome and Yvgeny stared at each other. Finally, Newsome broke the silence.

"How long's it been? Few months, I reckon?"

"Five months, to be precise."

Newsome nodded.

"And I hear you took that kid in and gave him a job. The one that chopped up that body."

The kid was Albert, Yvgeny's understudy. Albert was from the nearby town of Byron and currently studied at the hallowed halls of Harrison Hills School of Mortuary Science. He was ushered in with open arms following a glowing recommendation from Yvgeny.

Albert caught Yvgeny's attention the previous fall, when he was finishing high school. For a short time, the boy was also a murder suspect.

THE BODY IN THE BED

It all started one day when his gravedigger, Alfred, set out to prepare a freshly dug grave for a funeral scheduled for later that afternoon. When he arrived at the grave site, he discovered someone had dumped a body in the hole, then attempted to cover it up under a thin layer of soil.

Yvgeny tried to enlist the help of the detectives, but at first, he found their assistance sub-par, forcing him to try to solve the case himself. Yvgeny brought in several of his friends and tried to channel his favorite Sherlock Holmes investigative techniques; he had always wished for such a chance!

Later, when the detectives finally decided to step up their game, they pushed Yvgeny aside, and when they weren't satisfied with his removal from the investigation, they falsely accused Yvgeny and his confederates of obstruction. It became a race to the finish line as each team worked the case, sometimes independently, sometimes together. Eventually they solved the case, each side taking full credit and blaming the other for interfering.

Along the way, several suspects were considered and discarded. Albert was one of them. Some of the kid's antics made him look like a murderer, and, fearing the investigators at the sheriff's office would have fingered an innocent boy of a heinous crime, Yvgeny had to see the case through to the end despite the investigators' warnings. Thanks to Yvgeny, justice was served. Just like his idol, the great Sherlock Holmes, Yvgeny used his deductive reasoning and observation of even the smallest of details to solve the mystery.

When it was all said and done, Yvgeny was so impressed with the boy that he offered him a job, and the boy accepted. Although he had started as Yvgeny's temporary intern, he was quickly promoted to official understudy, having exhibited an incredible aptitude for the profession. By January, he had transferred from Middle Georgia Technical College and a boring future in automotive repair to the eternally exciting and rewarding field of mortuary science at HHMS.

"Small town hero, that boy," Yvgeny gushed.

"Right. Hero. More like felon."

"Potato, potato," Yvgeny responded, using both pronunciations, then added, "The kid's got talent."

JONATHAN B. ZEITLIN

"So, back to my question, Geny, you come to tell me you solved another murder?"

"I merely come to report facts, inspector. I must say, first resentment, now jealousy? Really, sir, I'm surprised."

Yvgeny tried very hard to hold his tongue, and Brianna noticed and squeezed his arm. She leaned in and whispered in his ear, "Don't do it, Geny!" but to no avail. He adjusted his hat, then held on to the lapels of his morning coat, channeling his best Victorian gentleman's pose.

"As I recall, inspector, I dutifully notified the sheriff's department of that murder, and was insulted and ridiculed right back out into the street."

For emphasis, he cleared his throat and tugged on his lapels.

"I did what any model citizen would have done, in order to ensure justice was served."

In fact, Yvgeny had grown quite fond of retelling his story to anyone willing to listen, regaling them with his epic tale of how he single handedly solved a terrible killing, how he drafted a unique and unstoppable group of confidantes to assist him in his zealous pursuit of the killers, and every step of the way, foiling the two gumshoes and their haphazard and negligent approach to the investigation.

I'm a modern-day Sherlock Holmes, he reminded himself. Batting at Brianna's hand squeezing ever harder on his arm, he took a breath to continue his history lesson for the detective, but before he could get another word out, Newsome interrupted him.

"Jealous? Jealous of what? You and your team of morons?"

Newsome quickly turned to Brianna and said, "present company excluded, of course." Then he turned back to Yvgeny and continued, "And why would I be jealous of someone who obstructed that investigation from day one? Oh, that's rich. Bubba's gonna love this!"

Yvgeny took a deep breath, then cleared his throat.

"I'm not interested in having collie-shangles with you, inspector, I'm here on a mission from deputy coroner Flowers, an important mission, dispatched from the sheriff himself."

"Oh, this oughta be good," Newsome announced, then

THE BODY IN THE BED

glanced backward at the woman behind the counter and called out, "Maxine, pay attention, you're gonna want to hear this!" Pointing backwards at Yvgeny with a thumb, he added, "dispatched by the sheriff himself!"

Yvgeny placed his hands on his hips and took a deep breath. He had rehearsed his lines in the hearse on the way over.

"Deputy Coroner Flowers wishes for me to inform you there has been a death at Sunset Manor Assisted Living Center. The man was on hospice and the death was attended by a doctor. However, Madame Jezelda the Psychic -"

"Madame Jezelda? Oh, Maxine, please tell me we got the recorders going in here. I gotta play this for Bubba. OK, sorry Geny, go on."

Yvgeny cleared his throat.

"Madame Jezelda has been informed by reliable spirits from the other side that the victim has been murdered, so in an abundance of caution, Deputy Coroner Flowers has taken the body for a brief examination."

There was silence as Newsome stared at Yvgeny, expectantly. After a few seconds his smile faded and he said, "That's it? That's the best you got?"

Yvgeny turned to Brianna and said, "I think I've had enough of his podsnappery. Let's go."

"No, no, you can't leave yet, Geny!" Newsome cried.

"Um," Maxine interrupted, then said in a small voice, "Harry?"

"Not now, Maxie!"

"OK, Geny, as you were saying? Tell me more about this psychic!"

As Newsome waited expectantly, Yvgeny turned back to Newsome, then looked over Newsome's shoulder and saw the sheriff himself had entered the room and was standing beside Maxine listening to their exchange.

Yvgeny's cheeks colored, but he couldn't hide the smirk that began to form.

"What are you expecting, inspector?"

"I don't know, maybe another dump job or something. Not some old man in an old folk's home."

"Well, I consider you officially informed. And remember, the order came from the sheriff himself. Who am I to question?"

Newsome's eyes narrowed.

Did I overplay my hand? Yvgeny wondered.

"The sheriff has more sense than that, Geny. If he ordered it, it's only because that place is full of voters."

"Damn straight," the sheriff called out. Newsome spun around, and Yvgeny's smirk morphed into a full smile.

"Didn't hear you come in, boss," Newsome muttered.

"The eighty-plus crowd. Them there's the toughest law and order folks I got. Gimme twelve of 'em in the jury box, they'd convict anyone."

The sheriff tugged up on his pants, which had sagged below his ample waist. They only stayed in place a moment before resuming their journey south of the belly button.

"Yessir, they'll know they're in good hands here. That autopsy's worth its weight in gold."

Yvgeny's smile faded, then turned into a frown when the sheriff turned his attention on him.

"Since when does an undertaker perform death notifications? Isn't that my deputy coroner's job?"

"Yes, but he had his hands full with the body. God knows you don't want him multi-tasking."

"At least you got that one right."

The sheriff had not been thrilled with the idea of appointing Flowers deputy coroner, but at the time it was more of an honorific than an actual job. As elected sheriff, he spent most of his time campaigning for his next election, so hiring someone to execute the ministerial functions of coroner was an easy and free way to increase the amount of hand shaking and baby kissing he could accomplish each week.

The sheriff was willing to overlook some of Flowers's idiosyncrasies because he was an actual medical doctor; according to state law, a medical license wasn't required for coroners in a county of their size, but the sheriff figured he'd get some good political mileage out of it. Even better, he'd save his county some money each year if he could pay Flowers for autopsies instead of the GBI.

Unfortunately, Flowers turned out to be more of a nuisance than the sheriff expected. First, the title went straight to his head. Business cards and monogramed Polo

THE BODY IN THE BED

shirts, those things he could stomach. But then his new deputy coroner wanted a converted ambulance. The sheriff resisted it as long as he could, then, in a moment of weakness, allowed Flowers to acquire an old van the county school board had salvaged, then left in the sheriff's yard to be auctioned. *How much trouble could he get in with something like that?* the sheriff thought.

The next thing he knew, Flowers had the van overhauled and beefed up with a set of glass packs, painted bright red, then he stenciled his name and new title on the sides. It looked more like a plumber's van than an ambulance. Every time he saw Flowers drive by, he wanted to punch the nearest wall. Flowers even had the gall to submit a reimbursement request for the work, which the sheriff personally shredded, then scooped the paper chips back into an official Sheriff's Department envelope and mailed it all back to him.

When the sheriff received Flowers's request for a permit to operate lights and siren, he briefly lost his mind.

Newsome looked at his watch, then clapped his hands together and said, "Well, look at the time. Great catching up with you, Geny. Make sure and not come back now, ya' hear?"

Newsome turned on a heel and walked back behind the counter to stand beside the sheriff.

"A pleasure as always," Yvgeny responded softly. He faced the sheriff and with a curt nod, said, "sheriff." Then he turned to Brianna and said, "Let's go."

Newsome returned to his old battered metal desk, which was pressed up against Bubba's so that they faced each other. Space was at a premium in the office, leaving little room for privacy. Bubba was leaning back in his chair, his feet on his desk, and glanced up at Newsome when he walked by.

"That who you thought it was?"

"In the flesh."

Bubba nodded, then spit tobacco juice into a Gatorade bottle.

"What'd he want?"

"Flowers is examining some dead guy from Sunset Manor who was on hospice."

Bubba narrowed his eyes.

"Why would we care about that?"

Newsome smirked and said, "because Jezelda said it was a murder."

"The freak with the bandana?"

"Yup."

"Whatcha gonna do about it?"

Newsome shrugged his shoulders and said, "If it was anyone else, I'd do nothing. But him? And that idiot Flowers? If they're involved -"

Bubba nodded his head. Newsome opened his desk drawer and grabbed his car keys.

"Come on, Bubba, let's go for a ride."

THE BODY IN THE BED

CHAPTER THREE

☦

By the time Bubba and Newsome made it to Flowers's office, Flowers had already withdrawn blood and was completing his visual inspection of the body. Bonnie, Flowers's secretary and assistant, was about to flip the sign from OPEN to CLOSED when they arrived.

Bubba and Newsome opened the door to Flowers's clinic and stepped inside. His lobby was very small, with room only for a small reception desk and two chairs.

Their noses were immediately assaulted by the thick smell of Bonnie's perfume. Bubba grimaced and waved his hand in front of his own face, but Bonnie didn't notice. She saw the badge on Newsome's belt, then turned to Bubba. Her eyes flashed down to his own badge, worn on a chain around his neck. Chewing and popping her gum, the secretary leaned to her right and knocked twice on a shut door, and when a muffled male voice inside called out, "What?" she said, "Cops are here. Wanna talk to you!"

After some commotion inside, the door opened an inch and Flowers peeked out from behind the door.

"Come on out Flowers, we need to talk."

"About what?"

"You take a stiff from Sunset Manor?"

"Maybe."

Bubba glanced at Newsome, who shrugged his shoulders. Bubba squeezed by Bonnie, stepped up to the door, and kicked it just hard enough to smack Flowers in the shoulder and push him backwards. While Flowers tried to recover, Bubba pushed the door all the way in and walked inside, followed by Newsome. Flowers rubbed his shoulder and back pedaled toward his desk, protesting softly.

As Flowers leaned back against his desk, he noticed his bong still sitting on his shelf. He hadn't used it in months, and it was empty of water, but no doubt still had resin in the chamber. He started to panic, but couldn't move. Bubba was staring at him.

"Maybe? You told the undertaker to tell us about it. Remember? What, did you think we wouldn't do our job and come check it out?"

"You- you can't come in here without a warrant."

Bubba looked at Newsome, then back at Flowers, his jaw open in amazement.

"A warrant? You work for the damn sheriff!"

Looking over Flowers's shoulder, Newsome saw the body lying on the exam table, and turned back to Flowers and asked, "You didn't even start cutting on him yet?"

Flowers's eyes grew wide and he said, "I'm not cutting him up! You know how much work that is?" Flowers stuttered for a moment, then spoke softly.

"You two sound just like Geny."

As Bubba walked toward the body, behind Newsome, Flowers quickly side stepped toward the shelving, but before he could reach it, Bubba turned to face him. Flowers froze, hoping his body was blocking Bubba's view of the bong.

"What's an autopsy without chopping up the body and seeing what's inside? How else you gonna see if it was a murder?"

Bubba crossed his arms and waited impatiently for Flowers to answer.

Flowers glanced back toward the body, then shook his head.

"He was on hospice. What would *you* do?"

The detectives said nothing, and after a moment, Flowers let out his breath in a whoosh and muttered, "Look, the sheriff only authorized a limited autopsy. I did a visual, took some blood, poked around a bit, then called it a day. It's good enough."

"Ain't ya supposed to wait for the results before sending him off to the funeral home?"

"Like I said, he was on hospice! He was almost 90 years old. He died in an old folks' home. The only reason I got him at all was that psychic went crazy and said his ghost told her he was murdered. You think I'm gonna cut a guy up for that?"

THE BODY IN THE BED

"Then why do it at all?"

"You kidding me? Quickest $600 I ever made."

The body was on an exam table, with a white towel over his privates. Bubba walked over to the window and looked outside while Newsome walked around the body. Flowers remained in front of his shelving; there wasn't a lot of space in his examination room anyway. He checked his watch, then sighed, a little louder than he intended. He forced himself to relax.

They're here for a possible murder, they're not going to sweat a guy for having a little bit of paraphernalia! Besides, it's legal now!

He shoved his hands in his pockets, leaned back against the cabinet.

Besides, he thought, *I'm already pretty much done with the body. As soon as the cops leave, I'm going to get Geny out here to haul the guy off. Easy money!*

Newsome moved in for a closer look at the body, moving methodically from head to toe. Without looking up, he called out, "Flowers, you didn't see anything strange?"

"Nope."

"You took blood."

"Yup."

"Gonna send it off for analysis?"

"Of course."

"You verify hospice status?"

"Yup."

"Talk to the attending?"

"Yup. Dude from Macon, said the stiff was on his list. Cancer. Had weeks, maybe a month."

"This his stuff?" Bubba asked, reaching for a large paper sack on the couch.

"Yup."

Bubba opened the sack, reached in, and withdrew a pair of pajama pants, held the pair up, glanced at the front, the back, then draped them over the couch. Reaching into the sack again, he poked around, then dropped the bag back on the couch.

Newsome walked around the body one more time, then stood straight, stretched his back with a groan. Then he turned to Bubba and said softly, "Come on, we're done here."

Flowers had to move to the other side of the couch to let them pass toward the door. On their way out, Newsome looked at Flowers and added, "I'd appreciate you letting me know when you get the results of that tox screen, maybe fax us a copy?"

Flowers nodded, adding, "Sure, why not?"

Newsome passed by the shelving, seemingly not noticing, then Bubba followed suit. Just as he passed the shelf, however, Bubba reached up and tapped the bong with a finger, sending it smashing to the linoleum tile. It shattered into a million smelly pieces.

"Oops! Sorry Doc, clumsy me!"

Back in their car, Newsome stared out the window a moment while Bubba reached for the tin can in his back pocket, took a pinch of Copenhagen, shoved it under his lip, and wiped his fingers on his jeans.

"This is a complete waste of time, isn't it?" Newsome muttered to himself. Bubba, looking out the window, nodded his head slowly, and added, "Yeah, probably. Any point in talking to the psychic?"

Newsome snorted and said, "Yeah, right."

Flowers waited for the deputies to leave, then collected the blood samples and paperwork and placed them in a lockbox bolted to the ground outside his office. A big sticker on the box said *Rocket Labs*.

"Bonnie, would you schedule a lab pickup? I'm going to get Geny over here to get the body."

Bonnie shuddered, then reached for the phone, adding, "Fine, just don't make me call that creep. And I'm getting out of here before he arrives."

Flowers chuckled and reached for his cell phone.

Yvgeny answered the phone by crooning, "Ah, Flowers, you done making stew out of that poor man?"

"Hardee har, Geny. Look, how soon can you come get him? I don't have any cold storage here and my place already smells like a high school biology lab." Flowers paused, then asked, "Hey, what's all that noise?"

"It's supper time, Flowers. We're at Luigi's grabbing a pie."

"Well hurry up, it's after five p.m. I don't want to wait around here all night."

"How is that my problem?" Yvgeny screeched. "You're the

THE BODY IN THE BED

one that just *had to* cut him up for your measly $600."

"If I cut him up, he'd fit in my refrigerator. Come on, I'll have him ready by the time you get here."

Yvgeny glanced across the table at Brianna, and sighed.

"I assume you found nothing worth informing the law?" Yvgeny asked as he reached for another slice.

"Nope, took some blood and sent it off for a tox screen, did a physical exam, nothing amiss as far as I can tell."

"Gee, Flowers, sounds like you really pulled out all the stops."

"Just hurry up, Geny."

Flowers and Yvgeny both hung up at the same time, each thinking he was the first to end the call.

Flowers opened his cabinet to fetch a body bag, but found the drawer empty. He cursed to himself.

She was supposed to keep up with this stuff!

He looked around his office, trying to remember where Bonnie stored the extras. He opened one drawer after another in his desk, rummaged through the bathroom, even wrenched open the file cabinet drawers, all to no avail.

"Dammit!" he muttered to himself, then glanced across the room at the small closet. Hopeful, he opened the door, and found a box against the wall filled with his body bags. With a sigh of relief, he grabbed a stack of them and returned them to their rightful spot in his cabinet.

These were no run of the mill standard body bags, but a box of bags designed especially for him, deputy coroner. That was exactly what he had stenciled on the top of each bag: *Gilbert County Office of the Deputy Coroner, James Flowers*. A box of twenty came at a 15% discount, setting him back just under $500.

He was quite proud of his design skills, just like the old van he convinced the sheriff to purchase for him. Flowers had it painted cherry red, had his name and coroner logo stenciled on the sides, and even added some glass packs to impress the ladies as he drove through town. The only thing missing (not for lack of trying on his part) was a set of red lights and a siren. Flowers had heard the sheriff turned the same color as Flowers's van when he got the written request for the red lights.

Flowers ordered the fancy envelope style bags to make it

easier to bag his bodies. His order even included special ink that changed color when the bag was exposed to moisture; an especially helpful hack if you want to ensure the contents have not been corrupted.

Yvgeny texted Flowers to tell him he was on his way, and just before seven p.m., he pulled into the parking lot of Flowers' office complex. Flowers had already taken the elevator down and was waiting outside, leaning against the gurney holding the late Mr. Ledbetter. Yvgeny backed into the nearest parking space.

Yvgeny emerged from Cerberus with a slice of New York style pizza in his hand, the cheese oozing off the crust. He approached Flowers, then tossed his half-eaten slice onto the top of the body bag. Yvgeny glanced at the gold stenciled lettering on the body bag, then turned to Flowers and said, "Really?"

Flowers didn't respond, and Yvgeny turned away, shaking his head.

"$600 bucks, huh?" Yvgeny asked as they loaded him into the hearse. Brianna waited in the passenger seat, a lazy smoke trail escaping from the window.

"Easy money."

"You got the paperwork?"

"Not yet. But it's fine, there's nothing to see."

Yvgeny poked at the body, then turned to Flowers.

"Still in one piece. What was the point of this again?"

"$600 bucks."

"Right."

Yvgeny made sure the body was secured in his hearse, then pressed the automatic rear gate button. Just as it started to close, Yvgeny shouted "whoops!" and reached in to grab his slice of pizza from on top of the body. He stuffed it into his mouth, then turned to Flowers and said, barely comprehensibly, "Gotta go."

Flowers saluted Yvgeny, then turned to bring the gurney back to his office.

Yvgeny drove maybe fifty feet, then screeched to a halt. He hopped out and yelled Flowers's name.

"That's my gurney, Doc."

Flowers cocked his head, then remembered he had taken Yvgeny's gurney at Sunset Manor. They stuffed it into the

THE BODY IN THE BED

back of Cerberus, then Yvgeny and Brianna were off again.

Inside his hearse, Yvgeny scrolled through his phone a moment, then sighed.

"Neither of them ever called back?" Brianna asked.

Yvgeny shook his head and said, "Apparently they are too busy to call back an undertaker who called to inquire about their father. Tragic."

It will really be tragic if I have to make a claim to the county to pay for the burial. They never pay enough to make it worthwhile.

Brianna flicked her cigarette out the window and smiled. Yvgeny didn't notice, as he was still musing to himself.

Sometimes a little crowdfunding can even things out, depending on how many friends the dearly departed had. But again, the best way to get paid was from the family.

He felt a smack on his arm and turned to find an irritated Brianna.

"You didn't hear a word I said, did you!"

"Sorry my dear, lost focus. What was it you were saying?"

"I said I put her address into my phone."

Brianna showed him her screen.

"Are you suggesting we pay her a visit?"

Brianna smiled again, and said, "Let's just go surprise her!"

Yvgeny checked his watch, thought about it, then smiled and patted her on the thigh.

╬

The decedent's daughter, Jeanine Ledbetter, had a ground floor apartment in Warner Robins. Yvgeny arrived just past eight p.m. All the windows were bare, and all her lights were on. From their spot in the parking lot, they could see her in the windows scurrying back and forth. They could also see clearly that the place was in shambles.

Yvgeny reached behind his seat and grabbed a large folding package reminiscent of something a traveling salesman might use. Brianna raised an eyebrow but had learned not to ask too many questions.

JONATHAN B. ZEITLIN

The woman answered the door within seconds of him knocking. She had one earring in her ear and was fiddling with the other one. She froze when she realized what Yvgeny was wearing.

"Who the hell are you?"

"Yvgeny Jedynak, from Schmidt and Sons. I left you a message."

"Right." She looked down at Yvgeny's outfit, then asked, "On your way to a costume party?"

Yvgeny made a prune face but didn't answer.

She finished putting her second earring on, then opened the door fully and said, "Well, come on in, I guess."

Yvgeny stepped inside and almost immediately tripped on a box. Brianna entered but remained by the door. The apartment was in complete disarray, clothing on the floor in piles, a broken chair in a corner, and cardboard boxes filled haphazardly with miscellaneous junk. Yvgeny looked around a moment, then turned back to Jeanine.

A lit cigarette was on the counter, sending up a trail of smoke toward the ceiling. Brianna immediately had an urge to light one up but restrained herself.

Jeanine was probably in her early fifties, although it was hard to tell for sure. Her hair had been colored, made obvious by the gray close to the roots, and she was wearing a decent amount of makeup. The skin exposed below her neck was freckled and slightly crepey. Seeing his focused glance, she shot him a withering glare but he did not notice.

"Moving in or out?"

"Out, of course. As soon as that check comes, I'm getting out of this one-horse town."

"What check?"

The woman looked at Yvgeny as if he was crazy.

"Duh! Dad's check! Now that he's gone, cha-ching!"

The woman made a pumping motion with her arm to emphasize her point.

"So, I take it he had means?"

"Yeah, but he was a cheapskate, kept it all socked away."

"He forked over enough for your brother to get a new car."

She snorted and started fiddling with her hair.

"My brother's a jackass."

Yvgeny nodded, slightly nonplussed, then looked around

THE BODY IN THE BED

for a flat surface. He walked over to a coffee table and started moving things around to make room. As he worked, he called out, "So, how would you like him prepared?"

Jeanine had returned to a nearby box and started wrapping glasses in newspaper. Without looking up, she said, "I don't know, just do whatever you normally do. How much is it?"

Yvgeny placed his three-fold display on the table and opened it up. On one panel were tiny samples of the various species of wood out of which his coffins were made. It looked similar to the large swatch books customers used at stores like Home Depot. On the middle panel were miniature sample urns, and on the right, fabric samples for the inside of the coffins. Jeanine, however, had no interest in inspecting them.

Yvgeny watched her pack for a moment, sizing her up, then turned to his display, quickly calculating some numbers. Then he doubled them.

"Depends. Preparations are $5,000. Standard funeral another $10,000. Paid up front. Cremations are charged on a different scale."

Jeanine glanced up at him a moment, then resumed her packing. Yvgeny tried not to smile; he had grossly overshot his usual fees, following a hunch that she would not care. In his experience, people expecting a windfall didn't sweat the details. He took a gamble and won.

"Fine. But no cremations, that's gross. Do you take credit cards?"

"No, but you can use a credit card to pay me with PayPal."

"Don't I need your e-mail address?"

Yvgeny produced a business card and presented it to her with a flourish. She took the card and glanced at it. Her eyes narrowed.

"PushingDaisiesforCash@Yahoo.com?"

"I find it's helpful to insert a little whimsy into an otherwise painful experience for the families of my clients."

Jeanine raised an eyebrow, muttered, "Right," then announced, "Is that it?" while pocketing the business card.

"Well, generally loved ones choose the casket, the headstone, and help decide who should be invited to the funeral. Of course, there's also the business of selecting the style of music, types of food and drink, a general theme. I don't generally arrange such things myself. And a photograph or two of the dearly departed would be quite helpful."

Jeanine sighed and turned to rummage through a shoe box. As she rooted through the box, she said, "Don't you just have some kind of package? Just a regular coffin, regular music, and stuff?"

"Well, I suppose, but who would you like to invite?"

The woman stood straight holding the shoe box, picked out a few photographs, then tossed the box onto the table. She considered a moment, twirling her hair with one hand.

"I don't know. Can I just e-mail you a list?"

Yvgeny nodded, taking the photos from her outstretched hand, then asked, "And what shall I inscribe on the headstone?" Yvgeny dramatically raised a hand and intoned, "Here lies Earnest Ledbetter, devoted father, loving husband -"

The woman snorted, picked up a half-wrapped glass from the counter and dropped it into one of the boxes.

"Yeah, right. Mom left him when we were kids, after she caught him nailing our babysitter. Do you charge by the letter? If you do, just chisel in his initials."

Her callous disregard for her own father was deplorable, but Yvgeny grudgingly found himself appreciating the woman's frugality and lack of tolerance for convention.

Yvgeny considered demanding a few extra fees, but stopped himself- $15 thousand was a good chunk of cash, and it was coming over PayPal. No bounced checks, no trip to the bank. Plus, for a fee like that, he could easily accommodate all the geezers at Sunset Manor.

Show 'em a good time; they'll be back! Soon!

Yvgeny opened a small black folder he had been carrying under one arm, and removed a few typed pages stapled together.

"Very well. If that's all, then I will leave you a copy of our standard contract, which I will need signed and returned before -"

She snatched the contract from his hand, produced a pen from the counter, signed the document, then handed it back to him. Then she looked at her watch and cursed under her breath.

THE BODY IN THE BED

"Sorry, I'm late."

"A prior engagement at this hour?" Yvgeny asked.

"When do *you* go out to celebrate winning the freakin' lottery?"

Yvgeny considered asking the crass woman whether she would like to come out to the hearse to take a look at dear old Dad, but he resisted the urge. Ever since meeting Brianna, he tried to be a better person.

On his way out the door, freshly signed contract in hand, he turned and asked, "By the way, how would you like him dressed?"

The woman froze behind him in the doorway, car keys in hand, and sneered.

"Who cares? Just put him in whatever."

"Well, usually they're dressed in something formal, something they have on hand."

She looked around her apartment, a sarcastic expression on her face, then made eye contact with Yvgeny and said, "You see anything here that would fit an old man?"

Yvgeny just stared at her.

"Didn't think so. Just do what you gotta do and send me the bill."

Yvgeny turned to leave, but stopped one more time, causing exasperated exclamations from both Brianna and Jeanine.

"Almost forgot, if you're moving out, you have a forwarding address yet? Are you changing your phone number?"

The woman let out a melodramatic sigh and said, her jaw tight, "Number ain't changing. And I don't know where the hell I'm gonna live yet. Depends on the numbers left of the decimal. Are we done here?"

Yvgeny smiled despite her rough demeanor and said, "Why, yes, yes we are. I will e-mail you the bill shortly."

After they returned to the hearse and shut the doors, Brianna whistled and said, "Damn, that's one cold-hearted bitch! I mean, I thought *you* were cold, but that's her own blood she's talking about!"

With a grim smile, Yvgeny started the hearse and said, "Yes, quite impressive, wasn't she?"

By the time they arrived at the mortuary, it was full dark, and the security lights had all clicked on. A large cloud of moths and other bugs were buzzing around the lights, drunk with excitement over the incandescent bulbs. Just to the left of the carport, under one of the security lights, Alfred was seated in a plastic chair. He was totally absorbed in whittling a piece of wood, his knife flashing rhythmically under the light. He was oblivious both to Yvgeny's arrival and the disco cloud over his head.

Alfred was a deaf mute of advanced age; Yvgeny honestly had no idea how old the man was. He was already a fixture at the place when Yvgeny's father took the place over. A young Yvgeny remembered Alfred when he had all his hair, before his eyes became the milky blue they now were, before his joints popped and crackled whenever he walked or worked. His skin had become like the bark of an ancient tree.

Yvgeny had no idea why Alfred couldn't speak, but after a few decades with him, he acquired enough facility with Alfred's grunts, clicks, and gestures to gain a rudimentary understanding of his communications.

Yvgeny emerged from the hearse, stretched, then approached Alfred. He waved a hand in front of Alfred's face to get his attention.

"My dear Alfred, so good of you to wait for us. Please see that Mr. Ledbetter is ensconced in our finest refrigerated drawer."

Alfred watched Yvgeny's lips as he spoke, then asked, "Nnng. Ng ngh nghh?"

"Yes, I said Ledbetter. Just some old guy on hospice, Alfred, nobody you know."

Alfred creaked into a standing position and, motioning with his knife, repeated, Nnng. Ng ngh nghh?"

Yvgeny looked at the knife and took a step back.

"It's Earnest; Earnest Ledbetter. What's gotten into you, Alfred?"

Alfred looked over Yvgeny's shoulder toward the hearse, his eyes wide.

"Ng ngh ng ng ngh!"

"I don't know, he was on hospice, probably old age. Jesus, Alfred, are you getting soft?"

Alfred walked past Yvgeny and toward the rear of the hearse, knife in one hand, block of wood in the other. Turning to Brianna, Yvgeny shook his head, smiled a thin smile, then held out a crooked arm, and said, "I think my old friend's finally lost his mind. Now, my dear, would you care to join me for some tea?"

Brianna took his arm in his, but whispered, "Sure, but do you have any beer?"

╬

Flowers looked from the breezeway to make sure Yvgeny was gone, then, satisfied he wasn't coming back, he locked the door and flipped the sign around to CLOSED. As he walked back inside, his shoes crunched on more glass, and he sighed and glared down at the floor, seeing that he missed a few shards from his broken bong.

He retrieved his broom and dustpan, this time trying a little more carefully to clean up all the shards. The last thing he needed was one of his elderly patients to slice their feet on broken glass in his office. He'd never hear the end of it!

After he cleaned up the mess for the second time, he grabbed his paperwork off his desk, intending to sit on his couch and finish it. He cursed when he saw the old man's clothing and personal effects still draped across the cushions.

What kind of detectives were these guys?

Flowers made a mental note to hit up Yvgeny the next morning to hand over the old guy's stuff, then he returned to his desk to finish his paperwork. His bookkeeper handled all of his billing, but these forms were special; the sheriff required Flowers himself to fill out the paperwork for his autopsies. The GBI also required the personal signature of the referring physician. Luckily, each stack consisted of only a few forms, so he finished in about fifteen minutes. He stood up and stretched, then looked at the clock.

On most evenings, his wife griped when he got home late, so he made sure he was out the door just after five each day. Home by half past five, dinner at six, television at seven, most days of the week. But not on Tuesdays.

Tuesdays were special. As far as his wife knew, Tuesdays were paperwork nights. Tuesdays were catch up nights.

Mondays and Tuesdays were always busy, so Tuesday nights helped him stay ahead of the curve.

Flowers was usually closed Wednesdays. He never could figure out why, but none of his elderly patients liked to visit him, or anyone else, on Wednesdays. Mondays and Tuesdays were busy because some of his patients refused to go to the emergency room with their acute problems, preferring to suffer all weekend and see him at his office as soon as he opened.

Thursdays and Fridays were also busy; he had a theory for this as well; the elderly started to feel apprehension about being alone all weekend, and that apprehension started to build toward the end of the week, so they'd come see the doctor to head off any brewing infection, any lingering aches and pains. The phone calls started on Thursday mornings; by Thursday afternoon and all day on Fridays he usually had a packed waiting room. But whatever the explanation, Wednesdays were a breeze. Eventually, he decided to close the office on Wednesdays.

Good ol' paperwork Tuesday!

Paperwork Tuesday wasn't free, however. Paperwork Tuesday came at a price- Honey-do Wednesday. Flowers had looked forward to having an extra day off each week, and his wife had remained silent about the implications of his plan, waiting for the right moment to shatter his dreams.

She even let him have his first Wednesday to himself, preferring not to strike until he reached the point of no return. For her, that point came after he printed new business cards reflecting his new schedule; when he changed the sign on his door; when he submitted the change to the ad he maintained in the yellow pages; when he paid the teenaged neighbor an extra $20 to change his website.

She employed the frog in the pot of water method. The first Wednesday was all his; the second Wednesday, she merely asked him to gas up her car. The following Wednesday was laundry and shopping. Within six weeks, he realized his hopes were dashed. His Wednesdays became long, arduous days filled with painting walls, repairing leaky toilets, weeding the yard.

He had been outplayed and he knew it, but he kept quiet. He even kept quiet when his wife told him his Paperwork

THE BODY IN THE BED

Tuesday left the night free for her to go have fun with her friends. He kept quiet because as long as she thought he was still busy working Tuesday evenings, and as long as he gave her his Wednesdays, he would still have his alone time.

Either way, he thought, *the joke was on her, because what was Tuesday night really about?*

Party time!

For Flowers, Tuesday evenings really had involved paperwork and phone calls with patients and insurance companies. It was a real hassle, and it kept him up until the wee hours of the morning. There were billing codes, pre-authorizations, appeals, capitation arrangements, and forms.

Lord, the forms!

Every day he had to sort through the ICD-10 to figure out his billing codes, then submit those codes using the CMS 1500, or sometimes it's electronic cousin, the 837-P, for all his Medicaid and Medicare patients. Then there were EOBs, ERAs, company specific faxes and cover sheets. There were forms he had to submit online, forms he had to mail, forms he had to print, fill out, scan, and e-mail, even forms he had to print and type with a typewriter, then send off in an envelope with an actual stamp!

The rest of his Tuesday evening was filled arguing with insurance companies by e-mail, by phone, by paper, and by fax. Tuesday evenings started to bleed into Wednesdays, turning his life into a living hell; but all that vanished once he found the website Bigshotz.

Bigshotz matched people like him with professionals from around the world. Accountants, bookkeepers, medical billers, even logo designers. After searching through hundreds of profiles on this website, he found a medical biller to deal with the insurance companies, an accountant to handle his taxes, even a logo designer to design the logo that he put on his body bags and coroner van. Strangely, all three had the same first name, John, and all three hailed from different countries across West Africa. Their prices were rock bottom; so low, in fact, his wife didn't even notice the charges on the credit card.

Ever since he made the switch to "fully automatic," Tuesday evenings became all about relaxation. It was just past eight p.m. by the time he made it back up to his office

JONATHAN B. ZEITLIN

after handing the body over to Yvgeny; after finishing his paperwork and, once and for all, cleaning up the mess caused by that nosy detective, he shuffled through the lobby, made sure the doors were locked, the blinds all drawn, then he dimmed the lights.

Next stop, the stereo.

Flowers was an old school purist, and grabbed his old shoebox filled with cassette tapes. He thumbed through until he found his homemade mix tapes, each labeled *Groovy Jams, Vol. 1, Vol. 2,* and so on. He had labeled each of them in his own messy handwriting. Of course, he only used the best: TDK, which were just as great as they were in 1988 when he purchased them. With his old school HiFi system with Dolby noise reduction, he found the sound far superior to commercial CDs.

Carrying them over to his stereo, he popped in *Volume 3* and pressed play. The Sixties and Seventies started turning the ambiance from staid backwoods medical office to what he liked to call *Doctor Disco*. Next, he flicked on his lava lamp so the wax would start to melt inside. Finally, he unlocked his apothecary.

Behind the antibiotics, the codeine, the morphine, crazy old lady Eunice Stein's pills (Eunice was convinced Flowers was her late husband, and because of her fear of choking, she would only take her pills in his presence), behind it all was his private stash, and he smiled when he finally was able to reach it.

Burning herb in a doctor's office would have been a terrible idea, as the smell was so unique. His bong had become a shelf curiosity (an educational piece for his occasional teenaged patient), and he tossed his papers and his straight pipe. He experimented with a hookah, but the smell was still a problem. Some of his elderly patients had incredibly sensitive sniffers, causing him to blame "reckless teenagers" outside his office for the occasional smell. Even with the windows open, his patients occasionally picked up the scent. He needed a better solution.

There he was, thumbing through his latest edition of Cannabis Culture, when he saw the full-page advertisement for the GrapeVape, a small purple device a little bigger than a Zippo. He whipped out his credit card and ordered two; one

THE BODY IN THE BED

for home, and one for work; he couldn't risk driving around with it in his car. The Georgia Medical Review Board would not have been kind.

For him, it was love at first sight. His little nebulizing friend heated his liquefied marijuana emulsion to a temperature between 180 and 200 degrees Celsius, just short of combustion, which of course occurs at 230 degrees Celsius.

A few puffs, and you were off to the races!

It still smelled, but not nearly as strong, and dissipated much more quickly, especially when he opened the window and exhaled through a paper towel containing a couple of scented dryer sheets.

He vaped his first hit, then strolled over to his mini-refrigerator and pulled out a beer.

Let the good times roll!

A few puffs and a few sips later, he turned up the volume, then walked over and peeked through the drapes down toward the street. Satisfied, he shut the window, then walked over to the far wall and flicked one of the switches. His black lights came on, making his posters all come alive. They included all his favorites: Led Zeppelin, Jimi Hendrix, and many others, in all the groovy colors of his childhood. His white lab coat shone like a flashlight, revealing, in stark contrast, hundreds of little dark specks of lint, a tribute to his laissez faire approach to cleanliness.

He began to roll on the waves, the THC mixing with the alcohol and triggering all his dopamine receptors. Crunching his empty beer can against the table, he retrieved another, took a long pull, burped loudly, then leaned against the wall, smiling.

Tuesday was also movie night. His office had a large plasma on the wall which he kept on CNN during the day when he had patients coming and going. At night, however, it was a virtual smorgasbord of programming delight. He started clicking between his hundreds of channels, trying to settle on a good show.

He only had basic cable at their apartment, but at the office he chose the most expensive, most expansive package. According to his new accountant, the office cable bill was a deductible expense, so why not?

JONATHAN B. ZEITLIN

Two or three beers later, he was kicked back, enjoying a movie. He walked over to his doctor's stool, sat down, then slid across the floor toward the window with his vape. He cracked the window, took two more puffs, then with a good kick he sent himself twirling in a circle on the stool. He closed his eyes, a big smile on his face, then realized he was losing his balance.

Better keep 'em open so I don't fall off!

He opened his eyes and took one more twirl on the stool, enjoying watching his room spinning around, and he started to chuckle as he noticed his couch smiling back at him. He smiled back, but a few revolutions later, he frowned.

Why is my couch smiling at me?

He put his feet down to stop twirling, stared at his couch for a moment, then smiled again.

Problem solved. That's not my couch smiling, it's just a happy face hovering above it! Yes, that's much better.

He turned away, took another long sip of beer, trying to relax. Then he frowned again.

Wait, why is there a smiley face hovering by my couch?

He squinted and rubbed his eyes, then looked again. Sure enough, there was a glowing yellow circle, but it wasn't smiling. And it was a faded, uniform day-glow, unlike his posters. He stood and walked over to his couch. There was a roughly oblong circle partially glowing in the dim light. He reached out and ran his finger across the glowing blob.

Damp?

Truly confused, he walked over and flipped on the lights, then turned his attention back to the couch.

Ah, that explains it! He thought to himself.

It was the dead guy's pajama pants. The detectives had inspected all the guy's stuff from the evidence bag, then left the pants draped over the couch.

Oh, yeah, I forgot.

He grabbed the pants and shoved them back into the evidence bag, then tossed the bag on the far cushion. He plopped down on the other end of the couch and grabbed the remote, hunting for something good. After a few more puffs of his nebulizer, he wrinkled his brow.

Why were the dead guy's pants glowing?

Fresh beer in hand, Flowers began pacing in his office,

THE BODY IN THE BED

wracking his brain. Medical school was a distant memory for him, and he tried to run through his mental catalog of substances likely to glow under ultraviolet light. He remembered reading a study about a Woods lamp, which used ultraviolet light to reveal potential dermatological abnormalities. He tried to concentrate, but the pot and the beer had softened his memory. He let loose a loud, jaw cracking yawn, then checked his watch.

A glowing crotch- venereal disease? Urinary tract infection?

He took another sip of his beer, scratched his cheek. Another yawn escaped.

Kidney disease? Bladder tumor?

Plopping down on the couch, he grabbed his phone and typed in *Woods lamp* into the Google search window, then waited for the results. The little screen buffered. He waited.

"Hmmm -" he breathed.

Lord, the poor guy could've had it all. Cancer's a bitch.

As his thumb stood, poised, on the screen, his eyes drooped. He stopped focusing on the screen, and his chin began to make its way down to his chest. The television droned on in the background.

As the rhythm of his breathing fell into the steady cadence of someone fast asleep, he leaned sideways and he rested his head against the brown paper evidence bag containing the pants and personal effects of the victim. And he slept.

What he thought was a few minutes later, he heard a loud *thump*. He scrambled to his feet, kicking his phone across the floor in his haste. Then he heard another thump. He sped to his window just in time to see a large garbage truck dropping a dumpster in the far side of his parking lot.

Left the damn window open!

His heart still pounding, he shut the window, then walked back toward his couch, trying to relax.

I'll just chill for a minute and calm down. Yeah, calm down, chill, relax.

He took one more swig of his now warm beer, and crouched down to grab his phone. He stuck it on the table and sat back down on the couch. He had left the television on, and it was now playing reruns of *Magnum, P.I.*

Jackpot!

Flowers watched one episode, then another, but soon after

the third, his eyelids began to droop again, and he laid back on the couch. This time he used a pillow instead of the evidence bag. Within a few minutes, Flowers was snoring softly.

THE BODY IN THE BED

CHAPTER FOUR

☦

Flowers's office was closed the next morning, so there would be no secretary bursting into the place. His telephone was set to go straight to voice mail. (Sometimes his wife tried to get him started early on his honey-do list.) No patient appointments, no pickups, no deliveries. He had all morning to sleep in. By the time he woke up, groggy, still wearing yesterday's clothes, it was almost noon.

The television was still on when he awoke, and for a while he stared, mindlessly, at the screen. He knew his wife would be waiting for him at home with a list of errands, so he was in no rush to leave.

Eventually, Flowers stood, stretched, yawned, farted, then went to the bathroom. He opened the blinds, reveling in the sunlight of a beautiful and crisp February day. He straightened up his office, gathering his empties and cleaning up his vape equipment, storing everything away, well out of sight and far away from nosy patients. Walking past his couch, he noticed the evidence bag on the floor. The previous evening washed over him in a rush.

His mind was significantly clearer after a good night's sleep, and he remembered his mental stumbling over the glowing crotch of the old man's pants. He reflected back on the prior night's thoughts- and came up with a new one: *maybe it was from the chemotherapy.*

He grabbed his smartphone from the table, then cursed, realizing he had forgotten to connect his charger. He plugged it in and waited until it had enough juice to turn on. As he stared at it, he continued trying to think of why the man's pants would be glowing.

Why would chemotherapy make someone's pants glow? That didn't make any sense.

He didn't have a Woods lamp, and couldn't remember

what kinds of dermatological issues they revealed. It didn't matter, anyway; glowing pants were not a dermatological issue.

Finally, his phone started rebooting. After it loaded and he entered his password, he typed the words Woods lamp into his browser. Hits on numerous dermatological diagnoses appeared. Flowers thought a moment.

Wet spot on the crotch really only means one thing.

Flowers searched *Woods lamp* and *urine.*

The first search result was about detecting antifreeze in urine.

Of course!

Flowers refreshed his recollection as he read; ethylene glycol had certain phosphorescent additives to help mechanics trace radiator leaks. Those same additives would also phosphoresce when exposed to ultraviolet light. A vague memory of medical school danced around just beyond his consciousness.

So, the guy spilled antifreeze on his crotch. Problem solved!

Another swig of room temperature beer, and his self-satisfied smile faded.

He was like a hundred years old, on hospice, and bed ridden. Where the hell would he get antifreeze from? And why was he messing with antifreeze while wearing his pajamas?

Flowers almost dropped his beer when the implications hit him. He paced back and forth a moment, his heart racing, cursing out loud. He began chanting, "Stupid! Stupid! Stupid!"

He froze a moment, standing still in the middle of his office, then started pacing again.

I have to get that body back before Yvgeny gets his hands on it.

He hunted around for his shoes, shoved his wallet in his pocket, grabbed his keys, and was heading for the door with a determined stomp when he stopped, suddenly, shoulders slumped. The thought of having his medical and driver's licenses yanked for DUI quickly curbed his enthusiasm. He was frozen in place, stymied, keys in hand. He checked his watch. It was already after one p.m.

I have to do something!

He checked his watch again, then he grabbed his phone. It

THE BODY IN THE BED

was only at 5% so he had to keep it plugged in, tethering him to the corner of his office. He scrolled through his contacts looking for Yvgeny's number, dialed it, but it went straight to voice mail. He tried the main mortuary line, but the phone rang forever, and when it finally went to voice mail, Flowers was greeted by loud organ music and the voice of a woman who would be better suited for answering the phones at a strip club.

"Hi there, sweetie, this is Schmidt and Sons. Need a burial? Cremation? You've come to the right place! Leave us your name and number and we'll call you right back. And don't be caught dead without one of our buy now, die later plans!"

The speaker made a kissing sound, then the woman exclaimed, "Toodles!" and the voice mail beeped.

Flowers cried out in frustration, then grabbed his keys and headed for the door.

That's it! If I get pulled over, I'm done. But if I don't get that body, I'm done anyway!

He made his way to the stairs, stumbling once in the breezeway, then turned the corner and headed toward his red van. His office complex was at a busy intersection, and the parking lot was fairly large and was separated from the street by nothing but a couple feet of dead grass, weeds, and a cracked sidewalk. His van was parked nose-in in a corner spot facing the intersection.

As he got behind the wheel, he watched as a car came to a stop at the red light. Behind him was a black and white Taurus containing one of the City of Comstock's sharply dressed patrolmen. When the light turned green, the car sped off but then the officer activated his blue lights and stopped the car.

"Shit."

Sitting in his van, keys in hand, he looked on as the traffic stop unfolded. Then another patrol car came up from another street and parked behind the first patrol car.

"Shit. Shit."

Flowers grabbed his phone again and called Yvgeny. Still, no answer. He ended the call and redialed. Again, no answer. He scrolled through his address book to find Yvgeny's cell number and tried it one more time. It went to voice mail. He ended the call and redialed immediately. Again, voice mail. Cursing to himself, his panic increasing, he tried the mortuary line again.

"Schmidt and Sons Mortuary."

Yvgeny's elderly mother's thready voice sounded like music to Flowers's ears and he practically crooned, "Ms. Jedynak, it's Flowers, Jimmy Flowers. I -"

"I know who you are! You think I don't recognize the voice of the doctor who left me a cripple?"

Momentarily confused, Flowers said, "What?"

With a "humph!" Yvgeny's mother sneered, "Of course, I wouldn't expect you to remember any one specific act of malpractice. It must happen so often, how could you keep track?"

Flowers thought a moment, then said, "Wait, are you talking about your foot?"

"Humph!"

Months earlier, Mama had lost her footing on the stairs and crashed to the bottom. She half crawled, half limped to her car and drove to Flowers's office. Flowers ordered imaging, confirming she fractured her foot, but Mama refused a cast. With some coaxing, he convinced her to wear a boot, which she wore around the house but refused to wear to the supermarket or any other venue outside Schmidt's. As a result, her foot didn't heal properly, causing her constant pain and a slight limp. Of course, she squarely blamed Flowers for her decrepitude.

"So, what do you want?"

"I need to speak to Geny."

"He's busy."

"It's important. It's an emergency."

"My son doesn't do emergencies. He does dead people. Emergencies are *your* problem."

Flowers tried to maintain his composure.

"Look, I have to talk to him. It's important."

"I'll tell him you called."

Flowers heard rustling and knew what was about to happen.

"Wait! I have to talk to him, it's an emer -"

She hung up the phone.

Flowers started rhythmically cursing and smacking his

steering wheel. He stopped when he saw a third patrol car pull in behind the second. Three patrol cars on a traffic stop meant only one thing.

Someone's going to jail.

Flowers twisted a little more in his seat and watched with interest as the third officer got out of his car and approached the second.

Here it comes.

As Flowers predicted, the first and second officer approached on the driver side of the vehicle, and the third officer came around to the passenger side. They brought the driver out and handcuffed him, searched him, then brought him back to the first officer's car.

City cops; there's never more than three of them working the streets.

The second officer returned to his patrol car, then emerged a few seconds later with his metal clipboard. The first officer reached for his shoulder mike and spoke into it.

Yup, they're calling a wrecker, and he's gonna inventory that car.

Again, Flowers's prediction was accurate, as the officers started going through the car and jotting things down on the clipboard while the third officer sat in his patrol car catching up on paperwork. Flowers smiled.

Wrecker's going to take at least fifteen minutes, then another fifteen to load the car and handle the forms.

Flowers looked off into the distance, toward the interstate. The sheriff's department usually spent their time on the highway playing with the troopers, leaving the city streets of Comstock for the city cops to patrol. For the next thirty minutes or so, Flowers knew there wouldn't be one cop between his office and Yvgeny's place.

Now's my chance!

Flowers turned the ignition and put on his seat belt.

JONATHAN B. ZEITLIN

A few hours earlier, and a few miles away, Yvgeny had returned to Sunset Manor to meet with Beatrice to ask her about guests for the funeral. It was just after nine a.m., but well past breakfast for the over eighty set; they were already having mid-morning tea and cookies. Beatrice had just poured herself a tea, and offered a dainty cup to Yvgeny.

He tried cajoling Brianna into calling in sick from her new day job so she could join him, but he couldn't convince her. *Such a career girl!* Yvgeny thought with a smile.

Declining the tea, he followed Beatrice toward one of the sun rooms and they sat together on a green and white striped couch. Yvgeny tried very hard to be patient but couldn't help checking his watch while the old lady blew on her tea.

"Is Dr. Flowers, well, finished with his -"

Yvgeny resisted the urge to be sarcastic.

"Autopsy?"

Beatrice turned away and nodded.

"Yes, he completed his examination."

Beatrice's teacup started to rattle against the saucer.

"And, what did he find?"

As they spoke, someone pushed an old woman in a wheelchair into the room, leaving her in a corner facing a window. Yvgeny recognized her from his last visit.

Yvgeny shrugged, and said, "Well, I suppose nothing, I picked up the body last night."

"He would have taken blood, yes?"

Yvgeny cocked his head at the old woman.

"Well, I suppose, but why do you ask?"

"No reason, just, you know, of course I deal with death here on a weekly basis, and this is the first time there was any question about the manner of one's passing."

"I see," Yvgeny whispered, then looked out onto the lawn, anxious to be back in Cerberus and on his way.

"When is the funeral going to be?"

Yvgeny pursed his lips and looked off into space.

"Well, to be safe, I'd say we need to get him in the ground by tomorrow. If we wait until the weekend, there could be, well, problems."

The old woman in the wheel chair suddenly piped up and called out, "Better get 'em in the ground!"

THE BODY IN THE BED

Yvgeny glanced over, but the woman was still staring out the window, smiling ear to ear.

Beatrice looked away, running a finger along the rim of her tea cup.

Yvgeny turned back to Beatrice and said, "It's been over 24 hours already, and given his physical condition, the chemotherapy, I'd -"

"I understand," Beatrice interrupted, a little louder than necessary.

A silence ensued for a good twenty seconds. Yvgeny cleared his throat and crossed his legs. Finally, she spoke.

"Will it be a big affair?"

"Well, not sure. The next of kin seemed disinclined to take an active role in the preparations, leaving it all up to me."

Beatrice adopted an expression of sympathy, adding, "Oh, you poor dear. Ms. Jeanine can be rather gruff. And slow with her payments. The last two, she missed completely."

Yvgeny made a mental note to check his PayPal account when he got back home, then cleared his throat.

"As for the funeral, would any of your guests here be interested in coming?"

Beatrice smiled, and said, "Of course, he was rather popular around here, and I imagine there will be several that would want to see him off. Tomorrow, you say?"

Yvgeny nodded.

Beatrice smiled, and said, "OK, we can get Maury to bring them over in the shuttle bus after the mall. We can make a day of it! Tomorrow would be delightful- could we schedule it for mid-afternoon, say three p.m.?"

Yvgeny shrugged his shoulders and said, "Don't see why not."

"We'll be getting back from Macon by around two p.m., maybe later depending on traffic, you know how the highway can get around Stockbridge. So, three p.m. would be perfect!"

Yvgeny paused a moment, trying to seem considerate, then asked, "Um, so, does Mr. Ledbetter have any formal wear? Something he can be buried in?"

Beatrice gave him a blank stare, then shook herself out of it.

"Well, I've already scheduled his room to be leased, so it's on the list for cleaning. His personal effects may already be gone. And Jeanine, naturally, has not returned my calls, so I'm not sure whether he left anything at home. Feel free to go check his closet, but don't get your hopes up."

Yvgeny had already stood, and when Beatrice finished, he turned toward the stairs, calling out, "Just be a minute."

Beatrice waved him off, and he headed toward the stairs. He passed the day room on his way, and posted at the entrance watching him was Luther P. Telfair. Two older women were a few feet away, watching Telfair watching Yvgeny, like expectant hens.

"Back so soon, sport?"

"Just checking to see if the man had a suit I can bury him in."

The old man looked at Yvgeny, in an exaggerated up and down movement, then announced, "Maybe you can let him wear that getup!"

Yvgeny was wearing his standard office attire: morning coat with tails, black pants with muted stripes, and top hat. He had chosen a paisley cravat to offset the black- a little risqué for his taste, but Brianna thought it brought out his latent rakish bent.

"Very funny. So is his stuff still here?"

"Nope. Closet's empty. The minute someone croaks, the heathens go after the goods like termites in a wooden shit house."

The old chief chuckled, then continued, "Like locusts on a date tree."

He began to laugh harder, a choppy, raspy sound, "Vultures on the rib cage of a water buffalo. You catch my drift?"

Yvgeny, stony faced, replied, "Killing yourself with metaphors, I see."

Telfair stopped laughing and said, "They was similes, champ."

Yvgeny sighed with his mouth tightly shut and turned on his heel.

"Anyway, consider it caught."

"What?"

"Your drift. But I think I'll take a look anyway just to make sure. Good day."

Before the old man could fire off a retort, Yvgeny was gone,

THE BODY IN THE BED

shooting up the stairs two at a time. He walked down the hall to Ledbetter's room, and when he walked in, he was surprised to find an old woman sitting on the bed, looking out the window. She started at his entrance, and when she turned to face him, he saw tears streaming down her face. She stood quickly, fussing over the sheets as if she was making the bed, suddenly fully occupied with tucking in corners and straightening the angles.

"Oh, excuse me, I was just finishing up here. I'll get out of your hair."

She slowly approached, leaning heavily on her cane, wiping away tears with her free hand. Yvgeny cocked his head and watched as she tried to leave, then called out to her.

"Wait. Did you know the man who lived here?"

She stopped and leaned on her cane, looking down at her feet. She nodded her head and spoke, so quietly Yvgeny had to move in closer to hear her.

"Yes, I knew him. I knew him very well. We - we were very close."

The old man was right, he was *a horn dog!*

"I see."

"Will there be a ceremony?" She asked, risking a quick glance toward Yvgeny, then back down again.

"Yes, tomorrow at -"

"What are *you* doing in here, you shrew?"

Yvgeny whirled around to find another woman, even older, but without a cane, and full of piss and vinegar. Her wrinkled white skin was flushed red around the cheeks in anger, and her lips curled back to reveal yellow but intact teeth.

The woman who just moments earlier was a portrait of contrite and abject sorrow quickly collected herself and raised her cane to point it at the other woman.

"You take one more step into Earnest's room and I will knock your head off!"

The other old woman raised one of her feet in the air, lurched forward, and dropped the foot down, calling out in a sweet sing-song voice, "One more step!"

With a cry of rage, the first woman brought back her cane like Babe Ruth and prepared to take a swing. Without thinking, Yvgeny grabbed the hand holding the cane and steadied it, urging her to lower the weapon. The other woman watched, smiling, hands on hips.

"Let go of me, you bastard!" The woman cried out, struggling to break free of Yvgeny, but, being forty years older, she was unable to loosen his grip.

Meanwhile, as he continued to restrain the first woman, the second one hopped on one leg, then bounced forward as if playing a game of hopscotch, calling out, "And another!" then started hopping closer and closer to the bed, singing, "Tiptoe, through the tulips!"

The woman with the cane became completely unglued and turned to Yvgeny, her face a mask of rage. She chopped at his neck with the knife edge of her free hand, causing him to release his grip on her other arm. Before Yvgeny could recover, she launched herself at the other woman and they fell to the bed, clawing at each other.

"Damn, sport, nice work. You always this lucky with the ladies?"

Yvgeny twisted around to find the old chief watching the women from the hallway with a smirk on his face. He fiddled under his shirt and pulled out a gold whistle, raised it to his lips, and blew a series of staccato notes from it. The women immediately stopped and scrambled to their feet. The chief stepped inside.

"What's the matter with you two? He's dead! There ain't nothing left to fight about!"

"Oh, yes there is, chief," the woman with the cane said, then pointed at her enemy, adding, "he was with *her* when it happened. It's all her fault!"

With a scream, Myrtle tried to claw at Bessie again, but Bessie was quicker on her feet and was easily able to sidestep away from her. Bessie smiled at the frustrated growl she got from Myrtle, still brandishing her cane, and said, "Well, I can't help it that he liked me better than Myrtle. Must be because I'm more fun."

"Now ladies, that's about enough. Bessie, why don't you head on out of here? Myrtle, you wait a minute or two, then go on out the door. Us men got some talking to do in here."

"We do?" Yvgeny asked.

The chief pretended not to hear him.

Bessie headed toward the door, but right before leaving,

THE BODY IN THE BED

she turned back to Myrtle and said, "He died with *my* name on his lips!"

Myrtle hefted her cane and launched it like an Olympic javelin thrower at Bessie. Bessie, surprised by the attack, almost ducked too late, the cane hurtling over her head and missing her by less than an inch. It slammed into the bannister outside and clanked down onto the hardwoods in the hallway. Bessie stuck out her tongue and left, and Myrtle fell face down upon the bed and burst into tears.

Yvgeny watched her for a moment, then turned to Telfair.

"What the hell was all that about?"

The chief sat heavily on the bed and put one hand on Myrtle's back.

"Like I said, Ledbetter was a lady killer. They all loved him, but these two were his favorites. It was Bessie that found him. One of the other residents heard the sobbing, found them in the room, so he grabbed his phone and called 911."

He continued rubbing her back, then after a moment said, softly, "Myrtle, why don't you go relax, you can go lay down in my room if you like, nobody will bother you in there. I need to have a chat with twinkle toes here."

Then he turned to Yvgeny and winked. Yvgeny suddenly had the urge to jump out of the window.

Myrtle lurched into a sitting position, rubbed at her eyes with the backs of her hands, then sighed and stood. She limped outside to collect her cane, then disappeared. Telfair walked over and shut the door.

"You know, the EMTs almost never run code one to a 911 call here. They know we're like a bunch of milk jugs in the fridge a few days after the sell-by-date. You know what I'm sayin'?

Yvgeny watched Telfair, slack jawed, as he spoke.

"But today, tell you what, sport, the ladies on the lawn were yowling like a bunch of pole cats, causing a hell of a ruckus. I'm surprised they didn't send a few bubble tops."

Yvgeny regained his focus and stood, paying only half attention to Telfair as he walked across the room and opened the closet, finding it empty. He turned and took a harder look at the place, only then accepting it was completely devoid of habitation. The bed was made, but the flat surfaces were all clean and bare, and, opening a couple of the drawers, he found them all empty. He turned to a quietly gloating Luther Telfair, who nodded his head and said, "Told ya', sport."

"They don't waste any time around here."

"Nope."

Telfair checked his watch then said, "Yup, another thirty minutes, they'll be bringing in the next guy. Happens all the time. Once you run out of money and the checks stop coming, this place will toss you out on your ass before you can put your teeth back in."

Yvgeny grimaced.

"I thought this guy had money."

"Yeah, well, *he* didn't run out of money. *He* ran out of time. That happens too."

"You're not going to start rapping again, are you?"

Telfair didn't answer.

"Beatrice said his family skipped the last two payments. You sure he didn't run out of green?"

Telfair made a raspberry sound and said, "Positive. His family dropped the ball, but he was fully reconciled long before we lost him."

Yvgeny shrugged, looked around the room, then moved on.

"So, listen, where's all this guy's stuff? I need his suit."

"He didn't have no suit," Telfair said, "he wore a damn silk bath robe most of the time, like he was Hugh Hefner. Guess he was, in a way."

Yvgeny shuddered and turned away.

"Coroner do his piece?" Telfair asked.

Yvgeny snorted and muttered, "Coroner. Yeah, sure, he probably walked around the body, counted fingers and toes, then picked his nose and called it a day."

"Hope he ran a tox screen, all I'm saying."

Yvgeny looked hard at the old man.

"You serious? The old guy just ran out of steam! You said it yourself!"

"No, sport, I said he ran out of *time*." Telfair shrugged, cleared his throat, and chanted, "By knife, by gun, by stone, you kill."

"That sounds like Jezelda's drivel."

"Words fit for Junior G, you ask me."

"I didn't."

"Suit yourself, sport, but I'm telling you, you're in over

THE BODY IN THE BED

your head on this one. Time to call the cavalry!"

"Call the cavalry? I did better. I informed them in person. Look where it got me."

Telfair opened his mouth to reply but Yvgeny cut him off.

"Look, I'm just a squirrel trying to bury my nut. You think this guy was offed, talk to Flowers, or the cops; either way, like I said, it ain't my problem."

Before the old man could respond, Yvgeny held up the palm of his hand.

"I told you: squirrel. Nut. I've already done my part. I even told the sheriff's department about everything and what did they do? They laughed me out of their office!"

"Those dim bulbs? You really think they're gonna investigate this as a homicide? Nope, like it or not, it's up to you and me, champ!"

Yvgeny put his hands on his hips and looked at Telfair in open mouthed amazement.

"You and me? Playing detectives? And all because some freak with a scarf on her head claims she talked to the guy's ghost?"

"Yup, sure do. There's more here than meets the eye."

"And I suppose you're an expert."

"Call it cop's intuition."

Yvgeny nodded sarcastically and muttered, "mmm hmm."

Telfair narrowed his eyes and said, "I was collaring murderers since before you knew your bunghole from your ding dong. I'm telling you, this one ain't right."

Yvgeny stared at him a minute longer, then deflated.

"Look, old man," Yvgeny said, "even if I believed it was a murder, which I don't, the last time I tried to help out on a case, I didn't exactly win any awards."

"I know all about you, sport. Those numb-nuts wouldn't never have figured it out without you."

Around six months earlier, when Alfred found that dead body buried in an open grave, Yvgeny tried to assist the sheriff's department. What did he get for his efforts? He got constant harassment from the constables, even got arrested for interfering with an investigation. In the end, he solved the crime himself, prevented an innocent man from going to prison, all without so much as a thank you from the sheriff.

In fact, the sheriff's department took all the credit for

solving the case, when in reality, Yvgeny did all the work.

Yvgeny watched as the old man shuffled to the window and drew the blinds. Glancing at the closed door, he moved in close to Yvgeny and whispered, "Now listen, I'm going to sneak out the back door. Keep the car running, I'm going to come around the next house and meet you at the street. We got work to do."

"What are you talking about? I don't have time for this crap, I got a funeral to prepare for!"

"When is it?"

"Tomorrow at three p.m."

"Tomorrow is mall day!"

Yvgeny didn't react, so Telfair squinched his face up as he thought about his options, then started pacing back and forth slowly.

Yvgeny, growing impatient, said, "Beatrice is going to have some van take everyone over to my shop. Just come with everyone else! What's the hurry?"

Telfair scoffed, and as he paced, he spoke.

"Look here, champ, if we wait until tomorrow, we'll never solve this here case."

Telfair glanced toward the door, then peered through the blinds before moving in even closer this time, and whispered in Yvgeny's ear, "And it ain't just Myrtle and Bessie. Somebody's up to something around here."

Yvgeny opened his mouth to respond, but Telfair waved his hand at him with an audible "Shush!"

The old man looked away, calculating, chewing his lower lip. Then he shook his head.

"Nope, too obvious. Plus, they always do a head count when we go places."

"I wasn't suggesting -"

The old man waved at Yvgeny again to silence him.

"We need a war room. I'll sneak into the office, get the bank records. Yessir. Then we need all the records of deaths. I think she keeps them in -"

Telfair trailed off in mid-sentence, pacing slowly. A moment later he nodded his head.

"Gotta be in the dead of night. We only have until tomorrow afternoon, so we have a lot to do. I'm gonna need a gun, a pair of cuffs, and -"

THE BODY IN THE BED

"Are you nuts?"

Telfair stared at Yvgeny a moment, and when his eyes started to un-focus, Yvgeny cursed under his breath. Telfair began swiveling his neck back and forth and took a deep breath.

"Cruising down the interstate, sittin' in the back,
Lookin' for the exit, reachin' for my gat.
My homeys on my left and my hoochie's on my right,
Vengeance is my bitch, and it's goin' down tonight."

"No, old man, no it's not!"

"You ain't going to finish this without me, sport!"

"Who said I was finishing anything? This ain't my thing, Telfair. I just put them in the ground, then pocket my fee."

"You stepped up before, didn't you?"

Yvgeny shrugged his shoulders.

"Yeah, but that was different. They dumped that body in *my* cemetery and compromised one of *my* funerals. What's my angle here?"

Telfair raised his eyebrows.

"You're supposed to bury him tomorrow. If there was foul play, you ain't burying nobody. *That's* your angle!"

Yvgeny crossed his arms, and Telfair finally gave up.

"Fine, sport, blow it off. But I'm telling you, I've been in the game a long time, and I know when something smells. Coroner took blood, right?"

"Yeah, I guess."

"He'll probably be in the ground by the time you get the results."

"How long does it normally take?" Yvgeny asked.

"Depends on who he used, what he asked for, how many other tests are waiting. Few days? Few weeks?"

"Great."

"OK sport, last chance. Are we doing this, or what? I can have someone provide a distraction while we jet."

"Telfair, *we* aren't jetting anywhere. Now, *I* have to go."

Yvgeny made his way toward the door, leaving Telfair by the window shaking his head. As he started down the stairs, he heard Telfair yell, "You'll be back!"

Hitting the lobby again, he passed Myrtle, who seemed to

have been waiting for him. As he passed, she grabbed his arm. Yvgeny stopped, and Myrtle leaned in and whispered, "You know she killed him."

"You too? Did Luther put you up to this?"

When Myrtle looked at him blankly, he sighed.

"Who? Bessie?"

"She killed him. I can't prove it, call it woman's intuition, but I promise you, she's a murderer!"

Yvgeny pried the old woman's fingers from his arm and then patted her hand.

"There sure is a lot of intuition going around today. Listen, I will make sure the coroner takes a hard look at him. Now, I must be going."

Myrtle seemed to have more to say, but just then Beatrice rounded the corner and saw the two of them. She cleared her throat and said to Myrtle, "There you are, dear, why don't I make you a nice cup of tea! I'm sure our friend here has places to be."

Myrtle turned away, dejection across her face, and Yvgeny seized the opportunity.

"Yes, yes, I have a lot of business to attend to, I really must be off. Toodles!"

A completely wasted trip to the looney bin. No suit, no help.

Without another word, Yvgeny made a beeline for the exit. On his way, he passed by the sun room where he had spoken with Beatrice. The old woman in the wheel chair hadn't moved, and as Yvgeny passed by, she called out, "She's a real whore!"

Yvgeny stopped and stared at the woman a moment. She was still facing the window in her wheelchair, oblivious to the world around her. Shaking his head, Yvgeny raced out the door toward his hearse.

Back at Schmidt and Sons, Brianna was waiting for him. She was leaning against her Smart Car, smoking a cigarette. When she saw his hearse approach, she took one more drag, then flicked the cigarette across the lawn. Reflexively, he glanced up toward the top floor windows. Had Mama been posted at her window as she often was, he knew exactly what she would say, for all the world to hear.

Oh, my tygrysek, look how your girlfriend uses your father's property like her own little ashtray. Then, when

THE BODY IN THE BED

Yvgeny would shout back up at her, Mama would place her hands on the window, yell *shameful!* Then slam the window shut.

Thankfully, there was no sign of his mother. It was her nap time anyway.

Brianna did not give him time to park, let alone get out of the car. She approached the passenger side of the hearse and climbed inside, cursing.

"Where the hell have you been?"

"Um, I was working. What's the problem?"

"Just drive, I'll tell you on the way."

JONATHAN B. ZEITLIN

CHAPTER FIVE

☩

Yvgeny placed his hearse in reverse, and as he backed up, checking for traffic, he asked Brianna, "on the way where?"

"Zelda."

Yvgeny slammed on the brakes.

"As in Madame Jezelda? Why do you want to go see that freak?"

"Because she's got a plan, and it's a good one. She's going to help us solve that murder."

"The old guy? Jesus, first that crazy rapping geezer, and now you two? What's gotten into everyone? I'm an undertaker, not a cop. Remember?"

"Rapping geezer?"

Yvgeny continued as if he had not heard her.

"Look, though it disgusts me to think about it, I'm pretty sure that guy died in the saddle! There's nothing to investigate, except maybe how he was able to whip all those biddies into such a frenzy!"

"Jezelda's been communing with the man's spirit. It wasn't his horizontal activities that did him in, it was something else."

"Yeah, he had cancer."

"Nope, not that, either," Brianna said, then continued, "the spirit doesn't know, it only knows it was murder."

"How convenient."

"The spirit said he died from the inside out."

"Well, that explains everything."

"Just shut up and drive."

"You know, at some point I will actually need to prepare for tomorrow. I haven't even given Mama the details."

Brianna responded with a grunt.

"And, again, our taxes pay for a bunch of guys with badges down the street to do this stuff. Why am I getting

THE BODY IN THE BED

roped into this?"

Another grunt.

A few minutes later, Yvgeny pulled into the circular driveway in front of Madame Jezelda's converted brick home. In her large bay window was a red neon palm that flashed on and off, and a sign that advertised readings for $20. As Yvgeny placed his hearse in park he shook his head.

"I can't believe I'm actually parking here."

"Well, look at the bright side, your hearse will probably scare off her customers for a day or two, that oughtta turn your crank."

Yvgeny pursed his lips and said, "Don't try to cheer me up!"

Madame Jezelda opened the front door and stood waiting for them to emerge from the hearse. Brianna exited first and trudged through the grass to greet her with a hug. Yvgeny trailed behind her, keeping his hands stoically clasped behind him, back straight. He left his derby in the car, something no Victorian gentleman would do when preparing to enter a lady's home. Unfortunately, neither Brianna nor Jezelda would likely pick up on the snub, but it nevertheless made the visit more tolerable.

They followed her inside, and she escorted them into her living room. There were two couches, a chair, and a table. The windows were covered in wispy red drapes, and the walls were adorned with oil paintings depicting bizarre landscapes. The room had black lights, candles, and lava lamps. The chair; her chair, actually, was upholstered in a pale purple leather with gold filigree. Tiny bells hung from the armrests, and when she sat, the bells tinkled.

Brianna sat on the couch across from Jezelda's chair. Yvgeny chose to remain standing, his hands still clasped behind his back. Jezelda, looking at Brianna, motioned to a pot on the table between them, a curl of steam escaping the spout.

"Tea?"

Yvgeny looked at the pot and sneered, then asked, "Eye of newt?"

Jezelda made a sour face and said, "Chamomile."

Yvgeny snorted and looked away, but Brianna accepted a small teacup, then grabbed Yvgeny by the arm and forced him to sit beside her.

"So, sorceress, why are we here?" Yvgeny asked, trying to get comfortable on the couch.

"Small talk not your strong suit, is it, hole digger?"

Yvgeny looked around the room while saying, "no more than interior decorating is yours."

Brianna kicked him sideways in his shin and cleared her throat.

"Madame Jezelda has a theory how she can identify the killer."

Yvgeny crossed one leg over the other, rested his clasped hands on his top knee, and leaned into Jezelda, saying, "Oh, goody, I'm all ears."

Jezelda scowled at him, then turned to direct her response to Brianna.

"Your man, he will show me the body. I want to see him alone, talk to his *Loa*. I will find out who killed him dead."

"You want to interrogate my corpse? Tell me, do corpses have constitutional rights? You know, being dead and all, I would say he has tacitly exercised his right to remain silent!"

Brianna and Jezelda both glared at him until he finished with a chuckle, then the ladies turned back to each other.

"If that don't work, I will attend the funeral. I will bring my rods, and summon the *Loa*, sniff around for the killer. If he's there-"

"Or she!" Yvgeny hastily added.

"If he's there, maybe the *Loa* will point him out to me."

Yvgeny clapped his hands together and stood, calling out, "Bravo! Bravo!"

As he buttoned his top coat and straightened his pants he announced, "This has been a lovely treat, thank you so much!" Then he flamboyantly checked his watch, and said, "But ah, look at the time! We really should be going, dear, it's lunch time, and we have a whole funeral to plan!"

Looking at Jezelda, he adopted a pained look on his face and said, "Charmed, as always."

Yvgeny scooched by Brianna, then held out his arm, elbow crooked, hoping she would take it. Instead, she blew across the rim of her tea cup and turned back to Jezelda.

"Then wait for me in the car, I'm getting a reading."

Yvgeny looked at his watch again, exasperated, then

THE BODY IN THE BED

headed toward the door shaking his head. As he walked toward his hearse, he started fuming.

Jezelda is going to ruin my funeral!

He chirped his alarm and fell into the driver's seat.

She's going to scare everyone off with her shenanigans, waving chicken legs and spitting rum on everyone. They're all going to go get stuffed by Raj Brothers, or that other idiot in Warner Robins.

He cranked the engine and started to press the little button on his steering wheel with the face profile and the lines coming from the mouth. Then he paused, his index finger hovering over the button.

Mama always said, when life hands you lemons....

Smiling, he activated his Bluetooth and after the beep, said, "call office."

"Schmidt and Sons."

"Ah, Albert, my dear boy, picked up on the first ring, well done."

"Of course, Mr. Geny. What can I do for you?"

Still smiling, Yvgeny said, "Can you talk to Mama, let her know I sealed the deal on that stiff from Sunset Manor. The party will be tomorrow afternoon at three, a rush job, so we will need flowers and invitations. Have her get the guest list from Beatrice. And tell her to check the account, there should be a new payment. A big one, so tell her to get the caterers scheduled."

Yvgeny could hear the sound of scribbling as the boy dutifully took notes. Yvgeny smiled again.

"Got it. What about the body?"

"It's in storage, but if you'd like to begin preparations, that would be lovely."

"You got it!"

"Excellent. See you shortly!"

A moment later, the front door opened and Brianna emerged from the house. She looked slightly pale, and lit a cigarette as soon as the door closed behind her. She walked around to the driver's side of the hearse to finish her cigarette, and Yvgeny rolled down his window.

"Prophetic?"

"Depressing."

"You paid twenty bucks for, wait, let me guess," Yvgeny

said, then spoke in a high pitched, trembling voice, waving his hands, palm down, over the steering wheel, "I see a man, he is your dead uncle, his name begins with a B; no, a C. He misses you. He says you should-"

"Will you just shut up? She said she spoke to my grandfather, he said he loves seeing me at his stone."

"I could have told you that for only ten."

"She also said you don't have to believe, but that you should take your head out of your ass."

Yvgeny nodded, made a soft strangled sound, then looked up at Brianna and asked, "You about done with that? We have work to do."

Back at Schmidt and Sons, Albert brought out the body and was letting it warm up a bit. Next, he would wash the body with a special disinfectant and germicidal solution, then focus on bending, flexing, and massaging his arms and legs to relieve any rigor mortis.

Beatrice had already e-mailed a guest list to Mama, who printed out the list, then prepared the programs for the event. Beside her was a stack of premium paper stock, which she would later feed into the laser printer Yvgeny had installed in the parlor.

When Brianna and Yvgeny returned to Schmidt and Sons, Yvgeny sought out Mama and found her on the phone while fiddling with the printer.

"Mama, make sure the caterers only do soft foods. We don't need another denture incident."

Mama shushed him and waved him off, screwing the phone harder against her ear.

"Who is it?" Yvgeny asked, ignoring his mother's wave off. Mama put her hand over the mouthpiece of the phone and whispered, "caterers," then turned her back on him. Yvgeny turned to leave, but then heard his mother snapping her fingers. He turned around to find her shoving a stack of programs into his hands.

Leaving Mama to finish her conversation, he took the programs back out to Brianna.

"Can you set these up on that table by the door? I need to go have a chat with Alfred."

Yvgeny walked out the back door and over to Alfred's shed, finding him wandering through the headstones as he usually

THE BODY IN THE BED

did, glancing up toward the clouds, as if deep in thought. Deaf and mute, Yvgeny waited for Alfred to notice him, then approached. Seeing Alfred's eyes turn to his lips, Yvgeny began to speak.

"Alfred, we need to prepare a hole for tomorrow. I'm thinking 625 would be a good spot, next to-"

Yvgeny snapped his fingers a few times as he tried to remember, then pointed his index finger into the air and called out, "Ah! Rex Lancaster! The last stiff we got from Sunset Manor. Remember where he is?"

Alfred blinked a couple of times, then nodded his head, remembering the spot. He then turned away and resumed his wandering.

"Excellent, I will add him to the map."

Inside his office, Yvgeny maintained a large paper map upon which every single occupant of his cemetery was recorded. It was a task his father had asked him to complete many years ago, and he had avoided it until his tenth-grade history teacher assigned "home history" projects to the class. Always looking for a way to kill two birds with one stone, he made his cemetery map into his research project, one that made his father proud, earned him an A+, and the collective disgust of the entire tenth grade class.

Yvgeny made a mental note to scribble the old man's name onto his map. The original project involved a laminated map and a grease pencil, but Yvgeny worried over the implications such a setup suggested, and used a Sharpie instead.

Some things, unfortunately, were permanent.

Presiding over a cemetery required much more than a shovel and a lawnmower. It was a complicated endeavor that required painstaking attention to detail. When Albert showed up for his first day in the office, Yvgeny walked him out back to his cemetery and, with an arm lightly resting on the boy's young shoulders, he motioned out to the headstones and explained to him what Yvgeny's father once taught him.

"Albert, think of a stadium. Think of your favorite stadium, where your favorite team plays."

Albert gazed out upon the headstones with a solemn expression.

"Those with the deepest pockets get the closest to the action; they get the best views; shade in the sunshine, shelter from the rain. Some of them even get box seats. And it's important who your neighbors are. Who wants to watch a game next to some drunk and obnoxious lout?"

Albert listened intently.

"The cream of the crop gets the best seats, and for everyone else, there's the bleachers. The nose bleeds, if you will. This place is just like that stadium. Now, over yonder -"

Yvgeny motioned up the hill toward the edge of the cemetery.

"That's where everyone else goes. The nose bleeds."

"Yes, yes, I see!" Albert cried out.

"Now, over there," Yvgeny motioned toward another corner of the cemetery, "you would think those are also nosebleeds, yes? On the contrary! See the large stela, the one with the little fence around it?

Albert followed Yvgeny's pointed finger, then haltingly asked, "Is that the box seats?"

Yvgeny clapped his hands together and exclaimed, "Splendid! You see, that's the marker for J. Nesbitt Friar, a captain of industry and one of the first interred at Schmidt and Sons. Back then, it was just Schmidt's. Now, Mister Friar, he was a contemporary of Eldred Senior's. It's actually in a prime location, with a little shade, a view of the entire cemetery, and it's separated from all the commoners by a fence."

"Wow, Mr. Geny, I never thought of cemeteries this way!"

"Actually, that's a good example of what I'm talking about. You see, like all good rules, there are also exceptions. Think of an airplane. Sure, the closer to the front, the sooner you get the snacks, the earlier you get off the plane. But there's other considerations. Think of exit rows."

Albert furrowed his brow.

"Certain spots have unique intrinsic value, like Friar's spot. Or that area, over there," Yvgeny added, pointing toward a slightly overgrown area to one side. "See, past those old oak trees? It's one of the most distant points from the street, and there's no real view. But it's quiet, and it's in the shade of that last oak. Ms. Brianna's grandfather is over there. It's in the nosebleeds, but it's a choice spot."

Yvgeny let it all sink in, thoroughly enjoying his new role as teacher and surrogate father, then, for effect, added, "Yes,

THE BODY IN THE BED

my dear boy, as they say in the business, location, location, location!"

Albert nodded, captivated.

Yvgeny smiled at that memory, then moved toward the cold room, where he found Albert bent over staring at the dead man on the gurney. When he heard Yvgeny walk in, he straightened up and turned quickly, as if embarrassed. Yvgeny smiled.

"That's right, my young apprentice, death is fascinating, is it not? Just think, a few days ago he was happy as a clam, and next think he knew, poof! It was all over."

Albert swallowed, his Adam's apple bouncing from the effort, then he turned back to the body while saying, "Exactly."

The telephone started to ring, but both Albert and Yvgeny ignored it. It only rang twice.

Albert had the same fascination with bodies that Yvgeny himself had at that age, and it warmed his heart to see the boy fawning over the corpse. He stood for a moment, proudly observing his understudy staring at the body.

Death was the one experience eventually shared by everyone, and the one experience nobody could share. Staring into the eyes of the dearly departed, as Albert was doing, mere inches away, death was a question and the answer was on the tip of Earnest's tongue, a mystery shared with his dying breath. Some people spent their entire lives trying to solve that mystery. Yvgeny, however, wasted no time on such things, confident in his belief that its eventual unraveling was a certainty.

But enough of such mental gymnastics. It was time to get busy!

Yvgeny approached, leaned in close to the body, and took a long sniff. He smiled; it smelled clean as a spring morning. He picked up an arm, tested it for rigor, and confirmed Albert had done a good job of massaging out any stiffness.

After tousling the boy's hair, Yvgeny walked over to his red Snap-On tool chest, sorted through some of his trocars, decided on the right one for the job, then ushered his understudy over to a square box in the corner of the room against the wall. The box had two hoses, one emerging from each side of the box.

JONATHAN B. ZEITLIN

"Albert, are you ready for your first lesson?"

The boy's enthusiasm matched Yvgeny's, and both were momentarily overcome with excitement and began hopping up and down in unison. Yvgeny shook it off, then brandished his trocar. After presenting it to Albert, he demonstrated how to connect it to the box.

"Now, let me show you how this bad boy works!"

Yvgeny flicked the power switch on his device and got busy. He fielded frequent questions from the boy as he worked, but he started having trouble focusing, his mind wandering to other matters, such as what kind of snacks to serve at the funeral, whether he remembered to pick up his dry-cleaning, where he would take Brianna on their next date, and of course, which tuxedo he would loan to Earnest for his ceremony.

Of course! The Rex Lancaster tux would be perfect!

Naturally, Yvgeny chose to wear only authentic Victorian era garments, so it would be too obvious if he loaned one to Earnest for his funeral, but good ol' Rex, the Sunset sent him along with his old tuxedo, which was a much more modern cut. Nobody would notice if he used that one!

Thinking back to his preparations of Rex's body, Yvgeny thought, *It would be a perfect fit!* Then, after the funeral, he would have Alfred retrieve the tuxedo from the body and put it back in the closet. Yvgeny was a fervent believer in recycling, and there was no way he would let a perfectly good suit rot in the ground.

When they were finished with the arterial embalming, Yvgeny pulled a few more tools from his tool chest and placed them, side by side, on a rolling metal table. He presented each one in turn, explaining to Albert their uses and how to clean them. Of course, some of the tasks required a practiced hand, and in those tasks, Albert observed closely while Yvgeny worked; but for everything else, he let Albert take the wheel and drive.

As Yvgeny watched Albert working, totally focused on the task at hand, he imagined this was exactly what his father must have experienced all those years ago when Yvgeny was learning the trade. He swelled with pride, realizing, perhaps, this was how it felt to be a father.

Yvgeny and Albert spent the rest of the afternoon

THE BODY IN THE BED

preparing Earnest for his big day. Normally such a job only requires a couple of hours, but Yvgeny took his time, teaching as he worked and fielding questions from his young understudy. Yvgeny liked to refer to a decedent's funeral as their "coming out" party, and Albert giggled at the reference.

After they finished the initial preparations with the body, Albert ghosted Yvgeny as he collected all the materials necessary for the next step in the process: another application of disinfectants, deodorizers, plus a surface embalming solution for any areas on the skin that required restoration, and a good quality skin moisturizer for the last step.

Then it's off to hair and makeup!

As Albert studied Yvgeny in action, it reminded him of one of those cooking shows where the chef jittered hither and yon from cabinet to counter. Albert was completely fascinated by this elaborate dance, and Yvgeny reveled in all the attention, adding a theatrical flair to every movement.

A clean prep job, as stated previously, usually took a couple hours. However, just like an automotive body-man finding rust in a wheel well, sometimes a mortician found an issue under the hood that required a little extra attention. This was one of those cases. The late Mr. Ledbetter was old, and had suffered from cancer and a number of other maladies, and it took its toll on his body. At some point, Albert looked up at Yvgeny and asked, "Why are we working so hard on his body? Won't he be wearing a suit?"

Yvgeny stopped working and stood up, contemplative. He tried to think of the perfect response, then smiled.

"My young friend, let me ask you a question. If you are in a convenience store and the clerk is outside and nobody could see you, and there were no cameras, would you steal a candy bar?"

Albert made an affronted expression and said, "Of course not!"

Yvgeny smiled even more broadly, then asked, "And why not?"

"Because it's wrong!"

"Exactly. Even though nobody can see you do it, it's still wrong."

Yvgeny returned his focus on the body, speaking as he

worked.

"It's called thanatological integrity, my young friend, and it's no different from the candy bar in the convenience store. Nobody else may see, but it's still wrong. You and I will both know what lies beneath the fabric."

Albert considered, open mouthed, then nodded slowly. His face was pale, he was tired, but he gazed at Yvgeny in awe.

"Wow. This is amazing."

They continued for another thirty minutes or so, then Yvgeny clapped his hands together.

"Break time! Let me go whip up a nice pitcher of lemonade! Back in a minute. Would you care to start the cleanup on the tools? Then we'll start makeup."

Albert's eyes widened and he exclaimed, "Of course!"

Still smiling, Yvgeny skipped up the stairs and down the hall toward the kitchen.

His smile faded when he walked into the kitchen to find his mother sitting at the table reading the newspaper. With each page, she lifted up the paper and shook it out to straighten the pages, a sound which, over the years, became increasingly annoying. When he entered the room, she glanced up, then back down to her paper.

"Your friend called for you."

Flip, shake!

"Which friend is that, Mama?"

Yvgeny rooted through the cupboard looking for the sugar.

"That half-wit Jimmy Flowers."

Flip, shake!

Yvgeny froze a moment, then turned to face his mother.

"And what did *he* have to say?"

"How should I know? I'm not your secretary. I told him you were busy."

Yvgeny took a deep breath, then shook his head. Reaching beneath the sink, Yvgeny grabbed the pitcher and filled it with water, still thinking about Flowers.

Why the hell was he calling?

Pitcher on the table, Yvgeny reached for his phone and scrolled through his contacts until he found the entry for *Village Idiot* and pressed send. It went straight to voice mail.

Flip, shake!

Yvgeny turned to his mother. From his vantage point he

THE BODY IN THE BED

saw the stack of completed invitations. Brianna must have folded each into its own envelope and returned them to the kitchen.

"I'll have Albert deliver those later, Mama."

Mama shot him a withering glare but said nothing.

Great. She's in another one of her moods.

Yvgeny poured the sugar and lemonade mix into the pitcher and started to stir.

JONATHAN B. ZEITLIN

CHAPTER SIX

☦

Flowers made it about half way when he saw, up ahead, a Georgia State Patrol trooper on the side of the road watching traffic.
What the hell was he doing down here in Comstock?
His heart beating hard against his chest, Flowers put on his turn signal and pulled into a corner gas station conveniently located just a hundred yards from the trooper's car. He parked so he could maintain a view of the patrol car.
He checked his watch, then looked down the street at the trooper. He waited around thirty seconds, then looked again.
Come on! Pull someone over!
He continued dividing his attention between the trooper and his watch, and after a while, Flowers got out of his van and walked into the station. He poured a large coffee and grabbed his favorite snack from the shelving by the cashier's counter: an eight pack of mini-donuts; the ones covered in powdered sugar.
He checked his watch again- it was already well after two p.m.
Dammit! I need that body!
He slowly walked outside, trying to open the package of donuts while carrying his coffee. Frustrated, he put his coffee on top of one of the gasoline islands, ripped open the package, and popped a donut into his mouth.
While he chewed, he saw the trooper's car come to life as he accelerated from his parking spot to pull over another driver.
Hot diggity!
He grabbed his coffee and started walking toward his van, powdered sugar in a white ring around his mouth. He fumbled for his phone to call Yvgeny again. Juggling coffee, donuts, and a cell phone proved to be too much, and one of

THE BODY IN THE BED

his donuts flipped out of his fingers and down his shirt, leaving a trail of powdered sugar from neck to navel.

As he cursed and tried to catch the escaping donut, he heard a commotion coming from the other side of the parking lot. At first it sounded like a fight, with yelling and screaming. Then his distracted mind processed the sounds more clearly. It was someone yelling for help, and a female voice screaming. He turned toward the source of the screaming to see a taxi cab stopped between two of the gas islands on the other side of the parking lot. He walked toward one corner to get a better view. The taxi was parked sideways, the back doors open, and a woman was lying in the back-seat shrieking.

Flowers involuntarily took a few steps closer to get a better view. The woman appeared to be pregnant. The Indian taxi driver rushed toward the door of the station and poked his head in.

"Someone call the hospital, this lady's about to have a baby!"

The clerk behind the counter grabbed the phone and punched in 911. Flowers sighed, loudly, took a big gulp of his coffee and looked behind him, toward his van, and then back toward the screaming woman.

Shit.

Flowers reached into the cellophane donut package and quickly shoved two more donuts into his mouth; the imprecise movement sent even more powdered sugar sprinkling down his chin and onto his shirt. Then he dropped the donuts and his coffee on top of the nearest gas island and lurched into action, straightening his shirt and patting at the hair on his head. There was no shower in his office, so given the late hour and his prior evening's recreational activities, he smelled like a sour brewery filled with a celebrating rugby team.

"I'm a doctor!" he mumbled loudly, still trying to chew.

The taxi driver saw Flowers come around the corner of the station and led him over to his cab, turning back several times to make sure Flowers was following him. Flowers shook off his pounding headache and jogged the last several feet toward the woman. He turned to the taxi driver and yelled, "Tell the clerk to get you a bucket of the hottest water he can find, and some towels, stat!"

When he came into the woman's field of vision, she stopped panting a moment, and inspected Flowers, up and down.

"It's ok, I'm a doctor," he said. The woman scrutinized him a moment longer, then recognition set in. He started asking all the usual questions: when did the contractions start, how far apart were they, and then he reached for her wrist to check her pulse. She told him she had started feeling contractions earlier that morning and waited just a little too long to call a cab. No husband, no car, no neighbors available. "Bad timing," she said.

You don't know the half of it!
The head was already crowning.
The ambulance will be too late.

The baby was out before Flowers even heard the sirens in the distance, even before the Indian man returned with a mop bucket full of hot water and the clerk behind him holding towels. Flowers cut the cord with his pocket knife, then wiped the knife on his pants. The baby wasn't making a lot of noise, and seemed a little pale.

Flowers stood, dunked a towel in the hot water, then toweled off the new baby as well as he could. He rubbed vigorously, which stimulated the baby enough to start crying. As he cried, his skin reddened and finally the baby began to warm up and breathe. His crying intensified.

Flowers inspected the baby's airway to make sure he was breathing properly, swaddled him in one of the dry towels, then handed him to his mama.

People still pulled into the station to gas up, and several saw the commotion, then came running over with their cell phones to record the event for posterity. And for Facebook. And Instagram. And Tik Tok. And whatever new apps the kids were using. When he handed the baby over to the mama, the crowd applauded, surprising a bashful and sullen Flowers.

Flowers's shirt was a matted mass of blood, sweat, and powdered sugar.

A few minutes later, the ambulance showed up and the EMTs all crowded around Flowers and the woman. They took her vitals, checked the baby, then took statements from the

THE BODY IN THE BED

woman and a few others milling about. When they approached Flowers, all he could think about was getting to Yvgeny and recovering the body, but as he told the EMT what happened, the realization of what he had just accomplished hit him, and he puffed up with pride.

Flowers used another towel to wipe his hands, then checked his watch. He imagined Channel 2 interviewing him on television. Then, as if imagining it could make it happen, a news van screeched into the parking lot. It wasn't Channel 2, it was a local station, but who cares! He held his hand over his mouth and breathed into it to check his breath. Then he patted down his hair and straightened his shirt.

"Are you the man who delivered this baby?" asked the young and attractive reporter. Flowers blushed.

He imagined being awarded some fancy medal by the governor. Maybe a key to the city by the mayor. Another flunky hopped out of the van to set up something that looked like an opaque umbrella with a light in front of it. The flunky shot a quick look up at the setting sun, then adjusted the direction of the light a bit.

Flowers glanced behind him, also noticing the sun was already well past its zenith. Seeing it reminded him where he had been going before he stopped at the gas station. He started to panic again.

I gotta get that body!

"So, what does it feel like to be a hero?"

"A hero?" Flowers asked. He looked at the pretty reporter, at her microphone, at the cameraman, then he licked his lips, and forgot all about Yvgeny and his dead body.

Once the reporter solicited all she could from him, she called out to her flunky, "OK, that's a wrap!" and turned on her heel and walked off. Flowers, momentarily surprised, watched her go, then glanced over at the sun again. It was slowly melting from an intense yellow to a rich orange. He panicked. He checked his watch: it was already almost four p.m.

I really *gotta get that body!*

The reporter, microphone still in hand, had wandered over to the back of the taxi cab, where the new mother was arguing with one of the EMTs.

"I can't afford a ride in that ambulance! I ain't got no

insurance!"

All eyes turned to the cab driver, who was despairing over the mess in the back of his cab. When he realized everyone was looking at him, he backpedaled toward the driver's seat.

"No, no, no way! She ruined my taxi! And she didn't even pay me!"

The cab driver sequestered himself between the pumps and the side of his cab, palms raised in refusal. This time all eyes turned to Flowers.

Flowers started hyperventilating. The reporter had noticed the commotion and started walking over from the back of the ambulance, her camera-bearing flunky in tow. Even the EMTs had stopped to watch him, expectantly.

If I don't get that body, my career is over.

He looked back at the reporter.

But if I don't take her to the hospital, it's over anyway.

He sighed and painted an expression of warmth and confidence on his face.

"Come, Ma'am, I'll take you myself!"

As he retrieved his gurney from the back of his van, the EMTs surrounded the taxi, milling around the new mother like a cloud of winged insects, waving pens and clipboards stacked with disclosures, releases, and waivers, trying to get her to sign them. She swatted at the papers and pens, cursing at them to go away.

Flowers dropped the wheels from the gurney and jogged it back over to the woman, pried apart the EMTs, then enlisted their help loading her onto the gurney. The entire time, he focused on keeping his panic in check. He got her safely loaded and secured in the back of his van, then climbed into the driver's seat, his coffee and donuts forgotten. He grabbed his phone to try Yvgeny again, but was interrupted by a rapping on his window.

He looked up, and was surprised to find the reporter.

"Hey, we are going to follow you over to the hospital, maybe get a shot of you bringing her out of the van and wheeling her inside. It'll make for a great story!"

He swallowed his panic long enough to smile and nod his head. As they pulled out, his head started to pound, a mixture of anxiety and hangover. The sun's orange glow didn't help.

THE BODY IN THE BED

He tried calling Yvgeny again during the ride, but nobody answered at the mortuary or on the mobile. It was a short drive to the hospital, followed by a quick, choreographed photo shoot of him bringing the woman out of the van and wheeling her inside. Then, at the reporter's insistence, he posed with her while wearing a borrowed white hospital coat, both for effect and also to hide the powdered sugar and blood all over his clothes.

Finally, the ordeal was over, and Flowers was able to finish his trip. It was after five, and he had to flick on his headlights while he was en route. His worry grew, then metastasized.

The longer it takes, the more likely he's already embalmed him!

The longer it takes, the more suspicious this will look to the sheriff and the GBI.

It's after five and I still have to get the body and take it up to Macon.

The more he worried, the more things he found to worry about. He took a deep breath and tried to think of something positive.

Well, on the bright side, it's after hours, so I won't have to go through the standard intake procedure. I can drop old Earnest off and just fill out the forms and leave them on top of the body!

And, by the time they get to work in the morning, they'll see me on t.v. and understand why it took so long! I'll be a celebrity!

He continued driving, trying on a grim smile to keep his mood up. Then he thought of something else.

At this point, who cares if I get pulled over! I'd pass whatever drunk tests they got!

It was a short drive, but he constantly vacillated between elation at the activities of his afternoon and fear over the implications of not recognizing the obvious clues during his limited autopsy. His mind circled back to all his worries, then shed a positive light on his situation. The back and forth eventually brought back his headache.

Minutes later, with a sigh of relief, he parked his van in the driveway of Schmidt and Sons, right behind Cerberus. It was quickly approaching sunset. He rummaged through the back of his van until he found the cardboard box in which he kept his body bags. He pulled out an opaque white plastic bag, the kind used for evidence, and one of his fancy vinyl body bags with the gold stenciled lettering.

For appearances, he thought to himself.

He rang the doorbell, then waited, body bags tucked under his free arm. He rang it again. No answer. With a sigh, Flowers peered inside. There was no sign of life, no movement. He walked onto the grass and looked into another window. Darkness. With a muffled curse, he trudged across the yard and around the back, toward Alfred's shed. A light was on and he aimed for it like an excited moth.

Flowers opened the door without knocking. The shed was empty, and he cursed out loud, then walked back outside, studying the cemetery. The sun was resting upon the roof of the house across the street; once it fell behind the house, all that would be left on the horizon would be a glow like the embers of a low fire.

He stood gazing at the tombstones, at a loss. His shoulders slumped. Just as he started to turn and go back to his van, he noticed Alfred plodding between the headstones, shovel in hand. Flowers called out to him, momentarily forgetting he was deaf. He didn't want to traipse through the tombstones, so he waited for Alfred to return, impatiently shifting his weight from one foot to another. Alfred finally noticed Flowers standing by the shed, and started shuffling over.

"Alfred, I need to speak to Geny. Where is he?"

Alfred watched Flowers's lips moving, then shrugged his shoulders.

"Look, I know he's here, that damn hearse is in the driveway. It's an emergency. I have to get my hands on that dead guy."

Alfred pursed his lips and shrugged again, lifting his hands in the universal sign of *what the hell are you talking about?*

Flowers looked down at the shovel, caked with dirt, and momentarily panicked. Then he remembered the funeral wasn't until the next day, so Yvgeny couldn't have already buried him.

Not until he gets his money!

THE BODY IN THE BED

Flowers took a deep breath and collected himself. Alfred turned and entered the shed, putting down the shovel and grabbing a knife and a piece of wood that he had been carving. Flowers followed Alfred inside, angrily babbling, but his mouth cranked shut when he looked to his left on the shelf from which Alfred retrieved his carving. Alfred had a row of three wooden carvings, all presumably made by him. The first carving was a crawling baby, followed by what appeared to be a toddler, then a man, and so on. The one in his hand appeared to be a hunched over old man. For a moment, Flowers was surprised into silence. Then he shook it off.

"Look, that body Yvgeny picked up from me yesterday, it's gotta go to the GBI. It was a murder. Well, I think it might be a murder. He didn't embalm the guy yet, did he?"

Alfred turned the wood around in his hand a few times, deciding where to begin. Flowers glared at Alfred, then cursed as he remembered, for the second time, the man was deaf. He leaned in and waved a hand in front of Alfred's face to get his attention. This time, Alfred watched Flowers's mouth as he spoke, squinting to keep up with the moving lips.

"I need to speak with Geny now. It's an emergency."

There was a delay while Alfred processed the message, then Alfred cocked his head and stared at Flowers.

"Nnng ng?"

Flowers stared back, unsure what Alfred meant. Alfred, frustrated, motioned with his knife and took a step closer to Flowers.

"Nng ng! Nng?"

Flowers took a step back and held his hands up.

"Alfred, I don't know what you're saying. Where's Geny?"

Alfred took another step, sending Flowers backwards through the doorway. A sliver of fear took root as Alfred took yet another step, still holding his knife. Just as Flowers was ready to turn and flee, Alfred side-stepped around Flowers and headed toward the main house. With a sigh of relief, Flowers turned to follow.

Once they reached the back door, Alfred turned to Flowers and explained, "Nnng, nng ngg."

Alfred emphasized his point by cocking his head toward

the door a couple of times. Then without any further communication, he turned and headed back the way they came. Flowers watched him walk away, then opened the door.

The rear entry was below grade, and the lights all came on as the sensors were triggered by the fading light. With another sigh, Flowers walked inside, shutting the door behind him.

He felt like a burglar, and whipped out his phone to try to call him once more, then changed his mind. *Besides,* he reasoned, *I know he's here, his hearse is outside.* He took a few more steps, then thought, *Besides, a weirdo like him probably spends most of his time down here in the basement, where his neighbors can't see him!* He put away his phone.

He walked down the hall toward Yvgeny's work room. He suddenly felt an irrational fear that he would find Yvgeny emerging from a coffin like a vampire, but then set it aside.

Must be the hangover.

He had been down in Yvgeny's basement a few times in the past and remembered the way to his work room. He grabbed the doorknob, but froze when he heard noises coming from inside. Shuffling, muffled speech, a chuckle. His first reaction was disgust as he imagined Yvgeny and Brianna together on the stainless steel work table. He shuddered.

Then he heard an unfamiliar male voice. Flowers shuddered again, and, steeling himself, grasped the door knob.

Maybe I should knock, he thought.

Or maybe I should just run away!

Instead, he opened the door, slowly, silently, involuntarily closing his eyes in fear of what he would see. When he finally opened his eyes, it took a moment for his brain to process what his eyes were seeing.

Yvgeny was standing over a body, his back to the door. Albert, his pimply faced teenaged assistant, was on the other side of the body. They were close to the head. Resting on the hips of the body was a tray, and on the tray was a pitcher of lemonade. As Flowers watched, they finished their inspection of the man's head, stood straight and reached for their glasses, clinked them together, then slurped from their respective straws.

Yvgeny, glass in hand, started speaking to Albert in a low voice. Albert paid close attention, but when Flowers shifted on his feet, his movement caught Albert's eye. He waited patiently for a break in Yvgeny's dialogue, then Albert motioned toward Flowers.

Yvgeny stopped talking and turned around, then whistled when he saw Flowers. Staring at the blood and powdered sugar amalgamation on Flowers's shirt, he said, "What the hell happened to you, Flowers? You look like some kind of human cherry pie."

Flowers ignored him, and slowly approached the body, crestfallen.

"Is that my body? You didn't do anything to him? Oh Lord, you did something to him, didn't you? Did you do something weird? That's it, I'm going to the penitentiary. Oh no, no, no. Why? Just why?"

Flowers started pacing, tearing at his hair like King Lear at the precipice, while Yvgeny and Albert watched, amused.

"Why, indeed? Now, while we are on the subject, why are you here?"

"I need the dead guy back. I tried calling you!"

Flowers produced his cell phone and waved it in the air toward Yvgeny to emphasize his point.

"And I called you back," Yvgeny said, "Check your phone."

Flowers closed his eyes, shook his head, completely dejected.

"I thought you were done with him?" Yvgeny said.

"I was. But now I'm not. I think he was murdered."

"This again? What, $600 wasn't enough?"

"Very funny."

"No? Oh, wait, I know, you sewed your watch in the guy. Am I right?"

Flowers just glared at him. Albert started to chuckle. Encouraged by him, Yvgeny continued.

"Hang on, I'll figure this out. Did Jezelda put you up to this? It's gotta be Jezelda. Right?"

Yvgeny cracked his knuckles, then waggled his fingers at Flowers and shut his eyes. Adopting his best island accent, Yvgeny intoned, "Ooh, yes, I see it, Docta man, you got ta get the body back, ol' cracka done be murdered!"

JONATHAN B. ZEITLIN

His teenaged sidekick's laugh developed from a chuckle to more of a raucous snort, and Yvgeny reveled in it. Meanwhile, Flowers finally leaned in to take a closer look at the body.

"What the hell did you do to him?" Flowers asked.

"I embalmed him. What else? What's gotten into you, Flowers? You're even crazier than usual."

"I told you, I think the guy was murdered. I gotta get this body to the GBI. And now that you already embalmed him, I'm screwed. You still have his fluids?"

Yvgeny sneered at Flowers, then pointed toward the low sink behind the head of the body, responding, "Of course not, what would I do with his fluids?"

Albert snapped his head between Yvgeny and Flowers, then said, in between snorts, "Looks like your case," *snort*, "it done gone down the drain!"

Yvgeny laughed and held up his hand for Albert to smack, calling out, "Good one!"

Flowers looked down a moment, then resumed pacing and chanting, "I'm dead. I'm dead, I'm so dead!"

Finally, the doctor sighed, his shoulders slumping, and he said, "Well, time to face the music. Come on, help me get this guy into my van."

"You can't take him, tomorrow's the funeral. And it's open casket."

Flowers lit up again.

"Tough titty! This guy's the property of the State of Georgia now, until they do a proper autopsy."

"Flowers, are you nuts? You send this guy north because some whacko psychic says he was murdered and they'll take your license!" Yvgeny then rubbed his chin and looked toward the ceiling, adding, "Hmm, come to think of it, that's not such a bad idea."

"Psychic? No! That's not what I mean."

Flowers leaned against the table, then finally deflated.

"OK, look. You ever heard of a Woods lamp?"

"A what?"

"A Woods lamp. It's basically a fancy ultraviolet light. You know, a black light, like they have in discos."

"They haven't had discos since the Seventies, but go on."

"Well, the cops were at my office -"

THE BODY IN THE BED

Yvgeny rolled his eyes.

"And they left the guy's clothes draped over my couch. I had my black lights on, just relaxing, you know, and then I saw it."

"Saw what?"

"The crotch of the guy's pants was glowing."

Albert's eyes lit up, darting between Yvgeny and Flowers, waiting for the punch line. Flowers waited for recognition in their eyes, and when he failed to see it, he took a deep breath.

"There's only one good reason why his crotch would be glowing," Flowers said, arms crossed over his chest.

Yvgeny and Albert exchanged a glance, and Albert said, tentatively, "He was an alien?"

It was Yvgeny's turn to chuckle, but Albert continued staring at Flowers with an expression of earnest sincerity. Flowers stopped to inspect Albert a moment, open mouthed, then leaned in to Yvgeny and whispered, "Are you kiddin' me?"

Yvgeny clapped the boy on the back and turned back to Flowers.

"Come on, he's a genius in the making, Flowers. He's more like me every day. In fact, one day he might inherit all this!"

This time the boy snort-laughed.

"This is serious, Geny, wipe that shitty smirk off your face, he's gotta go."

Yvgeny checked his watch again, muttering, "Geez, Flowers, where's your sense of humor?"

"I think the guy was poisoned, ok? Ethylene glycol is the only thing I can think of that would make a guy's pee glow under a black light."

Yvgeny's shitty smirk disappeared.

"You're actually serious?"

"Yup."

Flowers reflected back on what he had read from his phone while standing over the body, then lifted his head high and began, smugly, to lecture.

"Ingestion of ethylene glycol makes its way through the digestive system, and eventually passes through the kidneys. When the kidneys metabolize EG, one of the byproducts is calcium oxalate crystals, a deadly substance which passes through the body in urine. The substance has phosphorescence, which means -"

"That it glows. Yeah, I get it. So, you're telling me the guy drank antifreeze?"

"Yup. And I'm guessing the guy didn't know it. I think someone poisoned him."

Albert had remained quiet, but suddenly raised his right hand in the air. Flowers and Yvgeny looked at him, and finally Yvgeny said, "You're not in school, Albert, you don't have to raise your hand to speak."

Albert's hand shot back down and into his pocket. He blushed a little, then said, "Or maybe he killed himself. He was dying of cancer, maybe he just got sick of waiting. Or suffering."

Flowers stared at Albert a moment, then nodded slowly, and muttered, "Yeah, I guess," then without missing a beat, he grabbed the table.

"Anyway, I gotta go, I gotta take this guy-"

"Like I said, Flowers, this guy's open casket tomorrow. *Tomorrow!* What am I supposed to do? Make a cardboard cutout of the guy? Stick *you* in there?"

"Dammit, what do you want *me* to do? Once they run labs on the blood that *I* took, they're going to find some crazy shit, then come back to *me* for the body."

Flowers crossed his arms and smiled, adding, "You know what, never mind. When they come asking for the body, I'll just tell them to talk to you, tell them you didn't want to give the body back. Then they can knock on *your* door. Oh, and you know what, I bet they'll show up with a search warrant, seeing as you wouldn't give him back to me."

"You know -" Flowers added, then looked slowly around the room, very pleased with himself, and hammed it up even further by running a hand along one of the counter surfaces, then tapping two fingers across the counter like little legs going for a walk. Then he turned and leaned back against the counter, arms outstretched, both palms on the counter, and in a grandiose air, exclaimed, "Who knows what else they might find here!"

Flowers sighed, looked up in the air, shook his head with a smile, and said, "Imagine, a bunch of cars from the GBI showing up, lights, sirens, guys in uniform everywhere. I

THE BODY IN THE BED

wonder, Geny, what would all your neighbors say? Geny? Hey, Geny!"

Flowers's performance was shattered when he realized Yvgeny wasn't paying attention, and instead had focused on some point on the ceiling. Yvgeny squinted, as if listening for something. Flowers stared at him a moment, then looked at Albert, who just shrugged his shoulders.

"Geny, are you even listening?" Flowers repeated.

Yvgeny cocked his head, as if deep in thought, then finally turned back to everyone with a broad smile. Clapping his hands together, Yvgeny turned to Albert and called out, "Albert, come quick, I've had a fit of inspiration!"

While Flowers watched, dismayed, Albert scurried behind Yvgeny as he approached a large cabinet. He opened the doors and started to rummage through the contents. He tossed a plastic bag over his shoulder, which Albert caught, then another. He dug around a while longer, then emerged with a cardboard box under one arm.

"Put them on the counter."

Albert walked them over to the counter closest to the body, then leaned in to read one of the labels.

"Alginate?" Albert asked.

"What the hell are you doing?" asked Flowers.

"No time to explain. Go over there, second drawer down. Get a big bowl, fill it with water. Quick!"

Albert rummaged through the cabinet, coming out with a medium sized bowl. He flipped on the spigot and filled it, then walked heel to toe back to Yvgeny, trying not to spill any of the water.

Yvgeny opened his Snap On tool chest and took out a pair of scissors and a long stirring stick.

"OK, let's get started. Get rid of that tray," Yvgeny ordered, pointing at the body.

Flowers moved in a little closer, his irritation folding into curiosity. Yvgeny walked up to the counter next to the plastic bags, then added his cardboard box to the collection. Yvgeny turned to face Albert.

Yvgeny leaned his hand on the box and said, "You're probably familiar with this stuff by its more common name, Plaster of Paris, but it's really just powdered gypsum, mined right here in Georgia. This is a kilogram, which should be enough."

Placing the box to one side, he grabbed the next container, then cleared his throat.

"Alginate is another product you're probably quite familiar with, probably had it in your mouth when you were a kid getting braces. Dentists use it to make molds of your teeth. Got this stuff at cost from a friend. I give him a lot of business."

When Yvgeny had a cremation job, state law required him to remove all metals from the bodies. That included fillings. Usually the fillings would be collected and dropped into the melting pot, but the legitimate outfits that did such work paid out pennies on the dollar, then sent you a 1099, forcing you to report the earnings. Yvgeny collected such fillings in a coffee can, and once the can was at least half way full, he took it to a sleazy dentist he found on the outskirts of Macon who had no objection to under the table transactions.

Tax is theft, and cash is king!

Yvgeny turned one of the plastic bags upside-down and shook out the contents: bandages, plastic sheeting, some fabric, and a container of Vaseline. Finally, he held up a small Tupperware bowl with a lid and shook it a moment.

"And, of course, sand."

With an earnest expression on his face, Albert asked, "So you're making a mask? Like the ancient Egyptians used to do?"

Yvgeny shoved a finger into the air and cried, "Yes! Exactly! Only not with gold. Ah, Albert, such a pleasure having you around, I must say. You finish my thoughts!"

Yvgeny started preparing the mixture, while calling out instructions to his apprentice.

"Albert, take this plastic bag and wrap his head. Cover it up real good. Yes, just like that. Now sprinkle some of this water on his face, especially his eyebrows. Get them nice and moist. Good, good, now take this cloth and tie it around his face. That's where the mask will end. Just like that, excellent –"

Flowers had been watching all the activity, flummoxed, but slowly it registered on him what was happening, and as Yvgeny and Albert crowded around Earnest's head, he spun into action.

THE BODY IN THE BED

"No, no, no! You can't do this!" Flowers cried, shoving himself between Yvgeny and the body. "He belongs to the GBI!"

Yvgeny ignored Flowers and, giddy, turned to Albert and started bouncing on his toes.

"OK, ready to make the magic happen?"

Albert watched as Yvgeny turned away from Flowers and the body and returned to the counter. He mixed two parts water to one part alginate, then quickly stirred with his stirring stick. While Flowers leaned against the body, as if protecting it, Yvgeny lifted the bowl and turned toward the late Ledbetter's head.

"Step aside, Flowers. This stuff dries fast."

"I can't let you do it."

"Flowers, this stuff dries up and then we will peel it off in one piece. Nobody will ever know we did it."

"I don't care! It's desecration!"

"It's an open casket funeral, we have to have something to work with," Yvgeny said, trying to sound reasonable.

Flowers slowly decomposed from angry to fearful.

"If the GBI sees any of this, they're going to go crazy. They'll kill me. They'll lock us up." He glanced at Albert, then said, "They'll lock us all up!"

Yvgeny took a deep breath, then tried a different tack.

"Listen Flowers, if they say anything, just tell them by the time you got over here, it was too late, I already embalmed him and took a mold of his face. Claim ignorance. That should come easy for you."

Yvgeny waited for Flowers to make up his mind, hoping it would be before his mixture started to harden. He waited about ten seconds, then added, "Dammit, I've already embalmed the guy! You think the GBI's gonna get any madder that I took a mold of his head?"

Flowers finally caved and, with his head hanging down, slid to one side. Yvgeny hefted the bowl again and began tipping it over Ledbetter's head. A moment later, just before the white material began to dribble out onto the corpse's face, Yvgeny stopped.

"Keep that cloth tight around his face! Good, just like that. Good boy!"

Finally, Yvgeny tipped the bowl over the man's head again,

and the white mixture oozed out across his features. When he finished, he took a step back and stared a moment. Then he looked down at his watch.

"So far so good, we- crap!"

Yvgeny turned and ran toward his cabinets and began opening drawers, then smacking them closed. He stopped and then scanned around the room, finally landing on the pitcher of lemonade and the two empty glasses. He jogged over and snatched the straws out of the glasses, then loudly yelled, "Got it!" and returned to the body. He carefully shoved one into each nostril on the corpse. Then, with a sigh, he turned back to Albert.

"That was a close one! OK, wait, wait, hold it, hold it, not much longer now -"

Flowers leaned in, and whispered, "Hey Geny, what are the straws for? The guy's dead."

Yvgeny stammered a moment, then sheepishly removed the straws.

"Of course," Yvgeny mumbled.

Yvgeny reached out and lightly touched the corner of Earnest's face, just enough to feel the material as it dried. He held his other arm up so he could stare at his watch, vaguely reminiscent of a doctor checking a patient's pulse.

As Yvgeny stared at his watch, Albert started fidgeting with the cardboard around Earnest's head. Finally, just when Albert's shoulders started to ache, Yvgeny dropped his arm and called out, "Ding!"

Relieved, Albert let go of the cardboard. He expected it to fall to the ground, but instead it remained glued to the material drying around Earnest's face.

"It's fine, Albert, now come, quickly, help me cut up this fabric."

Albert followed Yvgeny to the counter, and they both begun cutting short and narrow strips of the fabric. While they completed their task, Flowers slowly approached the body and crouched down to take a closer look at the drying alginate.

Yvgeny watched Albert cutting strips for a moment, then he went to go fill another empty bowl with water. Flowers, curious, approached the counter and looked over their shoulder.

THE BODY IN THE BED

"What are you doing?"

Yvgeny replied, "This fabric will protect the mold when we take it off his face. Without it, this stuff would crack pretty easily. Think of a pie without the crust."

Back at Earnest's side, Yvgeny handed the bowl over to Albert, then grabbed one of the cloth strips, moistened it in the bowl of water, then placed it over the quickly drying mask. He lightly ran his finger along the cloth to ensure it was in full contact with the alginate.

"Can't put them on too soon, pressing down on the fabric can distort the mask."

Flowers, too fascinated to think about his concerns, glanced up at Yvgeny and asked, "What the hell are you going to do with a mask?"

Yvgeny turned to Flowers, raised his eyebrows several times, rapidly, then returned his attention to Albert.

Flowers crossed his arms across his chest, then looked at the clock on the wall.

"OK, Albert, grab that edge, and when I start to lift, you match my movements, starting at the chin. OK, pull, slowly, slowly."

The two began lifting away the white substance, which had hardened into what looked to Flowers to be a rigid mask. The ends of a couple of the cut-up pieces of cloth loosened and hung from the mask, but enough of them were left to do their job. Once it was completely off, Yvgeny walked it over to the sink and placed it into a bowl he had filled half-way with sand.

"All yours, Flowers. Albert, please fetch our guest a body bag."

"No need, I brought my own."

Yvgeny looked down as Flowers held up his evidence bag and vinyl decorative body bag. Yvgeny wrinkled his nose, but remained silent. Then he turned to Albert and nodded.

Albert helped Flowers stuff the body into the white evidence bag, then into the black plastic bag. As they worked, Yvgeny noticed the gold cursive lettering on the vinyl bag Flowers brought and groaned.

Albert un-locked the wheels of the cart and began pushing it out while Flowers held the doors open. As they started walking down the hall, Yvgeny jogged over to the mold one more time to make sure it was drying properly, then, satisfied, he turned to catch up with the procession. As he turned, he noticed his notepad, pencil, and measuring tape on the counter. He snatched them up and ran after everyone, yelling, "Wait! Wait!"

He caught up with them at the double doors leading out. Beyond the doors, it was dark.

"What now?" Flowers asked.

Yvgeny started unzipping the bag, then calling out for Albert. He instructed Albert to lift up the man's head, and Yvgeny wrapped the tape around his forehead, studied the tape, then jotted down a number in his pad. He measured from at least a dozen angles, dutifully recording all the measurements. Flowers looked on, tapping his feet.

"Are you done?" Flowers asked, flatly.

Yvgeny stood back and started coiling up his tape. "Done."

Yvgeny shoved his pad in his breast pocket, tape in his pants pocket, then Albert held open the door so they could push Earnest through. On the sidewalk, Yvgeny walked beside Flowers, hands clasped behind his back.

"So, antifreeze, huh? You really think so?"

"Why else would his pee glow in the dark?"

Albert cracked a smile and was about to offer some alternatives, but caved when he saw the expression on Yvgeny's face.

"Why bother poisoning an old guy with cancer? He was on his way out already."

Flowers said, "Don't know. Don't care. All I know is he's going to Macon."

"Maybe young Albert is right. Maybe he got sick of suffering."

"Maybe. But what a way to go."

"Slow and painful?" Yvgeny asked.

"And then some."

As Yvgeny walked behind the body, he thought about old man Telfair and what he said about motive.

Love, sex, money.

Maybe he wasn't so crazy, after all.

"You told the sheriff, right?"

Flowers glanced at Yvgeny. As recognition set in, Flowers

THE BODY IN THE BED

started stamping his feet.

"Shit, shit, shit! I need to call the sheriff!"

"Only if you want to keep your job, coroner," Yvgeny said, with a smile. "Do give him my regards."

Flowers opened the rear doors of his van and smacked the gurney against the bumper. The legs of the gurney were designed to collapse upon impact, allowing Flowers to push the gurney down their tracks on the floor of the van.

"Oh, just a second!" Yvgeny cried out, then hiked himself up into the van.

"What the hell are you doing?"

Flowers leaned into the van and watched as Yvgeny produced his iPhone and unzipped the body bag.

"Just a couple quick pics for posterity!"

Flowers checked his watch again, and cried out, "You gotta be kidding me!"

Yvgeny first took a few close-up photographs of Earnest's face, then he crouched down next to the gurney and wrapped his left arm around Earnest's head. Holding out his phone with his right hand, he snapped off a few selfies of himself and Earnest. In the last shot, Yvgeny made the peace sign with his left hand.

A moment later, Yvgeny and Albert watched Flowers drive away, his glass packs rumbling into the night. After a moment of silence, Albert turned to Yvgeny and asked, "So, Mr. Geny, why did we make a mask of the dead guy's face?"

Yvgeny continued staring after Flowers's van a moment, then sighed. He had a brief feeling of unease- the funeral was mere hours away, and there was still much to do. Not only did he still have to build his own corpse, but there was music to select, flowers to purchase and arrange, snacks to prepare, caterers to hire, and he couldn't rely on Mama to do it all. He turned to Albert with a sad smile.

"Well, my young friend, when life hands you lemons-"

"You make lemonade?"

Yvgeny nodded, then with a smile, asked, "You want to make some overtime tonight?"

Albert nodded enthusiastically, and they returned to the mortuary.

JONATHAN B. ZEITLIN

CHAPTER SEVEN

☦

Once they returned to the workroom, Albert observed as Yvgeny started his preparations. He retrieved all the necessary materials, then, once everything was set out, he carefully removed the plaster mold from the sand and brought it over to his work area. With hands poised over the mold, Yvgeny turned to Albert.
"This is going to get really messy."
Yvgeny's brow crinkled in concentration as he worked. Albert watched, silently. Yvgeny began squeezing silicon out of a tube onto the mold. It was a laborious and exacting process, but Yvgeny was a master and made it look easy.
After Yvgeny had the majority of the task complete, he heard young Albert's stomach rumbling.
"We need to let this set. We missed dinner, didn't we? Shall we scrounge something upstairs?"
Albert nodded enthusiastically, and they plodded upstairs toward the kitchen. Yvgeny's mother was still at the table, newspaper on the table in front of her, but she was slumped over in her chair, her forehead pressed against the paper. Her prescription bottle of pain medication was beside her.
Yvgeny stared at her a moment, then shook his head. He started opening cabinets looking for something to eat, then swinging the doors shut, hoping the noise would wake her.
When he turned around again, his mother was sitting up, glaring at him.
"I had a terrible dream that idiot Flowers was here."
Mama's eyes were glazed, the pupils big and dark like saucers.
Great, she's rolling.
Yvgeny didn't waste his energy trying to tell her the whole story. She wouldn't remember anything he said.
"It was just a dream, Mama."

THE BODY IN THE BED

But then, as Yvgeny looked at her he realized, perhaps, it would be easier just to get it out in the open while she wasn't totally lucid.

His mother rubbed her eyes, then glanced at Yvgeny. Her eyes narrowed as she noticed he was staring at her expectantly.

"So -"

"So what?" his mother responded.

"So, for tomorrow, I was thinking maybe a closed casket -"

His mother closed her eyes.

"Oh no, you screwed up the body. What did you do, *tygrysek*? He's not blue, is he?"

Yvgeny remembered how mad Mama had gotten many years before, when she caught a much younger, much less experienced Yvgeny playing with a body that had been intended for cremation. As his father used to tell him, such bodies were always the best canvases for practicing one's skills. Thinking nobody would know, Yvgeny tried to create a real, full size Smurf. Unfortunately, the body ended up only somewhat blue. It was very disappointing.

"No, no, I just was thinking -"

"No, don't think. Just *do*. Our friends at Sunset Manor need to see his face. You know that! If they show up and see it's closed casket, they're going to think you're a hack and go to Lenny Updike." Mama snorted, then added, "They'll end up stuffed like a bunch of hunting trophies."

Yvgeny sighed. He knew she was right, but wanted to close the loop anyway. Earnest had to have an open casket, and Yvgeny knew it.

Mama started massaging her hip and wincing. She glanced at her pills. Yvgeny shook his head and grabbed the bottle, and when she objected, he held up a palm and said, "Mama, pace yourself."

"Oh, that reminds me, Beatrice called. Some lady there confessed to taking Earnest's favorite bath robe. He apparently made a comment once that he wanted to be buried in it."

"In a bath robe?"

"Apparently it's a very nice bath robe. Silk."

Yvgeny tried not to react visibly, but inside, he started to panic. It would be impossible to pull off his plan if he had to put the guy in a bathrobe! He took a deep breath, exhaled out of his nose, and tried to sound calm.

"Mama, it's getting pretty late. I can head over in the -"

"No, funeral days are always crazy, you'll never make it over there. Besides, tomorrow is mall day at the Sunset."

Yvgeny checked his watch, then said, "Mama, do you realize what time -"

"I already told Beatrice you were coming. She's expecting you."

Yvgeny sighed, and said, "Fine. I'll go get it." He looked off into space, pensive, then added, "Never done an open-faced sandwich with a guy in a bath robe."

"And one of the guys there wants to sing." Mama riffled through some papers on the table, put on her reading glasses, and said, "Wally Beaverton. He's bringing his own karaoke equipment."

Yvgeny let out a whoosh of air and said, "Well, that's a relief!"

One of the more difficult tasks in planning a funeral is finding musicians. In lower budget affairs, it's easy; a boom box and a few CDs are more than enough. But when the client's family has money, expectations go up.

First, musical acts aren't cheap, and they book well into the future; when someone dies, you only have a few days to put it all together, so you're left scraping the bottom of the barrel.

Even if you get lucky and find a band, then you might have compatibility issues. You might get a band that plays rock n' roll for a funeral in which the family wanted country.

Yvgeny devised an ingenious solution to all of those problems a few years ago, after burying the old retired band director at Comstock High School. He invited a subset of the current high school band's players to provide musical accompaniment, and they gleefully agreed to participate.

It was the perfect solution. Everyone clapped when children played instruments, no matter how terrible they were, and they worked for free. Yvgeny only had to provide them with snacks.

Wally Beaverton and his karaoke machine were a distant second place, but on the bright side, he was bringing his own equipment, selecting his own music, and whatever he did,

THE BODY IN THE BED

the rest of the elderly guests from the Sunset would applaud him.

Free entertainment. Like putting money in the bank!

Yvgeny found some cans of soup and dumped them in a saucepan, then scrounged some bread, picked off the moldy bits, and brought his finds over to the table. Albert ate quietly, occasionally glancing at Yvgeny's mother, but her medication had finally shifted gears up to highway speed, leaving her quiet and brooding. She sat staring glumly at Yvgeny, while Yvgeny pretended not to notice. Occasionally his mother turned away with a "humph!" but Yvgeny refused to take the bait. Finally, he and Albert plopped their bowls in the sink and they headed for the door.

"Don't forget the invitations!"

Yvgeny turned and jogged back to the table and grabbed them. Albert turned and asked, "Do we really need them? I mean, all those old people already know about it."

In unison, both Yvgeny and his mother replied, "Yes!"

Mama turned to Albert and said, "It's the proper thing to do, young man."

Albert turned to Yvgeny, who shrugged and said, "She's right."

The rare show of solidarity puffed Mama up with pride, but before she could launch into a lesson on professional integrity, Yvgeny anticipated what was coming and popped her balloon.

"Gotta go, Mama. Toodles!" he cried, and bounced out of the kitchen, Albert trailing behind him.

On their way out to his car, Yvgeny texted the love of his life.

Yvgeny: *On our way to Sunset Manor to pick up DG bathrobe.*

Brianna: *DG?*

Yvgeny: *Dead guy.*

Brianna: *You're gross.*

Yvgeny: *Kisses!*

Yvgeny first met Brianna at the cemetery, where she was visiting her grandfather. It was such an inspiring tale of grand-daughterly love! Brianna's father had regularly visited him, but after his conviction and life sentence, her father would never again see the man's headstone.

JONATHAN B. ZEITLIN

Her father grew very sick in prison, and, knowing the end was near, he had his lawyer draw up an arrangement, requiring Brianna to text the lawyer a picture of each of her visits. He didn't want Gramps getting too lonely.

In exchange, Brianna would eventually inherit her father's estate. She had no idea of the value of this estate; all she remembered was that her father never had a legitimate job, but he always had a nice car. And he had his own lawyer. She suspected his estate was fairly sizable, at least big enough to justify a weekly visit to the cemetery. After a year of dutiful visits (and text messages), the checks would start to come. She often wondered how big those checks would be.

Until then, she had to work. Her old job at the Golden Pantry had been a real drag; shift work, ill-fitting uniforms, crummy pay, rude customers, and an obnoxious boss, Ricky. Things got even worse when Ricky got arrested for selling marijuana out of the back of the store. With the manager in jail, Brianna got stuck working double shifts, and that put a big dent in her and Yvgeny's budding relationship. Then everything took a turn for the better.

It all started when one of her regular customers, Mr. Puffy (real name Paul Ruffy), was commiserating with her about the fact she couldn't smoke on the premises. Puffy owned a check cashing company across the street, Puffy's Pay Day, and at Puffy's, everybody lit up; the ceiling tiles were yellow from all the smoke. Even better, all their interactions with customers occurred from behind ballistic glass, and the internal motto at Puffy's was *Get Paid, Get Out*. It would be the perfect fit for Brianna.

When Puffy offered her a nine to five and a two dollar raise per hour, she accepted immediately and never looked back. She worked the rest of her shift, then went into the cooler, grabbed her old manager's weed (the cops only found part of the stash), then balled up her green smock and tossed it at her incredulous colleague as he walked in to start his shift.

It was getting late by the time Albert and Yvgeny arrived at the Sunset, but, surprisingly, the place was still bustling with activity. Even though it was February, it was a beautiful night and almost warm, and the porch was filled with people in rocking chairs, bundled under light shawls and blankets. Ceiling fans provided a warm yellow incandescent light, and

THE BODY IN THE BED

sconces provided an additional layer of radiance to the lawn. A couple was walking through the grass, and all eyes turned to the street when Cerberus pulled up, it's gleaming black paint reflecting whatever ambient light it could find.

As Yvgeny and Albert emerged, Beatrice appeared from the throng of people on the porch and waited for them. They met in the grass just at the foot of the stairs. She had a package under one arm. Behind her, on the railing to Beatrice's left, Yvgeny noticed a pot containing withered, dead petunias.

"Good evening, Yvgeny, how's your dear mother?"

"She's sturdy as an ox and about as stubborn."

Beatrice smiled and nodded. Then she produced the package under her arm.

"Myrtle had been hiding this in her dresser. She must have had a change of heart, as she told me she wanted to see him in it one last time. It's clean and should do nicely."

Yvgeny accepted the package with reverence, then leaned in to Albert and whispered, "Go get 'em!"

Albert produced the stack of invitations from his back pocket. They were a little creased in one corner, but Yvgeny let it slide.

It was his first time.

"Ma'am, here are the invitations to the funeral."

Beatrice accepted them with a smile, adding a quick "dear boy" reference.

Behind Beatrice, old man Telfair hobbled down the stairs and motioned to get Yvgeny's attention. When Yvgeny glanced in his direction, Telfair pointed around the side of Sunset Manor, then turned to start shuffling away. Beatrice noticed Yvgeny's distraction and turned to look back toward the porch.

"Everything ok, Geny?"

"Yes, yes, one of those ladies up there looked like she lost her balance."

Beatrice turned back one more time, then shrugged her shoulders.

"Ah, of course. Happens all the time."

Then, with a sigh, Beatrice held out her hand to Yvgeny and said, "Well, a pleasure as usual, dear boy! Send your mother my love!"

As Beatrice turned to walk away, Yvgeny handed Albert

the package and the keys to Cerberus and said, in a low voice, "Get in the car, wait a few minutes, then start it. I will be back shortly."

Albert crinkled his brow.

"How many minutes?"

"Just wait for a few."

"Five?"

"Sure."

Albert accepted the package and keys and turned to go. Yvgeny waited for Beatrice to climb the stairs onto the porch. Once she disappeared inside, Yvgeny quickly walked around to the side of the building, some of the old people on the porch watching him like a hawk, some with suspicion, others merely with curiosity. He found Telfair standing near the wall just around the corner, in the penumbra of darkness between two of the wall sconces.

Telfair skipped all pleasantries, and grabbed Yvgeny by the elbow and escorted him toward an even more shady spot on the lawn. There was a slight chill in the darkness, but Yvgeny could smell the wood siding, which was still warm from baking in the sun all day.

"How's the investigation going?"

"What investigation?"

Telfair grumbled in his throat, something like a dog growling.

Yvgeny sighed and said, "Well, Flowers said he thinks the guy had antifreeze in his system."

Telfair smacked Yvgeny's shoulder with a force that surprised him.

"I knew it!"

Telfair turned and started pacing back and forth, talking to himself.

"So that's how she did it. Of course! How could I be so stupid. Wily little vixen! No wonder I'm stuck here. Must be losing my edge."

"She? Who?"

Telfair turned back to Yvgeny, incredulous.

"Who? Are you kidding me?"

"One of those old ladies?"

"Bessie, she's got a temper on her, for sure. And she's a little loose with the men, you feel me?"

THE BODY IN THE BED

"Feel you?" Yvgeny shuddered.

"She became unglued when she caught him with Myrtle. That must have been the last straw for her. Must've poisoned him."

Telfair chewed on his lower lip a moment in the manner of old people, then muttered, "Sweet stuff. That's why people use it to kill cats."

Yvgeny remembered dipping his finger into the coffee beside Earnest's bed. It was sweet.

Telfair seemed to be deep in thought, then he turned to Yvgeny with a look of pure conviction. He leaned in close, and in a conspiratorial whisper, said, "We need to talk to Dub M."

Yvgeny pulled away from Telfair and just stared at him. Telfair, seeing the confusion in Yvgeny's eyes, raised both his hands, palms out, and nodded his head.

"I know, I know, it ain't his real name. That's just his street name."

"You want to introduce me to a guy with a *street name*? No, wait, you actually *know* a guy with a street name?"

"Dub M hangs out at the Money Bar on Cherry. You know it?"

"The black club? How the hell do you know anyone that hangs out *there*?"

Telfair shook his head and, with a smile, said, "Wasn't always a black club. Back in the day, Junior G's pe-paw and me, we was regulars! Used to be called the Rooster. Crowd's done changed, but it don't matter. It's still my spot. Every Wednesday."

"Luther, that place doesn't even open until midnight!"

"Exactly. You think we can just stroll out of here whenever we want?"

Telfair took a deep breath, then started to beat box a tempo, slapping his hand on his knee.

"Locked up, yo, but ain't committed no crime.
Nothin' doin' here but rottin and rhymin'.
The ladies be helping me pass my time,
But I gotsta bust out 'fo I lose my mind."

"Junior G," Yvgeny said, his voice flat.

"The one and only. Wrote that after coming to visit his pe-paw."

"Money Bar? Why not go somewhere like Natalia's, that nice piano place on Riverside?"

"Lame."

"Piccolo's? That place with ballroom dancing?"

"Lame!"

"So, you're telling me you sneak out of here and go to the Money Bar? Of all the places, you go to a gangster bar?"

Telfair cocked his head, and after a moment, Yvgeny took a deep breath and said, "Right."

"We got a guy on the outside. Leonard Make Rain. He's pure Cherokee, yessir. We call him Lenny Make Bacon. I don't remember why, but it stuck. He never had kids, so he ain't got nobody to lock him up and take all his money. He springs us every Wednesday night. Midnight. Like clockwork."

"Nobody says anything?"

Telfair snorted and waved a hand errantly around in the air and cried out, "Who? These gummers? What the hell are they gonna say? They're all passed out snoring into their CPAPs by nine. The ones that can *hang* are with me. We all pile into Lenny's Lincoln and away we go!"

Yvgeny just stared at Luther a moment, completely silent. When he finally responded, he spoke slowly, as if unsure of his words.

"I have never, in my life, met someone quite as strange as you, Luther."

The old man took it as a compliment and swelled up with pride. Then he started pacing, punching a fist into his open hand.

"So, here's the deal. Meet us there tonight, around one AM. I'll make sure you're on the guest list. And bring that healthy chick. The brothers will love her!"

It was Yvgeny's turn to hold his palms out toward Telfair.

"Whoa, whoa, why do I need to go talk to this guy?"

"You still don't think my boy had game, do ya? Well, Dub M saw it all. Ernie slayed more tang than most of the bangers at that club."

"I'm going to have to bring my intern with me just to translate what you're saying, Luther."

THE BODY IN THE BED

"No interns. Just you and the healthy chick. You'll see for yourself."

"But see what? You just said a minute ago you think Bessie did it. How is going to a club going to convince me of anything?"

"It ain't that, sport, it's Dub M. He, well, he just *knows* things. He don't say much, but he's got this way, he just sees right through people, he's got a crystal ball for a brain. He'll know if it was Bessie, he'll just take one look at her. Know what I'm saying?"

Yvgeny paused a moment, then said, "Nope. Not a clue."

"Look, MM doesn't say much, but I guaran-damn-tee he will have some answers."

"MM? I thought it was Dub M."

Again, Telfair just looked at him and waited.

Yvgeny rolled his eyes.

"Wait, Double M. Cute. And MM stands for what, exactly?"

"Double M, MM, 2M, Dub M, no matter how you slice it, he's the *Mime Master!*"

Yvgeny stared at Telfair a moment, slack jawed, then said, "You know what? I don't want to know." He paused, making a prune face, then asked, "I don't suppose you'd consider having the sheriff's department just go talk to your guy?"

"You kidding me? Whatcha think would happen if we showed up at Money Bar with a couple of cops?"

Yvgeny nodded slowly, said, "Guess you have a point."

Yvgeny sighed.

"So, one a.m. tonight? You realize I am presiding over a funeral in a few hours?"

"Yup. That means we don't have much time. You get your facts straight before tomorrow and maybe the killer will be in jail before it even starts."

"Right," Yvgeny replied with a snort, "Have you met the cops around here?"

With a broad grin, Luther said, "Of course, I've met 'em. That's why I'm counting on you!"

Yvgeny walked briskly back to Cerberus, finding Albert nodding off in the passenger seat. He was thankful he had parked toward the bottom of the drive, which meant everyone at Sunset Manor, including Beatrice, had probably already forgotten about him. He could coast to the street and be gone without anyone noticing.

Albert woke up with a start when Yvgeny slammed the door shut. He rubbed his eyes, then turned to Yvgeny.

"Where were you?" Albert asked.

"Just talking to an old friend. A very old friend."

Yvgeny set the hearse in neutral and let it roll back onto the street, then started it and jammed it into gear. Turning toward Albert he said, "We don't have a lot of time, so you better put on your seatbelt."

Cerberus was a beautiful specimen, a custom-built Cadillac XTS on a special chassis designed for a hearse. Front wheel drive, 304 horsepower, and plenty of torque. It was a pleasure to drive, but Yvgeny was in a hurry. Cerberus was made for straight lines and heavy loads, not precision handling.

Albert was slightly green by the time they returned to Schmidt and Sons, but Yvgeny had no patience for his complaints, shooing him back down to the office. He sat him down on a stool in his work shop, sliding another stool beside him and taking a seat.

"My dear Albert, we must work like the wind tonight, we only have a few hours to make the magic happen, there's no margin for error!"

"But Mr. Geny, I still don't know what we're doing!"

Yvgeny produced the photos Jeanine Ledbetter had given him earlier, and rummaged through them. Beside him on the table was the rubber death mask they made from the mold of Earnest's head.

Albert watched as Yvgeny occasionally raised up a photograph, compared it to the mask, then tossed it back into the pile. He did this several times, then sighed in frustration. After a moment, he produced his phone and scrolled through his photos to find the selfies he took with Earnest. After watching Yvgeny scroll through photos and hold up his phone next to the mask for several more minutes, Albert lost patience and asked, "So what are we doing?"

Yvgeny took a deep breath, then put down his phone.

"We have to find a few good photographs to make sure we can make the mask look like the dearly departed and not some rubber mask you'd buy at the supermarket on

THE BODY IN THE BED

Halloween." He snatched a few of the photos he got from Jeanine Ledbetter and handed them to Albert. "These photos are pretty old, so it's quite difficult, and photographs can be unreliable, especially with colors. If we don't get the coloring right, people won't buy it."

"We're selling the mask?"

"I'm speaking figuratively, dear boy. People won't believe it's him."

Albert just stared at Yvgeny, his mouth open, uncomprehending. Yvgeny took a deep breath and started over.

"We don't have the body anymore, and we promised an open casket funeral. We don't want to let everyone down. If I get fifty of those old geezers in here and they see a closed casket, they will scarf down half a bottle of wine, chomp on a bunch of crackers, shuffle by the casket, and that's it. When they die, they'll just go get stuffed by the lowest bidder."

Yvgeny stood, adopting his greatest P.T. Barnum imitation, one leg hiked up on the stool.

"But if they show up and find their beloved Earnest Ledbetter looking like the picture of health, full of life, as if he could hop out of the coffin any moment and do the Charleston, then that's another story, isn't it? They'll all leave at the end of the ceremony, but they'll all be back eventually, for the same deluxe treatment!"

Albert's slack jawed expression of confusion hardened into recognition, appreciation, even fascination.

"But, Mr. G, you don't have the body, so what are you going to do? Use a mannequin? Another dead guy?"

Yvgeny made a mental note; he had never thought of using another body.

Too bad I didn't get a cremation order this week.

"Excellent question, my dear boy, excellent question. This is where it gets fun."

Yvgeny ceremoniously leaned in, one arm around Albert's shoulder. Albert, sensing the importance of what was about to be imparted, dutifully leaned in and held his breath.

"This is top secret, and of course involves proprietary information and techniques. Needless to say, you cannot repeat my methods to anyone."

Albert, eyes wide with reverence, nodded without

speaking.

"OK. So, my father was a master at piecing together bodies. Car wrecks, farming accidents, whatever the case may have been, he could put them back together. He would have made Humpty Dumpty good as new."

Walking over to the counter, he leaned against it and crossed his arms.

"My father taught me everything I know. I will never be quite as good as him, at least I don't think so. However, I am probably the best in the state, conservatively speaking."

Yvgeny glanced toward the door, then spoke more softly, which required Albert to step a little closer.

"In this case, we don't have anything at all to work with, do we? So, we must ask ourselves, how can we have an open casket when we no longer have the body?"

Albert waited for an answer, and when none came, he cleared his throat.

"Um, I guess -"

Yvgeny waved away the rest of Albert's sentence, and clucked with his tongue, saying, "Ah, Albert, I was asking rhetorically. If we don't have the body, we will just have to make one!"

Albert's brow furrowed and he asked, "Make one?"

"Of course!"

Yvgeny glanced at his watch, then said, "Here's the thing. There's open casket, and there's open casket, you know what I mean? We could keep the bottom-half closed, which means we only need him from the waist up."

Yvgeny glanced over at the package he got from Beatrice.

"They wanted him to be buried in that awful silk robe, but I don't see how we can pull that off. We can use one of the loaner suits I've collected over the years. Then we just need a couple of hands and a neck. And the head, of course."

"You've done this before?"

"Well, yes and no. I've made limbs from scratch, reconstructed lots of body parts, but never a whole body. It will be a first! Quite exciting, really; Squee!"

Albert smiled and hopped up and down with Yvgeny.

"How will you make the body?"

"Well, if we had more time, I'd say we could do something really fancy, but given the late hour, I think we'll just make a crude metal cage packed with wadding. I'll probably just use coat hangers." Yvgeny started pacing, head down. "I have a big bag of stuffing from Home Depot, and if we run out, we can also use insulation. You know, the pink stuff?" He waited for Albert to nod, then continued. "Doesn't really matter. The only risk is if someone tries to touch the body."

Albert watched Yvgeny's every move as he paced.

"Not much I can do about that now. Again, if I didn't have to rush, I could rubberize the outer shell, make it a little more lifelike, but in this case, we'll do the best we can, and I'll just have to keep guard over it during the viewing."

Albert nodded his head, still star-struck by Yvgeny's ingenuity and prescience.

But Yvgeny trailed off as he thought of the two old women fighting over their love for Earnest.

I could see the one with the cane trying to climb into the casket with him. That could be a problem. And if she's the killer, it could really get ugly.

Looking at his watch again, Yvgeny said, "My dear Albert, we must hurry, no more time to lose!"

JONATHAN B. ZEITLIN

CHAPTER EIGHT

☦

Bubba was home on the couch in front of his television, digging at his fingernails with a large hunting knife, when his cell phone rang. It was late, and Bubba looked at the screen before deciding whether to answer. It was the sheriff.
Bubba stopped digging and took the call.
"Yessir?"
At first, all Bubba could hear was the sheriff's labored breathing, as if he was pressing the phone into his mouth. Then he cleared his throat, and grumbled, "That sumbitch Flowers. You know what time it is?"
"It's almost midnight, sheriff."
"I know what damn time it is, I'm rhetoricating!"
Bubba bit his tongue and waited.
"That sumbitch texted me. Not a phone call, just a damn text. You know what he said?"
Without waiting for a response, the sheriff switched his phone to speaker and started pressing buttons and swiping. The selections made electronic sounds that Bubba could hear.
"He says, 'Sending the Ledbetter case up to Macon for a full autopsy. Suspicious findings.'"
The sheriff then squeezed his mouth back against the phone and asked, "What the hell's he talking about, suspicious findings?"
"Not sure, sheriff."
There was another beep, and Bubba could hear the sheriff's breathing get softer. Then he yelled, "And now the damn GBI's calling."
"The GBI?"
The sheriff breathed into the phone a moment longer, then said, "You best get to the bottom of this. You and Newsome."
Bubba quickly responded, "Yessir."

THE BODY IN THE BED

"Listen here. Must be fifty voters over there at the Sunset. Don't let me down."

"Yessir."

Still grumbling, the sheriff ended the call.

Bubba got up and started getting dressed. Before he could finish, his phone started ringing again. The call was coming from a restricted number: his screen only showed the area code, "478." Bubba took a deep breath, then pressed the button to answer it, and the caller started yelling before Bubba could say hello.

"Who the hell embalmed this guy?"

Rufus Kincaid, MD, was the senior pathologist at the GBI's morgue in Macon. No-one knew his true age, but he had already been the senior pathologist for years when Bubba and his partner Harry Newsome were brand new rookies on uniform patrol. He was generally crabby and prone to fits of anger.

Bubba thought for a moment.

"Which guy?"

"How many dead guys you send to the GBI tonight?"

"We didn't send nobody. I reckon you're talking about Flowers."

"Yes, Flowers, he wheeled the guy in a couple hours ago, scribbled out an intake form, and left him in the damn lobby. One of the security guards found the body and called me. You know what time it is?"

Bubba checked his watch but this time he didn't answer.

"All the form says is possible EG poisoning."

"EG?" Bubba asked as he tried to put on his shoes.

"Ethylene glycol."

"Ah, right. Antifreeze."

"It was on the crotch of his pants. Must've found it with a Woods lamp. So, who embalmed him?"

"Well, I'd say it was the undertaker."

"Undertaker?"

Bubba paused a moment, shoe in hand.

"You know, that crazy Russian guy on Main Street."

"What the hell did he do that for?"

"He's an undertaker."

"Yeah, but this is a suspicious death!"

Bubba cleared his throat, spit into his wastebasket, then

said, "Yeah, well, it wasn't that suspicious at the time. The guy died in hospice at an old folks' home and he didn't have a gun shot or a stab wound. Not even a bed sore, far as I recall."

There was a brief pause.

"Well, he's here now, so why'd Flowers let this undertaker embalm him?"

"I reckon you'd want to ask Flowers that question, Doc."

"Maybe I'll have the medical review board ask him. Damn fool."

"Well, Doc, guess that's why they pay you the big bucks."

The doctor grumbled a moment about being awakened from his bed, then after a pause, Bubba said, "Why'd they call you in for this guy? Don't you got a midnight shift doctor or something like that?"

"Of course, we do. That's who called me when your damn coroner did his dump and run."

Bubba finished putting on his shoes, then after a pause, he asked, "Well, you got anything we can work with?"

"You're lucky that undertaker's sloppy. I found enough blood to do an EGT and –"

"A what?"

"An ethylene glycol test."

"Got it. But how could you find blood if the guy was embalmed?"

"Well, let me dumb it down as much as I can. Depending on how good the mortician is and how bad the body is, there's always something to test. You can pump all the blood out of the veins, but there's plenty of other places it can settle, especially with old, sick people. You can always find a pocket, and this guy was no different. He was a mess inside."

"OK," Bubba said. "But, wait a minute," he asked, "How long is it going to take to get the results of that test?"

"Already got it. It's a veterinary test, they use it for animals. Only takes thirty minutes and you get your answer."

"Well, that's great."

"Yeah, but it ain't something you can use in court. I still need to run a tox screen. My guess is his GA and FA will be through the roof."

"Huh?"

THE BODY IN THE BED

The old doctor sighed and said, "Glycolic – never mind. I'm pretty sure he was poisoned."

"Or he did it to himself."

"Nobody commits suicide with antifreeze. Maybe they drink it to get high, but not a guy like this one. Too old for such stupidity."

There was silence on the phone, then Bubba whistled and said, "Hot damn, Flowers actually solved him a crime."

"Would've been better," Kincaid said, "If he didn't send the body to a mortician first."

Bubba said, "So, you got anything else for us?"

Bubba grabbed a pen from the cup on his desk, slid a notebook over.

"Not yet. I ordered a serum osmolality test and some urine microscopy just to make sure I can -"

"A what and some what?"

Kincaid sighed, and asked, "That other guy around? The smart one?"

"It's midnight. I'm home."

Kincaid sighed again, then said, "I'm going to do some nice, fun tests to see if the nice man has antifreeze in him. Good lord, man, you ever work a homicide before? Antifreeze kills 5,000 people a year."

Bubba wrinkled his brow, then asked, "So, how much antifreeze you gotta drink?"

"Ain't you got a lot of questions. Well, it's hard to say, but I'd guess maybe a shot glass worth? It builds up in the system, so a sprinkle in a few drinks over a few days, that might just do it. Especially in a guy already compromised from chemotherapy. Should know for sure after I dig around a little bit. If I find birefringent oxylate crystals in his renal tissue -"

"English, doctor."

Kincaid muttered something, then said, "If his kidneys glow in the dark, then you got your cause of death."

"Got it. Thanks Doc, I'll tell Newsome."

After hanging up the phone, Bubba walked over to the window. He stared outside a moment, deep in thought. Then he picked up his cell phone and called Newsome's cell. He didn't answer.

Bubba called dispatch.

JONATHAN B. ZEITLIN

"Margie, what's Newsome's home number?"

"Hang on." Margie started fiddling with the keyboard at her station. "Wait a minute, system says he's Code 5 at his part time, tonight."

Bubba cursed and smacked himself on the forehead. On Wednesday evenings, Newsome worked at the movie theater in downtown Comstock. The place was always packed on Wide Screen Wednesdays, and after a few hormone infused teenager riots, they hired an off-duty officer to discourage such behavior.

That's why he didn't answer his cell.

Due to a number of factors, such as the cinder block construction and local topography, the theater had virtually no cellular service inside. You might get lucky if you walk outside into the parking lot, but Bubba knew better. When he was at his part time, Newsome usually snuck into whatever movie was playing and hovered by the door to watch it, occasionally peeking out to make sure the place wasn't getting robbed. Bubba knew the only way he'd reach Newsome was in person.

Bubba headed out toward his car and drove to the theater. He started to chuckle during the drive as he thought about Newsome in his old uniform.

Most of the detectives at the department kept at least a few of their uniforms from way back when they pushed a patrol car on a beat. Most of those detectives needed them because they had to supplement their meager incomes with part time jobs. Bubba was one of the few who didn't bother; his farm brought him enough extra income to make ends meet.

Newsome's uniforms were most likely from the Nineties, which was many years and pounds ago. Bubba smirked; when Newsome was stuffed into his old brown and tan uniform, he looked like a human sausage.

Fifteen minutes later, Bubba parked in one of the two spots close to the door marked *police vehicles only*. The theater was in a new and free-standing building; the corporation that owned it bought an old sod farm a few years earlier, bribed the right county officials, and within two years the sod farm became a huge, well-lit parking lot and a five-screen movie theater.

THE BODY IN THE BED

Just like every other Wide Screen Wednesday, it was crawling with families and suspicious looking teenagers. He found Newsome leaning against one of the walls right next to a huge cardboard cutout advertising some romance movie soon to hit the theatres. Bubba's smirk returned.

Newsome's brown uniform pants were threadbare and shiny from dozens and dozens of visits to the drycleaners, and the uniform shirt, no doubt a perfect fit twenty years ago, was a little too tight around the middle, causing the polyester between those buttons to gap out, revealing his undershirt. Bubba stifled a chuckle.

Newsome smiled when he saw Bubba approaching.

"Well, well, you're out late. Midnight movie just started."

"Yessir. Couldn't sleep, seeing as my phone's been going crazy."

"Whatcha mean?"

Bubba said, "Got a call from the sheriff."

"Well, that ain't good."

"And Kincaid."

Newsome frowned, and said, "Kincaid? At the GBI? What'd he want?"

"Looks like Flowers sent that old man up to Macon."

"Flowers sent the guy to Macon? What the hell for? I thought we called that one a natural."

"Apparently Flowers saw differently." Then Bubba placed his hands on his hips and added, proudly, "said our dead guy died from EG poisoning, yessir."

"Ethylene glycol? How's he figure? Did he find crystals in his renal tissue?"

Bubba deflated and cursed under his breath. Newsome, at first animated at the news, sobered up and shoved his hands in his pockets.

"Wait a minute," Newsome added, "How does he know? Last we heard, Flowers was sending blood to the lab. He already got the results and told Kincaid?"

Bubba shrugged.

"Well, Kincaid did some kind of quick test at the morgue. And Flowers, he found antifreeze on the guy's clothes."

Newsome just stared at Bubba, then started pacing back and forth.

"How the hell did we miss that?"

Bubba shrugged his shoulders, then, with a sly smile, added, "We didn't have a Woods lamp."

Newsome stared at Bubba a moment, cocked his head, while Bubba stared back, smugly. Newsome pursed his lips, then said, "You know, you could've just called, you didn't have to drive all the way out here to give me this news."

"I tried. Ain't no signal here."

Newsome grunted, then said, "Why don't you give Flowers a call, tell him we want his ass in our office first thing in the morning."

"Think he's still awake?"

"Keep calling him until he is!"

Bubba smiled, then asked, "How late you working tonight?"

"Gotta stay until the midnight movie's over, then escort the manager to the bank. Probably just after two, I guess."

Bubba nodded his head and turned to go.

"Hey Bubba!"

Bubba stopped and turned around.

"On second thought, let's make it nine or ten."

Bubba chuckled and walked out the door.

⁓

A couple hours earlier, at Schmidt and Sons, Yvgeny rushed down the stairs back to his work room, where he had left Albert.

"Splendid!" Yvgeny exclaimed when he walked in. As instructed, Albert had gathered as many wire coat hangers as he could find and was in the process of uncoiling the top hook of each one.

As Yvgeny watched his understudy working, he thought about his dear friend Louise, the curator of Humperdink's Waxen Personalities in Macon, Georgia. She was an old master, and had worked with his father. Several of her creations were worthy of a prominent place at Madame Tussaud's. Her creations were so realistic their lack of a heartbeat was the only clue they weren't alive.

I could really use her help.

THE BODY IN THE BED

Some of his fondest childhood memories were the times his father brought him to Louise's to see her in action. He spent an entire glorious summer as her assistant, learning her tricks. He wished he could enlist her support for this latest project.

If only there was time.

It took at least three months of toiling to create one of her masterpieces. Yvgeny had less than one day. It was also dreadfully expensive. For years, she did contract work, making them to the client's specifications, payment in advance, in full. But now, at this stage of her life, Louise was content simply to display the ones she had.

But I bet she'd love to dig into a project like this.

Her last contract kept her busy for months; a big-time drug dealer out of Atlanta wanted one made of himself. She could do much of the work on her own, but for the fine tuning, the facial features, she needed the real thing. The dealer spent two weeks in a chair at her shop modeling while she worked. The final product was indistinguishable from the man. Yvgeny once asked her why he commissioned such a work, and she said she didn't know for sure, but she had some ideas.

Just a few weeks ago, she was complaining about being bored.

The core pieces in her collection were a group of four that she recycled every year, freshening them up in new displays, new hair, new features, a "new look." Her latest "scene" featured them lined up together around an empty barber's chair, each dressed in red and white stripes, one holding a comb, the other, a pair of scissors. She named the display "Barbershop Quartet." Before that, they were pushing lawnmowers and hedge clippers in a scene she had titled, *Hecho en Mexico*. His favorite rendition was the four models, barefoot, walking in lockstep across a street, dressed just like a certain musical group in their pose for a certain iconic album cover. He sighed.

It can't hurt to ask!

Yvgeny, still smiling from his memories, walked over to one of his cabinets and opened a drawer, retrieved wire snips, needle nose pliers, a caulking gun and a tube of Liquid Nails, then approached Albert.

"Just straighten them out the best you can, I will do the rest."

While Albert got back to work, Yvgeny texted Louise.

Emergency. Need advice. And some hair. Straw colored, maybe code 14 or 15.

Yvgeny then disappeared, returning a few minutes later with several items of clothing under his arm. He lay them over his work stool, then grabbed a pair of scissors and a small tool Albert could not identify. Yvgeny cut the undershirt all the way up the back, then did the same with the dress shirt. For the coat, he used the small tool to pull apart the seam in the back, then cut apart the thread in the seam with quick, practiced flicks of the wrist. He glanced at Albert and said, "Hugo Boss. Too nice to ruin."

Yvgeny looked up suddenly from his work, looked off into space, then grabbed his phone. He texted Louise again.

And bring hands.

Yvgeny then walked over to the pile of hangers Albert had straightened out. With Albert watching, he picked a few up, one at a time, inspected them approvingly, then chose a few and carried them over to his work station. He started to work the metal with his pliers.

"I usually start with the neck. You need to make a mesh, no more than three inches between each main line. See how I'm doing it? Sort of like weaving, only with metal."

Yvgeny continued to work, sending Albert back to his wire pile to fetch more product.

"You can do an entire body this way, but in our case, we only need to worry about from the waist up."

Slowly, the jumble of wires was taking on a distinguishable shape.

"Now, if there was a hardware store open," Yvgeny counseled, "we could just buy some chicken wire. That would make things go much more quickly."

Yvgeny's phone buzzed, and, with a wink at Albert, he checked the message.

On my way.

"Albert, you're in for a real treat tonight. You're going to be in the presence of greatness. Even greater than myself!"

Albert adopted an expression of reverence as he watched Yvgeny in action. With nimble fingers, he rapidly bent the

THE BODY IN THE BED

coat hangers, one after the other, and as Albert watched, the mass of bent metal became a neck. Occasionally, Yvgeny reached for his caulking gun and added a generous dollop of Liquid Nails, careful to provide additional reinforcement in the areas that were most important.

Then Yvgeny moved on to the shoulders. A fine sheen of sweat started to glisten on Yvgeny's brow, and he stopped several times to wipe at it with the back of a hand. It took over an hour, but finally, Yvgeny stopped and stood back from the mass of metal, wire snips in one hand, pliers in the other.

"Amazing," breathed Albert.

"Come help me prop Mr. Ledbetter up."

They stood the wire mannequin on the table, then Yvgeny produced a large roll of silver duct tape and carefully wrapped it around the body's torso. He did it in stripes, leaving gaps as wide as a fist in between each round of tape. The mass of coat hangers and tape gradually acquired the appearance of a human form.

"Now, step three!"

Yvgeny retrieved a garbage bag filled with fiber batting. He began shoving large fistfuls of stuffing in between the strips of tape, starting at the bottom and working his way up, then handed the bag to Albert with a growl.

"Come on, help me shove it in, as much as you can squeeze in there!"

Yvgeny checked his watch with increasing frequency, urgently stuffing the batting into the mannequin. Finally, he stepped back and studied his work. He slowly walked around it, looking for even the smallest imperfection, then he nodded.

"Good enough."

Yvgeny filled in the open strips with more duct tape, then punched his fist down into the hole in the neck to make sure the batting filled the entire body cavity. He shoved in a few more fistfuls of batting to make sure, then put a temporary piece of duct tape over the neck hole to keep it from coming out. He also shoved an extra handful of batting into the arms through the holes where the hands would eventually go, then adding a piece of tape around those holes.

Yvgeny grabbed the cut undershirt and gently fitted it

through the arms, careful not to rip the material on any of the wires. Once he arranged the undershirt, he added the dress shirt, then sport coat, careful to set each piece just right. He used liberal amounts of fashion tape and safety pins to make everything sit on the frame perfectly. Albert stood back and watched as the master worked. Shortly after, they inspected the final product. It looked like a man from the waist up, ready to go to his wedding, or the opera, or some other formal event. All that remained were the head and hands.

"So, what's missing?" Yvgeny asked.

"The head?"

"Exactly."

Yvgeny retrieved his pad and paged through it until he found his measurements. Satisfied, he opened one of his cabinets and came out with several Styrofoam heads. He grabbed his measuring tape, then took several measurements of each of the heads, compared them to his notes, then rejected first one head then the other. He was left with one head, which he measured all over again.

"Time for the mask?" Albert asked, expectation and excitement in his voice.

"Almost. Just need to make some alterations."

Yvgeny grabbed a few more coat hangers and carefully bent them around the Styrofoam forehead, adding more Liquid Nails to the back to keep them secure. While frequently consulting his notes and checking his work with the measuring tape, he formed a metal cage around the head.

When he felt confident with his work, he grabbed a tub of some kind of clay-like material, and started filling in the gaps between the wire cage around the head. As he worked, he talked.

"You see, it doesn't have to be perfect, just enough for the mask to fit snugly over the top. We want to avoid what I like to call the 'squish factor.' One wrong move, and things could go sideways. Literally."

After he finished, he stood and walked around his work. Albert came up close and inspected the head, with lots of whispered "oohs" and "ahs." Then he looked over at Yvgeny and asked, "So, now do we put on the mask?"

THE BODY IN THE BED

With a smile, Yvgeny shook his head and said, "First, we have to beef up things a bit."

Yvgeny returned to his cabinet and fetched the same cloth wraps he used to make the mold of Ledbetter's head. He ran them all under the faucet, then wrung them out carefully. He wrapped the first one tight around the wire framed head, rounding out all the edges, then reached for another piece.

"I see," Albert exclaimed, "you're softening all the edges so it looks more real."

Yvgeny smiled and whispered, "Exactly right, my young friend."

"And it will keep the wires from cutting the mask?"

Yvgeny smiled again and crooned, "I do believe you've found your calling!"

"Darling!" Came a female voice from behind them.

Yvgeny turned to find Louise standing in the doorway, a large folded clapboard under one arm. He rushed to her and they embraced while Albert watched, surprised by her sudden appearance.

"What's the emergency?" Louise asked.

"Funeral's tomorrow, open casket, and we don't have the body."

Louise took on a solemn expression, patted Yvgeny on the back, and intoned, "You poor dear!"

After a moment, she pulled him away, hands on his arms, and in a low voice she said, "Don't you worry, Louise is here now. We are going to pull this off." She glanced at the wire Mr. Ledbetter and nodded approvingly, adding, "And I see you've already got down to business. Good."

Yvgeny disengaged from her and turned to Albert.

"Albert, come, I want you to meet the one and only, Louise Humperdink! The Wizard of Wax! The Princess of Perfect!"

Louise smiled at the boy, said, "Ah, yes, the understudy!" but then returned her attention to Yvgeny without more than a nod to Albert.

"I came as soon as I got your message. I have my hair samples here, and I brought all my stock, it's in the car."

Without another word, Louise walked over to a clean spot on the counter and propped up her clapboard display. She pulled apart the corners, revealing a collection of hair locks in various shades. She pointed to one corner.

"Here's the 14s and 15s. You have a photograph or two?"

"Of course," Yvgeny said, and produced his photographs, handed them to her, then scrolled through the pictures on his phone until he found the selfies Yvgeny took from the back of Flowers's van.

She placed the phone beside her hair samples, laid the photograph beside the phone, then studied them. After a few moments, she nodded and said to Yvgeny, "Good eye, Geny, Code 15 it is." She slammed her sample panels closed and cried, "Be back in a jiff!"

After she disappeared, Albert muttered, "Wow."

Yvgeny rubbed his hands together.

"Told you!"

Louise returned a few minutes later with a Ziploc bag filled with hair in a color and size approximating the few remaining strands of the late Earnest Ledbetter's hair. She also had an old children's metal lunchbox, decorated with a Star Wars motif. She handed the bag to Yvgeny, then walked over to the mannequin. Albert followed her over and watched her as she inspected Yvgeny's handiwork.

"How long you spend making this?"

"Maybe two hours." Yvgeny called out.

Louise nodded and continued walking around the mannequin.

"Excellent work," Louise breathed, "especially considering the timeline."

She motioned for Albert to come closer, then waved a hand toward the mannequin.

"It's kind of like making a mummy in reverse, you know. Instead of removing all the insides and taping him up, you tape him up, then add the insides."

Albert nodded, then yawned.

"What's in the lunchbox? Lunch?" Albert asked.

"Oh no, no, something much more exciting than that. Geny, come see, look what I brought you!"

Yvgeny turned to watch Louise open the lunch box. Inside were two perfect wax hands, carefully packaged in Styrofoam peanuts and separated by wax paper.

"When you said you needed a pair of hands, I assumed you were being literal."

"Oh, Louise, how could I ever repay you? They're perfect!"

THE BODY IN THE BED

Yvgeny walked them over to the counter and placed them in a safe place.

"I'd wait until you're almost done before you put on the hands. They're prone to warping if you're not careful."

Yvgeny continued wrapping the strips around the head until it looked more like a human head missing its face. Once it was shaped to his satisfaction, he lifted it up over the torso and connected it with a series of wires he had left protruding from the neck area.

He retrieved a small clear bottle and unscrewed the cap. Attached to the cap was a brush, leading Albert to assume it was some kind of glue, and Yvgeny began to brush in spots around the head.

Finally, he returned to the cabinet and gingerly took the mask, carefully slid his hands inside, and stretched it over the metal wire head. It was an almost perfect fit.

Albert took a step closer and watched as Yvgeny walked around the mask, nodding in some places, squinting and looking more closely at others. As he inspected, he made small, micro-adjustments to the mask.

"Amazing," Albert cooed.

Yvgeny, seemingly satisfied, tucked the neck piece of the mask inside the collar of the shirt, then buttoned the top button.

"Lucky the old man was almost bald. The good stuff is really expensive."

"Hair?" Albert asked.

"Yup."

Yvgeny wheeled over one of his small tables, and placed upon it his bag of hair from Louise, a small vial of liquid with an eye dropper, tweezers, and a special pair of eyeglasses that had, mounted over them, a pair of magnifying lenses. He also had his phone with one of his close-ups of Ledbetter displayed, and his collection of photos from Jeanine Ledbetter.

"It's go time," Yvgeny said to no-one in particular.

Yvgeny donned the glasses, retrieved a small lock of hair from the bag with his tweezers, then studied the photographs. He awakened his phone screen to check his selfie with Ernie, then returned to the mannequin. Using the special glue, he attached the first lock of hair. It was a very slow process, but luckily, he didn't have to attach too much hair. When he was finished, he took a step back.

Yvgeny slid the glasses down on the bridge of his nose, then held up one of the photographs next to the mannequin's face. He squinted, turning from the picture to the mannequin, then back again, then walked around the table while consulting the picture. Finally, he clucked his tongue and said, "Just a little makeup and he will be perfect!"

Albert had wandered over to the lunch box and was looking inside. Turning to Yvgeny, he called out, "Mr. Geny, what about the hands? Don't we need to finish them, too?"

"Yes, but one step at a time. Hands are very delicate things, and I will need a short break before starting."

Albert nodded his understanding, but then another involuntary yawn escaped him. Yvgeny took off his special glasses, and said, "Well, young man, you've had quite a busy day. Why don't you go home, relax, but I need you back here bright and early, tomorrow's the big day!"

Yvgeny then reached into his back pocket and withdrew his wallet, peeled out a crisp $5 bill, and presented it to his intern with a solemn expression on his face.

"Here's a little bonus. Get some ice cream on your way home. Try Nelson's, they're open 24/7. And it's on me!"

"Wow, thanks Mr. Geny!"

Yvgeny ushered him out, then returned to his work room, where Louise was gathering her things.

"I should also be going; you still have a lot of work to do. Wish I could catch the funeral."

Yvgeny frowned.

"You can't make it?"

"No, I'm afraid I can't. I finally broke down and decided to mold some new talent."

Yvgeny's eyes lit up. Louise swore she was finished after the drug dealer job.

"How exciting! Who will it be?"

"Well, ever since I met that lady friend of yours, I've been wanting to do a big boned Viking type woman. You know, a Helga, or a Brunhilda. So, I've been courting some of my old benefactors."

The big outfits like Tussaud's pulled out all the stops when they made their sculptures; doing it right took several

THE BODY IN THE BED

people working together over at least a few months, full-time, and a lot of money, well over $100,000 for just one of them. Louise preferred to work alone but at her age, she grudgingly had to hire some part-time help. And for Louise, such a project required an investor.

"One of them introduced me to this wealthy gentleman who actually owns a few wax figures of his own. He had one commissioned for each of his ex-wives over the years."

Yvgeny glanced sideways at Louise, who only shrugged.

"Each to their own, I guess. Anyway, he agreed to fund my project, and I agreed to visit him once a month to take care of his wives."

Wax figures required constant maintenance. A nip here, a tuck there, a little smoothing around the edges.

Yvgeny asked, "That's it?"

Louise's smile faltered somewhat, and she said, in a lower voice, "Well, and I have to change the name of my museum to *Humperdink and McCloud's Waxen Personalities*."

"Oh Louise, I'm so sorry."

Louise took a deep breath, then painted a smile on her face.

"Don't be! After all, I'm finally breathing some new life into that mausoleum! It feels so good to be working with fresh wax again! I feel twenty years younger! Now get to work, you have a funeral to prepare for!"

Louise insisted on letting herself out, leaving Yvgeny alone in his workroom. He took one more walk around his mannequin, nodded his head, then approached the lunchbox. He reached in and sifted through the Styrofoam peanuts, then withdrew the first hand, inspecting it carefully. They were original parts, and, having never been colored, resembled raw white fish meat.

Next, Yvgeny laid the hands on his rolling table, wheeled it over to sit beside the new Earnest Ledbetter, then he mixed his paints, eyeballing it with frequent glances back at Earnest's latex face.

This won't be perfect, but it's the best I can do.

He worked quickly, approximating the color of the mask, then laid them out on the counter to dry. He approached the mannequin one more time. He needed to keep it sitting upright on the table to make sure the head stayed where it belonged. He had added extra cement to keep everything secure, but one can never be too careful!

With one more look around the room, Yvgeny let out a loud sigh, then turned out all the lights and went to his study to change into fresh clothes. On his way, he slammed his shin against his old Army surplus cot. Frugal by nature, the cot sufficed as his bed, but then he met Brianna, and they got serious. Now the cot was nothing more than another horizontal surface for him to store junk. He knew he needed to get rid of it, but was unreasonably superstitious about taking that next step.

Finally, with a sigh, he gathered up everything that had collected on the cot, stacked it all on a shelf, then folded up the cot and shoved it into a corner.

What does a white man wear to a black bar?

He stared at the options hanging from his wardrobe, and finally selected a fresh black suit. He didn't have too many other choices anyway. He chose a matching silk cravat and his best top hat, then headed toward the door to grab Brianna. Thankfully, his mother wasn't in the kitchen as he left.

Yvgeny made the drive to Brianna's apartment complex, thinking, *this better be worth it*. After he pulled into the parking lot, he sent Brianna a text.

Your chariot awaits!

After a pause, he felt his phone vibrate and looked down to see a flashing "poop" emoji. He smiled.

Minutes later, Brianna came hoofing down the external metal staircase leading from her apartment. The metal creaked under the stress, but held fast. His phone vibrated again, and he looked down, surprised.

Schlepping around so late at night. With her. Hope I don't fall down the stairs.

Yvgeny regretted giving his mother a cell phone, and especially regretted showing her how to send a text message. Once she got the hang of it, she couldn't keep her thumbs still. He considered responding, then realized it would be futile. He put away his phone and hopped out of the car in time to open the door for his date.

"My dear, ravishing as usual."

Brianna had stuffed herself into a very snug, very cherry

THE BODY IN THE BED

red sheath dress that left nothing to the imagination, and topped off the ensemble with black shiny clogs. Her shoulders were bare, but sheltered beneath a black silk scarf. She had curled her hair and left it loose, resting against her scarf. She stopped at the car, but made no move to get in. Instead, she reached into her bosom and withdrew a pack of Marlboros. As Yvgeny inspected her, wondering where she would have room for a lighter, she plucked one from the box of cigarettes and lit up. After a deep drag, she spoke.

"Are you actually going to wear that?" she asked, looking up at his top hat.

Yvgeny narrowed his brow.

"What? You don't think it goes with the cravat?"

"It hasn't gone with anything in a hundred years."

Before he could respond, she blew out her smoke with a whoosh and asked, "So, why the hell are we going to Money Bar? You realize you're the wrong color for that place."

"So are you."

Brianna paused, took a drag, and muttered, "That's different."

Yvgeny inspected her again, then shrugged.

"Well, like I said, the old guy at the Sunset convinced me I should go."

"But why? Are you playing police again?"

"No! Yes! I mean, well, sorta." Yvgeny moved from indignant to proud to conciliatory in one sentence. He took a deep breath, then leaned against the fender.

"That quack Flowers found antifreeze on the stiff's crotch. He thinks the guy was poisoned."

"With antifreeze?"

"Yes. Why?"

It was her turn to shrug. She took one more drag, then flicked the cigarette across the parking lot.

"Nothing, just I remember people leaving it out to get rid of stray dogs, cats. It's a terrible way to go."

"Well, didn't seem like he suffered that much."

"That's because he had a few other things killing him at the same time."

Yvgeny waited a polite moment, then continued.

"Anyway, the cops aren't doing anything, so if I don't dig

around a little, there could be another killer on the loose!"

Brianna rolled her eyes.

"Plus, this was supposed to be a nice, easy, open casket affair, paid in full, up front. But no! Flowers and his damn wet crotch cost me the body, so I had to make it from scratch!"

"You did what?"

"I made my own Earnest Ledbetter. He's drying out in the office."

Brianna muttered, "Jesus," and made a look of disgust, but she held her ground.

"Still doesn't explain why we are going out to a black bar at midnight."

"Old man Telfair thinks it would be illuminating for us to go. There's some guy there that he thinks will convince me of motive. Oh, and the killer might be there."

"What? You're taking me on a date to meet a murderer?"

"She's pushing ninety years old, my dear, I'm not too concerned."

Brianna exhaled loudly but didn't respond.

"So, what's her motive? That the old guy was a stud?"

Yvgeny just shrugged.

"He says when we go there, everything will make sense."

Brianna shook her head and squeezed by Yvgeny and got into the car.

"And how are we supposed to figure out if she did it?"

"Apparently this guy Telfair wants me to meet is psychic or something like that. Like a crystal ball."

"This should be interesting," she said.

The drive to Macon was uneventful, and they arrived a little early, around 12:30 a.m. The line went down the length of the building and around the corner. They drove by slowly, scoping out the Sunday best church outfits the worn by the hopeful patrons.

"Ain't one single white boy in that club."

Yvgeny didn't respond, suddenly and painfully aware of how much he would stick out in the crowd. He turned the block and started looking for a parking spot.

"And there damn sure ain't no white boy in that club wearing a suit like that."

Brianna turned and glanced behind her, into the back.

THE BODY IN THE BED

"You sure about that top hat?"

Yvgeny didn't respond.

"Do you *want* to get your ass beat?"

"We've got a crew here, I'll be fine."

"A crew? This is getting better and better. You're meeting a bunch of geriatric white folk!"

Brianna turned away, inspecting the crowd. She muttered, "Oh, if my Daddy could see me now."

Yvgeny shook his head and turned to drive in another circle.

"Just valet park it."

Yvgeny's jaw dropped.

"Are you kidding me?"

The minutes ticked by as Yvgeny looked for a spot, finding none.

"Um -" Brianna pointed out her window and said, "Are *those* your friends?"

Yvgeny turned to see a huge, old Lincoln pull up to the valet line. The driver's door opened, and a very tall and ancient Native American man emerged from the driver's seat. He was wearing a leather cowboy hat with a hat strap of rainbow colors. He wore a matching leather jacket with fringe that hung from the breast and sleeves. His hair was long and white, and he kept it swept back into a ponytail.

"That must be Lenny Make Bacon," Yvgeny breathed.

"Lenny what?" asked Brianna, but when Lenny opened the rear suicide door of his Lincoln, Brianna's jaw dropped.

Lenny reached into the back of the car and half dragged out a tiny old white woman grasping a cane. She stood and straightened herself out, then Lenny reached in one more time as if to assist someone else, but then he yanked his arm back as if he had been bitten by a snake.

"I can get out my damn self, Jesus Christ, Lenny, whatcha think I am, an invalid?"

"And that would be the Right Honorable Luther P. Telfair."

Brianna glanced over at Yvgeny but was too shocked to comment. Several more elderly occupants slowly emerged from Lenny's Lincoln, then Lenny tossed the keys at the valet and they started toward the club.

"I can't believe we are doing this," Yvgeny mumbled, then he put Cerberus in drive and did a U-turn, parking behind the Lincoln. All eyes were on him as he hopped out of the driver's seat and jogged around the hood to open the door for Brianna. At the last minute, Yvgeny decided to leave his hat in the hearse.

Once Brianna got out, the hushed mumbling stopped completely. Brianna straightened her skin tight dress and stood tall, facing the car. Recognizing the sudden silence, Brianna turned to face the crowd and found at least a hundred pairs of eyes focused on her, ogling her, drinking her in. Then came a whistle.

Several girlfriends turned to smack their boyfriends, to no avail.

The whistle was followed by a cat call, then another whistle, and within seconds it was pandemonium. Brianna reached into her cleavage for her smokes, and the men in line went wild all over again. Brianna's cheeks began to color, and she quickly linked her arm in Yvgeny's.

"I ain't standing in this damn line," she said.

As if on cue, Yvgeny heard the familiar voice of Luther P. Telfair coming from the door.

"What the hell y'all doing? Signing autographs? Get on in here!"

"I believe that's our signal."

They quickly walked past the long line, past the drooling male patrons, past several of their jealous female dates, and past the podium and the three-hundred pound bouncer guarding the door. The bouncer unfastened the rope for them to pass through.

Luther was waiting just inside the club. The bass of the stereo was strong enough to thump against Yvgeny's chest, and the flashing lights made it feel like he was walking through a bottomless cloud. Brianna smashed her cigarette into an ashtray on a table, and the men seated at that table just stared at her, speechless.

"Aren't *you* a hit?" Yvgeny chided.

"Shove it."

Luther Telfair puffed up and held out his arms.

"Welcome! This my hood and these my homies!"

Brianna stared at him, mouth agape for the second time that evening.

Yvgeny looked around a moment, then said, "Luther, you

never cease to amaze me."

With a big smile, Telfair turned and said, "Come on, let me take you back to our table."

The walk was surreal. The club was packed with well-dressed patrons, and the three of them were the only whites in the place. They walked behind a very slow-moving Telfair, and although Yvgeny felt self-conscious about sticking out so much from the crowd, amazingly, none seemed even to notice him. In fact, several of the patrons gave Telfair a high five as he shuffled past.

All the way in the back of the club was the VIP section. It was separated by another very large black-outfitted bouncer and a series of blood red velvet movie theater style stanchion ropes. Telfair shuffled toward the huge bouncer, who grinned ear to ear when he saw him. They did some kind of elaborate hand shake that ended in the man enveloping the old guy in a bear hug, then he unclicked one of the ropes to let him in. He turned to the rest of the entourage and motioned them forward.

The group that had poured out of the Lincoln were all seated at a round table in the corner, a bottle of champagne in a silver chiller, and two bottles of red wine at each end. Yvgeny recognized Bessie and Myrtle, Lenny Make Rain, and two unknown old ladies. Telfair stepped forward, turned to face Yvgeny, raised his arms up again, and cried out, "Welcome to my crib!"

It was loud in the club, so Yvgeny leaned in and yelled in Telfair's ear, "You brought the killer with you?"

Telfair turned to look back at Bessie, then leaned in and yelled back, "If she offers you a drink, just say no!"

Yvgeny looked around the place, astonished. He had never been inside before, never realized how large the place was. In two of the corners were what appeared to be large bird cages hanging from the eaves. Inside were women wearing very little and dancing to the music. He briefly wondered to himself how they got up and down from the cage, then realized the cages were on huge motorized hooks.

Where were the controls?

Yvgeny turned to whisper something sarcastic in Brianna's ear, but she was not standing beside him. He turned to find her still talking with the bouncer, and whatever they were discussing, she was smiling from ear to ear. His cheeks coloring, Yvgeny took a step toward them, preparing to defend her honor, but just as he did so, she turned around to return to the group. Looking at the biceps on the man with whom she had been talking, Yvgeny felt a bit of relief.

"Making friends?"

Brianna glanced back at the man, who was still watching her out of the corner of his eye.

"L gasses up at my old store."

"L?"

"Laverne."

"Guess I'd go by L, too."

Telfair approached and put an arm around each of them to guide them toward the table, explaining, "Come on, grab a seat, I'll introduce you."

"Listen up, folks, this here is Geny the Undertaker, and his lovely girlfriend Brianna."

The elderly group squinted at them, then smiled. Yvgeny leaned into Brianna and whispered, "The killer is that one there, with the sullen look on her face. Keep your eyes on your drink."

Telfair turned to Yvgeny and began introducing each person by pointing at them and announcing their name. Bessie and Myrtle briefly glared at each other.

"This here is Lenny Make Rain, the guy that drove us here. That there is Bessie, and of course Myrtle, I think you already met them. And right there is Helouise. She likes to be called Hella! And at the end there, the lovely Victoria."

Victoria smiled, revealing a set of yellowing, crooked teeth. Telfair leaned in close and whispered, "Vicky's a party girl fo sho!"

Yvgeny shuddered, and turned toward the packed dance floor. Telfair followed his gaze, then said, "Yup, Dub's out there showing 'em all how it's done."

From behind them, one of the old ladies cried, "There he is! Get it, Dub!"

Yvgeny turned back to the dance floor in time to see a black man wearing a black suit bustin' a move. The crowd on the dance floor parted, revealing Mime Master as he moonwalked toward a corner, then fell backward into a crab position, then began to spin like a break dancer from the

THE BODY IN THE BED

Eighties. Yvgeny could not see his face, only his body and the impressive dance moves. He was older, which Yvgeny surmised from the man's somewhat brittle form and stiff movements.

"That guy's got some game," Brianna whispered in Yvgeny's ear. As they watched, the man spun around, then dropped onto the floor and continued spinning again, legs swinging around in the air. There was something strangely familiar in the movements, but Yvgeny couldn't place it. He turned to Telfair and asked, "Who is this guy?"

"He's the Mime Master."

"Yeah, but what's his story? Does he live at the Sunset, too?"

"Nope. He don't say much, but we see him here every week, rockin' out on the dance floor."

"And that's what I came all the way to Macon to see? Some guy wearing a suit break dancing?"

"That ain't break dancing, sport! That's free style!"

Yvgeny shook his head and turned to face the old man.

"Look, Luther, this ain't really my kind of place. You promised me I'd get answers."

Telfair scratched his cheek, then shook his head and turned toward the table.

"Come on, you'll see soon enough."

When he returned to the table, he discovered the group had rearranged the seating so that Yvgeny was forced to sit between Myrtle and Bessie. Brianna was relegated to a spot between Telfair and Lenny. The expression on Lenny's face was similar to the look of a child watching his mother bringing him a birthday cake, candles lit. As Yvgeny took his seat, both women descended on him immediately.

"Did you get Ernie's robe?"

"Yes, but-"

"Bessie, you can't dress him in a robe for a funeral, that's just tacky."

"Myrtle, since when are you an expert on funerals?"

"He always said he wanted to be buried in it. Are you going to go against his wishes?"

"Any idiot knows you don't dress a man in a robe, he's gotta wear something formal, like Yvgeny here is wearing."

"Well, he should be comfortable, you know how much he

liked wearing it."

"He didn't wear it all that much with me."

Myrtle adopted a look of disgust and muttered, "Tart."

"Prude."

"I am not a prude, you trollop!"

"At least I can walk, you three-legged wet blanket!"

"How dare you, you, you streetwalker!"

"Ladies, enough already! Yes, I got the robe, but no, I'm not putting it on him. This is a formal event; he will need to wear a suit. But I tell you what, when it's all over, I can put the robe back on if you want."

"Yes."

"No."

As they both launched into another stream of invective, Yvgeny looked over at Brianna, who was busy listening to Lenny tell her some kind of story. Dub M was still burning up the dance floor, and Telfair was staring at Yvgeny with marked interest, as if he was watching a television show. With a sigh, Yvgeny turned back to Myrtle, who had stopped swearing at her nemesis and had crossed her arms, fuming silently.

"So, what's really going on here?"

At first, she did not act as if she had heard him. Then, after a moment, she deflated. She eyed Bessie briefly, but Bessie had already lost interest and was looking out at the crowd. Myrtle leaned in and spoke candidly.

"We had always fought over him like this, but over the last few months, he seemed distracted. At first, I thought he started seeing someone else. We had grudgingly accepted the fact he split his time between Bessie and me, but this was different."

"Maybe he didn't want to hurt your feelings."

"No, this isn't high school, young man, I'm going to be ninety soon, and Bessie is eighty-seven. If it's fun, we do it. If it ain't, we don't. We don't have time to stand on principle and social mores."

"Then why care?"

"Well, he was, I don't know, he was just so distracted."

"Well, maybe he had a lot on his mind. He was dying!"

"Yeah, I guess. Maybe the cancer was getting worse."

Telfair was virtually gloating from across the table. Yvgeny

THE BODY IN THE BED

tried to ignore him.

Yvgeny considered for a moment, then turned to Bessie, who had been refilling her wine glass. He leaned toward her, and said, "So, Bessie, is it?"

Bessie turned to Yvgeny, slugged her wine, and slammed the glass on the table.

"What's that nincompoop telling you?"

Ignoring her tone, he asked, "how do you really think Earnest died?"

Bessie sized Yvgeny up, then leaned toward him, emitting a strong and unpleasant smell of sour wine. She raised her voice, glaring at Myrtle as she spoke.

"I know exactly how he died. I was there."

Yvgeny tried to curb his revulsion. Myrtle glowered back at her when she heard her claim.

"You mean -"

"You got it, darling."

Yvgeny shuddered and turned away a moment. Brianna was still nodding and listening to whatever long story Make Bacon was weaving. Telfair was still watching him intently. Yvgeny sighed.

"When we were finished, I went downstairs to get him a cup of coffee. I don't drink that stuff, but just about everyone else does. Beatrice was pouring mugs for everyone and said she was about to bring one up to him. I told her I'd save her the trip."

"So, you don't think he was murdered?"

"Of course he was murdered! Where have you been?"

"OK, then who did it? And how?"

"Obviously someone must have poisoned him."

"Obviously?"

"Well, let's see, he wasn't shot or stabbed -"

"True," Yvgeny said.

"And he wasn't smothered or thrown out a window."

"Yes, I know, but -"

"He wasn't run over by a car, and obviously he wasn't thrown -"

"I get the picture."

The old woman leaned in even closer and said, "It's the quiet ones you have to worry about."

She then jutted her chin out, motioning toward Myrtle,

sipping forlornly on her glass of wine.

"Let me tell you something, if I knew who did it, I wouldn't need any poison. I'd kill him -"

"Or her!" Yvgeny interjected.

" - with my bare hands!"

Yvgeny decided it was time for him to leave, but just as he prepared to get Brianna's attention, he noticed the music had changed, and there was a lull from the dance floor.

He looked around and realized the DJ was taking a break and had put on some radio station. Next, he saw the two bird cages grinding their way back down to the floor. He glanced up, wondering how they were getting down, then looked closer and saw they each were holding onto levers inside their cages.

Most of the crowd had stopped dancing but remained standing in place. A few turned to leave, and that's when Yvgeny noticed Dub M approaching them from the dance floor. In the dim lights of the club all he could make out was a black man in a black suit. It appeared he had injured himself on the dance floor, as he was dragging one leg.

Telfair started trying to explain something to him, and Yvgeny tried to pay attention, but he was increasingly distracted by Dub M and his injury. The closer he got, the better Yvgeny could make out features, details. He recognized the suit. Recognized the hair, although it was combed. And the face. Yvgeny stood, and as Dub M and he made eye contact, his smile opened into an expression of complete surprise.

"Alfred?"

THE BODY IN THE BED

CHAPTER NINE

╬

Meanwhile, at Schmidt and Sons, Mama was awake again.

She checked her phone for the hundredth time, then stared at the ceiling. She couldn't sleep. She couldn't sleep knowing he was with her, *that wieloryb!* She couldn't sleep because her joints ached. She couldn't sleep because her son was an *idiota*!

He thinks I'm an idiot. He thinks I don't know he doesn't have the body.

A few hours earlier, she had watched from her window as Flowers piled the carcass into his stupid red van and sped away.

Finally, with a huff, she struggled into a seated position, then she stood. On wobbly legs she grabbed her cane and waited for her vertigo to subside. Then she went walking.

Perhaps a nice cup of tea would help me get back to sleep.

Down the stairs she went, one at a time, careful not to lose her balance, muttering the entire time about her no-good son not being around when she needed him. Her medication made her groggy, unsure on her feet, and it was worse at night.

She held tight to the railing, trying to avoid a fall. The last time she fell, she had to drag her battered, bruised body all the way to that quack Jimmy Flowers all by herself. Her gait hadn't been the same since.

Finally, she hit the heart of pine of the main floor and shuffled toward the kitchen, still grumbling. With one hand grasping her cane, she slid her other hand against the wall until she found the light switch, flicked it on, walked into the kitchen. She approached the corner, then stared at the empty countertop. The teapot was gone.

"Dammit!"

When Yvgeny was in the middle of a project, he sometimes

took food, drink, whatever tickled his fancy, and scurried down into his work room with it. She often found wrappers from potato chips on bodies, cookie crumbs on the floor, and, most egregiously, the teapot. She started the long, arduous trek across the hall, down the stairs to the basement, gingerly stepping down each one, grasping the bannisters with each hand with her cane tucked under one of her armpits. Her mind was still swimming in the medication that kept her alive and relatively pain free, but also blurred her senses and compromised her dexterity.

"That ingrate. That slob. That slouch. If his father could see him now, cavorting like some, some *fircyk.*"

Having reached the basement, she lumbered down the hall toward his work room. The door was cracked open, and it squeaked when she pushed on it. It was dark inside. She could hear the rhythmic squeak of what must have been the ceiling fan, an unnecessary waste of electricity. In her state, it felt like she was walking through a swimming pool.

She thought of her son's frequent references to himself as a supporter of the Green Movement recycling craze.

"Environmentalist, my eye!" she mumbled, then wobbled inside. A few steps in, she squinted. In the darkness, everything seemed to be moving around, swaying like kelp in the ocean. She focused on one swaying object, the largest one in the room, then squinted. She struggled to sharpen her vision, and the shape slowly coalesced into the outline of a man. Sitting? Standing? She couldn't tell, and didn't trust her vision, especially under the influence of her medicine.

"Yvgeny? Is that you, *tygrysek*? Why are you sitting in the dark?"

His mother back pedaled a couple steps and felt around on the wall for the light. She turned it on, then stared at the figure. Her eyes took a moment to focus.

She screamed as she realized it was some stranger. Instinct took over, and instinct didn't like to wait around for questions or deep thoughts. She lifted her lightweight cane in her hands like a pole vaulter running toward the launch point. On tottering legs, she drove forward and plunged the four-legged tip of the cane against his forehead.

He wobbled but remained standing! She readied her cane again, this time like a baseball bat, and delivered a withering

THE BODY IN THE BED

blow to his temple. Her attacker almost fell over, but righted himself. With a war cry, Yvgeny's mother wailed on the man's body, head, arms, but he was too strong. She started to back pedal. The man sneered at her, his face stony, resolute. She thought she saw his arms begin to reach up and out toward her.

"Bastard! I'm calling the police!"

She hobbled over to the telephone and dialed 911, quickly, before he could attack her.

"9-1-1, what's your emergency?"

"There's a man in my home! He's trying to kill me!"

"What does he look like?"

She turned and looked over at the man, then squinted. The attacker hadn't moved, and was taunting her, menacing her. The coiled telephone cord was very long, and she walked closer, in short mincing steps, her neck craned forward to inspect the intruder.

"He's older, and he's wearing a black tuxedo. He's sitting on a table."

She reached up and rubbed one of her eyes while holding the phone screwed into her ear.

Wait a minute. Where are his legs?

She walked a little closer, the phone cord starting to grow taut.

And why isn't he moving?

Hold on.

That's no man at all.

"Um, never mind, false alarm, there's nothing to see, um, forget it!"

She hung up before the dispatcher could confirm she was safe, so she sent two cars. Within minutes, there were sirens quickly approaching Schmidt and Sons, but Mama didn't hear them. Her hearing was no better than her eyesight, and as they slid through the deserted city streets, Mama was focused only on the intruder. Now that she wasn't tethered to the telephone, she was able to get up close and personal.

Beneath the nice suit, right where she nailed it with her cane, was a mess of batting covered in cloth kept together with a cage of what looked like wire coat hangers. The head was a mangled mess of latex and dented Styrofoam. The face had makeup, which Mama had smeared with one of her strikes, and there was a tear in the latex over one ear where Mama had plugged him especially hard, a glancing but solid blow.

"Uh oh."

Finally, her ears perked up as she heard the sirens approaching outside. She cursed again, then backed out of the room, turning off the lights and shutting the door out of habit. She scuttled down the hall toward the double doors leading out of the basement.

She shuffled out as quickly as she could, coming out onto the carport just as the cops screeched to a halt outside. A set of flood lights on motion sensors clicked to life, thus bringing both her and the nervous cops face to face.

"Where is he?" one of the officers asked, reaching for his gun.

"Downstairs, but listen-"

"Come on, Frankie."

The first cop dashed inside while the younger one took two deep breaths, looked around, then warily stepped inside. Neither gave Yvgeny's mother a chance to explain what happened. She turned around and started shuffling after them, poking her cane against the concrete with each step.

"Wait, you don't understand!" she called out as they started down the hall, their flashlight beams creating shadows with strange angles and corners.

The officers, weapons drawn, covered each other while they cleared each room. When they got to the last door on the left, Yvgeny's work room, they staged on either side of the closed door. The larger officer grasped the doorknob with two fingers, the rest of his hand still holding his flashlight, then looked silently at his partner. The partner mouthed *one, two,* and on the three count the officer turned the knob, pushed the door open wide, then performed a buttonhook maneuver, one going left and the other right. They sighted down with their flashlights and engaged the man in the suit.

"Freeze asshole!"

Just as the older officer engaged the man with his verbal command, the other one's flashlight moved across the suspect just the right way, and as it did so, the officer saw something flash. Something silver. Something *metal.*

"Gun!"

THE BODY IN THE BED

Both officers started to shoot. Two, three, four, five shots, they kept coming until finally the man fell to one side and rolled over. While the older officer turned to find a light switch, the younger shuffle-stepped closer and closer to the body with his flashlight trained on the man. As he approached, he yelled, "Don't move! Let me see your hands! Let me see 'em, your hands! Your hands! Stop resisting!"

Under the stress and excitement, the younger officer's voice cracked like a teenager. He reached up to his shoulder mic and yelled into it, "Shots fired! Shots fired!"

The other officer found the light switch and turned it on, then he hurried back to his partner's side, weapon still drawn. As they approached, and as the adrenaline started to fade, they caught their breaths and studied their subject a little more carefully. Their weapons began to sag.

"Shit."

Just then, Yvgeny's mother walked into the room and saw the officers' handiwork. The "man" had sustained significant damage to his head, chest, and arms. The officers studied their burglar, determining the flash of metal they had seen was actually just a collection of metal wires sticking out of the mannequin's sleeves.

Yvgeny's mother brushed past the officers and looked down, still swaying from the medication. She squinted, cocked her head, then nodded.

"Yup, it's Earnest Ledbetter. You killed him again. I better tell Yvgeny it's going to be closed casket after all."

⛩

Alfred glanced in each direction, as if debating whether to turn and run. Telfair and his friends all watched as if they were on a sidewalk watching a car crash, mouths open in surprise that turned into horror.

"Nnng! Ng nng ng ng!" Alfred wailed.

"*This* is your Mime Master?"

"The one and only!"

Telfair observed Yvgeny's and Dub's expressions, and, after studying them both, he asked, "Y'all know each other?"

Yvgeny put his hands on his hips and said, "I don't know, why don't you tell him, *Mime Master*"

He put great sarcastic emphasis on the words Mime Master, and when Alfred didn't open his mouth, Yvgeny added, "Well, Alfred is my gravedigger!"

Yvgeny leaned in and inspected Alfred, then he took in a few very deep breaths.

"Alfred, you showered? With *soap*?"

Alfred normally presented an unkempt and unwashed appearance around Schmidt and Sons, such that most, including Yvgeny, avoided getting too close.

"How nice it would be if you maintained this level of hygiene around the workplace."

After a pause, Yvgeny turned to Telfair and said, "So, I came all the way up to Macon so my own gravedigger, a deaf mute, can help me solve a murder?"

Yvgeny looked down at his shoes and, in a voice too soft for anyone in the club to hear, he muttered, "Oh, Holmes, Holmes, *this* is to be my Watson?"

Yvgeny fell heavily into his seat, and Brianna, rarely the emotional type, patted him on the back. Alfred slowly creaked into a seat across the table, and chugged a glass of water. Telfair, grinning broadly, leaned in to Alfred and clapped him hard on the back and yelled, "Alfred? I like it. I like Mime Master better, but Alfred ain't bad! Like the guy on Batman!"

With his arm still around Alfred, Telfair looked over at Yvgeny and said, "Check it out, ladies, it's black Alfred from Batman!"

Yvgeny rubbed his temples a moment, then looked up again.

"Why the hell do you call him Mime Master?"

"I think you know exactly why! You know the way he talks!"

"Wait a minute. What do you mean, 'the way he talks'"?

"What do you mean, what do I mean? He talks with his hands, gets all crazy. Can't understand a damn thing he says, but *sure* he talks. Just like a mime."

Yvgeny stared, expressionless, at Telfair, then slowly turned back to Alfred.

Telfair leaned across the table and whispered, "Part of

THE BODY IN THE BED

working a murder case is *eliminating* suspects. Just as important, if you're asking me."

"OK Dub," Telfair continued, "tell me, remember Earnest?"

Alfred watched Telfair's lips, then nodded, solemnly. He put his head down. Telfair looked over at Yvgeny and asked, "He already knows?"

"Of course, he's the one that unloaded him from my hearse and brought him over to my workroom."

Telfair still had his arm around Alfred, and he squeezed the man's shoulder, saying, "Sorry, old sport."

Alfred looked down at the table a moment longer, dejected, then stood and began to windmill his arms and pour out a stream of "nng nng ngs!" Telfair glanced over at Yvgeny, said, "See what I mean?" then held up his palms to Alfred and cried out, "Whoah! Give me a minute!"

He took a deep breath, asked Alfred to repeat what he said, and both Yvgeny and Telfair listened intently. Looking at each other, Yvgeny said, "He was found dead a couple days ago. Dead in bed."

Alfred looked around at the people seated beside him, then glared at Bessie and Myrtle. He turned back to Telfair and raised his hands up in the universal sign of *why*?

"Well that's the question, ain't it, Dub?" Telfair said. Telfair's eyes unfocused, then, and Myrtle rolled her eyes and said, "Aw, hell, here he goes again."

Telfair started beat boxing, and chanted,

"Didn't have the chills, felt fit as a fiddle,
Never suffered no ills, didn't anger no hoes,
Nothin' in his system,
No cuts, no holes.
Paid all his bills, still dug the thrills,
But why he rottin' in his crib, now *that's* the riddle."

"Junior G, I suppose."

Myrtle looked at Yvgeny, dismayed, and warned, "Don't encourage him."

Telfair, smiling, turned back to Alfred and said, "Sorry, couldn't help myself. Now, as you were saying?"

"He wasn't saying anything, Luther. He can't talk."

"Right. Ah, yes, now I remember. Alfred, I've been trying to explain to Geny here that Earnest was a lady's man. You remember how he carried on in here?"

Alfred smiled a sad smile and shook his head as if recalling his antics. Then he mimed having his arms around two women, and turning and kissing each one, then he let each arm slowly drop down until it appeared he was feeling the bottoms of two invisible women. Yvgeny made a look of disgust, and out of the corner of his eye he noticed Myrtle suddenly appear fascinated with a dark corner of the club, refusing to take her eyes off whatever distant object held her attention. Bessie reveled in Myrtle's discomfort and leered at Alfred.

Telfair watched their reactions and smiled again. Then he turned back to Alfred and said, "Now, Dub, the other ladies we bring here to the club, they all give him the googly eyes, don't they?"

Yvgeny turned to the two unfamiliar women that had emerged from Lenny's car, but they were too engrossed in the sights of the club to be paying attention. Luther, sensing his distraction, raised his voice and said, "Forget it, Vicky's nuts and Hella's dumb as a doorknob."

Telfair turned back to Alfred and said, "All the others, Dub, they always had a thing for good ol' Earnest, am I right?"

Alfred nodded, shrugged his shoulders. Telfair turned to Yvgeny, smug, and smacked his hand on the table, announcing, "I rest my case!"

Unfortunately, Yvgeny wasn't paying attention. He was focused on the two bird cage girls approaching from behind Telfair. They wore skin tight silver-sequined shorts, heels, and tube tops. One had a long afro and the other was bald. They enveloped Dub M/Alfred and Telfair in their arms and one of them cooed, "Where's my Ernie?"

Yvgeny couldn't hear Telfair's response, but as he whispered in their ears, they adopted the universal expression of one receiving bad news. A moment later, one of them ran off in tears.

Telfair turned back to Yvgeny and winked. The second bird cage girl walked over to the table and sat on Lenny's lap, grabbed his drink and guzzled it. Yvgeny, however, was still not impressed.

THE BODY IN THE BED

"Luther, what's the big revelation here?"

"You kidding me? Motive, sport! Don't you remember nothing I taught you? The women loved this guy. And he loved the attention. I done told you about those two here," he said, pointing a thumb toward Bessie and Myrtle. "Take a minute and think about what Bessie might do if she thought Ernie was playing the field."

Telfair turned back to Alfred.

"Now, Dub, we think we know who did it. And we think she's here tonight, at the club."

Dub M, or Alfred, started looking around uneasily into the crowd.

"No, I mean here, at the table!"

Dub M took a step back and narrowed his brow.

"No, not one of us. But maybe Bessie. Whatcha think?"

Alfred glanced over at Bessie, then started shaking his head violently.

"You sure, Dub? You sure it wasn't her?"

The swivel grew more violent, more quick. Yvgeny finally raised his hand to stop him.

"Ok, ok, don't kill yourself, we get it." Yvgeny turned to Telfair and muttered, "So much for your big revelation." Yvgeny paused, then added, "Maybe it was the other one."

"You got wax in your ears? We done gone over this. Myrtle ain't got the spunk to whack him. Right, Alfred?"

Alfred glanced behind Yvgeny toward the table, then shook his head.

"I'm telling you," Telfair continued, "I had my eye on Bessie, but if Dub's not feelin' it, then it's gotta be someone else."

"Great, then who killed him?"

Telfair pursed his lips a moment, then shrugged.

"Maybe there was another man... someone jealous of Ernie getting all the ladies. Maybe another woman who didn't get what she wanted."

"Jealousy, anger, desperation, madness, that sort of thing?"

"Just like Jezelda said! That's where I'd place my bet."

"What about his good for nothing family?" Yvgeny asked.

"He was poisoned, sport."

"Yeah, so? I didn't get the feeling that daughter of his would have lost any sleep over doing it."

"Sure, sport, but you actually have to show up at the place in order to poison someone."

"Right," Yvgeny said, then started to rub his temples with his fingers.

"Luther, I am not feeling very confident about this whole murder thing."

"Suck it up, buttercup, you know the sheriff's office ain't going to go interrogate a bunch of little old ladies. You're all we got!"

"Well, until now, you were telling me it was one of these ladies here!"

"I stand corrected."

Yvgeny sighed.

Telfair chewed on his lower lip again, glanced over at the other ladies, then leaned in and spoke in a softer tone, "We been over this already. Myrtle's half soft in the head, she'd never be able to pull off a murder, and besides, she fell hook, line, and sinker for Earnest, she cries every day for him. Not a chance."

"As for Bessie, well, maybe I had blinders on with her. Dub didn't think she did it, and let's face it, she might have the stones for it, but if she killed anyone, it would be Myrtle. And, I tell you what, if she was gonna do him in, it wouldn't be with poison. She'd push him down the stairs, or just strangle him. She's infantry, she ain't no sniper."

Something started to nag at Yvgeny. He glanced back at Bessy, who was sipping her drink and occasionally glaring at Myrtle. He reflected back on what she said. She said she was there when Earnest died. Then she said, "When we were finished, I went downstairs to get him a cup of coffee."

Yvgeny pushed past Telfair and approached Bessy. He squeezed his way over and sat beside her on the table.

"You said you saw him die."

"What?"

"You said you saw him die, right?"

"You got it."

"You two were *in flagrante delicto* when it happened."

"Not sure what the hell that means, but sure, yeah, probably."

Yvgeny prepared himself for his *Aha!* moment.

"If you two were together when he died, then why would

THE BODY IN THE BED

you have gone downstairs afterwards to bring him coffee?"

Bessy's combative expression faltered. She glanced over at Myrtle again, and, seeing she was in a deep conversation with Hella, she leaned back into Yvgeny, contrite.

"OK, you caught me, undertaker. We weren't in the sack when he died. I just said that to piss Myrtle off. I got a good rise out of her, didn't I?" She smiled, then said, "I wanted to surprise him. Usually Beatrice brings around a coffee cart a couple times a day. I met her in the kitchen and grabbed Ernie's mug. He had his own special mug, you know. When I walked in, I found him dead."

Yvgeny nodded, and chided her, "You know, it's quite bad form to lie about such things. Luckily, I am not a detective."

Bessy shrugged and took a sip of her drink.

"What's anyone going to do? At my age? Ain't a jury in the world that would convict me of lying about that!"

Yvgeny was again impressed by the old woman's clarity of thought. His mind wandered off, then, away from Bessy and Myrtle. Telfair and Alfred, to the extent Alfred actually said anything, were right: these two women were not the murderers.

He shimmied his way around Myrtle and back to Telfair.

"So, it looks like we are back to square one."

Telfair put his hands on his hips and nodded sagely. He said, "Must be someone else at the Sunset we haven't thought of." He smiled, and added, "But don't worry, I'm sure you'll sniff it out!"

Yvgeny's face twisted with surprise.

"Luther, how many people live there? And how do you propose I narrow it down? Check myself into the place? Go in undercover as an old man?"

Movement at the table caught Yvgeny's attention. He turned in time to see Vicky wincing, then she popped out her dentures, ran a finger along them, studied them a moment, then, with a shrug, she plopped them into her wine, stirred them around with a spoon, then took a long pull from the glass. Her friend watched the entire affair then turned away as if nothing happened. Yvgeny felt himself melting a little inside.

Telfair, however, didn't miss a beat.

"Not a bad idea, sport, but that's a lot of work. I say we

wait until tomorrow's funeral, pay close attention to everyone, see what they do. Maybe set up a camera so you don't miss nothing!"

"I usually record my events anyway."

In fact, he recorded his events as part of his marketing package. For $299 he made the entire event available on VHS or DVD, checks made payable to Schmidt and Sons. Ledbetter's funeral would be no different. *Hell*, he thought, *I might even offer a senior citizen discount.*

"What about suicide?" Yvgeny asked. "Maybe he ran out of money, or he just couldn't handle the cancer."

"Nah, I doubt it. Hell of a painful way to go. Slow too, not like a bullet in the noggin. And where in the hell would he find antifreeze, and sneak it inside without anybody seeing him?"

"Accident?"

Telfair cocked his head and said, "What the hell kind of accident?"

Yvgeny's phone started to vibrate in his pocket, and he checked it to find another text message from his mother. He cringed, then read the message.

Policccccre here. Wevee a sichuation.

Yvgeny leaned in to Brianna and said, "We have a problem. We need to go."

"What kind of problem?"

"Not sure yet. Mama's on her meds."

Yvgeny turned to Alfred and said, "I suppose you need a lift back home, Twinkle Toes?"

Alfred glanced back to the dance floor, then crossed his arms and shook his head.

Yvgeny pursed his lips and stood.

"Suit yourself. Brianna, shall we?"

Brianna chugged the rest of her drink, then stood.

"Well, Luther, see you tomorrow, I guess."

"Wouldn't miss it for the world."

Then Yvgeny turned to Alfred, and with a smile, called out, "See ya tomorrow, Mime Master!" Then Yvgeny leaned in and added, "And do have that suit of mine dry-cleaned before you return it."

Once they were back in Cerberus, Brianna cleared her throat and grumbled, "So what the hell happened in there?"

THE BODY IN THE BED

"Not a lot. Telfair thought his friend, 'Mime Master,' would magically be able to convince me good old Ernie was a ladies' man, and whether Bessy did it. I was hoping for something a little more convincing."

"I bet. Kind of a wasted trip."

"If he died of antifreeze poisoning, then it had to be someone that lives there. Or maybe he killed himself," Brianna said.

Yvgeny smiled and replied, "Well, who's the detective now? We talked about that. The old man said nobody would do themselves with antifreeze. Guess it's too painful and takes too long."

Brianna looked out the window for a moment, deep in thought.

"What if his kids wanted all his money, so they hired someone to do it? Someone that lived there? Someone on the inside."

Yvgeny pursed his lips, nodding slowly. He remembered the old man that scurried out to meet one of the Singhs out in the street to report Ernie's passing.

Everyone's got their side hustles to make a few extra bucks. Why would these old people be any different?

"Possibly. Haven't thought of that."

Yvgeny stole a quick glance at Brianna, then risked commenting, "Well, anyway, *you* made a new friend."

"What, that bouncer? Just talking about the weather."

"Mmm hmm."

Brianna's mouth opened and she turned and stared at him.

"Are you jealous?"

"Of course not. Just making conversation."

"Mmm hmm," she replied, then turned to look out the window, smiling.

Just over half an hour later, they returned to the mortuary. Two city police cars were parked outside and all the lights in the place were on. Yvgeny and Brianna looked at each other but didn't say a word. He had to consciously will his feet to move forward. Brianna grabbed his hand and said, "Geny, if something was wrong with your mother, there'd be an ambulance. Besides, she was the one that texted you."

He looked at her blankly, then shook his head quickly, as

if clearing from a fog.

"What? No, I'm worried we've been burglarized. That battle axe will outlive us all!"

They came in through the side door and found two officers seated at the table, with Mama at the stove waiting for the tea pot to start whistling. The officers fumbled to their feet when they saw Brianna, then slowly returned to their seats, forlorn.

Yvgeny recognized the younger officer from an earlier visit, and he called out, "Constable Frankie, welcome back!"

Yvgeny had never liked the city police, and the last time Frankie had been to Schmidt's, Yvgeny pulled out all the stops, capitalizing on the officer's obvious fear of coffins, dead bodies, and funeral homes. To Yvgeny's delight, his gruesome antics had the poor officer running to find a barf bag.

The pot started whistling, and Mama took it off the heat and started shuffling toward the officers.

"I don't know how you live here, Geny," Frankie quipped, then reached into his shirt pocket with trembling fingers and pulled out a plastic can of Skoal Bandits.

Just as Yvgeny was about to respond, he saw his mother shuffling toward the officers with her scalding hot tea pot. She was so unsteady from her medication, scalding water was tumbling out of the spout with each step she took. One drop arced through the air and landed on the wooden surface of the table, sending up a tiny plume of steam. He rushed in to snatch away the pot before she dropped it on one of the officer's heads.

"Such a good son, my little *tygrysek*! See boys, you have nothing to worry about!"

Yvgeny narrowed his eyes as he placed the teapot on a trivet on the table and turned to his mother and asked, "What should they be worried about, Mama?"

Brianna stepped in to assist, grabbing two tea cups from the pantry and placing them before the officers. Then she poured the tea into the cups. His mother turned to the older officer and said, "Come on Henry, just tell him, no sense prolonging it."

Henry picked at his uniform shirt a moment, then looked at his friend Frankie. After taking a deep breath, he started.

THE BODY IN THE BED

"Well, dispatch sent us here, said your mother called in a signal 6."

Yvgeny stifled a sigh and checked his watch.

The younger officer nudged him and whispered something. Henry nodded and said, "Sorry, a burglary in progress. Anyway, the dispatcher said she could hear her yelling at someone. So, we hauled ass over here."

Yvgeny looked up at Henry, his ears perked. He waited another moment to hear the rest of the story, then impatiently turned his hand over and over in a circular fashion and coaxed him with a long, "And?"

Henry sighed.

"And, well, we hauled ass over here, ran in and stuff, and you know, well, it was really dark, and we saw a guy, this guy, you know, well, he was holding something shiny. It looked like a gun! I mean, we thought it was a gun! So, you know, we did what any good cop would do."

"There was a guy here?"

"Well, you know, we thought there was this guy, you see -"

Yvgeny started to realize what happened. His heart skipped a beat.

"You shot my mannequin?"

"Well, Frankie yelled *GUN!*"

Yvgeny's jaw dropped.

"So, you shot him? How many times? No, scratch that, how bad is he?"

The two officers looked at each other and shrugged. Yvgeny stormed out of the kitchen and headed downstairs. Brianna jogged to catch up with him, glaring at the two cops as she passed. The officers stood, but then him-hawed around the table as if unsure whether to follow or run out the front door. With shoulders slumped, they trudged toward the stairs after Brianna.

His mother had watched the whole affair on wobbly legs, and when everyone left, she sat at the table, grabbed one of the officer's empty cups, and blew across the rim.

"Oh, Earnest, you poor dear," murmured Yvgeny when he saw the damage. He crouched and ran a hand down the mannequin's chest, cursing softly. Then he began to inspect the damage more carefully.

"You shot him *and* beat him? With what, a nightstick?"

Henry cleared his throat, then mumbled, "No, I believe someone else beat him before we got here. Maybe with a cane."

Hope she's enjoying her tea, Yvgeny thought.

He checked his watch again, then ran his fingers across the mask. He stood slowly, a rueful smile on his face.

Brianna said, "Well, guess you need a plan B."

"That was my plan B. I need a plan C."

Yvgeny circled around the Earnest mannequin, sticking his finger in several of the bullet holes.

"This was a Hugo Boss suit. How am I going to fix all this before tomorrow's funeral? This could take hours!"

Brianna approached the mannequin opposite Yvgeny and inspected the damage. She turned to Yvgeny and muttered, "What kind of medication is she on?"

Yvgeny stood, listless, then turned to the officers.

"Well, constables, I think we can take it from here. Please don't shoot anything else on your way out."

"No sir, we can't leave, we had to call a detective and a supervisor."

"And why is that? More target practice?"

"Anytime there's a shooting, we have to call a detective and a supervisor."

Yvgeny sighed and looked over at Brianna, who shrugged her shoulders.

"Brianna, my dear, would you please escort our new friends back up to the kitchen? I believe Mama was about to reward them with a nice cup of tea for their efforts."

☩

Bubba had finally returned home from his visit to Newsome and was fast asleep when his telephone started ringing. In his dream, he was hiding from a phone the size of a Chevrolet, but after several rings the real phone cut through his dream phone and he answered it, groggy and with a thick tongue.

"Got a Code 10 and you're next on the list."

THE BODY IN THE BED

"Call Newsome, he's probably still awake."
"Don't worry, he's next."
Bubba opened his eyes.
"Newsome, too? What is it?"
"Shots fired."
Bubba sat up in bed and shook the fog away.
"Where?"
Bubba could hear the dispatcher's jaw smacking up and down as she worked on what sounded like an entire package of chewing gum, then she said, wryly, "That creepy old Russian guy's place. You know, the cemetery and everything."
"What? Schmidt's?"
"You know any other Russian cemeteries around here?" *Smack, pop.*
"He's Polish."
"Whatever." *Smack, pop.*
"Who's the shooter?"
The woman stopped chewing and smiled.
"It's y'all's friends, Henry and Frankie. Mutt and Jeff. The Bobsey Twins." *Chuckle, snort.*
The woman began laughing in between words, and when she laughed, she snorted, making her sound like a talking pig.
"I get the picture."
Undeterred, the woman kept going.
"Frick and Frack. *Chuckle. Snort.* Dumb and Dumber."
Bubba pursed his lips and before hanging up, he told her, "Just tell 'em we're coming."
Bubba slammed the phone down, picked it up again, then punched in Newsome's number. After about seven rings, he answered.
"Grab your shit, there's been a shooting at Geny's place."
"You freakin' kidding me?"
"Nope. Frankie and Henry."
Newsome sat up in bed just as Bubba had done.
"Should've fired their asses last time."

CHAPTER TEN

☦

When Newsome and Bubba pulled into the driveway at Schmidt and Sons, they saw the two city squad cars and Yvgeny's hearse parked in the street. The front door was cracked, so the detectives let themselves in. They followed the sounds down the hall and into the kitchen, where they found Yvgeny's mother teetering on her cane, and the two uniformed officers shuffling from one foot to the other, dejected.

"Evening, Ma'am," Newsome said.

Mama opened her mouth to respond, but before she could get even one word out, the two uniformed officers came to life, flanked her, and started yelling, each trying to drown out the other.

"Frankie yelled 'Gun!' so I did what I had to -"

"Henry just started shooting, it's all his fault -"

"Yeah, well if Frankie wasn't still hung over from -"

Every time Mama opened her mouth to speak, one of the officers interrupted her. She grew more and more irritated.

"Shut up, Henry! At least I don't sit watching porn on my cell phone all night!"

"I do not!"

Frankie mimicked scrolling on a phone while grabbing his crotch and moaning, "Ooh, ooh!"

Newsome raised his hands, palms out, and yelled, "That's enough! What the hell's wrong with you two?"

Yvgeny's mother pushed past the two uniforms, smacking her cane down hard on one of their feet, causing the officer to hop up and down in pain.

"Here to collect your friends?" She asked. Her speech was slurred, causing Newsome to ask, "Are you ok?"

"Just fine. Except for these bozos here turning my home into the OK Corral."

THE BODY IN THE BED

Frankie pointed accusingly at Mama and yelled, "Yeah, well, she beat him with her cane!"

Mama slowly turned and pointed her cane at Frankie and, in an ominous tone, muttered, "You're next."

Frankie opened his mouth to issue a retort, but saw the two detectives staring at him. He averted his eyes, looking down at his shoes instead. Newsome asked Yvgeny's mother, "So, what the hell happened?"

"I came downstairs to get my teapot. It was dark. You know, my vision isn't what it used to be. I thought that dummy was a burglar, so I called 911. Once I got the lights on, I realized it was just one of Geny's projects. I told your people to cancel *these* dummies, but here they are. They pushed me aside and ran downstairs."

"And shot the dummy."

"Exactly."

Newsome looked back over at Henry and Frankie, who were still whispering and motioning at each other, and said, "Is that about right?"

They both looked at Newsome like children in the principal's office, and nodded. Then one elbowed the other and said, "This is all *your* fault!"

"Enough!" cried Bubba.

After glaring at them for a moment, Newsome looked over at Bubba and asked, 'What do you think, should I take away their guns and send 'em home?"

Bubba smiled dryly and inspected the two officers, who were now silent, rapt with attention, their faces having lost all color. Bubba took a step closer, hands on his hips, and spoke slowly.

"Well, maybe so, maybe so. Let's go have us a look downstairs, take us a few pictures, then figure out what to do with them. Meanwhile, why don't you fellas go out to your cars and think about what y'all did."

The uniforms filed out the front door, heads down, while Newsome tried to withhold a smirk. Once the door closed behind them, Newsome chuckled, winked at Bubba, then put on a serious face and turned to Yvgeny's mother. He said, "You mind if we go check it out?"

She raised one shaky hand and said, "Go right ahead!"

They walked down the stairs and into Yvgeny's work room,

finding Yvgeny busy with the mannequin. Bubba looked around and shivered, then whispered to Newsome, "Harry, this place gives me the creeps."

Yvgeny continued working, but glanced up quickly at Newsome.

"Inspector."

Newsome nodded curtly and responded, "Geny."

"Here to inspect the crime scene?"

"Not much of a crime scene if you ask me," Newsome said.

Yvgeny feigned surprise, exclaiming, "Lucky it wasn't *me* on that table!"

Bubba snorted but didn't speak. He walked slowly over to Yvgeny and looked over his shoulder at the mannequin. He whistled, then said, "Damn, Geny, that's some good work. I'd say it ain't no surprise they shot his ass, that thing looks real!"

Yvgeny shrugged his shoulders and said, "Yeah, but would *you* shoot an 80 year-old man in a suit?"

"Well," Newsome replied, "that depends if I was hung over."

"Or if I'd been surfing porn all night." Bubba added.

Newsome sighed, then walked past the mannequin to the wall. He crouched and ran a finger along the cinder blocks.

"Those fools are damn lucky they didn't kill nobody."

Bubba took one more look around, and said, in a small voice, "OK, great. We done here?"

Newsome shook his head and grumbled, "Almost," then approached Yvgeny.

"So, Geny, you still messing around with that hospice case?"

Yvgeny stood up from his project and eyed Newsome suspiciously.

"Why do you ask?"

"Just makin' conversation."

"Oh, really," Yvgeny said, flatly.

"Actually, ain't a hospice case no more. It's a murder case."

Newsome stuck his thumb out toward the mannequin and added, "And this looks just like my victim."

Yvgeny had finally righted the remains of the Ledbetter mannequin on the bench, then turned to face Newsome. He

THE BODY IN THE BED

put his arm around the mannequin as if they were old friends.

"I will take that as a compliment, inspector. And, as a matter of fact, it *is* the dearly departed. Thanks to Flowers, I have no body for my open casket funeral tomorrow. Gotta make do with what we have!"

"Geny, funny thing about that body. Flowers took him up to Macon a few hours ago for a full autopsy."

"Flowers must have realized he was in over his head. What a surprise."

"And then the ME called. Said the body had already been embalmed."

"Sounds like you're having a busy night. What's your point, inspector?"

Newsome took a step closer.

"Did you embalm my victim, Geny?"

"I did my job after Flowers supposedly did his. No crime there."

Newsome continued to stare at Yvgeny, then, in an ominous voice, said, "Maybe not, undertaker, but I don't like where this is going. This is how it started last time."

"And what is that exactly?"

"Your meddling. Remember, last time you got crossways with me you ended up in a cell."

Yvgeny clasped his hands behind his back and puffed out his chest a bit.

"Funny, inspector, what I remember is cracking that case way before you and your friends."

Newsome pursed his lips, and he leaned back a little, resting his hand on the butt of his gun.

"Right. What would we do without you, Geny?"

Newsome glanced over at the mannequin again, shaking his head.

"You'd best just bury this dummy and move on. You're out of your league on this one."

"You know, inspector, I'm shocked and appalled at your insinuation. I told you days ago that you might have a death to investigate and you scoffed at me. Now I'm out of my league?"

Yvgeny started pacing like a lawyer in front of a jury.

"My only interest here is preparing for tomorrow's funeral

and collecting my fee. Solving a murder, well, that's your job."

Newsome stared at him a moment longer, then turned away. Bubba asked, "Funeral's tomorrow, huh?"

"Yup. Should be a lot of fun. Live music, booze and snacks, and everyone will be there. The family, all his friends at Sunset Manor, even Jezelda will be making a guest appearance."

Taking a conspiratorial tone, Yvgeny leaned in and whispered, "Maybe the killer will even show up!"

"What time does the party start?" asked Bubba.

"Promptly at two p.m."

Bubba glanced at Newsome, who was still staring at Yvgeny. Keeping his eyes on him, Newsome said, "You hear that, Bubba? Sounds like we just got invited to a party! Save us a couple chairs, Geny!"

"You two are more than welcome," Yvgeny replied. "But your friends upstairs, you can leave them at home."

Yvgeny and Brianna escorted the detectives up the stairs, through the kitchen, and out the door. On their way out, Newsome turned around and asked, "Almost forgot. You were out awful late tonight, weren't you?"

"You checking up on me?"

"Nope. But these uniforms said when they got here, you weren't home."

"Perhaps I was just out for a walk, clearing my head."

"Your hood was still hot."

Yvgeny cocked his head.

"And you were parked *behind* the marked cars."

"Ah, you caught me! You cracked the case of the missing undertaker! I was out on a date, if you must know."

Newsome gave Yvgeny one final look, then walked toward his car. Bubba approached the uniforms, still sitting glumly in their patrol cars, and sent them on their way.

Back in the kitchen, Mama was finishing her cup of tea. After Yvgeny walked in, Brianna turned to Yvgeny and asked, "You really think the killer will show up?"

Mama snorted, then muttered, sarcastically, "My son, the big shot detective," then turned away to begin her precarious climb back up the stairs. Yvgeny stared at her a moment, then turned away.

THE BODY IN THE BED

"Well, probably, assuming he was murdered. I still haven't ruled out suicide, or maybe even some kind of crazy accident. But no matter what happened, Ernie hadn't left the place in days, so someone at this funeral will know something. And whoever that somebody is, they live at the Sunset. Beatrice says everyone is going, so that's an entire van full of potential witnesses. And maybe a killer or two!"

Yvgeny looked up, nodded his head to himself, and added, "You know, maybe if someone conspicuously *doesn't* show up, that just might be interesting."

"But those two old ladies, you don't think either of them did it?"

Yvgeny shrugged.

"Well, you heard Telfair. He's now convinced it wasn't them." Yvgeny rolled his eyes and added, "Apparently *Double M* ruled them out."

Brianna thought a moment, then asked, wide eyed, "And Jezelda, you think she'll be able to identify them?"

Yvgeny stared at her, incredulous.

"Are you kidding me? She's just looking to capitalize on some free advertising tomorrow."

"She's the one that called out the death before anyone said a word!"

Yvgeny waved away her comment and said, "Beginner's luck!" Then he chortled and shook his head, a broad grin on his face.

"Ah, Brianna, what would I do without you? Things would be so mundane, so boring."

Yvgeny turned to the mannequin and shook his head while clucking his tongue.

"Ah, Earnest, it's no use, I don't have time to repair you! I'm going to have to go to plan C."

"And what's plan C?" Brianna asked.

"Well, Earnest was a smallish guy, pretty skinny. I just need to find someone with his frame, then I can handle the rest."

"What? Who the hell are you going to get to lay in a coffin and pretend he's a dead guy?"

Yvgeny looked at her a moment, then slowly a wide, toothy smile splashed across his face.

JONATHAN B. ZEITLIN

⹋

Thursday morning was warm and cloudy, a perfect middle Georgia day. Bubba was sipping coffee in the sally port with one of the dispatchers when Newsome arrived, his hair disheveled and a dour expression on his face. He walked past them and into the building without even a nod of his head.

"He always that cheerful?" asked the dispatcher.

Bubba waited for the door to slam shut, then shrugged and said, "He had a late night."

The dispatcher put down her coffee cup, lit a cigarette, then tossed the match into the cup.

"So I heard."

"Plus, he did his part time."

The dispatcher took a drag of her cigarette, then asked, "Why is he still doing that? He need the money that bad since his divorce?"

"Dunno, but I don't think it's because of the divorce. I think he just likes to get out of the house and pretend he's in uniform again. Good old days and all."

They were quiet a moment, then he asked, "You hear about our on-call thing last night?"

"The Frankie and Henry show? Who doesn't! Dummies."

A few minutes later, Newsome returned, holding a paper cup of coffee. He leaned against the bricks and took a sip. Then he checked his watch and muttered, "Where the hell is he?"

The dispatcher asked, "Where is who?"

Neither Bubba nor Newsome responded, and a few minutes later they heard the low throaty rumble of Flowers's van. Soon enough, they saw his shiny red paint and bowling shirt style cursive lettering on his doors identifying him as Deputy Coroner. The dispatcher watched him a moment, then scuffed her cigarette butt against the brick of the building while muttering, "Him? Dumb ass."

Bubba glanced over at the dispatcher. Noticing his interest, she looked up and said, "What? I can't believe the sheriff lets him drive that stupid thing."

THE BODY IN THE BED

They continued talking, and occasionally one of them would glance toward the parking lot to see if Flowers had emerged from his van. After several minutes, Bubba said, to no one in particular, "What's he waiting for?"

A moment later, a late model Mercedes pulled in and parked next to Flowers's van. The Georgia license plate read NGRI 2.

"This day's just getting better by the minute," Newsome growled, then tossed his coffee cup in the trash. He paced for a moment, then stood beside the door, arms crossed over his chest. Bubba waited at the edge of the sally port next to the dispatcher.

Soon after the Mercedes parked, Flowers hopped down from his perch behind the wheel of his van and hiked up his pants. His Hawaiian shirt hung on him as if he was a deflated balloon. He was disheveled and seemed sullen.

The woman that emerged from the Mercedes was in her fifties and her hair was dyed dark red, set off by a pair of huge gold bangly earrings. She was armed with a briefcase. Bubba's jaw dropped.

"Her?"

The dispatcher glanced over at him and said, "You know her?"

"Everyone does. That's Donna Proctor. Worst criminal defense lawyer in middle Georgia."

"By worst, do you mean best?"

Bubba nodded glumly.

"Why the hell did Flowers bring *her*?"

Flowers and Proctor approached the sally port.

Newsome remained at his post against the brick wall and called out, "Jimmy, you bring a friend?"

Flowers's cheeks reddened somewhat, but he didn't speak. Instead, the woman stepped forward and held out her hand toward the nearest person, which was Bubba.

"Morning, deputies, Donna Proctor, counsel for Dr. Flowers. How do you do?"

Before either of them could reply, the woman flicked her wrist and produced business cards as if she was a magician with a deck of cards, and presented them to Bubba and Newsome.

"I don't just do criminal defense, men. Wills, estates, civil litigation, immigration, you name it, I got you covered. And of course, divorce," she added with a wink. "I'm an expert in essentially every practice specialty."

With one of her long, red nails, she pointed at the business cards she shoved into their hands, and added, "Check out my website. And did I mention? 10% discount for law enforcement!"

For a moment, both deputies stood staring at her, too surprised to respond. The dispatcher finished her cigarette, dropped the butt into her empty coffee cup, and left, muttering, "I'm out."

Newsome cleared his throat and, after a brief glance at her business card, turned to Flowers and asked, "Damn Flowers, we just wanted you to tell us what you saw on the body."

"Detective, please address your questions to me."

Proctor turned to Flowers and started rubbing his back.

"Jimmy, they'd like to ask you what you saw on the body."

Bubba rolled his eyes as Flowers turned to face his lawyer. He rubbed the stubble on his chin a moment, and started to narrate.

"Well, there I was, turning off the lights to leave for the evening. As I passed the couch in my office, I noticed something glowing. You see, these detectives left the victim's clothing draped over the couch."

Flowers emphasized his words by pointing a thumb towards Newsome.

"Anyway, I thought to myself -"

"No, Jimmy, just the facts, no opinions."

Flowers squinted as she spoke, then nodded quickly, muttering, "Right."

"I moved in more close-like to inspect the source of this strange glowing, and determined it was coming from the crotch of the victim's pants."

The lawyer nodded and said, "Good, now go on, Jimmy."

Nodding, Flowers continued.

"So, I tried to figure out why it would be glowing, and I remembered learning about Woods lamps in medical school. A Woods lamp is a special device -"

"I know what a Woods lamp is, Flowers."

Everyone turned to Newsome in surprise. Newsome grimaced, then said, "Back off, I've been to a dermatologist."

THE BODY IN THE BED

Flowers cleared his throat and said, "Right. Anyway, I have an ultraviolet light in my office, just for fun, and I had forgotten to turn it off, hence the discovery. That's when I realized something was up."

"Great, Jimmy, just great!" the lawyer crooned, then rubbed his shoulder. Energized, he continued.

"So, I started thinking to myself-"

"Jimmy," she chided.

"Sorry, right, so I said to myself, 'Jimmy, remember, ethylene glycol has additives to make it phosphoresce. That's how mechanics can figure out where your radiator is leaking from. So I concluded that this man was likely poisoned with antifreeze."

The doctor turned to the lawyer, seeking approval, and she rubbed his back again and called out, "Good boy!" as if he was a puppy.

Newsome and Bubba glanced at each other, then Newsome asked, "So you sent off the blood work to the GBI? And sent the body?"

"I sent the blood work to Rocket Labs. They already picked up the blood by the time I figured it all out."

"And you sent him to the GBI because you found antifreeze on the guy's clothes."

"You got it."

"And you felt you needed a lawyer to tell us that?"

Flowers's face reddened and he looked away.

"It must've been after midnight when Bubba called you. You found a lawyer between then and now?"

The lawyer rubbed Flowers's back a little harder.

"Don't answer that, Jimmy."

Ignoring the lawyer, Newsome leaned in and said, "Something tells me there's more to this story. Whatcha hiding, Doc?"

"Sorry, detective, you can't question my client like that. You'll have to direct your concerns to me."

"We ain't in court, Counselor. And your client ain't a suspect. But the fact he showed up with you makes me wonder."

"Well, you're prohibited from drawing any negative inference from my client's wise decision to have competent representation when being shaken down by the police. And I am here for my clients 24/7/365."

Bubba looked at Newsome and asked, "Did she say shaken down?" Then he looked at the lawyer and said, "If we was shaking him down, we'd -"

"Be violating his civil rights, no doubt," she quipped. Then she turned to Flowers and said, "I think we're done here. Let's go before this becomes a case of police brutality."

As Flowers and his lawyer turned to leave, Newsome muttered, "I'm getting too old for this -"

"Oh, and detectives, next time you want to talk to my client, make sure you direct those questions to me." She looked at her watch, then said, "Jimmy, we need to go! We have an interview to attend!" She turned back to the detectives and added, "Your good doctor here saved a baby's life yesterday. The world wants to hear all about him! Good day!"

Bubba and Newsome watched as the two walked toward the parking lot. They spoke quietly, the lawyer occasionally rubbing Flowers's shoulder, then they each piled into their respective vehicles and lurched into traffic. With a sigh, Newsome and Bubba returned to their desks.

Bubba rocked back in his chair for a bit, then reached for a plastic Gatorade bottle half full of tobacco juice. He spit into the bottle, then asked Newsome, "Should have mentioned that bong in his office."

Newsome didn't respond, still fuming over the encounter with Flowers. Bubba continued rocking, then asked, "So, I reckon that old fart was murdered."

Newsome shrugged.

"Well, that or he killed himself."

Bubba nodded, said, "Yessir, Kincaid said it was suicide or murder."

They both rocked in their chairs in silence for a moment. Then Bubba smirked and added, "or maybe Geny spilled antifreeze on the clothes."

Newsome shrugged again, then patted on his shirt pocket. He had given up cigarettes years ago, but occasionally had a craving, especially when he was irritated. Bubba withdrew his can of Skoal from his back pocket and offered it to Newsome, who pursed his lips and turned away. A moment later he turned back to Bubba and asked, "Thought you was

THE BODY IN THE BED

a Copenhagen guy?"

Bubba shrugged and said, "It was all they had at the store."

Newsome nodded slowly, then a moment later, he stood.

Newsome said, "Maybe we should go over to Sunset Manor and have a chat with the manager."

"We really think some senior citizen whacked this guy with antifreeze?"

"Well, Bubba, unless you got a better idea?"

Bubba remained seated, distracted.

"Something on your mind?" Newsome asked.

"Harry, we don't both need to go to that damn funeral, do we? Geny's funerals will give you nightmares."

Newsome sighed.

"One thing at a time, you big baby. But yes, we are both probably going to the funeral."

Newsome had to park in the street because the Sunset Manor van was in the driveway, door open, ready to take its passengers to the Macon Mall. The driver was leaning against the van smoking a cigarette. Newsome parked, then grabbed his clipboard. Bubba remained in the car while Newsome walked around to the passenger side and, after a moment, turned to Bubba and opened his car door.

"You coming or what?"

"This place gives me the creeps."

"Duly noted. No funerals, no old folks' homes, no mortuaries. What the hell kind of detective are you? Now come on."

Still, Bubba sat, his Gatorade bottle filled with tobacco juice between his legs. Newsome watched him a moment, then sighed.

"Jesus. You're getting soft, Bubba."

As Newsome prepared to go, Bubba took a deep breath, then let it out in a whoosh. He got out of the car, spit, then hiked up his pants. He rolled his shoulders, then swiveled his neck, and took in a deep breath. Newsome glared at

Bubba's ritual, then said, "OK, Princess, *now* can we go?"

It was just after 10 a.m., and on any other morning, the crowd would be gathered for mid-morning tea, and Beatrice would be at her hallway post to greet any visitors. But this was no ordinary day. It was Mall Day, and most of the residents had their tea early and were already gathered in the day room, ready for the trip. Beatrice was nowhere to be found.

All eyes turned to the detectives when they stepped inside. Visitors were always a welcome source of entertainment. Some of the bolder residents tottered over, overcome by curiosity.

"Ooh, they have badges!" one lady crooned.

"Vincent, stay back!" another lady pleaded, grabbing at an old man's walker as he shuffled toward the detectives, a huge smile plastered across his face.

"Quick, someone go tell the chief!"

There was hushed whispering, then the old men and women began to part in two directions, forming a pathway down the middle. Telfair appeared at the other end of the room like Moses parting the sea, and began walking toward the detectives.

"Well, well, well, look who's here. Ya'll finally came to your senses!"

Bubba narrowed his brow and said, "Whatcha talking about?"

"This was a murder all along, champ, but y'all didn't have no interest until someone else got interested."

Newsome narrowed his eyes at the old chief and, with hands on hips, declared, "And who else is it that's interested?"

Telfair smiled and shook his head.

"Well, let's see, there's that quack Flowers for one, that's a good start."

"You're pretty well informed for an old man in a nursing home."

Telfair looked around, theatrically, and scoffed.

"How many times I gotta explain this? This ain't no nursing home, it's assisted living. Know what that means? That means somebody cleans my room, makes my meals, pays my bills. Got Cinemax all day long and ain't got nobody

THE BODY IN THE BED

to tell me to turn it off. I'm fifteen again, sonny boy, living at home with Mom and Dad. Just because I live here don't mean I'm soft in the head. Anyway, what I'm sayin' is, you're a day late, dollar short here."

The old man started bopping his shoulders up and down as he spoke, and Bubba winced.

"Oh no, Harry, he's about to start rapping."

Telfair stopped, glanced at Bubba, and said, "Know what? I ain't gonna give you the pleasure."

"Look," Newsome interrupted, "where's Ms. Beatrice? We need to talk to her."

"Check the front desk."

"Already did."

"Then ring the bell. You're a detective, I've got confidence in ya'!"

"Real helpful, chief."

They returned to Beatrice's station while Telfair cackled behind them. They stood a moment, then Bubba tapped his palm on the silver bell in the corner. A moment later there was rustling coming from down the hallway. They heard Beatrice before they saw her.

"Dammit, what'd I tell you folks about smacking that bell and running away! I'm gonna take -"

She rounded the corner and came face to face with the detectives and stopped mid-sentence.

"Oh, hello detectives, what can I do for you?"

Newsome leaned against the desk and asked, "Well, I suppose we should start by having us a little conversation, if you have a few minutes?"

Beatrice's cheeks colored slightly, then she said, "For you two? As long as you need. Let's go have a seat outside, we will be more comfortable there. But I should warn you, my residents are getting anxious. It's Mall day, you know, and we have to leave early so we can make it to the funeral on time."

Beatrice led them back down the hall and out the front door while patting at her silver hair and straightening her dress. The three sat together on a set of rocking chairs, her in the middle, Newsome and Bubba on either side. Bubba started unscrewing his Gatorade bottle.

"So, Ma'am, we -"

"Call me Beatrice."

"OK, Beatrice, we are taking a look at the Ledbetter death. How well did you know him?"

Beatrice sighed and looked out in the distance. Her cheeks colored again.

"You're taking a look? The Ledbetter death? What do you mean, exactly?"

Newsome sighed.

"This might be a murder."

Beatrice didn't say anything for a moment. Then she took a deep breath and said, "Oh, poor Earnest."

She picked at her dress, and continued.

"I knew him about as well as I knew everyone else here. Maybe a little better than most, as he was one of my longest surviving residents. Three years, give or take."

"Is that a long time?"

"Well, most don't make it that long once they get here. Some run out of money. Some move to be closer to family, or family starts to feel guilty and takes them in. Did you know the national average is 28 months? And only 16 percent stay three years or longer. Earnest was breaking the odds. He was a real fighter."

Beatrice made a strange face, one that Newsome could not decipher.

"Were you two close?"

Beatrice started smoothing out the lap of her dress.

"Whatever do you mean? Earnest was a client. I suppose I could call them all friends, but really they are all just paying guests at the Sunset."

Newsome nodded. Bubba spit, started rocking.

"Let me rephrase. Is there anyone you know that might want to hurt him?"

Beatrice also began to rock in her chair. She seemed to be deep in thought for a few moments, and when she spoke, she was very careful with her words.

"Earnest had it all. He had his looks, he had all his teeth, even had a little hair, and he still had a great personality. A lot of people might have been envious of that. And he liked women's company, so whichever woman didn't have it at that moment might have been a little jealous. But to kill for something like that? I just don't know."

THE BODY IN THE BED

"Any women in particular he was close with?"

More rocking. Then she spoke, her words measured, clipped.

"He spent most of his time with Myrtle and Bessie. They were apparently his favorites. They couldn't stand each other, but it seemed like they were always together. Them and the old chief, Luther."

"Luther Telfair?"

"One and the same. Those three -" Beatrice clucked her tongue and shook her head. "They think I don't know about their late-night antics."

Newsome and Bubba exchanged a quick glance as Beatrice continued rocking, a little faster now.

"And what late night antics are we talking about?"

"It's like parenting a bunch of college kids. Every week they sneak out of the house and pile into some outsider's car. They come back hours later. I can smell the alcohol in the air."

"Outsider"

"Some old Indian guy in a Lincoln."

"You don't know where they go?"

"Obviously some bar!" she replied, a little too loudly. She seemed to have surprised herself a bit with her tone, and visibly collected herself before continuing. "I'm sure it would be easy to figure out. How many late-night bars have visitors of their . . . vintage?"

Newsome nodded.

"Any reason you think we should have a chat with Telfair?"

"Well, detectives, I wouldn't tell you how to do your job, but at the very least, he would have more insight about Bessie and Myrtle."

Newsome turned to Bubba and asked, "Got anything?"

Bubba asked, "Was he making his payments on time?"

"Well," Beatrice replied, "I'm afraid I can't discuss the financial matters of my clients. Financial privacy, you know."

Newsome and Bubba looked at each other.

"Sure, I get it," Bubba said, "But, being that he's dead and all, I don't think dead guys have any right to financial privacy."

"Well, they do to me." Beatrice said, a little snippier than she intended, because she followed it with a rueful smile.

Newsome asked, "How about if we come back with a subpoena. Would that help?"

Beatrice stopped rocking.

"Well, then I guess I wouldn't have any choice, would I?"

All three fell into an awkward silence, then Beatrice looked out at the waiting van, and said, "If that's all, the van is waiting for me."

"Of course. Well, thank you for your time."

They stood up, but before the detectives could leave, Beatrice asked, "One question, Detective, if you don't mind."

Newsome turned and looked back at her.

"How was he killed?"

Newsome considered her request for a moment.

"We think he was poisoned. Antifreeze."

Beatrice turned and looked back out toward the street, away from the detectives, her cheeks turning red.

"That poor man," she said in a shaky voice.

"Beatrice," Bubba said, "you keep antifreeze on the property for any reason?"

Beatrice looked at him with surprise and declared with a giggle, "Are you kidding? Ain't no cars here, just mine, and I don't even pump my own gas!"

Newsome considered her a moment, then asked, "You know what? You have any objection to us having that chat with Luther Telfair?"

"Of course not. I'll fetch him, but remember, that van is on a schedule, so you'll only have a few minutes."

"Understood. Thanks a lot."

After Beatrice walked back inside, Bubba leaned in and muttered, "If this was just about anywhere else, I might be scratching out a search warrant to take a look around the place."

"You're damn right."

"Whatcha gonna ask the old chief? You think he knows anything?"

"Sounds like he's been holding out on us. He's old, but he's still po-lice, and po-lice don't keep secrets from po-lice. Something smells here, and I betcha he knows more than he's saying."

A moment later the screen door opened with a creak, and

THE BODY IN THE BED

Luther Telfair emerged. He looked Bubba up and down, turned to Newsome, then snorted, shoved his thumbs behind his suspenders, and whistled.

"Ya'll still here? What's Gilbert County's finest need from me?"

Newsome leaned against the side of the porch.

"Just figured we'd ask you a few questions."

Telfair grinned and said, "Hot diggity, a real live interrogation! Better make it fast, the van leaves for Macon in about three minutes. Whatcha got?"

"Well, I hear the vic and some of you guys liked to go hit the town, sneak out of the place and everything."

"Sneak? I'm eighty goddamn seven years old, I don't need to sneak nowhere!"

"Doesn't really answer my question, chief."

"I didn't really *hear* a question, sport."

"OK. Is it true that you and a group of others that included the victim used to go to bars together?"

"Decedent."

"What?"

"The decedent. As of right now, Earnest is the decedent. Ain't a victim unless you have a crime."

"I see. So, you don't think he was killed?"

"Don't matter what I think, sport."

Telfair looked down at his watch, then said, "Tick, tock!"

Newsome's cheeks colored, and he made a fist.

"Look, chief, you and Earnest and some old ladies hit the bars, is that right?"

"Imprecise, but I suppose so."

"Couple of ladies here fancied him, right?"

"I guess so."

"You think either of them had the stones to kill him? Maybe with antifreeze?"

Telfair nodded, then turned and gazed out on the lawn, chewing on his lip. Then he shuffled over to one of the rocking chairs and sat.

"I'll be damned. Maybe you two aren't a complete write off."

Telfair rocked for a moment, then turned back to Newsome.

"Ain't nobody here got a car, and we ain't got us a stray

cat problem. You hear what I'm sayin'?

"Right," Newsome said.

Telfair started rocking.

"You check the register? He have any visitors?"

"Nope," Bubba said.

"Hmph."

Telfair started rocking harder and chewing on his lower lip.

"Well, couldn't have been Myrtle or Bessie."

"How do you know?"

"I have my ways. It wasn't them. They'd kill each other if they had the chance, but not him."

"Then who you think did it? You know the drill, chief, it's love, sex, or money," Newsome said.

Telfair glanced at Newsome, and muttered, "True that." Then he shrugged.

"In this case, I'd say it was sex or money. But it wasn't either of them. Must've been someone else. Ernie was a player, you know. And jealousy's a bitch."

"Maybe someone at the bars you go to, maybe someone poisoned him there?"

Telfair shook his head and said, "Not a chance. He ain't been feeling too good the last few weeks. Pretty sure it was the cancer, not anything else. Besides, he hasn't been out with us for a long while."

"So, who would you put on your short list?"

"Well, nobody comes to mind. Listen, if they killed him with antifreeze, that was real up close and personal. That takes some detachment."

"Well," said Newsome, "I reckon it has to be one of these old folks, then. He ain't had no other visitors lately, at least not according to the register."

The three sat in silence a moment, then Telfair began the laborious process of getting out of the rocking chair.

"Well if you can't dig in on the sex angle, you need to start looking at money."

"Did he have any?" Bubba asked.

"Yessir, and he cut off his kids, before they blew through it all."

"Kids ain't been around here?"

"Last time one of them showed up was a while back, so

THE BODY IN THE BED

unless they hired someone, made it an inside job, it wasn't them."

The detectives and Telfair stood together a moment, each chewing on the facts. Telfair checked his watch just as the van driver started to blow his horn and yell, "Last call!"

"That's my cue. Good luck, fellas," he said. Then he added, "By the way, you check the financials here at the Sunset?"

Newsome glanced at Bubba.

"Not yet."

The screen door suddenly opened with a creak, and the Sunset's residents started their slow procession down the stairs toward the waiting van. Telfair fell into line behind them, and called out, "Well boys, the proof's in the paper. Should be the first thing you check in a case like this. Now I got me a bus to catch. See you at the funeral!"

JONATHAN B. ZEITLIN

CHAPTER ELEVEN

☩

Yvgeny had set his alarm on his iPhone to wake him around seven a.m. It was the theme song from the Adams Family, and it was programmed to get louder and louder until he reached over to turn it off.

Yvgeny grabbed the lip of his coffin and heaved himself up high enough to peer over the top and check his phone's display for the time. He turned back to Brianna, still asleep, and smiled. The Goliath brand Galaxy 52 incher was one of his floor models, and he had wheeled it in when he felt their relationship had sizzled to the point where she would tolerate it. It was the perfect size for when Brianna stayed the night: nice and snug, but roomy enough for them both to fit.

His mother barely even noticed the Galaxy's disappearance from the showroom. Brianna, however, noticed when it showed up in his parlor. The first time he suggested they share it, she flat refused, but over time she relented.

And why wouldn't she?

This Galaxy had a dove gray silk interior, sterling fittings, extra cushioning (added by Yvgeny to make it more comfortable for the living), custom paint job, and every upgrade available. It screamed high class! Brianna's final, last ditch attempt at avoidance was to say she was afraid of getting stuck inside, after which Yvgeny removed the sliding lock bar that was part of the sealing mechanism, leaving her without further objections to the new arrangements.

And the rest is history!

Yvgeny carefully extricated himself from the coffin without waking her, showered, and made coffee, and by the time Albert arrived at nine a.m. sharp, he was already dressed, caffeinated, and ready to go. He met Albert at the front door as he entered, and ushered him straight downstairs.

THE BODY IN THE BED

On the way down, Yvgeny said, "OK, Albert, I have great news. Today's the big funeral, right?"

Albert nodded eagerly.

"Well there's been a slight change, and it's an exciting one! Are you ready?"

"Of course! What is it?"

"The mannequin isn't going to work out. We need a live model. Someone I can trust; someone I know will be able to pull it off. I'll give you one guess who I think can pull it off."

The eager expression on Albert's face faded a bit, and his shoulders slumped.

"What's wrong?"

"Nothing. Well, it's just that, um -"

"Speak, man! We don't have a lot of time. All you have to do is lay there! Here's how it will work. You just climb in; we will shut the lid -"

Albert started to turn pale, and reached out to lean against the wall for support. Yvgeny watched his young understudy's reaction and cocked his head.

"You're claustrophobic, aren't you?"

Albert nodded, perspiration beading on his brow. They resumed heading down the hall and into the work room, where Yvgeny started pacing, then cursed under his breath. He turned back to his mannequin, inspected the damage again, and shook his head. When Albert saw the damage to the mannequin, he sucked in his breath in surprise.

We are out of time.

He closed his eyes and steepled his fingers together as if he was praying, trying to collect his thoughts. He looked out the small basement window that looked out on the cemetery. In the periphery of his view was the shed which served as home base for Alfred, and as Yvgeny watched, Alfred lumbered out, then grabbed his lower back and stretched.

Yvgeny got another idea.

Yvgeny put on his best smile and launched himself out the back door, leaving Albert standing in the middle of the room with a look of surprise. Then Yvgeny ran back inside, grabbed the mask from the mannequin, and while stuffing it in his coat, called out to Albert, "Come! Come! We only have a few hours!" and ran out of the room again.

Alfred saw them coming and narrowed his eyes,

suspicious. Yvgeny waited to make sure he was close enough for Alfred to be able to read his lips.

"My dear Alfred, we have a situation of the utmost importance, and I do believe you are the only one who can save the day!"

While Alfred processed the words, Yvgeny inspected Alfred's frame, sizing him up- height, weight.

Yes, he will do just fine. And he still has my suit!

"This afternoon is the Ledbetter funeral, you know."

Alfred nodded morosely.

"He was your friend, wasn't he?"

Alfred watched Yvgeny's lips moving, then nodded again, this time almost imperceptibly. Yvgeny smiled.

Yes, that's the angle.

"Well, my dear Alfred, there is something you could do for him. Consider it a parting gift, something that only you can give him. Would you like to hear about it?"

※

"Are we seriously going to that funeral?" Bubba asked.

"You got a better idea?"

Bubba stared out the window of his favorite morning haunt, a small coffee shop just down the street from the sheriff's department, succinctly called Cofee Donut. The owner, a very hard-working elderly Korean man, created his sign all by himself and refused to change it despite the misspelling. At Cofee Donut, cops got free coffee and half price donuts.

Newsome sipped his coffee and shrugged.

"Look, Geny's a psycho, but he made a good point. Chances are, the killer will be there. You know killers like to show up at funerals, right? Why would this be any different? And he's also right about the fact the killer's probably one of those senior citizens living there."

"I reckon," Bubba replied, but in a forlorn voice.

"So, it can't hurt to go sit in the back and keep an eye on things."

THE BODY IN THE BED

"You ever been to one of his funerals?"

"Hell no. You?"

"Once," Bubba said, then shook his head as he reflected on the experience. "A few years back, when that janitor died. Remember old man Cecil? The old janitor at Central High?"

Newsome smirked and said, "Of course. He was taking out the trash back when I was in school!"

"Yeah. He died five or six years ago. He was a good old dude."

"So Geny did the funeral."

"Yup. It was a nightmare."

"You were there?" Newsome asked.

"Yeah. Figured I'd drop in. Saw it in the newspaper. Said anyone that went to Central was welcome to stop by."

"So why was it a nightmare?"

Bubba shifted in his seat, swigged the last of his coffee, then shoved a few napkins into the bottom of the cup and reached for his Copenhagen.

"He got some band kids from Central to play a bunch of weird songs. Like, I'm talking ninth graders here. Then, he opened the lid of the coffin."

Bubba paused, then shivered.

"Poor Cecil. He wasn't wearing no suit or nothing. He was in his work clothes, you know, that dark blue shirt with that patch with his name on it and everything. He had a broom in one hand and a mop in the other, crossed over his chest, you know, like one of them Egyptian mummies. I mean, what the hell?"

Newsome just stared at Bubba, his mouth open.

"Then, afterwards, him and his mother laid out snacks for everyone. Cheetos, Fritos, chips and dip, Little Debbies, and fruit punch. It was more like a seven-year old's birthday party than a funeral. I'm telling you, it was just weird."

Newsome shrugged and said, "Well, maybe he's upped his game since then. Unless you have a better idea. We can always go back to Sunset Manor and spend the whole day there interviewing people."

Bubba sat a moment, then spit into his coffee cup and said, "Guess we're going to another funeral."

"You must have been so close with Earnest. Dear Earnest, may God rest his soul."

Yvgeny advanced slowly on Alfred, speaking in a soothing, calming voice, like a dog catcher, knowing Alfred couldn't hear him but doing it just the same.

"I bet he would have done anything for you. Such a bond you two had. Isn't that right?"

Alfred's eyes darted left and right, frantic, realizing too late he was entangled in another of Yvgeny's webs. He nodded, and it was a quick movement, but enough for Yvgeny."

"And look at you now, you have the chance to take care of your dear friend, do him one last favor, a present for Ernie before he disappears for good. You want to do that, you want to help him, don't you, Alfred?"

Again, the tentative nod.

Yvgeny's hands had been clasped behind his back as he advanced, and finally, once he was merely inches away, Alfred's back against the wall of his shed, he leaned in and produced the mask.

"Earnest needs you. Do it for him, Alfred, do it for Ernie."

Alfred shook his head, his eyes wide, staring at the mask.

"Let's just try it on, make sure it fits."

Yvgeny stretched out the mask a bit, careful not to make the rip on the cheek any worse, then slowly lifted it over Alfred's head. Alfred held his breath as it went on, then let it out in a whoosh. Yvgeny fiddled with it for a few moments, then took a step back. Yvgeny did not know his age, but Alfred was probably a little younger than Earnest, with a fuller face, making the mask, and thus Earnest's face, a little misshapen. Earnest's pointy nose hung off Alfred's, making him look like a distorted Cyrano de Bergerac.

"Hmm. Nothing that can't be adjusted, just a nip and tuck, here and there. Fantastic, Alfred, fantastic! I'm sure dear Ernie is smiling down on you right now."

Yvgeny checked his watch, then clucked his tongue. He turned to Albert and motioned for him to follow, then led Alfred away from the shed and into the mid-morning sun.

THE BODY IN THE BED

"Come, come, no time to wait!"

Alfred shuffled his feet like a condemned man on his way to the gallows, Yvgeny pushing him along, Albert trailing behind, his brow still glistening with sweat from his fear of having to climb into a coffin.

Pushing through the back door, they took the stairs slowly, forced to follow Alfred's plodding gait. Once they returned upstairs, they found Yvgeny's mother in the kitchen putting away dishes. She was unsteady on her feet, and when she heard them approach, she spun around and almost lost her balance.

After she recovered, she glanced over at the clock on the wall, then sized the three men up and down. With a humph, she said, "Better late than never, right, my little *tygrysek*?"

"There's no time for your theatrics today, Mama."

His mother turned her attention to Alfred, still wearing the mask.

"And what the hell happened to Earnest? He was white, you know."

"Would you like a reminder of why Alfred has to wear this mask? And it has to be Alfred; my dear boy here suffers from claustrophobia. I can't stuff him into a coffin for three hours pretending to be dead."

His mother stared at Albert, then Alfred, then with another "humph!" she turned around and picked up the teapot.

"Oh, and, Mama, considering you destroyed the suit I was going to put on Earnest, perhaps you could clean up the one Alfred's been wearing.

Mama didn't turn around, but let out a much more muted "humph."

"Come now, Alfred, we may get some guests early, we must be ready. And Mama, is the karaoke guy coming?"

Without turning from her teapot, she called out, "What, you don't trust your mother to set things up? She doesn't know how to do her job? Do you think I'm incompetent?"

She poured her tea, then with her mug in one hand and her cane in the other, she shuffled toward the door, a few drops of tea spilling over the top with each step. She continued muttering to herself the entire time. Yvgeny waited for her to leave, then turned to Albert.

"Come now, Albert, let's go get set up. Alfred, take Mama

my suit, and meet us in the work room in ten minutes. Hurry!"

Alfred retrieved the suit, left it with Mama, then joined Albert and Yvgeny downstairs.

The first order of business was for Yvgeny to address the damage to the mask. Latex was fairly easy for him to work with, so repairing the rip was easy. The more difficult part was making the mask look right on Alfred. Alfred and Ernie had very different features, different head circumference, pretty much different everything. Working with some clay and some extra latex, Yvgeny arranged the mask on Alfred's head and got to work. By the time he was finished, it looked almost as convincing as it did on the mannequin.

The next step was makeup. Some of the angles had changed slightly, so the makeup requirements also had to be modified. After perfecting the face, Yvgeny turned to the neck, using a special foundation product to make Alfred's neck into that of an elderly white man.

Albert paid close attention to Yvgeny's ministrations as he stood over Alfred with his makeup brush, inspecting his face carefully from various angles. An hour went by in the snap of one's fingers, and just as Mama returned with a freshly pressed suit, Yvgeny and Albert stood over Alfred, inspecting every inch of Alfred's face and neck, carefully, with a critical eye.

"It's a masterpiece," Yvgeny breathed.

They assisted Alfred in carefully putting on the suit, then escorted him over to the corner, where Yvgeny had placed the coffin into which Alfred would be climbing. It was a highly polished wood, and had a lower and upper lid, like a horizontal version of the Dutch doors leading into Yvgeny's kitchen.

Alfred's pace slowed as he approached the coffin, requiring a little extra coaxing from Yvgeny, but eventually he got Alfred safely settled into the coffin. Once inside, Yvgeny had to make some minor adjustments to the tuxedo to accommodate the fake hands.

"OK Albert, let's go check on preparations. We need to get the chairs set up and make sure Mama has the bouquets all ready."

Yvgeny turned toward the coffin and looked in to make

THE BODY IN THE BED

sure Alfred could see his face, then said, "Alfred, just relax, we'll be right back."

╬

Yvgeny and Albert returned to the main floor just as Brianna and Jezelda arrived in Jezelda's BMW. Yvgeny held the door as the two walked into Schmidt's, each with an armload of things, which they placed on a table unobtrusively staged in the rear corner of the room. Yvgeny checked his watch, then looked outside toward the street; the van carrying the occupants of Sunset Manor had likely already deposited its payload at the mall. They had time, but they couldn't afford to dawdle. Given the number of setbacks in preparing for this funeral, Yvgeny needed to build in even more time to accommodate any unexpected problems.

In the back of the room was a pile of white plastic folded chairs. Yvgeny started arranging them in rows, with Albert watching and copying his every move. Yvgeny's mother tottered back and forth between the kitchen and the parlor, griping at the caterers. Every time she returned to the parlor, she looked disapprovingly at Yvgeny's rows of chairs, then adjusted one or two of them. When one of the caterers stopped working for even a moment, she stopped whatever she was doing and, with a practiced glare, forced them back into action. After a while, they scurried away whenever she entered the room.

"You gonna have any music? It's quiet as a cemetery in here," Jezelda whispered to Brianna.

Brianna looked around, then shrugged.

"Apparently some guy at Sunset Manor thinks he sounds like Sinatra. He's bringing a karaoke machine."

On the table, Jezelda had spread out a red velvet cloth, upon which she placed a red candle, a black candle, and a bowl. Next to the bowl she laid a pair of longish wooden sticks, and a chicken's leg with a braided rope around the end.

"What goes in the bowl?"

Jezelda took a flask from her purse and dribbled the contents into the bowl. Then she took a pull from the flask and handed it to Brianna with a wink.

Brianna took a swig and returned the flask. Then she wiped at her brow and cursed softly.

"Jesus, it's hot in here."

Yvgeny's mother entered the room again, in the middle of delivering a pointed rebuke at one of the catering staff. As she shuffled past, Brianna interrupted her to ask about the air conditioning. Mama raised one eyebrow and said, "It's the best we have, dear. Why don't you go and open a window."

Brianna sighed, then turned and opened a couple of the windows, the screens long ago rotted away.

Mama straightened some of the chairs he had just staged. As she turned to hobble back into the kitchen, Yvgeny stopped her.

"Mama, where are the flowers?"

Mama pointed toward the kitchen.

"And how are the caterers?"

Mama rolled her eyes and glanced behind her toward the kitchen.

"Well, by now they've probably stuffed half our good silver into their pockets. But the food is coming along. Relax, my *tygrysek*, you have bigger things to worry about."

Just then, a brown Ford Taurus pulled into the driveway. Newsome and Bubba remained inside for a while with the engine running, engaged in a conversation. Brianna noticed the movement from the open window and returned to Jezelda, muttering, "Great, the cops are here."

Jezelda shrugged and said, "Da man be murdered and the cops be looking for the killer. Just like me."

"Humph," Brianna said.

Yvgeny also saw them coming, and turned to Albert.

"Albert, it's about time; let's go prepare the body."

Just as they left, the detectives finally emerged from their car and approached the entrance.

When Yvgeny and Albert walked into the work room, they found Alfred staring at himself in a mirror, shoulders slumped.

"What are you doing out?" Yvgeny asked.

When Alfred saw Yvgeny behind him in the reflection, he

THE BODY IN THE BED

looked glumly toward the coffin, then turned toward the door.

Yvgeny noticed and nonchalantly placed himself between Alfred and the door to prevent any escape attempt. Finally, Alfred accepted his fate and walked over to the coffin, head down, and climbed inside.

"Albert, fetch me the hands, they're over there beside the lunchbox."

Albert cooed in awe when he saw Yvgeny's work on the hands. He returned them to Yvgeny, who laid them on Alfred's abdomen as Alfred stared at the ceiling, holding his breath. Yvgeny inspected one of the hands, then walked over to his desk and rifled through a few drawers until he found what he was looking for.

Returning to Alfred, he held a popsicle stick over his face and explained, "Alfred, I'll need you to hold on to these, ok?"

Yvgeny carefully tried to shove a popsicle stick into the base of the first hand. The base had a slot built into it for mounting, but the slot was just a little too small. It took some effort, but eventually, Yvgeny was able to insert the stick, leaving enough of it protruding for Alfred to grab. He then duplicated his effort with the other hand.

Yvgeny the popsicle sticks and hands to Alfred, one at a time.

"OK Alfred, here you go. Wait, wrong hand!"

Yvgeny took the first hand from Alfred and replaced it in Alfred's other hand. Once Alfred had both hands, Yvgeny arranged the tuxedo and shirt so that it minimized the improper dimensions of the arms.

Yvgeny stood again, carefully inspecting his handiwork.

"Albert, what do you think?"

"Makes his arms look a little too long."

"Exactly. Nothing we can do about it. If we keep the bottom door closed, it will make it less obvious."

Yvgeny took a step back and studied Alfred in the coffin. Then, with a slow nod, he called out, "Perfectamente!"

"And with time to spare!" Albert added.

"Yes, yes," Yvgeny responded, glancing at his watch.

Leaning against the lower door, Yvgeny smiled down at Alfred and said, "OK Alfred, just a few more minutes before the party starts. Now, usually, I like to seal the coffin and spring it open at the last minute for effect, but given you're still breathing, I will leave the top cracked open a couple inches. Albert, come see, don't you just love the peek-a-boo doors?"

Yvgeny slowly eased down the lower door, but he only made it half-way when Alfred began to mumble and struggled to sit up. Alarmed, Yvgeny rushed forward to block him.

"Alfred, what are you doing?"

Alfred struggled just a little, mumbling incoherently.

"Alfred, don't tell me you're afraid of small spaces, too. It's a little late in the game to turn back now."

Alfred slumped, but did not struggle further. He glumly accepted his fate as Yvgeny eased down the lower door over Alfred's legs.

"You're going to be fine, Alfred. Now remember, don't open your eyes, don't do anything crazy. You're supposed to be dead!"

Yvgeny started to lower the top door, but, as promised, left it cracked open several inches. Yvgeny could hear Alfred's respiration increase, as if he had dove into icy waters.

The coffin was on a large cart with heavy casters, and Yvgeny turned the cart around and started pushing it toward the doors. He leaned in and whispered, "Now, Alfred, you know there will be a graveside service. But don't worry, we won't bury you."

Alfred stared at Yvgeny in horror.

"We will lower you down, maybe let Bessie and Myrtle toss a shovel or two of dirt on top, and call it a day."

Alfred began to struggle again, and in a shrill voice, said, "Nng! Nngh ng ngh!"

Yvgeny stopped in the hallway and drummed his fingers against the top of the coffin for a moment. Albert cocked his head, then asked, "What's wrong, Mr. Geny?"

"Well," Yvgeny said, "Alfred has a point. I have to seal the coffin to drop it in the hole, but if I seal it, he won't be able to breathe very long. I'm going to have to get him out of it before we take it out to the cemetery."

Yvgeny thought for a moment, then turned back to Alfred. He cranked the door up so Alfred could read his lips.

"Tell you what: after the service, I'll wheel you back out to

THE BODY IN THE BED

the hall, let you get out and run downstairs, then we'll bury it empty. You just have to make sure nobody sees you getting out. How does that sound?"

Alfred processed what Yvgeny said, then nodded.

"Now relax," Yvgeny said, in a soothing tone, "you don't want to mess up the makeup."

Yvgeny lowered the door again, and they pushed him over to a coffin sized elevator. While Alfred went up the elevator, Albert and Yvgeny bounded up the stairs two at a time to meet him on top and open the elevator doors.

Fetching his tall hat from the parlor, Yvgeny turned and checked his appearance in the mirror, then turned and faced Albert. He studied the boy from head to toe, then nodded his head. Albert did not own a suit and was too small to borrow one of Yvgeny's Victorian masterpieces, so he chose black jeans and a white cotton Oxford.

"Splendid, my boy."

Yvgeny pulled his shoulders back, held his head high, and glided into the room.

It's go time!

The Sunset van had just arrived, and was coming to a stop in the driveway. Beatrice was the first to climb down the steps onto the grass, then she turned to inspect the grounds, hands on her hips.

Once she was satisfied with whatever concerned her, she turned and waved at the van, and the Sunset crew started unloading. First off, and first at the door to Schmidt's, was Wally Beaverton, who clutched the banister and slowly eased his way up the steps, careful not to rub his white tuxedo against the wall of the mortuary. One of his lady friends had tied his bowtie a little lopsided, and his cummerbund hung a little loosely around his waist. He made it inside, adjusted his bottle bottom glasses, then made his way through the rows of chairs Yvgeny had arranged. He looked around carefully, then pointed toward a corner of the room, turned, and called out, "Put it here, Danny!"

Danny was an orderly at Sunset Manor, and was second off the van, lugging Wally's equipment. At his command, Danny brought forth Wally's karaoke machine. Around his shoulder was a bag containing the cords, the microphone, and Wally's little black book containing all the words to all his favorite songs. Nodding his head at Wally, Danny lifted the handle and rolled the karaoke machine in the direction of Wally's pointed finger, then began setting everything up.

The detectives had posted themselves outside to scrutinize everyone. Bubba shifted his weight from one foot to the next, occasionally turning to spit in the bushes. Bubba watched the group disembark from the van and file into Schmidt's, then turned to Newsome and said, "Bunch of geriatrics, Newsome. You really think there's a killer here?"

"Don't know, Bubba, but unless you got a better idea, this is all we got."

Bubba shifted his weight, and then started scratching one calf with the toe of his other boot.

"Antifreeze. I mean, hell, could've been a big accident."

"Sure, Bubba. Maybe they were out of sugar, so he used antifreeze in his coffee. Happens all the time."

"Well, I'm just sayin' –"

"No, what you're sayin' is that you were so freaked out by the last funeral here that you got some kind of complex about it. Jesus, Bubba, I ain't never seen you like this!"

Bubba turned and spit again. Then he turned to Newsome.

"Look, you know I just had a birthday."

Newsome smirked and said, "Well, happy birthday. I'll bake you a cake."

"It was the big four zero."

"OK. Congratulations?"

Bubba turned and spit again.

"No. Point is, ever since I turned forty, I can't stand being around old people. Old folks' homes, funerals, dead people in general, they all just creep me out."

Bubba looked off into space, took a deep breath, then spit again.

"Can't explain it."

Newsome looked at Bubba a moment, then said, "You're serious."

"Yup."

Newsome looked away, thoughtful for a moment, then said, "Hit me like that when I turned fifty, but it didn't last more than a day or two. You can't go around feeling sorry for yourself, it's just a freakin' number."

"I know. Like I said, I can't explain it."

THE BODY IN THE BED

"Well, try to keep it together, Bubba, we got us a murder to solve."

After everyone else had climbed off the van, the Right Honorable Luther P. Telfair gingerly stepped down off the van and onto the driveway. He stuck his thumbs behind his suspenders and snapped them when he saw the detectives.

"Well, lookie there, you two hot dogs showing up at the funeral, gonna catch you some killers!"

"Afternoon, Luther. You're awfully revved up today."

"Yessir, had me one of them damn big ass cinnamon rolls at the mall. More sugar in that thing than a dozen hookers at a Navy yard!"

Luther snorted loudly a couple times, then turned and spit a large amount of phlegm onto the sidewalk.

The three stared at each other a moment, Luther pulling at his suspenders, Bubba kicking at the dirt.

"So, you get that subpoena?"

"Working on it."

"Working on it? Damn, whatcha waiting for?"

The detectives remained silent, but Telfair wasn't finished.

"So, whatcha gonna do? You got some leads? You get a warrant for the Sunset? You gonna search the place?"

"Sorry Luther, that's all classified," Newsome said dryly.

"Classified, my ass! This here's a murder! Ain't no terrorist plot!"

Before the detectives could respond, Beatrice poked her head out the door and called out, "Luther, get on in here, it's about to start!"

Luther, grinning broadly, turned back to the detectives and said, "Well, come on, hot dogs, you don't wanna miss the show!"

Inside, the elderly visitors began taking their seats. Wally was fiddling with the knobs on his karaoke machine, and Jezelda was busy in the back with Brianna. Yvgeny had left a gap in the chair staging to create a pathway straight through the center of the room, and he and Albert wheeled Alfred and his coffin through that pathway. They set him up in front beside the dais where Yvgeny would emcee the event. He raised up the top lid, then looked inside to make sure Alfred looked dead. Satisfied, Yvgeny stood directly in front of it just in case one of the old people got too close. He didn't want to take any chances.

A living person can only play dead for so long.

As the visitors approached Yvgeny to try to get a glimpse of old Ernie Ledbetter, Yvgeny did his best to block their view. Every time he had a free moment, he turned to check the makeup, and to make sure Alfred was remaining immobile.

So far so good.

Two more old ladies approached, deep in conversation, and Yvgeny smiled as they passed. Being hard of hearing, they both spoke much louder than they realized.

"Oh, Margaret, Hank died the same way, remember? That poor, poor man. One day he's fine, then suddenly he had those awful headaches, then, oh dear, do you remember the filth that came out of his mouth, like he was a sailor! Such foul language! Downright loony, he started acting, then smack! That's it!"

The lady accentuated her point by clapping her hands as she shouted, "Smack!" Her friend made the sign of the cross over her chest.

The driver of the van came in, pushing a wheelchair containing the eternally smiling woman Yvgeny remembered from the Sunset. He parked her toward the end of the middle row so as not to disturb any of the chairs.

"Test, test, test."

Old Wally started tapping a finger against his microphone, then carefully crouched down to fiddle with his knobs again. Yvgeny turned one more time to inspect Alfred, and found him slack-jawed, fast asleep. He quickly faced the crowd, then, while leaning back with his fist and rapping at the side of the coffin. Glancing back at Alfred, he found him still asleep.

He tried, as nonchalantly as possible, to lift his foot and softly donkey kick the coffin. A few guests in the front row looked at him strangely, but soon forgot about it once Wally got their attention. Finally, Alfred opened his eyes and smacked his lips a couple times.

"Alfred! For Heaven's sake don't go to sleep! You start snoring, you're going to give these old ladies a heart attack! Remember, you're dead!"

Alfred nodded just enough for Yvgeny to see it.

After a few more taps on the microphone, Wally looked

THE BODY IN THE BED

over at Yvgeny and nodded. Yvgeny, hands clasped behind him, approached Wally and took the microphone from his hand.

"Ladies and Gentlemen, dearly beloved, we are gathered here to pay our final respects to our dear friend, Earnest Ledbetter."

Both Myrtle and Bessie immediately began to sob. Luther put his arm around Myrtle, who curled into him and wept into his shoulder. Luther continued watching Yvgeny, smiling broadly and showing off all his teeth.

Jezelda grabbed her chicken leg from the table, dipped it in the bowl of liquid, then placed it around her neck. Gingerly grabbing her rods, she crossed them, faced them down, and quietly staged herself in the back corner of the room. As Yvgeny addressed the crowd, she held them out before her and started to walk along the outskirts of the back row, pointing her sticks at the back of each guest's head, pausing briefly, then moving on. One after the other, she shifted behind the crowd.

Yvgeny made a prune face as he watched her work, annoyed by the constant distraction. As he continued his speech, Jezelda moved on to the next row, this time crossing the rods in an "X" pattern and rattling them around behind each guest. Those in the back row, now able to see what she was doing, watched her carefully, then exchanged confused glances.

Yvgeny's mother remained in the doorway leading to the kitchen and was also following Jezelda's movements, but hers was more of a disapproving glare. She punctuated her glare every few minutes by turning around and peeking through the doorway to check on the caterers.

Bubba and Newsome also posted themselves in the rear, close to the doorway to the kitchen. Newsome studied the crowd, looking for clues, but Bubba was too distracted, staring at his shoes and scratching at his arms. His continued nervous fidgeting finally drew the ire of Newsome, who first turned to inspect Bubba; then, with a smirk, he leaned in and whispered, "Hey, Bubba. Take a look up there. I think I just saw that dead guy in the coffin move. Wait- yup, he did it again. Ooohh!"

Bubba's eyes widened, then darted to and fro, anywhere

except toward the front where the coffin was staged. Then he leaned in and hissed, "Shut up, Newsome. Just wait, this is going to give you nightmares." Then, under his breath, he added, "Just like with Cecil."

Newsome, having cast his bait, began reeling it in.

"Hey Bubba, did you know back in the old days, undertakers buried people facing down, just in case they came back to life, you know, they'd start clawing their way out, but the joke was on them, they were just digging themselves further into the hole!"

Bubba took a deep breath, then kicked Newsome in his shin.

"You ain't funny, Newsome!"

"I wonder if your buddy Geny over there buries 'em face up or face down. Whatcha think?"

Bubba gave Newsome a withering stare, then moved away from him, taking a post by Jezelda's table. Newsome watched him leave, chuckling to himself. Bubba leaned against the table, but he leaned too much and scraped the table a couple inches across the wood floors. One of the candles knocked over, extinguishing the flame in its own wax. Luckily, none of the guests heard the noise, as they were all focused on Yvgeny. Bubba straightened the candle while Jezelda continued shaking her sticks at the back of the guests' heads.

"And now, I give you the caramel voice of your beloved Wally Beaverton. Hit it, Wally!"

There was a brief feedback squeal as Wally fired up the karaoke machine, then the music started. It was a classic hit from none other than 'Ol Blue Eyes himself. While the audience sat, transfixed by Wally's voice, Yvgeny turned to inspect Alfred one more time. Alfred had been looking up at the ceiling, and the moment he sensed movement from Yvgeny, he squinched his eyes shut. Then he cautiously opened one eye.

"Caught you, you rascal! Now, no more playing around, once the eulogy is over, they're going to start filing up. *Kapisch*?"

Alfred nodded, almost imperceptibly.

Newsome and Bubba both saw Yvgeny lean in toward the coffin. Smirking again, Newsome walked over to Bubba and

THE BODY IN THE BED

leaned in close.

"Hey Bubba, you see that? Geny's talking to the dead guy. You think Ernie's talking back?"

Bubba clenched his jaw and looked back down at his shoes. He fumbled in his back pocket for his tin of Copenhagen.

Beatrice had taken a seat in the front row, next to two empty chairs upon which Yvgeny had left placards with *Family* written upon them with a Sharpie. Jezelda had worked her way up to the first row, waggling her sticks at each guest. She posted herself behind Beatrice and started working. She stopped, cocked her head, then started moving the in a different pattern. After about a minute, Beatrice turned to give her a dirty look. Jezelda finally moved on.

Wally's voice trailed off as the song came to an end. One elderly woman in the back row yelled "Bravo!" and began clapping, but stopped when she realized no-one else had joined her.

"Dear friends and family, let this not be a day of suffering, but a day of rejoicing, a day of celebration of the life of this man."

As he began his speech, Yvgeny waved a hand behind him, toward the casket. Inside the casket, Alfred was fighting the urge to scratch his arm. He took a risk and cracked open one of his eyes. Seeing no-one standing over him, he decided to scratch it, but then realized his hands were holding popsicle sticks attached to two fake wax hands. He took a deep breath, then let go of one of the sticks, pushed the hand out of the jacket sleeve, then satisfied his itch. Then he grabbed the stick again and pulled his fake hand back into the sleeve.

No sooner did he scratch one arm then his other arm itched. He reversed hands and repeated the process. Finally, he sighed and shut his eyes.

Unfortunately, relieving his itches only stimulated his nerve endings elsewhere. His face started to itch, then his arms again. He let loose of both fake hands and scratched his face, his arms, his leg. In the process, one of the hands slid to the side and got lodged in between his thigh and the coffin. He struggled to retrieve it, careful not to rock the coffin.

Finally, he recovered the hand, but then his face started to feel like it was on fire. He began to wonder what kind of makeup Yvgeny had used.

Am I having an allergic reaction?

He scratched and scratched, then froze. He worried about whether he was scratching off the makeup.

Alfred began to panic.

What will I do? What if they see brown skin?

"In a moment, I will ask you to come approach the casket and wish your dear friend Ernie a *bon voyage*. And as you will see, he's the picture of health. That's what you can expect when you come here, to Schmidt and Sons Mortuary. I'm sure you've all heard our industry pledge:

If you're dead and gone and stuck on ice,
Schmidt and Sons will make you look nice,
Full package funerals at one low price!"

Yvgeny paused a moment so his jingle had full effect, then continued.

"Now then, I'll be passing out cards that will give you a 10% discount, but first, Wally has one more song to strum on your heartstrings, followed by a brief but tasteful eulogy by one of his dear friends, Luther P. Telfair."

As Wally burst into another old Sinatra song, Newsome watched Jezelda. She had returned to her table, shooed Bubba away, and started fiddling with her chicken leg. Newsome pursed his lips.

What a phony, he mouthed silently at Bubba.

Newsome grew up on a farm, and he remembered his Daddy coming home at night, dusty and dirty from working his fields. His Daddy used to tell him stories about his crazy Uncle Jocephus who believed in dowsing rods. The farmers in his time used to walk around with two sticks crossed together, and the sticks would tell them where to dig to find water. Total hocus pocus.

He slowly wandered toward the front, posting himself in a position where he could see everyone's faces. His eyes narrowed. He looked for something out of place, anything that didn't seem right. He tried to pay attention to body language, to expressions, strange behavior.

I got nothing.

He turned toward Bubba, relieved to see he had finally

THE BODY IN THE BED

gotten back into the game and was also desperately trying to find the needle in their haystack. Newsome sighed.

This is a total waste of time.

Yvgeny, still standing before the crowd, was conducting his own survey. It was a sea of pale, white haired, heavily medicated octogenarians. Toward the back was his beloved Brianna, and toward the front, Beatrice. He watched Jezelda return to her station in the back, apparently having struck out. He also saw Newsome in front studying the crowd, Bubba in back doing the same thing. Their body language said it all.

This is a total waste of time.

Just as Newsome abandoned all interest and turned to get Bubba's attention, the atmosphere changed, ever so slightly.

A very large bumblebee buzzed into the window Brianna had opened and buzzed around toward the crowd. Some of the old ladies removed their Sunday church hats and began waving them at the bee and swooning with anxiety. The activity distracted Bubba and Newsome from their worries, and both started to follow the dive bombing with a smirk on their faces.

Wally, somehow thinking all the activity was directed toward him, sang even more loudly, with more feeling. He stuck his microphone a little too close to his mouth, and Yvgeny winced at the resulting feedback whine from the karaoke machine. Yvgeny maintained his composure, though, at least until the bumblebee made a beeline toward the coffin.

Don't land, don't land, don't land.

As Yvgeny, Newsome, and Bubba watched, the bumblebee initiated a downward spiral straight into the open lid of the coffin. Yvgeny froze.

Being a deaf mute, Alfred's other senses compensated for his lack of hearing; he would have sensed the bee buzzing around his face. However, behind the mask, and with his hands hidden beneath his specially tailored sleeves, he didn't notice anything, at least not until the bee landed on his cheek. The landing was enough to get his attention, even from underneath a layer of makeup and latex, and he jerked his face to one side. This movement scared the bee, which did exactly what scared bees do.

JONATHAN B. ZEITLIN

A moment later, the coffin began to buck to and fro. There was a gasp from the front row, then another. Yvgeny tried to stabilize the coffin, but Alfred started groaning and climbing out.

"Nng! Ng Nghh ng ngh!"

Alfred struggled to get out of the coffin, then swatted at the bee with one of his wax hands. He moved too quickly, and the hand came loose from the popsicle stick and flew across the room and into the lap of an elderly woman, who looked down at the body part in her lap and immediately fainted.

Alfred had dropped the other hand to the floor and was clutching his cheek in pain, using his own brown hand. Beneath the mask, his face was already swollen from the sting, and his swatting at his own face had re-opened the break on the other side of the mask, causing his brown skin to show there, too.

Two more old ladies in the front row fell forward, having fainted from the frightful scene. Another stood and began quoting Leviticus. A few more were screaming their lungs out. Bessie, a little tipsy from lunch at the mall, struggled to her feet and tried to run toward Alfred, yelling, "Ernie it's me! Bessie!"

Suddenly the old smiling woman in the wheelchair sprang to life and yelled, "She's a real whore!"

In the middle of it all, Luther Telfair sat transfixed, a smile on his face, as if he was at the movies.

Alfred started angrily yanking on the bottom lid to get his legs free. He struggled so hard that he fell sideways and over, then oozed out like an inchworm, landing on the floor. Still groaning, he climbed back to his feet and lurched toward Yvgeny.

"Nng ng! Nggh ngh ng!"

Alfred reached out with one arm toward Yvgeny. Behind Yvgeny, and unbeknownst to him, Jezelda was approaching fast.

"In the name of *Baron Samedi*, release this soul!" cried Jezelda. She held a small spade, as if she was on her way to plant some tulips. She began waving the spade in a circle toward Alfred.

"*Papa Ghede*, hear my prayer! Tell *Baron Samedi* to release

THE BODY IN THE BED

this man!"

Yvgeny noticed Beatrice staring open mouthed in horror at the spectacle. Then, collecting her wits, she stood slowly and fled from the room. As she turned, she almost knocked over his mother, who was shuffling toward Alfred as fast as she could, her walking stick clacking against the wooden floors. While Alfred stood, alternating between reaching out toward Yvgeny and clutching at his face, Mama lifted her walking cane high above her head, then brought it crashing down on Alfred.

"Why won't you just DIE!"

Alfred almost lost his footing from the blow, then let out a wail like a wolf howling, then resumed rending at his mask, and finally removed enough of it for Mama to realize it was him. She took a step back and fell into the empty chair marked *Family*. Jezelda stopped in mid-chant, cocked her head, and then called out in a small voice, "Alfred, that be you?"

By the time things calmed down, most of the residents of Sunset Manor had already climbed into the van. Still in his chair, Luther shook his head and started clapping his hands.

"Bravo! Bravo! Best show I've seen in years!"

As Telfair's clapping wound to a halt, Newsome turned to Bubba to tell him something, but was surprised to see he had vanished. Newsome started looking around and found him huddled under one of the tables in the back of the room.

"Unbelievable," Newsome muttered. Bubba sheepishly crawled out from beneath the table and stood quickly as if nothing had happened, brushing down his pants. Trying to model nonchalance, he staged next to Newsome and stuck his thumbs in his pants pockets. Newsome, disgusted, turned back toward Yvgeny.

"So, what's next? Dancing zombies? Maybe your voodoo priestess here can stab a few Geny dolls, see if they work?"

Yvgeny pursed his lips. Behind the detectives, he saw Albert approaching, a look of concern on his face. Before Albert could make it to Yvgeny, both Myrtle and Bessie pushed Albert and the two detectives aside and confronted him.

"Where's the *real* Earnest?" Bessie demanded.

"What have you done with him?" Myrtle inquired, then

turned to inspect the coffin.

"It's complicated, ladies. He's at the GBI. It's now an official murder investigation."

The change in the old women was immediate, anger and anxiety melting into sadness and dejection. Forgetting their hatred for each other, the two wandered off together, the wind having been taken from their sails. Albert turned to watch them leave, then approached Yvgeny.

"Mr. Geny, Mr. Geny, what happened?"

"Ah, long story, my boy," Yvgeny said, wrapping his arm around Albert's shoulders and leading him away from the cops. After one more sidelong glance toward the detectives, he turned and leaned into Albert and whispered, "Change in plans. I need you to leave the coffin here. Maybe you can go help Alfred get changed."

"What about the gravesite service?"

"I'll explain later," said Yvgeny, "but there's not going to be a field trip to the gravesite after all."

Yvgeny's original intent was to have the service, let a few people shovel in some dirt, then when everyone left, haul out the coffin and put it back on display. When and if he got the real Earnest back, he would just cremate him.

Why waste a perfectly good coffin?

Now, with the cat out of the bag, there was no need even to pretend.

"Alfred should have placed the marker already." Yvgeny glanced back at the two detectives, then leaned in to Albert again.

"I want you two to fill in the hole. If anyone asks, just tell them it's unsafe to leave an open grave. Tell them we will just dig the hole again when we get Earnest back."

Albert nodded, then approached a battered and bruised Alfred, who was leaning against the wall holding his hand over his cheek. Yvgeny watched Albert lead Alfred away, then called out, "and get the man some ice!"

"Thought maybe we'd get some leads here," Newsome said dryly. "Wasn't expecting a show like that."

"Well, inspector, sorry to disappoint. Now, if you'll excuse me, the show must go on."

"Boyo boyo boy, that was a doozie!"

The detectives and Yvgeny all turned at once to find old

THE BODY IN THE BED

man Luther Telfair watching them.

"Chief, the public part of this show is over," Yvgeny muttered.

Telfair glanced out the window and saw the Sunset Manor van backing out into the street, then the driver put it in gear and floored it. Telfair shrugged his shoulders and turned back to the detectives.

"Well, missed my ride. Guess I'll hang around a bit."

Suddenly the front door burst open and a slightly disheveled and irritated Beatrice walked in. In the background, they could hear two women screaming at each other. Beatrice turned and glared at Telfair.

"You'd best get out here and settle this once and for all! Those two are at it again like a couple of school girls. I had to send the bus on without us. I do declare, this is ridiculous!"

Telfair thumbed his suspenders out and let them smack against his chest. He leered at the two detectives and said, "Duty calls!"

The door shut behind him, and soon after, Yvgeny heard the staccato sound of Telfair's whistle. Newsome walked toward a window to watch. Then he snorted.

"Those two are going at it! Hey Bubba, maybe you should get out there and help the old man out."

Bubba looked over Newsome's shoulder and out the window, horrified. He whispered, "Jesus, Mary, and Joseph!" then high-tailed out the door. Beatrice straightened her hair with her hands, then sat heavily into one of Yvgeny's folding chairs and began to fan herself with a Sunset Manor pamphlet she retrieved from her handbag.

"Well, Geny, you sure know how to throw a party," Newsome said, deadpan.

"I'm gonna go to the grave site, maybe the soul of the man will speak to me."

Jezelda had gathered her belongings into a fringed backpack and had approached the group, holding a napkin filled with snacks from the snack table.

"What happened to your islander accent, snake charmer?"

"Stick it, hole digger."

Yvgeny smiled grimly, then shrugged. "Look, there's not going to be a graveside service. Obviously, there's no body."

Jezelda chewed on her lip for a moment, then shrugged.

"That don't mean the man's soul ain't out there, looking for a place to rest!"

Newsome looked at Jezelda, then smiled at Yvgeny and said, "Count me in! I ain't got nowhere to be."

Yvgeny sighed, then his shoulders slumped.

"Great, it's a party. To the gravesite we go."

THE BODY IN THE BED

CHAPTER TWELVE

☩

Yvgeny followed Jezelda outside, where Myrtle and Bessie were still struggling with each other. Telfair stood a couple feet away blowing his whistle. Bubba give them a moment to respond to the whistle, then stepped in to pull the two women apart, holding each at bay with one hand on each woman's shoulder. They continued verbally assaulting each other.

"You killed him, you worm!"

"He would've killed himself before being with you again, you troglodyte!"

"Prostitute!"

"Tramp!"

"Trollop!"

As they started to tire, Bubba was able to loosen his grip on them. Tears streamed down Myrtle's face, and Bessie's face was flushed and pinched with anger.

Bubba saw Newsome, Yvgeny, and Jezelda emerge from Schmidt's, then turned to address the women.

"Ya'll two need to start acting right, this here's a funeral!"

Beatrice also emerged and joined them. Bessie was still standing tall, chin jutting out, defiant. Myrtle blew her nose, then lowered her gaze.

In a low voice, Myrtle said, "She's a murderer. I know it. She killed him."

Beatrice's face froze, then she asked, sweetly, "Just who are you talking about, dear?"

Without looking up, Myrtle pointed over at Bessie. Before Bessie could respond, however, Beatrice moved in and put her hand on each woman's shoulder.

"Come now, that's about enough. Why don't we head back to the house, and I will make you each a nice hot cup of coffee and we can talk through all this nonsense."

"I don't drink coffee," Bessie said.

Myrtle muttered, "warm and sweet, just like Ernie was to me."

Bessie snorted.

"See? You didn't know him like I did. Ernie drank his coffee black and bitter. Just proves my point!"

"I said *he* was warm and sweet, not his coffee, you tramp!"

Yvgeny listened to this exchange with interest. He glanced over at the detectives, but their expressions revealed no recognition.

Of course not, they don't know what I know!

Jezelda waited a moment longer, then hiked up her backpack and began to trudge up the hill toward Earnest's grave. She arrived to find Alfred leaning on his shovel while holding a bag of frozen peas on his cheek. He had changed out of the tuxedo, but his face and neck still bore remnants of his white makeup and the mask, contrasted by his otherwise black skin.

A few minutes later, Yvgeny, the detectives, the old women, and Telfair, all approached. Alfred finally put down the bag of peas and started filling the empty hole with dirt. Albert fell in behind Alfred, watching him work and trying to mimic his body language and posture.

Newsome watched Albert and Alfred a moment, then asked, "Where's the coffin? And why y'all filling the hole?"

"There's no body, inspector, at least not yet. Who knows how long the GBI will keep him! I can't leave an open hole indefinitely."

Newsome nodded in understanding.

"Either way," Yvgeny added, "his plot will be here waiting for him."

While Yvgeny and Newsome spoke, Jezelda shook a small rattle and started singing under her breath in a language no one else understood. While she worked, Bubba started to get distracted and turned and glanced at some of the headstones around him.

"Hmph."

Newsome turned to Bubba.

"What?"

"Nothing."

Newsome turned away. Bubba continued looking around,

THE BODY IN THE BED

then, in a lower voice, said, "Hmph."

Newsome turned back to Bubba, put his hands on his hips, and said, "What the hell is it?"

Bubba didn't respond for a moment, then pursed his lips and pointed at one of the headstones.

"Hank Mumford. Remember him? Worked at the car wash where we used to take our slick tops, over there off 247 and Peffley. Must've been over 90 years old. I heard he went over yonder to the old folks' home like our dead guy here."

Telfair heard most of the exchange, and clucked his tongue.

"Assisted living center, dammit. Ain't no old folks' home. And Hank was good people, don't be dissin' him."

Newsome looked at the headstone, then said, "93. Says so on the damn stone. What's your point?"

Bubba shrugged his shoulders again, and said, "I ain't got no point. Just saying I remember him."

"Great."

Newsome turned back to the group, turning his attention to Jezelda, who had started shaking her little rattle at the partially filled hole in the ground.

"Hmph."

Newsome exhaled in a loud whoosh and spit, "Now what?"

"And right there, next to him, Mervyn Littler. I remember him, too. Helped out at the country store."

"You just taking a walk down memory lane, aintcha?" Newsome growled.

"Mervie the Pervie!" cried Telfair. Who could forget that old hound dog!"

The detectives turned to Telfair.

"Yessir. Almost as much of a stud as my man, Ernie!"

Yvgeny turned to Telfair and the detectives and declared, "Please, inspectors, let's have some decorum."

Bubba snorted. Yvgeny turned his attention back to Alfred, but he was lost in thought.

Two cops. No, three cops, a voodoo psycho, and a walking corpse. This day is a complete disappointment.

Yvgeny sighed.

Then again, full payment, got to keep the coffin, and maybe the GBI will just keep the body.

Jezelda approached the headstone and started shaking

her rattle against it. Her chanting got a little louder. Albert watched her, fascinated.

Yvgeny, still stuck in his own head, replayed Bessie's words.

Ernie drank his black and bitter.

Yvgeny chewed on the facts, and started to piece everything together. He felt an urge to cry out *A-ha!* but his musings were interrupted by the detectives.

Bubba, having apparently overcome his fear of cemeteries, had wandered a few feet away, and cried out, "Newsome! Newsome! It's Ms. Millie, remember her? She was my fourth-grade teacher. No, fifth! Fifth-grade teacher!"

"Dammit, Bubba, what the hell's got into you? I -"

The exchange continued between the detectives, with Telfair occasionally adding a barb or two to keep the verbal sparring going. Yvgeny stopped listening, however.

Mervyn Littler. Hank Mumford. Earnest Ledbetter.

Something in the back of Yvgeny's mind was nagging at him. He felt a shiver go up his spine just like in the movies.

Who was next to Hank Mumford?

Yvgeny closed his eyes and pictured that old map he had in his office. He didn't want to risk the detectives seeing him and sensing something was on his mind.

Something important.

Mary Beth Casey. Of course.

He had to get everyone out of his cemetery. He needed to see his map. He needed to think!

"OK, folks, show's over. Time to go home!"

Jezelda checked her watch, then leaned against the headstone and fiddled with her pack, shoved her rattle inside, fished around for her car keys, then stood.

"I ain't getting any vibes from the dead man no way," Jezelda said, then leaned in close to Telfair and whispered, "Come on, old man, you need a lift. I'll get ya back to the house."

"You still got you that slick Beemer, dontcha?"

"Ya."

"Then I'm in!"

Telfair started beat boxing as he followed Jezelda toward the car, causing Yvgeny to wince. Fortunately, by the time the words came, he was out of earshot.

THE BODY IN THE BED

"Jesus, you gotta be kidding me," Newsome muttered.

Yvgeny turned to Albert and Alfred.

"Thank you, my dear Alfred, that will be all for today. There's more frozen peas in the house if you need them. We can finish filling the hole tomorrow."

Yvgeny turned to Albert and said, "Come now, Albert," and started the walk back to the mortuary, hands clasped behind him. Albert remained at his side, studying his every move, then mimicking his movements perfectly. Newsome watched Yvgeny go, narrowing his eyes. He let Yvgeny and Albert walk ahead several paces, then he fell in behind them. Bubba watched Newsome for a moment, then elbowed him to get his attention.

"What is it?"

Newsome didn't respond.

"Newsome, what the hell?"

Newsome quickened his pace and caught up to Yvgeny.

"You're onto something, aren't you? I can smell it."

Yvgeny remained silent.

"Those others, they all died while they were at Sunset Manor, didn't they?"

Yvgeny debated whether to respond, but then answered him.

"I believe so."

As they reached Schmidt's, they saw the Sunset Manor bus heading up the street, this time with Bessie, Myrtle, and Beatrice.

"So, what do you make of it?" Newsome asked.

Yvgeny thought about the question a moment, then shook his head.

"I'm not sure yet, but if you give me a little while, I might come up with something."

☫

When Yvgeny returned to Schmidt's, he stomped past Brianna without a second glance. Brianna had been smoking, her hand holding the cigarette up and through the window; it was the compromise she and Yvgeny worked out when she started spending so much time at his home and place of business. She watched him pass by, eyed him with a look of surprise, then flicked her cigarette out onto the lawn.

She followed him down the hall and into his work room, where he had started rummaging through his desk drawers and talking to himself.

"What's up?"

He continued rummaging, then pulled out a bound journal of some sort. He seemed not to have heard her. Brianna walked over, rapped him on the head lightly with her knuckles, and said, "McFly, McFly, anybody home?"

Yvgeny looked at her as if surprised she was in the room. He took a deep breath, swallowed, then suddenly let loose with a torrent of words. Brianna tried to comprehend, but could barely keep up. When he stopped to take a breath, she reached out and grabbed his arm.

"So, let me get this straight. You've buried over twenty people from Sunset Manor over the last few years, all in their nineties."

"Right."

"And because one of them was killed with antifreeze, you now think all of them were killed the same way? How the hell did you reach that conclusion?"

Yvgeny stood staring at Brianna, his journal in his hand.

"Are you kidding me? Don't you see it? They were all around 90!"

"Yeah, so what? It's an old folks' home."

Yvgeny waggled a dismissive hand toward Brianna.

"No, not all twenty. I mean yeah, they all died, but the most recent ones, I remember them. They were all around 90, and I bet they all had the same symptoms before they died."

He brandished his journal and declared, "It's all in here!"

Yvgeny continued pacing and babbling, and Brianna grew more frustrated.

"What are you talking about?"

"Mervyn Littler. Hank Mumford. Earnest Ledbetter. Mary Beth Casey."

"Geny!"

"Don't forget Meredith Hauptmann."

THE BODY IN THE BED

"Earth to Geny. You're rambling!"

"Meredith. I remember talking to someone about her. Can't remember the lady's name, but I remember her saying she was the picture of health, then one day she didn't feel good. Chest pain, stomach pain, then a day or two later, she started acting crazy, like she was losing her mind. Next thing you know, she was dead."

"It's called getting senile. It happens. You ain't making any sense, Geny. Even less than usual."

Yvgeny seemed not to have heard her.

"And then, right before the funeral, I heard those two old ladies talking about someone named Hank. One day he was fine, then headaches, then he lost his mind, then poof! He's worm food. That's not normal."

Yvgeny looked at Brianna, a pleading expression on his face. He asked her, "Don't you see? They all died at Sunset Manor. Don't you get it?"

"No! It's an old folks' home. Of course, people are dying there."

Yvgeny started pacing again.

"Something ain't right. I just know it. Mervyn Littler. Hank Mumford. Earnest Ledbetter. Mary Beth Casey. Meredith Hauptmann." Yvgeny stopped, then turned to face her abruptly and with a pointed finger, yelled, "I know!"

Yvgeny spun around and snatched his marked-up cemetery map off his wall, then brought it over to his desk. He slammed his journal down on the desk beside the map. Then he fished around in a coffee mug on his desk filled with pencils and pens. He finally found his Sharpie and sat down at the desk. Brianna produced her package of cigarettes, looked toward the window, back at the cigarettes, over to Yvgeny, then sighed and put them away. She walked over to Yvgeny.

Yvgeny took his Sharpie and pressed it against the map, then stopped. Then he slowly put away the Sharpie and dug through his mug again, finding his old grease pencil. He circled plot number 312.

"This is Earnest Ledbetter."

Then Yvgeny circled four more plots and their corresponding plot numbers.

"These are the others."

JONATHAN B. ZEITLIN

He stopped a moment, studying the map, lightly tapping his grease pencil against the end of the desk. Then he circled a few more.

"OK. These are all the Sunset Manor people, at least for the last ten years or so. It's, um -" Yvgeny did a quick headstone count, then said, "twenty-two people."

"Is that a lot?"

"Well, seems a little light a number to me, but I suppose a few got buried elsewhere. Or cremated."

Yvgeny started thumbing through his notebook, first quickly, then slower and slower, then seemed to have settled on a particular page, and began running his finger down the handwritten lines.

"Aha!"

Brianna leaned in over his shoulder, and Yvgeny breathed in the scent of her hair. He took a deep sniff, then tried to focus on the task at hand.

Yvgeny tapped his grease pencil on his map, counting headstones, then circled one. Brianna leaned in and said, over his shoulder, "Mary Beth Casey?"

"Yup," Yvgeny replied, then started reading his notes. "Survived by a lousy son and a poodle named Pookey. How could I forget; she left her entire estate to the caretaker for that dumb dog. And they still owe me."

Yvgeny had stared into space a moment, then shook his head and looked back down at his book.

"She'd been feeling sick for a few days, then ended up in the hospital. Stomach pain and nausea, and quickly increasing psychotic behavior. Dead three days later."

Yvgeny grabbed his grease pencil wrote beneath Mary Beth's name the words *pain, crazy, dead.*

"Why do you keep these notes on people? What difference does it make?"

Yvgeny shook his head and clucked his tongue.

"We've talked about this, my dear, it is important to know what killed them so I can better prepare them!"

For Yvgeny, the art and science of embalming was very similar to cooking. There was a handful of methods, and, like his mother's old-world dinner recipes, there was always wiggle room depending on the ingredients at hand. The manner of death, the drugs that had sustained the client, the

THE BODY IN THE BED

condition of the body, all were relevant factors in helping him tweak his preparations to maximize the outcome.

They call me the Chef of Death!

"Right."

Yvgeny patted her on her leg, then turned back to his notebook. He flipped forward a few pages, then smacked the page.

"Meredith Hauptmann, aged 92. No survivors. Stomach pain, nausea, then she lost her mind. Dead in two days. See a theme yet?"

"Maybe."

Yvgeny found her headstone on his map, and beneath her name he wrote *pain, crazy, dead.*

"But, Mervyn Littler. Interesting."

Beneath his name, Yvgeny wrote *heart attack.*

"Hmm...."

Yvgeny continued scanning page after page, running his finger down his shaky handwriting, nodding his head on occasion. After each review of his notes, he found the relevant headstone on his map and jotted down, in shorthand, the symptoms. The further back in time he went, the longer it took him to thumb through his notes and find the right entries. When he was finished, he put down his grease pencil and leaned back in his chair. Brianna watched him, expectantly. Then he turned to her.

"Interesting."

"What?"

Yvgeny didn't immediately respond. He thumbed through a few pages, grunting as he scanned, then flipped to another page, nodded, then looked off into space.

"What the hell is it?" Brianna demanded.

"Well," Yvgeny responded, "look at the last ten years of Sunset clients. Twenty-two people. Most of them died of all the usual natural causes: cancer, heart conditions, diabetes, right?"

Brianna just looked at the map.

"Then this guy here, Jim Reynolds, five years ago he died of 'natural causes,' but in my notes I said his daughter took him to the hospital because he was having stomach pain, blood in his urine, and then, the last day or two, she thought he lost his mind. He got violent, started hallucinating, then dropped dead."

Yvgeny moved his grease pencil over a few headstones, tapped it on the map, and continued.

"See, then a few more died of the usual stuff, then, about a year later, Nathan Oberholzer. Same basic symptoms: stomach pain, digestive issues, bizarre behavior, death."

Brianna stared at the map, then said, "OK, so what?"

"Twenty-two people in ten years. They're all dying of the usual things, then once, five years ago, this guy dies of something else. A few more die, then four years ago, another weird one. Then, over the last year, maybe fifteen months, five die of the same thing. It's *accelerating*."

Brianna stared at the map. She studied the twenty-two headstones Yvgeny circled, the years, and the causes. Yvgeny put check marks over the ones that died of the same suspicious symptoms. She felt a chill rise up her back.

"Are you saying -"

Brianna was interrupted by the sound of Mama smacking her cane as she hobbled down the hall toward his office. She burst in without knocking, but before Yvgeny could object, she held up her mobile phone.

"Where is it?"

"Where is what, Mama?"

"The money? We have another freeloader. You said this one was guaranteed! You know how much I had to pay those caterers?"

Yvgeny stood, snatched the phone from her hand, and looked at the screen.

"Mama, that's the wrong account."

Yvgeny clicked through a few screens until he found the proper account, then handed the phone back to her.

"See, it's all here."

Mama looked at the screen, then sighed.

"Well done, my little *tygrysek,* I never had a doubt!" Mama said, then pinched him on the cheek. Mama briefly eyed Brianna before leaving. Yvgeny shook his head as she left.

"Now then, where was I?"

"I think you were about to tell me there's a serial killer on the loose at the Sunset."

"I'm afraid so. But who? And why?"

Yvgeny and Brianna both glanced back down at the map.

THE BODY IN THE BED

Mama's smacking of her cane against the wood floors slowly disappeared, but as Yvgeny listened, he started thinking.

"Hmph."

"What?" Brianna asked.

Yvgeny grew pensive, brooding.

"Hmph."

Brianna smacked his shoulder and said, louder, "What?"

Yvgeny held up his index finger and stood, then walked over to his file cabinet and pulled open one of the drawers. He rifled through the contents of the drawer, coming out with a couple of large ledgers. Placing them on the desk beside the map, he started digging into them.

"What are those?"

"Payment ledgers. Helps me keep track of who paid and when. A lot of people pay funerals off in installments. Some claim they paid me when they didn't. I've learned the hard way, if it ain't in writing, it didn't happen."

Yvgeny started researching dates and payments, and making little notes on another sheet of paper. Brianna followed along beside him. When he was finished, they both stared at the obvious results.

Brianna put her hands on her hips and whistled.

"So, all the ones with the suspicious deaths had trouble paying you."

"All except for Ernie."

"But this doesn't really tell you anything, does it? They could have still been paying the Sunset."

Yvgeny shrugged, and said, "Sure. That's why it's only a theory."

"But it's a good one," Brianna replied.

After a moment staring at his notes, Brianna asked, "So, now what?"

Yvgeny sat, brooding over his map, then spoke slowly.

"Well, I'd love to find out if these guys were in arrears at the Sunset. Maybe Telfair could steal the records -"

"Geny!"

"I know, I know. He'd never go for that. That leaves us with a search warrant. Maybe a subpoena. But I'd have to convince the sheriff's department to do it. And even then, there's only one way to know for sure how they died."

"How's that?"

"We gotta exhume them."

"What?"

"Dig them up. Then test them."

"Who's we?"

"Exactly."

Yvgeny paused for Brianna to process his suggestion, waited a moment longer for dramatic effect, then swiveled in his chair to face Brianna.

"We need a court order to exhume a body. I don't have one. I suppose I could just do it anyway."

"Are you kidding?"

Yvgeny smiled, ruefully

"It's pointless anyway. Even if I dig them up, I don't know how to test them for antifreeze poisoning. I'd go to jail for no reason."

Brianna waited a moment, then cocked her head.

"What about Flowers? He's a doctor."

"Good Lord, woman, I can't trust him with a task of this magnitude!"

"So, what are you going to do?"

He sighed and said, "the only thing I *can* do."

Yvgeny got on the office computer for a few minutes, hoping to do some quick research. He had never found statistics compelling, but in this case, it wasn't him that needed to be convinced. When he finished, he grabbed Brianna, and fifteen minutes later, Yvgeny was parked in front of the Gilbert County Sheriff's Department. Yvgeny squinched his face in displeasure.

"I can't believe I thought *this* was a good idea."

"Actually, you didn't think this was a good idea, you just thought it was the least bad of all your ideas."

"Right." Yvgeny got out of Cerberus, then leaned into the open window and said, "Well, wish me luck."

Yvgeny turned, walked a few steps, then returned to the hearse.

"Actually, my dear, will you join me? You seem to keep things a little more, well, civil, when you're there."

Brianna grudgingly got out of the hearse and followed him into the precinct.

When the polyester wearing secretary saw them coming, she immediately rang Newsome's line.

THE BODY IN THE BED

"Your buddy's here, the weirdo with the funky suit. And that girl."

As Yvgeny approached, the secretary hung up the phone and, without looking at him, said, "He's on his way."

"Tremendous."

Newsome hung up the phone and glanced across his desk at Bubba.

"We've got company."

Bubba and Newsome both got up and headed toward the lobby to meet Yvgeny. When they reached the lobby, Newsome gave Brianna a short nod, then turned to Yvgeny. Neither extended a hand.

"Whatcha need, Geny?"

Yvgeny glanced behind Newsome, toward the secretary, who was pretending to be busy with paperwork.

"Is there somewhere we can speak, well, freely?"

Newsome raised his hands expansively and said, "You're in the sheriff's department, speak as freely as you want."

Yvgeny rolled his neck one direction, then the other, then turned to Brianna.

"My dear, if you would be so kind."

Brianna approached and smiled.

"Yvgeny has some information about the murder at Sunset Manor. I'm pretty sure you're going to want to hear it."

Newsome sighed.

"Ma'am, nothing good ever comes out of your friend nosing around in a murder. Trust me."

"No, this time you should trust *me*. He's got a theory, but he's got evidence, too."

Newsome stared at Brianna for a moment, then turned to Bubba. Bubba shrugged his shoulders, and finally Newsome grumbled, "Fine," and turned toward the door. He waited for the secretary to press a button, and when he heard the buzzing, he pushed open the door.

Newsome escorted everyone into a large interview room, and chose a chair that faced the door. Bubba reached behind him and removed a notepad from his back pocket and turned a chair around and straddled it backwards, using the chairback as a table for him to lean on. Brianna and Yvgeny took chairs across the table from Newsome.

"OK, Geny, let's hear it."

Yvgeny wasted no time.

"I believe whoever killed Ledbetter killed several others, using the same *modus operandi*.

"Keep going."

Yvgeny stood, clasped his hands behind his back, and started pacing back and forth, across the table from the detectives.

"Well, Ledbetter was killed with antifreeze, right?"

"We don't have official cause of death back from Macon yet, but let's assume yes."

Yvgeny channeled his best Sherlock Holmes.

I need to get a pipe.

"Of course. Now, if I may, have you inquired with anyone about how the decedent was feeling in the days prior to his death?"

Newsome glanced over at Bubba, sighed, then answered him.

"Of course. But you aren't here to ask me questions, I believe you're here to tell me *your* theory."

Yvgeny smiled.

"As you wish. In the one, two, maybe three days prior to his expiration, old Ernie probably complained of stomach pain, and toward the end he would have been acting really weird. Would've had a headache, too."

"That doesn't mean anything, Geny. Lots of people get headaches and stomach aches. I'm starting to have both right now."

"Ah, inspector, you haven't heard my theory yet. Or the facts. I implore you to be patient."

Newsome shook his head and checked his watch.

"Make it fast, Geny, it's getting late."

"I checked ten years' worth of records for all the funerals from Sunset Manor. I keep meticulous notes, of course."

"Of course, you do," said Newsome.

"Twenty-two people in ten years. Most died of all the ordinary things that kill old people."

"Like cancer," Newsome said, "heart attacks, stuff like that."

"Exactly."

Bubba took his Copenhagen from his back pocket and started thumping it against his leg. Yvgeny paused while

THE BODY IN THE BED

Bubba took a pinch of dip and placed it behind his lip. When Bubba finished, Yvgeny glared at him a moment, then continued.

"Where was I?" Yvgeny asked, then said, "Oh yes. Then, about five years ago, I got Mary Beth Casey. Chest and stomach pain, headache, and some kind of bizarre behavior."

Newsome didn't bother looking up, only said, "Great. But that doesn't mean anything."

Yvgeny ignored him.

"Then, a year later, Meredith Hauptmann. Same symptoms."

Newsome, who had only been half paying attention, stopped fiddling with his cuticles and looked up at Yvgeny. Bubba had been doodling in his notepad, but stopped and started watching Yvgeny as he paced.

"Go on," Newsome said.

"Since December of 2010, I've buried twenty-two Sunset residents. Of them, seven had the same strange symptoms as Ernie Ledbetter. Of those seven, I've buried five of them in the last fourteen months."

Yvgeny, now on a roll, continued lecturing the detectives.

"Now, statistically speaking, and of course I'm using proven numbers from the CDC, for people 65 and older, the two leading causes of death are heart disease and cancer. One third will die of a heart problem. Another twenty-two percent will die of cancer. That's a total of fifty-five percent. Another twenty percent die of things like accidents, Alzheimer's, suicide, respiratory disease, blah, blah, blah, you get the picture. That leaves around twenty-five percent to other things. Seven out of twenty-two dead guys? That's a thirty-two percent ratio. Know what that means?"

"It means we got a problem," Newsome answered.

There was silence in the room as everyone chewed on Yvgeny's statistics. Then Newsome leaned in toward Yvgeny and asked, "What's their names?"

Yvgeny, realizing he finally had their undivided attention, sat back at the table and clasped his hands behind his neck.

"These names are in order, chronologically. Mary Beth Casey. Meredith Hauptmann. Jim Reynolds. Nathan Oberholzer. Rex Lancaster. Hank Mumford."

Yvgeny smiled as he watched Bubba furiously scribbling

into his book. Then suddenly he stopped and looked up at Yvgeny and said, "that was only six."

Yvgeny shook his head and declared, "Don't forget Earnest Ledbetter."

Newsome pursed his lips, then asked Bubba, "Who's taking warrants today?"

Bubba checked his watch, then looked up at the ceiling, deep in thought. Then he nodded.

"By the time we get there it'll be way after five, so I believe it'll be Welch."

"Perfect."

Newsome stood and looked over at Yvgeny.

"Anything else?"

"Of course, inspector. Surely you didn't think I was resting my case on statistics, did you?"

Newsome sighed and sat back down. He checked his watch again.

"Now then, where was I," Yvgeny said, then started pacing again.

"Ah yes. As I'm sure you can imagine, I also keep meticulous records on all financial matters in my business. I cross referenced my embalming notes with my financial records. Of course, when you run a business, there's always a few clients who are late with their payments. Some never pay at all. Just an unfortunate reality for entrepreneurs like me."

"Come on, Geny, get to the point."

"Each of these seven clients I've mentioned also had difficulties making their payments. Well, each of them except for Ernie."

Bubba narrowed his eyes and processed this information. Then he said, "Wait a minute. What do *your* bills have to do with anything? By the time you get involved, they're already dead."

"True. But if there were money problems *after* they died, it's not unreasonable to think, perhaps, they were having money problems *before* they died."

Bubba nodded his head slowly, then started jotting into his notebook. Newsome stood again.

"Well, Geny, I hate to say it, but nice work."

"Thank you, inspector. But, I just have one more thing."

THE BODY IN THE BED

Newsome started tapping the palm of his hand against his thigh, then pressed his lips together for a moment. "Go for it," Newsome said, his words clipped.

Yvgeny took a deep breath, then said, "The day I came to pick him up, there was a cup of coffee by his bed. It was sweet."

Newsome just stared at Yvgeny a moment. Then he blinked a few times, quickly. He looked over at Bubba.

"Bubba, didn't that old lady say the vic took his coffee bitter?"

Bubba nodded.

"And didn't Beatrice offer to make those old ladies a cup of coffee at the funeral?"

Bubba nodded again, then said, "You don't think -"

When Newsome shrugged, Bubba stood and grabbed the car keys off the table. Newsome poked his head out of the interview room and yelled out to the dispatcher, "Send a couple of squad cars to Sunset Manor."

Everyone stood and started filing out of the room. Yvgeny, however, was deep in thought, his eyes unfocused. Their conversation triggered a memory of his visit to the Sunset and meeting Beatrice outside. There had been a pot of flowers on the landing, and they were all withered, dead. It didn't register at the time, but now he remembered. The day he picked up Earnest, the flowers were bright and beautiful. Beatrice had poured the contents of his coffee mug into that pot.

"Now listen here, Geny, you ain't dug up those bodies yet, have you?"

Yvgeny shook his head briskly to clear his mind. He focused on Newsome.

"Of course not, I'd need an exhumation order to do that!"

"Good. Good. We're going to go get us those orders. Don't you touch those bodies, ok?"

Yvgeny made a half bow, and said, "Of course, inspector, you're the expert. I just sell holes."

"All right, Geny. Good work. Actually, really was some good work. Give us a few hours to get the paperwork in order and see the judge. Don't suppose you brought any copies of those notes of yours?"

Yvgeny reached into his coat and pulled out a sealed

envelope and presented it as if it was a holy relic.

"Of course. I never leave home unprepared."

Newsome walked Yvgeny and Brianna to the front entrance, then on their way out, Yvgeny turned back and waved a hand and yelled, "Toodles!"

After they left, Newsome took the envelope and walked by Bubba, saying, "Come on, let's get this done."

As they walked past, Wanda called out to them. She was standing behind her desk and still wearing her dispatcher's headset.

"Hey, 215 and 217 are over there at Sunset Manor. They want to know what they're supposed to do."

"Don't let that old lady kill anybody!" Bubba said, a little more sarcastically than he intended. Wanda relayed the message, then waited for a response. Wanda rolled her eyes, then turned to Newsome.

"They want to know which old lady, there's like twenty of them."

Newsome walked over to Wanda and held out his hand.

"Let me see that microphone."

Wanda had an external microphone on her desk, and she reached down, flipped a switch to move the conversation to the microphone and an external speaker, then handed the microphone to Newsome.

"215 from Code 10, just speak with the manager, Beatrice. Make sure everything is Code 4. You copy?"

There was some static, then the officer at Sunset Manor keyed his mic.

"Copy. Make sure Beatrice is Code 4."

Newsome sighed.

"Negative, I'm asking you to make sure everyone *else* is ok, not Beatrice. Clear?"

"Clear. We'll ask Beatrice is everyone ok."

Newsome turned to Bubba and mumbled, "Are you kidding me?"

"215, are you 10-12?"

"Negative."

"Do you see Beatrice?"

"10-4, she's here."

"In front of you?"

"No, in the other room."

THE BODY IN THE BED

"OK. Is anyone dead?"

There was a pause.

"Negative."

Newsome took a deep breath.

"And how do you know?"

Another pause.

"We asked Beatrice?"

Newsome closed his eyes, put his palm over the microphone and took a deep breath.

"OK. I want you to stand there and keep your eye on Beatrice. Don't let *her* kill anyone. You copy?"

After the officer acknowledged the instructions, Newsome returned the microphone to Wanda.

"Who is 215, Wanda?"

Wanda smiled broadly and said, "I thought y'all knew! It's your buddy Frankie!"

"Let me guess. 217 is Henry."

Wanda mimicked a basketball player shooting a basket and yelled, "He shoots, and he scores!"

Newsome motioned to Bubba.

"We better hurry before that idiot shoots someone. Come on, let's go write this up."

On their way back to their office, Bubba asked, "You really think someone killed all them old folks?"

"I don't know, but if Geny's even half right, well, you know."

"You reckon Beatrice killed them all?"

Newsome stopped fiddling with his computer and gazed out the window for a moment.

"Maybe. Or the kitchen staff, or some other old guy. But I don't like this, not at all."

Bubba nodded, thought for a moment, then declared, "Hot damn, Newsome, we ain't never had a serial killer in Gilbert County. We better nail this down before the GBI swoops in and snatches it away from us."

"Better tell the sheriff, too. You know he will want to get on t.v. and talk about it."

Bubba checked his watch again, but didn't say anything. Newsome started typing, but then looked over at Bubba and asked, "Hey, while I do this, how about you go grab us a couple sandwiches."

Yvgeny and Brianna returned to the mortuary, and Yvgeny summoned Albert and Alfred out to the cemetery. He looked up, then checked his watch.

"So, I think we have maybe an hour or two of daylight left."

Brianna watched him, disapprovingly, and when he glanced over at her, she said, "You know he said don't touch those bodies."

"Of course, and I have no intention of touching those bodies. I am merely preparing for the inevitable exhumations."

Turning on his heel, he started pointing and barking orders.

"OK, Albert, I want you and Alfred to start digging here, here, and here," Yvgeny said, holding out a shovel for the boy.

Albert glanced uneasily at Brianna, and said, "But, Mr. Geny man, are you sure?"

"Ah, Albert, relax, Brianna is right, to exhume a body we need a court order and a county permit, but all we are doing is moving the dirt on top of them. Big difference!"

Yvgeny rolled his eyes and approached Brianna.

"Ah, the innocence of youth! I am a strict constructionist of the law, and the law says you may not disinter a body without an order from a judge. We aren't disinterring."

"Disinter? Or exhume? What's the difference?"

"Apples and apples," Yvgeny said, dismissively.

Albert tried to follow the conversation, then just shrugged and accepted the shovel. Alfred had already started digging. Yvgeny stood over them, his arms crossed and his face a study in satisfaction.

THE BODY IN THE BED

CHAPTER THIRTEEN

☦

"You ever do one of these before?" Bubba asked.

Newsome looked up from his draft affidavit, then nodded. "Once, a long time ago."

He finished reviewing his affidavit, then sent the document to the printer. On the desk were the remains of their sandwich wrappers. Once the affidavit printed, Newsome grabbed it and they left for the courthouse.

As they drove, Newsome said, "Glad it's Welch on duty. Ever since that last thing with Geny, he's signed whatever we give him."

Bubba shivered with the memory of how they discovered Welch involved with Geny's mother. Then he leaned into Newsome and whispered, "Why you gotta bring that up? Can you imagine him over there with Geny's mother? In a funeral home? Doing -"

Bubba stopped himself and shuddered, muttering, "Never mind."

They reached the buzzer outside the on-call magistrate's office, buzzed, then waited for the click. Once they heard it, they let themselves into the office and began to greet Welch, then stopped dead in their tracks.

"Can I help you?"

Behind the desk was an old white man in his seventies wearing a blue and white seersucker suit and a navy bow tie. His hair was white and he had a very carefully trimmed beard. His expression revealed no mirth whatsoever.

Neither Newsome nor Bubba spoke, but both had the same reaction.

God help us, it's Judge Mather.

Judge Mather retired from the bench, but took "senior status" which essentially meant he could preside over any case, at any time, whenever he felt like it. He also had the authority to practice as a magistrate whenever he needed a little extra spending money. Before taking the bench, he was a private bar attorney that specialized in wills, estates, and trusts. He had virtually no working experience in criminal law. However, or perhaps as a result, as a judge, he was particularly hard on cops.

Newsome painted a smile on his face and stepped forward.

"Afternoon Judge, we were hoping to get a few exhumation orders signed."

"Exhumation orders? As in plural?"

"Yes, Judge."

"How many?"

"Seven."

"Denied."

"What"

"I said denied."

"You haven't even seen them yet, Judge!"

"Doesn't matter. Exhumation orders must be submitted by the sheriff or medical examiner of the county in which the body is located, and must be made to a judge of the superior court."

"But we work for the sheriff, and you're a superior court judge."

"Devil's in the details, deputy. At this moment, I am sitting as a *magistrate*, not a superior court judge. And you're a *deputy* sheriff, not the sheriff, and I'm not aware of a delegation order on file in superior court."

Newsome just stared at Judge Mather a moment, sputtering. Bubba stepped in and asked, "OK, Judge, do you know who's on call for superior court?"

Judge Mather swiveled around in his chair so his back was to the deputies, then typed into his computer. He scrolled down with his mouse, then nodded his head. He swiveled back around to face them and said, "That would be me."

Bubba and Newsome exchanged a glance. Newsome cleared his throat and said, "So, Judge, we are hoping to get a few exhumation orders signed."

"Well, you came to the right place."

Newsome tentatively held out his affidavit. The judge took it, flipped to the last page, and checked the signature. Then

THE BODY IN THE BED

he slid the papers across his desk back to Newsome, and said, "Denied."

"What?" Newsome said.

"Only the sheriff, coroner, or medical examiner or their designees can request such an order."

Newsome rolled his neck and took a deep breath. Bubba stepped forward again and withdrew his mobile phone, typed in his password.

"Judge, you said it had to be the sheriff *or his designee*, right?"

"Right."

"So, Judge, if I showed you this text here from the sheriff sending us out here for these orders, would that satisfy the requirement of a delegation order?"

The judge cocked his head a moment, deep in thought, then answered, "Somewhat unconventional, but I'll allow it."

Bubba held out his phone, and the judge read the text message. Then he took out his own mobile phone and took a picture of the text. He slid the affidavit back, turned it around on his desk, then carefully squared it dead center on the surface. He steepled his fingers together over the document and started reading.

When he finished, he looked at each of the detectives, then turned back to the paper before him. He read it again, slower this time. His face remained completely expressionless. Before he reached the end of the first page, he reached into a desk drawer and removed a red pen. Bubba glanced at Newsome but neither said a word. The judge circled something, then moved on.

"Mmm hmm," the Judge said, his eyes going left to right as he read.

"All the bodies are in the same place?"

"Yes, Judge."

"Mmm hmm."

The judge continued to read, and the detectives grew more worried. Finally, he reached the last page again, then stopped, returned to the first page, and did a quick third read. He made a few more marks with his red pen. Bubba had the urge to shout at the man, but remained silent. Finally, he stopped, squared the affidavit on his table again, then slid it toward Newsome.

"Sorry. Denied."

Newsome and Bubba both exclaimed, "What?"

The judge remained expressionless and stated, "You don't have sufficient probable cause to exhume the bodies."

"How do you figure? All seven died in the same place, within a few years of each other, all with the same symptoms. The last guy was confirmed to have died from antifreeze poisoning. How is that not enough?"

"Well first, the only one for which you've collected evidence is already in the custody of the GBI. The other six, that's all pure conjecture."

"But -"

The old judge cleared his throat and said, "The other six all died at an assisted living center. Each no doubt had a number of maladies, and each complained of a few vague symptoms that could mean a hundred different things."

Newsome and Bubba exchanged another glance.

"And these statistics you cited, while interesting, are not dispositive."

"But -"

"Not to mention, your sole source of evidence for their vague symptoms was taken from a mortician who claims to have taken it from his handwritten notes. Now, remind me, isn't this the same guy you two arrested a few months ago?"

"That was something completely different."

"Right. Tell me something else, is this mortician a physician?"

"Of course not!" Newsome said.

"And did you get a chance to see his original notes?"

"No."

"Get copies?"

"Yes."

"Regarding these copies, did this mortician sign an affidavit attesting to their authenticity, and detailing the circumstances in which he created these copies?"

Newsome sighed.

"No."

"How about an affidavit establishing the manner in which he stored these records?"

Newsome didn't answer.

"I figured. So, you're unable to establish, for me, whether

THE BODY IN THE BED

the notes were made contemporaneously to his obtaining the information. That means you are also unable to swear that his recorded observations were made sufficiently close in time to establish their veracity."

Newsome remained silent.

"Mmm hmm. But you think this story establishes sufficient justification to exhume seven bodies?"

"Definitely."

"Right. Let me ask you something else. In your affidavit you mentioned this mortician told you six of these people owed him money. Did he provide you any evidence?"

"Says so in his notes," Bubba blurted out.

"Any bills? Letters of collection?"

Silence.

"Any idea whether any of these people owed anyone else? Were they up to date on their payments to Sunset Manor?"

Again, silence.

"Oh, and by the way, of the seven people you detail, the only one for whom you actually have any evidence of antifreeze poisoning has paid his debt in full."

The judge paused a moment, and when neither of the detectives responded, he continued.

"Right. Tell you what: for these seven people, I'll sign a court order for you to get their medical records. I mean real medical records, not the musings of some glorified taxidermist."

"That will take weeks!"

"They're already dead! What's your hurry? Maybe by then the GBI will give you an actual cause of death on this Ledbetter fellow, God rest his soul."

Newsome stood and started pacing in front of the judge's desk.

"And I'll sign a subpoena for Sunset Manor to get their billing and payment records."

Newsome stared, open mouthed, at the magistrate.

"What if we're right?" Newsome asked. "A subpoena will give them a month to gather the records. Or challenge it in court. Meanwhile, we'll be alerting some serial killer that we are on to them. What happens when we get ten more bodies stacked up at the morgue?"

The judge stared back at Newsome a moment, then turned

away, started drumming his fingers on his desk. Then he rested his palm on Newsome's affidavit and slid it an inch or two further toward Newsome.

"Here. Take this back and make all the corrections I've circled. And add that serial killer part. I'll use it to issue a forthwith subpoena."

Newsome sighed, said, "well, it's better than nothing. Thanks, Judge."

"Don't get too excited. I'm also giving you a forthwith subpoena for those books of notes your friend at the funeral home has."

Newsome and Bubba gathered themselves and headed toward the door.

On the way out, Bubba muttered, "Might as well just get a search warrant for the Sunset."

The judge perked up, and called out, "What did you say?"

Newsome stopped, hand on the doorknob, then closed his eyes and whispered, "Way to go, Bubba."

Bubba turned back toward the judge and said, "Just that we should get a search warrant"

"For Sunset Manor?"

"Yup."

The judge steepled his fingers together and pursed his lips. A moment later he said, "Get those original notes and payment records, and give me a proper description of Sunset Manor, you might just have enough probable cause for a search of the premises."

Newsome let go of the doorknob, and he and Bubba walked back over to his desk.

"How about we get the mortician to sign an affidavit authenticating these copies of his notes? He can detail how and when he made them, where he kept them, who else had access to them, how he knows they're his notes, and whatever else you want us to put in there."

"That would be acceptable."

Newsome reached up to his shirt pocket, patted on it.

"And, respectfully, if we serve a forthwith subpoena on the Sunset, we will have to wait for the records, then we will have to analyze them, and the whole time we'd have to freeze the entire place until we can write another affidavit for a search warrant. That could take twelve hours, maybe longer. That's a lot of inconvenienced elderly folk, and a lot of police man-hours."

"That's the price of living in an ordered society, deputy."

Newsome nodded, and after a glance over to Bubba, Newsome uncrossed his legs and leaned back. He stretched, then leaned his arms across the seat back. He smacked his lips, then, with a smug expression, he said, "Of course, your Honor. I'm just thinking ahead. That would probably generate a few complaints from the Comstock police chief, not to mention the sheriff, because you know all those old people at the Sunset are going to start making phone calls."

Judge Mather's expression got even more dour.

"What, exactly, are you insinuating, deputy?"

"Nothing, your Honor, nothing at all. But, you know, next week is the sheriff's big rally. And you know who's the guest of honor? Judge Sam Moon. Sorry, I mean *Chief* Judge Sam Moon."

Judge Mather's eyes narrowed, his expression becoming even more grim.

"Judge, isn't your contract with the county renewable each year? I think the chief judge has to sign those every summer. That's just a few months away."

Bubba started to fidget in his seat.

"The sheriff and the chief judge are tight, you know. Real tight. In fact -"

"You're on thin ice here, deputy. Choose your next words carefully."

"I'm just pointing out that there might be a much easier way to do this."

The judge started drumming his fingers on his desk again, but in a low voice, he said, "I'm listening."

Newsome leaned in toward the judge.

"How about I make those corrections you wanted, then we get that affidavit from the mortician, and I write this up as a search of a crime scene. We have a deputy coroner who already made preliminary findings one of the victims was poisoned. Kind of sounds like a no-brainer, wouldn't you say?"

The judge's eyes lost focus as he considered.

"But you only have one victim. How would that justify a search of the entire premises? Or the financial records of the others?"

Newsome was silent for a moment, his mind racing. He started tapping his foot against the floor. Then he cocked his head. He squinted. He looked up toward the ceiling. Then he gazed back at the judge and smiled.

"Motive."

"What?"

"We will argue our theory is that the murders were all perpetrated because the victims weren't making their payments, and the business was going to go bankrupt if they couldn't clear the beds for paying customers. We know from the manager that Ledbetter missed his last two payments."

"Yes, but in your affidavit you said he eventually made those payments."

"True, but we don't know *when* he made them. For all we know, he was killed before the payments cleared."

The judge pursed his lips, then nodded.

"We also know that most of the victims had payment problems with their funerals. We need to seize the Sunset's financial records to prove their lack of financial solvency."

It was the judge's turn to contemplate the ceiling. He considered Newsome's argument, then nodded, saying, "Not bad, deputy. Not bad. Get it all together and I'll review it."

"Um, judge, what about those exhumation orders?"

"Don't overplay your hand, deputy. Like I said earlier, they're dead and buried, what's your hurry? One step at a time."

⁜

Yvgeny looked at his watch again, then glanced up at the clouds. He could barely make out the top of Albert's head as the boy stood in his freshly dug hole.

Where's the cops?

Albert turned, tossed the shovel out onto the dirt, then climbed out. Alfred had already finished digging his hole and had heaved his ancient and arthritic body out and back to a

THE BODY IN THE BED

standing position outside the hole.

"Well, that's all six, Boss!" said Albert. There was dirt caked all over his arms and his cheeks.

The six graves had been dug all the way down to the coffins. The lifter was nearby, and all that remained was to bring the bodies back to the surface.

"Now all we need is that court order."

Yvgeny checked his watch again, then sighed. Brianna flicked a cigarette out over the headstones, then wiped the back of her neck. She turned to Yvgeny and said, "How much longer we gonna stand out here? Mosquitoes will be out soon."

"Patience, my dear. I'm sure we will hear from the inspector at any moment."

As if on cue, Yvgeny's mobile phone began to vibrate. He answered it, and then furrowed his brow.

"Yes. Yes. Right." Yvgeny glanced over at Brianna, then turned away, muttering, "What? But, he can't . . . well . . . fine."

He replaced the phone on his belt, then turned back to Brianna, who was waiting expectantly. Yvgeny had a grave expression on his face, but he tried to paint on an air of nonchalance.

"That was Newsome. They want me to sign some paper explaining how I kept all my notes. My copies are apparently not good enough."

"We think we have a serial killer on the loose, and they're worried about how you kept your notes?" asked Brianna, incredulous.

"Well, on the bright side, it looks like they'll have enough probable cause to search the Sunset."

"Yeah, but the bodies are here, not there," Brianna said. "And what about the exhumation orders?"

Yvgeny stood for a moment, then turned away and muttered, "They're still working on them."

Brianna and Albert exchanged a worried glance. Alfred had been watching Yvgeny's lips moving, and once he processed the message, his eyes widened and he looked down at the open graves.

"Albert, why don't you go check the office email, see if the detectives sent me this affidavit I'm supposed to sign."

Yvgeny turned to Alfred, and said, "Alfred, let's get some tarps over these holes."

"Then what?" Brianna asked.

Yvgeny shrugged his shoulders.

"Then we wait!"

Yvgeny and Brianna started walking back toward the mortuary behind Albert. As they walked, they heard the sound of a rapidly accelerating car, followed by hard braking. Yvgeny picked up his pace, and as they walked through the carport, they saw Jezelda jogging up the driveway, her car parked in the street, smoke drifting up from the tires. Ignoring Yvgeny, Jezelda beelined toward Brianna.

"Girl, why you don't be answering your phone?"

Brianna retrieved her phone from behind her bra and glanced at it. There were several missed calls from Jezelda.

"Sorry, I must not have felt it buzzing."

"Listen honey, we gotta talk!"

Brianna and Jezelda walked off into the grass together. Yvgeny watched them go, then rolled his eyes and turned to Albert.

"Come, my young friend, check that email then let's get cleaned up. Things might get interesting tonight."

"Wait!"

Brianna trudged back toward Yvgeny while he waited, a smirk on his face.

"Let me guess -"

"Shut up! Jezelda's on to something. Let's go inside."

Yvgeny followed Brianna into the house, Jezelda following from a distance, eyeing the neighbors furtively, then studying both sides of the street with a gaze filled with suspicion. Once they were all safely ensconced in the parlor, Brianna spoke.

"Jezelda's cousin works at the auto parts store on Main Street. She was telling him about what happened at Sunset Manor, you know, the day the old guy died, and her cousin got all weird, said old people freaked him out. Like, he had this weird fear of old people. Said they were creepy."

"So?"

"So, he told this story about how this old lady came into the store a few years ago to buy some antifreeze. He said she started asking him all these weird questions, like how she

THE BODY IN THE BED

needed it for her car, but she was so clumsy, what if she accidentally drank some, and would it kill her, and what would it taste like, and whether he ever drank it. He said he was so creeped out by it he called in sick the next day."

Yvgeny's smirk disappeared.

"Does he remember what she looked like?"

Jezelda spoke up.

"All you white folk look the same. Especially the old ones."

Brianna put her hands on her hips and glared at Jezelda, who sighed, then said, "He said he'd probably know her if he saw her again."

All three remained silent, deep in thought. Then Jezelda added, "He thought she was asking maybe because she wanted to kill herself."

Yvgeny glanced at Jezelda, then Brianna, then looked off into space for a moment. Then he nodded.

"OK. This cousin of yours- is he at work right now?"

"Yup."

"OK, have him meet us over at Sunset Manor and -"

"You not be hearin' me, hole digger! Old people freak him out, I can't tell him that!"

Yvgeny started pacing in the parlor, then clapped his hands together.

"OK, got it. Let's talk to Telfair and see if he's got a picture book or something. Maybe we can show him a lineup!"

"It ain't a high school," Brianna said, "it's an old folks' home! You think they have graduation photos?"

"Of course not, but what if one of them wanders off campus? Need a photo to give the police. Surely they keep photos!"

Brianna nodded, and said, slowly, "I suppose that's true," then added, "But either way, it sounds like more of a police job to me. Maybe we should tell *them* to handle it."

Yvgeny cocked his head a moment, thinking.

"Sound good, but they're busy with this search warrant business."

Yvgeny chewed on his lip as he considered the options. "Besides, they're not going to drop everything to talk to some kid who had a weird experience with some old lady a few years ago."

Yvgeny gathered steam as he spoke. "Not to mention, if we

let *them* handle it, they'll probably trample all over this poor kid's rights. I'm sure they'll thank us, in the end."

"You mean like last time, when they put you and Alfred in jail for obstructing an investigation?"

Yvgeny considered Brianna for a moment, then let out an exasperated sigh.

"My dear, sometimes the right thing to do is not the best thing for the doer. And, as everyone knows, integrity is my middle name!"

Jezelda made a gagging sound and turned away.

Brianna raised her voice, her cheeks flushing.

"So, what happens when you go do your little talk with Telfair, and the cops show up? They'll throw your ass in jail for obstruction. If you're lucky!"

"Ain't gonna happen. They have to send me some paper to sign. Once they send it, and I sign it and send it back, then they have to go to the judge. I'll have at least an hour to talk to Telfair and get away."

"Do you hear yourself? You sound like a criminal!"

Yvgeny just stared at Brianna. Movement outside one of the windows then caught his attention and he looked out to see Alfred dragging out some tarps from his shed.

Just then, Albert wandered in with a piece of paper and handed it to Yvgeny. It was a draft affidavit laying out, generally, the circumstances in which he created and maintained his notes. He read it quickly, then grabbed a pen and signed it, then offered it back to Albert.

"Please scan it and send it back to whatever email it came from."

Yvgeny turned back to Brianna and clapped his hands together.

"OK! Now the clock is ticking. This could be an essential part of the investigation, and I believe the juice is worth the squeeze. Let's go talk to Telfair about those pictures."

"I think you're making a big mistake," Brianna said.

As Yvgeny and Brianna argued back and forth, the minutes passed. About ten minutes later, Albert wandered back into the room and looked from face to face, trying to figure out what he missed.

Yvgeny started pacing again.

"OK, here's the deal. Let's get in touch with Telfair. If he

THE BODY IN THE BED

can scrounge up some photos, we will show them to that cousin. If he fingers someone, we go talk to the detectives. If he doesn't, we drop it, and no-one's the wiser. How does that sound?"

"For a hole digger, that ain't half bad," Jezelda said.

Brianna jutted out her lower lip and nodded slowly, said, "I guess."

Yvgeny produced his phone and tried calling Telfair, but after several rings he got a recorded message that the user had not yet set up his voice mail. Yvgeny texted him, then called again. Yvgeny waited around ten minutes for a response, then started pacing again.

"Well, I guess we have to do this in person."

Brianna and Jezelda each nodded, solemnly. Albert turned from each person, gauging their reactions like an expectant puppy.

"I wanna come with you!"

"Of course, my dear boy, of course."

"I'm staying here with Jezelda," Brianna said, "I've had enough of that place."

"Divide and conquer, my dear," Yvgeny said.

Brianna furrowed her brow and said, "What if your mother comes down asking questions?"

Yvgeny considered a moment, then said, "Just tell her we went out for a drive. And don't let her fall into any of the holes."

Brianna nodded, and said, "Be careful."

Yvgeny smiled broadly and kissed her on the cheek. Jezelda started making gagging sounds while Yvgeny grabbed his keys and headed for the door, Albert in tow.

Yvgeny and Albert raced for Sunset Manor, but then Yvgeny came to a stop down the street from the place.

"What's wrong, Mr. G?"

Earlier, when Yvgeny had declared to Brianna that he surely had at least an hour once he sent back his affidavit, he felt confidence surging through his veins. However, the closer he had driven to the Sunset, the less confident he felt. Now, down the street from the place, he thought, *we could have minutes, or we could have hours. How long does it take to get a search warrant?*

"Well, what if Brianna's right? If the detectives show up

and find Cerberus here, things may get, well, complicated. Let's try to call the old man one more time."

"Great idea!"

Yvgeny called Telfair's cell again, to no avail. Then he used his hearse's Bluetooth to dial Sunset Manor, but before it started ringing, he ended the call.

"Why'd you hang up, Mr. Geny?"

"Well, what if the inspectors subpoena the Sunset's phone records? I don't want my number to show up."

Yvgeny looked out the window, tapping on the steering wheel with both hands.

Albert asked, "Maybe we can drive by and just see if he's outside?"

Yvgeny considered, then shrugged.

"I suppose. We don't really have a lot of options, do we?"

Yvgeny put the hearse back in gear and approached Sunset Manor slowly. There was no-one on the lawn, but there were a few elderly residents rocking in the chairs on the porch. He continued driving to the end of the street, then turned around.

"What to do, what to do."

Yvgeny looked out the window, deep in thought. After a while, he turned to Albert and said, "OK, here's what we're going to do. I'm going to let you off around the corner. I want you to go talk to those old guys on the porch, see if you can get Telfair to come out and get in the car. We will go for a drive, tell him the story, then bring him back."

"OK, boss."

Yvgeny drove up the street, just out of sight of the Sunset, then let Albert off.

"I'll wait here."

Albert crept up the street and walked up the neighboring business's yard, head on a swivel, then angled over toward the porch of the Sunset. He did so carefully, hugging the side of the assisted living center so those at the windows would be less likely to see him. Finally, he made it to the porch and, after a furtive glance in each direction, took the stairs quickly. There were three old men in rocking chairs, and one of them piped up, "Lookie here, we don't need no magazine subscriptions!"

Another of the men grew animated and said, "That's right,

THE BODY IN THE BED

no trespassing!"

Albert shook his head.

"No, no, I'm looking for the chief. Chief Telfair. Is he around?"

One old man looked at the other and said, "He's still alive, isn't he?"

The second old man nodded, said, "Well, he was this morning," then turned back to Albert and asked, "Whatcha want with the chief?"

Albert collected himself and tried to sound authoritative. *What would Mr. Geny say?*

"Criminal activity is afoot and we need the best!"

The old men studied Albert, head to foot, then both straightened up in their chairs. One of them went through the laborious process of getting out of his chair and said, "Well, why didn't you say so?"

He went inside, leaving Albert with the other man, who resumed rocking in his chair and studying the lawn as if Albert wasn't there. It only took a few minutes for the chief to emerge.

"Ain't you that understudy?"

"Yessir. Mr. G needs you!"

"I bet he does."

Telfair looked behind him into the lobby, then held the door so it shut without a sound. Then he leaned in to the other old man in the rocking chair and said,

"If anyone asks, I'm in the bathroom."

The old man nodded silently.

"All right youngster, let's go. Where is he?"

Telfair followed Albert down the same path he came, hugging the side of the Sunset, then cutting across into the neighbor's yard and down to the street where the hearse was idling. Telfair climbed into the passenger seat and turned to Yvgeny.

"OK, sport, whatcha need?"

"The detectives are getting a search warrant for your place."

"Hot diggity!"

"Listen, we might have a witness, but we need pictures of all the women that have lived here for the past couple years."

"You kidding me? We ain't got nothing like that!"

Telfair then turned away and squinted out the window, chewing his lip.

"Well, on second thought, I might have an idea."

Yvgeny waited, impatiently, then said, "What is it? What idea?"

"Well, Betty in 312, she likes to take pictures at all the funerals. She was too sick to go to Ernie's, that's why she didn't get a picture of him. But she's been here for a while, couple years, maybe, so she probably has most of them."

"Hmm. So, she only takes photos of them when they're dead?"

Telfair chewed on his lip a moment while looking out the window.

"Not too sure. I think she takes a few shots of everyone at the funerals, too. She's always got that damn phone in her hand, guess I never thought too much about it."

Telfair lit up, briefly, and turned to Yvgeny.

"Remember the old lady that videotaped Jezelda's performance? You know, when she was carrying on about Ernie? That was her!"

Yvgeny rubbed his hands together.

"Excellent. OK, why don't you get back over to the Sunset. I want you to go find this Betty and get her phone. We'll take the phone and- wait, what are you doing?"

Telfair was wearing denim overalls, and pulled an iPhone 11 out of the bib pocket and started scrolling around.

Yvgeny stared, open-mouthed, at the iPhone, and asked, "I've been calling you for the last hour."

Telfair studied his phone, then said, "Yup, see 'em right here. Sorry, I keep my ringer off. I'm retired, I don't answer phones no more."

He continued scrolling around in his phone, then felt Yvgeny's stare, and said, "I forgot, she puts all her pics on Facebook. See?"

Telfair held out his phone and Yvgeny saw the woman's Facebook page was a collection of close up pictures of the faces of the dearly departed, and groups of old people standing around punch bowls and snacks. Yvgeny shuddered, then picked up his own phone. When Brianna answered, he skipped the pleasantries.

"My dear, listen, I want you to get on Facebook and find

THE BODY IN THE BED

the page for Betty, um -"

He turned to Telfair, who whispered, "Fraticelli."

"Betty Fraticelli. Get over to that auto shop and show that page to Jezelda's cousin and see what happens."

After hanging up, Yvgeny sat quietly for a moment.

Telfair shoved his phone back into his bib pocket, then opened the door.

"Well, I better get back. Today's gonna be a real hoot!" Telfair said gleefully.

Yvgeny waited for the old man to shut the door, then they sped off.

A mile down the road, Albert and Yvgeny were waiting at a red light when they saw a line of police cars approach. Yvgeny slowly sunk into his seat as they passed. He recognized Newsome's brown Taurus, and the two made eye contact for a moment. As soon as the light turned green, Yvgeny accelerated away.

JONATHAN B. ZEITLIN

CHAPTER FOURTEEN

╬

Brianna ended her call with Yvgeny, then typed Betty's name into Facebook. When she found the page, and with Jezelda looking over her shoulder, they inspected a few of the pictures.
"This should be good enough. Let's go see that cousin of yours."
They started walking toward Brianna's Smart Car. When Jezelda saw it, she balked.
"I ain't gettin' in that machin, girl. We take mine."
With a shrug, Brianna followed Jezelda to her BMW.
Meanwhile, at Sunset Manor, Telfair had just entered the Sunset when Bubba and Newsome pulled up the driveway in their brown Taurus, followed by three uniform patrol cars, two officers in each car. The detectives waited for the uniforms to pile out of their cars, then they approached the front porch.
One of the younger officers popped his trunk, and came out with a battering ram. As he lugged it up the grass, Newsome stepped forward to greet him, hands on hips.
"What the hell you bringing that for?"
The young uniformed officer looked down at the ram, then back up at Sunset Manor, and shrugged.
"Well, just in case -"
"Just in case what? You see the door?"
The younger officer looked up to see the front door was wide open, and the only thing separating them from the inside was a flimsy screen door.
Now go put that thing away!"
Newsome turned and hiked back up the lawn while the younger officer stood, shoulders slumped. Another officer walked past him, shaking his head. The officer muttered, "dumb ass," as he walked past.

THE BODY IN THE BED

A crowd of elderly men and women gathered at the windows, on the porch, even in the yard. Newsome and Bubba approached the screen door, trailed by a handful of uniform police officers. They were met at the door by Telfair.

"Chief, we have a search warrant. Where's the manager?"

Telfair clapped his hands together and said, "Aintcha supposed to yell, 'Sheriff's department! Search warrant?'"

"Just tell me where she is so we can get started."

Telfair turned to one of the old ladies nearby and ordered, "Go scrounge up Beatrice, tell her the po-lice are here!"

Telfair watched the woman walk away, then turned back to Newsome.

"Hot damn, let's see the affidavit!"

Telfair reached out a hand toward the paperwork in the detective's hand, but Newsome pulled away.

"You kidding me? Hell, you're a potential suspect! Besides, we don't bring the affidavit with us on searches, you know that better than anybody."

The old chief snapped his fingers, said, "Aw shucks, but it was worth a try. So, I'm a suspect now? Hot dog! What's my motive, sport?"

Bubba said, "Maybe you was jealous of Ernie."

Telfair leaned back and laughed, then stuck his thumbs behind the straps of his overalls.

"Jealous? Hell yes, I was jealous, just like every other old ass sumbitch in here. But antifreeze? That's no way to kill a man. Ain't no sport in it!"

Bubba took a deep breath, then turned to the uniforms behind him.

"Ya'll secure the first floor, we'll head upstairs."

The uniforms spread out into the rest of the Sunset while the detectives went upstairs. Telfair watched them go up, a broad smile on his face. Then he reached into his bib pocket and withdrew a tan plastic cylinder and unscrewed the top. Inside was a long cigar in cellophane. As he removed the wrapper, he muttered to no one in particular, "Been saving this for a while!"

Just as he lifted the cigar to his mouth, he heard a commotion to his side, and he turned toward it in time to see Beatrice hustling by him and toward the back door with a large bag of garbage.

JONATHAN B. ZEITLIN

"Po-lice are here!"

Beatrice glanced at Telfair, mumbled something, then huffed out the door, lugging the bag. As Telfair watched from the window, she walked to the side of the building, opened the wooden fencing camouflaging the dumpsters, and tossed the bag inside. When she returned, Telfair was watching her intently. Beatrice began running her hands across her hair.

"Just trying to tidy up, I wasn't expecting visitors."

"Mm hmm," Telfair said.

Beatrice began climbing the stairs after the detectives. Telfair watched her climb, then stood for a long moment, staring at the empty staircase. Then he walked outside.

"This is the room, right here," Newsome said, while glancing at a piece of paper in his hand. Bubba came in behind him and opened the door. There were two suitcases by the bed and a framed photograph of an elderly black couple.

"Not no more, it ain't!" Bubba said, picking up the photograph.

Newsome shrugged and walked inside.

"Well, let's poke around a bit anyway."

A few miles away, Brianna and Jezelda arrived at the auto parts store. Women were a highly unusual sight in the place, and several of the patrons hunting for parts watched them pass like hungry sailors returning from a month at sea.

Behind the counter was a young black man with dreadlocks helping a customer look up a part on his computer. As soon as Jezelda saw him, she called out, "Philipe! Take a break, we need to talk."

Philipe looked up from his computer, saw his auntie, then he turned to Brianna. He looked her up and down, mouth open, eyes glazed over. Jezelda, recognizing what was happening, snapped her fingers and called out again, "Put 'cho eyes back in ya head! We got bid-ness!"

THE BODY IN THE BED

Philipe shook his head back and forth and blinked several times. He was a tall and attractive young man, and Brianna blushed as he came around the counter.

"No, we come to you. That computer have internet?"

Still looking at Brianna, he nodded slowly. Jezelda shook her head and pushed him out of the way. She accessed Facebook and found the old lady's website.

"Check out these women. Any of them match the one you told me about?"

Philipe scrolled down, looking at all the photos.

"No; nope; no, no, yuck! Hell no! Nope. Wait- all these ladies be dead!"

Philipe dropped the mouse and made the sign of the cross.

Jezelda rolled her eyes and demanded, "You don't recognize none of them?"

He shuddered, then looked up and shrugged.

"Wasn't none of those old ladies, sorry."

Brianna and Jezelda both sighed. Philipe started clicking around on the Facebook page, stealing glances at Brianna whenever he thought it was safe.

"Now what we gon' do?" Jezelda exclaimed. Brianna checked her phone.

"Wait! It's her! It's her!"

Philipe began hopping up and down and pointing. Brianna and Jezelda both crowded next to him to look at the screen. Philipe leaned in and took a deep whiff of Brianna's perfume.

He pointed at the center of the screen, which depicted the front of Sunset Manor and a group of elderly people. In the center was Beatrice, smiling and holding a bouquet of flowers.

"Which one?" Brianna asked.

Philipe pointed to the woman in the dead center of the photograph.

"Beatrice?"

"Her! Her! She's the one! She was the one."

"You're sure?" Brianna asked.

Philipe looked back at the screen, shivered, and nodded.

Brianna was still holding her phone, and clicked Yvgeny's name to call him.

"Yes, my darling?"

"Jezelda's cousin just identified the woman."

"Really? Which one is it?"

"Beatrice."

There was a pause as Yvgeny processed this information.

"Beatrice? Really?"

Brianna didn't answer. Yvgeny glanced over at Albert, who was waiting expectantly.

"I suppose I must alert the detectives."

"*Tygrysek! Tygrysek!*" his mother called out from the top of the staircase.

Yvgeny made a noise in his throat and yelled, "Not now, Mama!"

Before Yvgeny could return to his call, however, his mother called out again.

"Channel Four! Turn on the t.v.!"

Yvgeny narrowed his eyes and turned to Albert, who rushed over and turned on the television.

"Geny? Geny? What's wrong?" Brianna asked.

Yvgeny stammered out a quick, "Gotta go," and ended the call. On the television, Albert and Yvgeny watched as reporters surrounded the lawn of the Sunset, filming a collection of police cars and reporting on the search warrant.

"We have to go alert them, Albert. Come on! No time to lose!"

They raced to the Sunset in Cerberus, but the roadway was blocked. He parked the hearse down the street and briskly walked toward the Sunset. A uniform city police officer was waiting for them on the sidewalk and held up a hand in the universal gesture for *stop*! But before he could open his mouth to speak, Telfair called out from the doorway.

"He's ok, Danny!"

The officer looked toward Telfair, seemed to struggle a moment, then put down his hand and waved Yvgeny and Albert on. They hiked up the lawn toward Telfair, who was waiting for them at the doorway, a huge cigar stuck in the corner of his mouth. He wasn't smiling. The news crews were all staged on the sidewalk, filming everything. Yvgeny quietly applauded himself for choosing to wear one of his finest Victorian suits that evening.

Just as they approached Telfair, he came through the doorway and down the stairs. Yvgeny turned to Albert and said, in a low voice, "Let me do the talking, ok?"

THE BODY IN THE BED

"Listen, we need to speak with the inspector!"

"Hold your horses, cowboy, we got bigger problems."

"What do you mean?" Yvgeny asked.

Telfair shuffled past Yvgeny and out onto the lawn. Yvgeny and Albert followed him.

"Something ain't right. Cops walked in, and a minute later, Beatrice made a beeline for the back door with a big garbage bag."

"That's what we need to talk to the detectives about."

Telfair asked, "What do you mean? You get something from those photos?"

Yvgeny nodded his head, then checked his watch. "The kid fingered Beatrice."

"Hot damn!" Telfair cried out. "I think we just done solved us a murder!"

Telfair started beat boxing again, and Yvgeny looked down at his toes. Albert cocked his head at Telfair like a confused golden retriever.

"Court's in session
And my impression is
He's gonna die soon by
Lethal injection."

"That's it?" Yvgeny asked.

Telfair looked away and said, softly, "I forgot the next line."

Yvgeny shook his head, then turned to Albert.

"Come, my friend, let's go inform the inspector!"

Yvgeny and Albert walked briskly back toward the entrance, Telfair in tow. There was another uniform police officer staged at the door with a clipboard, and he barred their entrance. Telfair shouldered past Yvgeny and called out, indignantly, "I live here, sport. Now step aside!"

The officer slid a pen out of his pocket and said, "Name?"

"Luther P. Telfair, the third!"

The officer slowly started writing, then stopped and looked up.

"Telfair. That have one L or two?"

"Are you kidding me? When's Telfair ever had two Ls?"

The officer resumed writing, then shuffled to one side, allowing him entry, then blocked the entrance again. He looked up at Yvgeny, then asked, "You live here, too?"

"For heaven's sake, do I look like I live here?"

The officer looked at him blankly, but before he could say anything further, Newsome's voice came ringing out from within.

"Barry, step aside, we're coming out."

The officer guarding the doorway moved out of the way, and Telfair came out with Newsome and Bubba. Newsome immediately squared off with Yvgeny.

"Well, I'll be damned. So, he said it was Beatrice?"

"That's right."

Newsome turned to Telfair, and said, "And you saw her running a bag of trash out right after we arrived?"

Telfair just smiled and nodded. Newsome turned to Barry and said, "Hey Barry, go fish out that garbage bag."

Newsome then looked at Bubba.

"Go fetch Beatrice, tell her we'd like to talk to her out here so we're out of everyone's way. Tell her it's because she's in charge, something like that. Don't let her get all hinked up."

Barry walked around the corner of the Sunset. His expression clearly registered his disappointment over his new assignment. Newsome waited for Bubba to walk inside, then turned back to Yvgeny.

"Maybe y'all can find somewhere else to congregate, somewhere Beatrice won't see you. I want to try to get a confession right now, get it over with."

Before they could disperse, Beatrice emerged from the Sunset with an apologetic Bubba in tow. When she saw Telfair, Yvgeny, and Albert standing beside Newsome, she got nervous.

"What's going on here? And why are *they* here?"

Newsome muttered a curse, then called out, "Don't worry about them. Why don't you and I walk over here and have a chat?"

Bubba and Newsome led Beatrice across the lawn, and the three of them had a conversation out of earshot. Telfair continually glanced toward the dumpsters, and finally, the officer walked around the corner holding a large black trash bag. Newsome and Bubba had faced Beatrice away from the building so she couldn't see what was happening. Bubba motioned to get Barry's attention, indicating for him to stand

THE BODY IN THE BED

by.

Suddenly, the group heard Beatrice raising her voice.

"Financials? What for? What's this all about? I demand an explanation!"

"Well, Ma'am, I think you know why we're here, and I think you know a lot more than you've been pretending."

Beatrice summoned her most insulted expression, hands on hips, glaring first at Newsome, then Bubba.

"How dare you two accuse me of anything! I've never so much as had a parking ticket in my entire life. On my mother's grave, I have no earthly idea what -"

Newsome did not let her finish. He said, loudly, "We got the tox screen back on Earnest. He was poisoned. Antifreeze. Next stop is the judge to get exhumation orders on every other geezer that came out of this place on a stretcher."

"What does that have to do with me?"

"Well, we have a witness that watched you sneak out of here and toss a bag of trash after we arrived. What's in that bag?"

Beatrice turned red but said nothing.

"And another witness places you at a store asking all kinds of questions about antifreeze."

Beatrice looked away.

"So, I'd say this search has everything to do with you. Best thing you can do now is talk to us."

Beatrice stood a moment, silent, looking away. Newsome got her attention and motioned for her to look behind her. She did so, and saw Barry standing on the lawn next to a full black garbage bag.

"I think I want to talk to a lawyer."

Newsome nodded, then turned to Bubba.

"Come on, Bubba, let's take her in. Cuff her in front."

Bubba handcuffed her with her arms in front, then started walking her toward the Taurus. Newsome ran interference, pushing back the news crews who were pushing against each other to get their camera the closest. Several reporters had their microphone arms extended, trying to get a statement. None said a word.

Once Bubba had stuffed Beatrice into the back seat, Newsome turned and approached Barry. He kneeled and opened the garbage bag. Inside was a full collection of garbage, along with two half full jugs of antifreeze. He re-tied the bag, then told Barry, "Don't open this bag, let's send the whole damn thing back to the office and process it there. Got it?"

Finally, Newsome returned to Yvgeny, Albert, and Telfair, patted his hand against his shirt pocket, then sighed. He looked at Yvgeny and asked, "Listen, can you get the kid who identified her over to the precinct? And can you give me that Facebook page?"

"Of course," Yvgeny said, then turned to Albert and said, "Shall we?"

Newsome walked away, and Albert and Yvgeny prepared to leave. Telfair stood, cigar in his mouth, thumbs in his overall straps, with a huge smile on his face.

"Best damn time I've had in years, yessir!"

Telfair reached into a pocket and produced a book of matches, then proceeded to light his cigar. Once he had it properly lit, he took a few good puffs, then shoved his thumbs behind his overalls.

Yvgeny smiled and said, "Well, that's that!"

Telfair took another puff and said, "Not so fast, sport. Murders don't never get solved so quick and easy."

After Telfair walked away, Yvgeny and Albert returned to Cerberus and headed toward the auto parts store. It was only a few minutes away. They arrived to find the ladies inside with Philipe.

"Newsome wants me to bring the boy in to give a statement."

"He ain't getting in that *korbiyar*, hole digger. I'll take him myself!"

"I'm going, too," Brianna said, with a sidelong glance at Philipe.

"Well, he entrusted me to do it, so I guess we are all going."

A few minutes later, everyone arrived at the precinct. It was already dark, but the parking lot was well lit, and they could see Newsome's brown Taurus already parked outside. Beside it was a Mercedes with a vanity plate NGRI 2. Yvgeny raised his eyebrows but didn't say anything.

They approached the door to the precinct together. The receptionist was already gone for the evening, so they had to

THE BODY IN THE BED

ring the buzzer. Someone inside buzzed them into the lobby.

There was a row of chairs against one of the walls, and seated in the far chair was a matronly middle-aged woman in an expensive suit and well-manicured nails. Her hair was coiffed perfectly, and she was clearly angry.

"Great, now it's a party," she said.

The woman then walked across the lobby to a red phone on the wall, picked it up, and a moment later started yelling, "I've been waiting for ten minutes, and now there's a bunch of other people out here. You better not be talking to my client or -" She pulled the phone from her ear and stared at it.

"She hung up on me!" She looked at the group, incredulous, and added, "Can you believe that?"

Yvgeny smiled and said, "Yes, I absolutely do believe that. I would expect nothing more."

The woman inspected Yvgeny and his attire, then stood and approached him with a tentative hand outstretched.

"Donna Proctor, counsel for Beatrice Long."

Yvgeny took her hand and said, "Yvgeny Jedynak, undertaker for all," then he swept his arm in the direction of his friends, "and these are my associates."

"Undertaker, huh? I think I've heard about you. Schmidt and Sons, right?"

Yvgeny made a formal bow and said, "The nail is hit on the head."

Proctor looked at each of them, then said, gravely, "I suppose you are here because of this alleged murder."

No-one replied, so Proctor started pacing back and forth, speaking to no-one in particular.

"Just like the cops, arrest some poor little old lady based on spurious evidence and flimsy deductive logic. If ever there was a case to be made for intentional infliction of emotional distress, it's here."

Yvgeny and Brianna exchanged a glance, and Albert stared at the woman, mouth open, his face demonstrating a complete lack of comprehension.

"Mark my words, she'll be out of here in an hour. And if they're questioning her without me present, this town will be called Proctorville, and this sheriff will be passing out flyers at Wal Mart."

She started punching a fist into her open hand as she paced.

"Elder abuse, too, I'm sure. God, this place is swimming in torts."

Suddenly she froze and looked at Yvgeny and asked, "Ssh! Do you hear that?"

Yvgeny narrowed his eyes and said, "I don't hear -"

The woman held up her hand to silence him, and said, "It's the sound of a Montblanc pen writing the biggest check this county's ever written." She looked out into space and, theatrically, intoned, "Will you just look at all those zeros!"

The group heard a buzz, after which a door on one side opened up and Newsome and Bubba emerged. The lawyer spun toward the sound of the door and instantly attacked.

"What have you done with Beatrice? Where is she? I hope, for your sakes, you didn't question her."

"Of course not. She's being processed at the jail, then they're bringing her here for questioning," Newsome said.

"Questioning? She's not answering any questions! Are you out of your mind? You have no evidence!"

"With all due respect, how do you know what the hell we have?"

As the lawyer sputtered in righteous indignation, Newsome turned to Philipe.

"Hey Geny, is this the guy?"

Yvgeny smiled and said, "Sure is."

Before Newsome could speak again, an unmarked police van pulled up right outside the doors of the precinct, and two uniformed deputies emerged and opened the rear sliding door. Beatrice was seated inside, dressed in jailhouse overalls. Her hands and feet were shackled in chains.

When Proctor saw her, she stumbled back clutching her chest, her other hand behind her reaching for the wall. She started to hyperventilate.

"Oh my God, what have you done to my client!"

Yvgeny watched her with amusement, then turned to Jezelda and said, "Her theatrics are even better than yours!"

The glass doors of the precinct had a film that kept out the heat of the sun. This film was reflective, even at night, so neither the deputies outside, nor Beatrice, realized the lobby was filled with people. As the group inside watched, Beatrice

THE BODY IN THE BED

struggled with the deputies, clearly not wanting to get out of the van. At one point, she began to kick at the deputies, and when another reached in from the other side of the van, she moved in with her head to try to bite him. In the end, she had to be physically removed, and she spewed invective at the deputies the entire time. The film on the glass prevented the sun's rays from entering, but did nothing to muffle sounds.

"Who do you think you are, you sons of bitches, unhand me this minute! How dare you treat a poor, old woman like this! Ooh, if I knew your mothers, I'd give them a call right now! Wait until I see my lawyer!"

She continued her tirade as the deputies assisted her into the lobby, and as she shuffled in, she was too busy yelling at them to notice people were watching.

"Beatrice, Beatrice!" Donna yelled.

Beatrice stopped and turned around, and her cheeks turned beet red when she realized the room was full of people. Suddenly she relaxed, smiled, and adopted the demeanor of an elderly dotard.

"Oh, Donna, it's so good to see you! How's your family? I'm so sorry to bring you out so late in the evening."

Most of the occupants of the lobby rolled their eyes in unison, but Proctor ignored them.

"You poor dear, have they hurt you? Did they try to question you?"

Blocking her body with her own, Proctor turned her back on her client and addressed Newsome.

"How dare you put her in prison garb and chain her up like a common criminal!"

Bubba, dryly, said, "She is a common criminal. She's a murderer."

"She's nothing of the sort! Oh, when I'm done with this place, Beatrice is going to own this county, and both of you!"

Newsome stepped forward, hands on his hips.

"Your client is a serial killer. Why don't you ask her why she had two gallons of antifreeze in her room? Her fingerprints were all over them." Newsome looked at Beatrice, then, and asked, "We had a few minutes to look at your financials, too. They're not pretty. Is that why you killed them?"

A flash of anger spread across Beatrice's face, but she successfully buried it and smiled.

"Detective, how could you say such a thing?"

"That's enough, Beatrice, let me do the talking," Proctor said, then looked at Newsome and added, "Don't you question my client. You got something to say, you direct it at me."

"No problem," Newsome said, "Why don't you ask your client how much Rex Lancaster owed her before she killed him. And Nathan Oberholzer. And Jim Reynolds. And -"

"Stop that," Proctor said.

"We already have exhumation orders for six bodies. Yvgeny has people digging them up right now. Why don't you ask your client if we're going to find ethylene glycol when we test them?"

"That's enough!" Proctor cried out.

Newsome turned to Bubba and smiled. "You know, Bubba, once we have more time to study her bank records and compare them to the bodies she poisoned, we won't even need her statement. It will all be right there, for any jury to see for themselves."

"You think it's easy to run the Sunset with these damn freeloaders?" Beatrice shrieked, "If *you* rented an apartment and stopped paying the rent, you'd get kicked out on your ass, but if you're over eighty, no, heaven forbid you boot out some geriatric! You're stuck until they croak! The ones that pay always die, and the others, those cheapskates, they always *linger,* sucking at the teat until they suck it dry. Well, let me tell you something, buster, the profit margin is way too thin to let someone squat for free. Someone had to thin the herd, or they'd all be out on the street!"

Beatrice took a deep breath and collected herself, her head high. Even Proctor was silent, open mouthed with surprise.

"So, you had to do it. You did it to save the place and to protect the rest of them," Newsome said slowly, softly.

"You're damn right."

"Ma'am, you told us Ernie missed a few payments. But we checked the records. He was paid in full. And he was dying anyway. Why him?"

Before Proctor could silence her client, Beatrice said, "I just didn't like him, the way he carried on, like some adolescent fool, two timing those ladies."

The lawyer finally collected herself and said, softly, "Beatrice, I think that's enough. Please, no more talking."

She looked over at Newsome and said, in a low voice, "You realize none of this is admissible."

Newsome smiled.

"Au contraire, Counselor, she has her attorney present."

"Yes, but you never Mirandized her."

"No, but I wasn't questioning her, I was talking to you. What do you call that, Bubba?" Newsome asked, then started snapping his fingers as he dramatically tried to remember. "It's on the tip of my tongue. Oh, yes, you call them *excited utterances*." Newsome smiled, then said, "Besides, I don't need her statement, the evidence really is enough to convict her!"

Newsome turned to the deputies and said, "Put her and her lawyer in the interview room, let them talk." Then he turned to Philipe and said, "You mind coming back to our office for a few minutes?"

Philipe nodded his head, then Newsome waited for Beatrice and Proctor to leave with the deputies. Once the door closed behind them, Newsome turned to Yvgeny and held out his hand.

"Nice work today. All of you."

"Of course, inspector. Just doing our civic duty. But if I may ask, do you really have exhumation orders?"

Newsome said, "Not yet, but tomorrow we will probably go get them. Just be ready, ok?"

Yvgeny smiled and said, "Of course, inspector, always ready to help."

Newsome nodded, then looked at Bubba and muttered, "She's toast."

JONATHAN B. ZEITLIN

CHAPTER FIFTEEN

☦

Mama was in the kitchen puttering when the doorbell rang. She trudged to the door to find Newsome and Bubba outside. She turned to yell, "Yvgeny, your friends are here!" then she opened the door.

"Ma'm. Geny around?"

Mama turned to yell one more time, then motioned for them to come in.

"Just have a seat wherever. Tea?"

"No, thank you, we won't be long."

Newsome had a folder tucked under his arm, which he placed on the table beside him. A moment later, Yvgeny emerged from the back and smiled. He looked over at the folder.

"Well, inspectors, how punctual. Is that what I think it is?"

Newsome patted the package he had placed on the table, then slid it across to Yvgeny.

"Exhumation orders, as promised. Once you dig them up, we'll get Flowers to cart them over to the GBI."

"Splendid," Yvgeny replied, and took a seat across from Newsome.

"Did she talk?"

"She confessed. The DA made a deal with her."

"I've been thinking," Yvgeny said, "Ernie. What you said about him not missing any payments. Is that true?"

"Sort of. He was late with a few payments, but he was paid in full before she killed him."

"So, he didn't go broke?"

Newsome chuckled.

"Broke? Hell no. That man was loaded. Cut his kids out of his will a year ago, just never told them. Then he signed over everything to Luther P. Telfair. I guess they were really close."

"Now Luther's rich?" Yvgeny asked, incredulous.

THE BODY IN THE BED

Newsome smiled. "Filthy rich. Ledbetter was late with a couple payments because it took them a while to set everything up. They wanted to do it right, to make sure nobody knew about any of it. None of that matters, though, Beatrice had already made up her mind to get rid of Ernie because of his antics with the ladies."

"That's pretty damn cold," Brianna said.

"Yeah, but by then, Beatrice had already killed six people. It gets easier, killing. I think she would've killed Bessie and Myrtle next, if we didn't arrest her."

Yvgeny nodded slowly. "So, Telfair got everything. No kidding."

"You got it. How's that for a happy ending?"

As they wrapped up their meeting, they started to hear the low thump of bass in the distance. The thump got steadily louder as the car got closer. Bubba muttered, "Damn kids."

They turned toward the windows as a brand-new Cadillac Escalade pulled into Yvgeny's driveway. The bass coming from the stereo was deafening. Because of the angle and the tinted windows, none of them could tell who was inside. In a fit, Bubba jumped to his feet and stormed out, followed by Newsome and Yvgeny.

Bubba held out the badge around his neck and yelled, "Gilbert County! Turn off that damn radio and get out of that car!"

For a moment, nothing happened, making Bubba even more angry.

"Forty dash six dash fourteen requires -"

Yvgeny turned to Newsome and asked, "What's he talking about?"

Newsome winced, and said, "He's quoting the state law on loud music."

As Bubba screamed at the Cadillac, the occupant finally turned down the stereo and turned off the engine. Bubba marched toward the driver's side, right hand on the butt of his weapon.

"Hot damn, tiger, you memorized the Code? I'm impressed!"

Luther P. Telfair emerged from his new Cadillac, passed a dumbfounded Bubba, and approached Yvgeny. He was wearing a brand-new pair of denim overalls that he had pressed until there was a stiff crease in the legs. He raised up his new wraparound Oakley sunglasses, made a flourish toward his car, and said, "Not too shabby, right? Always wanted me one of these."

Yvgeny admired the vehicle and shook his head.

"I'm speechless."

"You should see the honeys at the Sunset!"

After gloating for a moment, Telfair turned to Newsome and said, "Let me tell you something, that measly police retirement check ain't enough to cover the bills. I sure hope you two have a plan."

Bubba nodded, said, "Got me a farm."

Telfair smiled, nodded in approval.

Newsome cocked his head and said, "I gotta ask, chief, when did you find out he was going to hand it all over to you?"

Telfair looked off into space and thought about it.

"It was maybe a couple weeks before he missed those payments."

Telfair looked out into the distance. He lowered his voice.

"We never really talked about money, but I always figured he was pretty well to do. I mean, his kids were always humping his leg for it, the ladies at the Sunset were always fawning all over him, even the men, they were always sniffing around for an easy score. Seen it a thousand times back in the day. He couldn't trust anyone, and then he got sick. Real sick. I guess he knew I'd take care of him."

"And he knew you'd take care of his ladies." Bubba commented.

"Guess so."

Telfair turned back to Yvgeny and shoved his thumbs into the straps of his overalls.

"What say we go for a ride? And where's Dub?"

THE BODY IN THE BED

☦

☦

THE END

Here ends **The Body in the Bed**. If you haven't read the first book in the Undertaker Series, **The Body in the Hole**, be sure to visit your favorite online distributor and pick up a copy. While you are there, you can also find other books by Jonathan B. Zeitlin.

JONATHAN B. ZEITLIN

Praise for The Body in the Hole

"Zeitlin has created a constellation of colorful characters worthy of Carl Hiaasen's finest work. The plot races, the dialogue crackles, and macabre meets mayhem. Don't be caught dead without The Body in the Hole on your reading list."

Robert Blake Whitehill, Author/Screenwriter, The Ben Blackshaw Series, RobertBlakeWhitehill.com

"I enjoyed this novel for its dark humor and Yvgeny's unique perspective on the case.... [I]t's just a good, fun mystery novel."

Reviewed by Sherri Fulmer Moorer for Readers' Favorite

"The Body in the Hole is interesting, entertaining, and well-written. As the mystery grows, Zeitlin draws the reader in, painting a lively picture of a small town, its inhabitants and way of life, and driving the novel to its conclusion with a full tank of graveyard humour."

Matt McAvoy Book Review Blog

"It's a mixture of Wes Anderson, Monty Python and Mr. Bean. It's snarky and satirical and it is not the least bit politically correct. I loved the zaniness of the plot, the smart-aleck dialogue, the disgusting habits of the characters and their penchant for carnival sideshow vehicles and uniforms. The characters embrace their own personal crazy, like a dog rolling in poo and loving it."

Jean M. Roberts, author WEAVE A WEB OF WITCHCRAFT and BLOOD IN THE VALLEY

THE BODY IN THE BED

Made in the USA
Middletown, DE
12 June 2024